DuPont

A Novel

Mingo Twain

ISBN-13: 978-0692646243

ISBN-10: 0692646248

Library of Congress Control Number Pending

Other novels and books by Mingo Twain

Burning Rock

The Remnant Stump

Beyond the Stars and Stripes

Yardbirds

Acknowledgements

I could never give Bonnie enough praise. Thank you for your love and unending support. To Randy, for your expertise and the wisdom you graciously shared. To Sara, thank you for believing in me.

Jacket design by:

The Cover Collection - West Yorkshire, United Kingdom

Preface

His father was a successful commercial real estate agent, and his mother a prominent federal judge. Seth Boone had everything a young boy could ask for. He was the brightest of students, with the ambition of someday becoming a doctor.

Leaving a bar drunk one night, Seth's father crashes the family SUV. He loses both legs and suffers tremendous damage to his lower abdomen, but survives. Returning home after surgery and months of rehab, everything changes in the Boone home. Seth becomes the victim of unthinkable and unimaginable abuse.

Late one night, Seth peeks into his brother's bedroom and witnesses something that will haunt him for years to come. He loses control and takes matters in his own hands, committing an act that ends his parent's lives and forever changes his own.

Demonized by the media, shunned by the community, and ostracized by the family lawyer, Seth's only hope lies with a rookie defense attorney and a stunningly attractive psychologist named Rita Logan.

The next three years becomes a daily struggle for survival in a world filled with hardened criminals, corrupt politicians, dirty cops, and a government organization that isn't supposed to exist. Seth's only reason to go on living is Rita, but he can't reach out to her – because he's supposed to be dead.

1

Aside from his parents, Seth didn't know a soul at the wake. He was the only one there from school, as he'd expected. He wasn't surprised none of the other kids from class came. Still he'd hoped one or two of the teachers would show up, although that wasn't the case. He'd never seen a dead body before. Although he'd been to several wakes in the past, it was always some distant relative, and he'd never approached the casket.

It was a dark overcast evening in the middle of April. The sad and gloomy sky hung low, as if to hug those present, offering some degree of comfort. Instead, it only seemed to amplify the awfulness of the tragedy.

Standing in a slow-moving line of aunts, uncles, and other family members, Seth inched along, toward the door of the Lillyhaven Funeral Home. His palms were sweaty and his face felt hot. He wasn't sure he could do this. He feared people would notice him, and he hated that. He never liked attention and avoided it whenever possible. His guts were one large bundle of knots.

Directly behind him, his mother pushed his father along in his wheelchair. A seemingly unending number of people purposely made their way over to say hello to her. Most greeters were overly loud. They hoped those within earshot would notice that she knew them. They were even more hopeful others would think she was a friend. Forcing smile after smile, Seth's mother softly claimed how good it was to see them and stated how she wished it were under other circumstances. Seth detested the fakeness of it all.

He'd held himself together, until now, and seemingly convinced himself that his best and only friend in this world wasn't gone forever. Soon enough though, he'd be inside the funeral home, nearing the casket. He wondered if he'd be able to continue suppressing his feelings, keeping them hidden, keeping them all inside where no one could see.

The reality of the situation, the litmus test of his true feelings, was about to be revealed – he only thought he was in control. Yes, Seth Boone, a young man who had learned over the last three years to hide all feelings and emotions, was about to be slapped across the face with a reality check. Being close to someone then having them being ripped away from you in a flash was something no one, especially a teenager, should have to go through.

He met Sarah a year and a half ago, well after his troubles at home started. She'd been in his class at school for nearly two years prior to that, but just like everyone else, he refused to speak to her. She seemed not to care. She hardly ever spoke to anyone herself, and never put forth any effort to make friends.

Seth never thought he'd have another friend in this world, neither did Sarah, but sure enough it happened. Sarah became more than just a friend - she was his reason to go on living. Sarah Cabell was the one person in the world of billions that he trusted. She was the one person in this world he could confide in. What was he to do now that she was gone? Having Sarah, meant neither of them had to live a life of solitude. They knew each other's secrets – secrets of the horrors they faced at home. She was gone now, dead – how could that be real?

Sarah and Seth had to meet secretly unless it was during or right after school. God only knows the treatment she would have endured at home if her parents knew she'd been talking to a boy. Seth, although he'd told his parents about Sarah, presented her as just a classmate, nothing more. He was careful not to mention her too much. He was afraid how his mother and father would react knowing he not only had a friend, but a girlfriend. Although he feared his father, he was more concerned about what his mother might do to him.

He thought how differently it would have been if Sarah hadn't been killed. In less than two months, school would be out of session. Their plans to run away that summer were gone now. Sarah escaped - taking those plans with her. His heart felt as though it were weighted down with lead. Sarah was only sixteen, same age as him. Her life was over – gone before it had begun. How could that be? He'd spoken to her just hours before the accident.

The police found the man who did it. The drunk that ran Sarah over while she was walking home from school never knew he'd hit someone. He crashed his car into a parked garbage truck a mile beyond the place he'd killed her. If the driver had been sober, the crash would have killed him too. When the police arrived, he was slumped over the wheel, unharmed of course. An officer opened the driver's door, and a half-empty bottle of sour mash whiskey fell into the street.

The line edged closer to the funeral home door. In a few minutes, he would be inside. His palms were wet from sweat as well as his forehead. A large lump had moved into his throat. Because of the trauma to Sarah's head, the casket was going to be closed. Seth was glad. He wanted to remember Sarah the way she was. If the casket were open, Sarah's hair wouldn't be fixed the same, and they would have covered her face with make-up, something Sarah never wore. He would have been standing there thinking how unnatural she looked, while listening to stupid people walk by and say how good she looked and what a nice job they'd done with her.

The line continued edging forward, and he was at the door now. Memories of Sarah flooded his mind. Random thoughts of the recent past and an ocean of raw emotion engulfed his every fiber. His chest tightened, and he was finding it hard to breathe. Sarah was dead. She had found her peace, something she'd never known while alive. She'd left him behind though. He was still alive on the outside but dead within.

Seth pulled the big door back and stepped to the side, allowing his mother to push his father's wheelchair past. He hated them being there. It was all for a show. They didn't know Sarah. Aside from the few things he told them, they knew nothing about her. Them being there was all for the benefit of his mother - the judge. She loved the attention. It wasn't uncommon for her to come to the funeral home when someone died, even if she didn't know the person who had passed. Everyone in town knew her. This was somewhere she could mingle and hear people praise her, while pretending to be compassionate.

His friend had died, not hers. Couldn't she have just stayed at home and let him go there alone to grieve in peace? He despised her at that moment more than he ever had in his life. He wished she were the one laying in the coffin. If the people in town knew the real Janie, they'd distance themselves from her as far as possible.

§

Seth's mother, Janie Gail Preston Boone, was the hometown girl, having been born and raised there in Abingdon, Virginia. She was an attractive forty-four year old, slender, with perfect brunette hair that hung around her shoulders with natural curl. Going along with her looks were her charm and charisma, which had most definitely played a part in propelling her into the position of a judge.

She'd risen fast up through the food chain - finding herself behind the bench as a federal judge at age thirty-three. Despite the fact there were several good men more qualified than her, when the seat became vacant, they were all overlooked. Uncle Sam looked around the courts and determined there were too many white male judges. The president was promoting diversity and women's rights, so the young, charming, Janie Boone from Abingdon fit the bill. She was not only the youngest, but also the first female to sit as a judge in the 14th District.

Janie was a beautiful woman by any standard. Men were constantly making eyes at her, and the brave ones would approach her, making subtle sexual gestures, testing the waters to see if they could swim. They all sank. She never once flirted back. She'd smile politely and excuse herself. To Janie, her reputation meant everything. She was a judge after all, and had an image to uphold. Any immoral act, especially adultery, could easily lead to her losing her seat on the bench, and she wasn't about to let that happen. Everyone viewed Janie as sweet, law abiding, an excellent wife, and of course the perfect mother. In the public eye, no one was more admired and loved in the town of Abingdon than Janie Boone.

Abingdon was a charming little southern town, nestled in the Appalachians just off Interstate 81. It's rich in history and culture, attracting those who wish to live a quieter life at a slower pace. It has a low crime rate, and the taxes are reasonable. There's a murder occasionally, but it's rare, usually linked to the drug trade that flows through Abingdon and every other city and town in the nation. A short drive west is Bristol, famous for its racetrack, part of the NASCAR racing circuit.

Raised in an upper-class neighborhood in Abingdon, Janie sang in the Presbyterian Church choir, donated hundreds of hours doing volunteer work - and of course, she was head cheerleader in high school. While in college, both of her parents died in a tragic parasailing accident while vacationing in Cancun. Janie was expected to inherit the wealth of the estate, but it was soon discovered her father was head over heels in debt from bad investments. He even owed the town barber, Jesse Wharton, over a hundred dollars for unpaid haircuts. After the creditors and IRS staked their claim in the estate and everything was settled, Janie received a little over eighty-grand of an alleged three-million dollar treasure chest.

A year later, Janie met and fell in love with Gordon Boone, a charming young man getting his start in the real estate business. Puppy love quickly turned into burning lust. Two months after meeting, they were married. Shortly after Janie finished law school, she and Gordon moved back to where her roots were, Abingdon, Virginia. Pulling a few strings with old family friends, she landed a job with the D.A.'s office. Gordon went to work for Southland Realtors, where he became an overnight success in commercial real estate.

The only Boone family member not present at the funeral home that evening was Julian, Seth's older brother by fourteen months. Julian was born with Downs Syndrome. He was quite small for a kid who'd just turned eighteen, but made up for his size with a killer smile and a heart as big as Texas. Aside from regular visits to the doctor or barbershop, Julian was seldom seen outside the house. Most often, it was Gordon or Seth taking Julian out because Janie was embarrassed to be seen with him. Why everyone had an angelic view of Janie Boone was a mystery to Seth.

Seth was shocked when his father called for a sitter that evening while they visited the funeral home. He expected his father to stay home with Julian, but that expectation never materialized. Hiring a setter was rare. He only recalled that being done once or twice. It wasn't that the Boone's couldn't afford a housekeeper or a sitter - they were quite wealthy. Seth suspected Janie didn't want strangers in the house because she was afraid they might somehow discover her secrets.

Day after day, Seth was the one who watched out for Julian. He cleaned up the messes Julian made, helped him bathe, washed the clothes, and cleaned the house. Seth was the Boone's household slave. He worked his tail off to keep the house in order. More often than not, if a hot meal was served, he was the one who prepared it.

It wasn't uncommon for Gordon and Janie to go off on vacation for as long as two weeks, leaving Seth to fend for himself and take care of Julian. That had been going on since Seth was eleven. In the beginning, he was devastated and scared senseless when they left him and Julian alone, but not anymore. Now he looked forward to the trips his parents took, and encouraged them to do so. With his parents out of town, it meant a few days of not having to take care of his mother's special needs.

Except for Sarah, Julian was the only person in the world Seth truly loved. Julian was innocent about anything and everything, and he loved his brother. Julian couldn't say the words the way he wanted to, but Seth knew how he felt. He and Sarah had already talked about it. After they ran off and found a place to settle in, they'd sneak back into town one night and take Julian away.

Seth thought Julian looked a lot like Janie. He had the same nose, same cheekbones, and he looked even more like her when he smiled. Seth didn't know who he looked like, grandparents perhaps. He certainly didn't look like his mother, and his build and facial features didn't resemble his father much. The thick hair was similar to his father's, but that was about it.

Seth used to adore his father. They played hard together. Gordon used to take him places and they'd spend time together. That all changed four years ago, when Gordon had his drunk-driving accident.

It was late one evening, around 11 p.m. Gordon had taken a potential commercial property buyer out for dinner and a few drinks. The few drinks turned into a few more. Gordon left the bar drunk. He tried to drive home but smacked the front end of an eighteen-wheel log hauler parked beside the highway. At seventy-miles per hour, there wasn't much left of the SUV Gordon was driving. The seatbelt was unbuckled. The airbag system saved his life. Gordon didn't escape without injury though. He lost both legs above the knees, nearly lost his arms, and suffered considerable damage to his lower abdomen. It was touch and go for three months. After he was stable, it was another six months of painful rehab. It was soon after Gordon came back home when the trouble started.

§

Once inside the funeral home, the line split into a half-dozen directions. Most people, including Seth's parents, veered off into small social clusters where insincere hugs and meaningless handshakes took place. The line going toward the casket moved quickly.

Soon enough, Seth found himself standing in front of the nicely polished box that held his sweet Sarah. He fought hard, trying to suppress the pain, the hurt, the heart tearing grief, but couldn't do it any longer. It was too much, too much to hold in. He loved Sarah, loved her with all his heart and soul. They'd held hands, hugged, and even kissed a few times, but their love was far more than physical desire.

Sarah was less than an arm's length away, but he couldn't touch her, hold her hand, or see her familiar sheepish smile he loved so much.

He draped his arms over the casket, and placed his head against the wooden box that held his sweet Sarah. Losing all control, his sudden, loud wails shook the walls of the building. His outburst of loud cries and calling out Sarah's name shocked Sarah's parents and deeply embarrassed Gordon and Janie. Finally, an elderly man who worked at the funeral home took Seth by the arm and led him aside, to an empty room reserved for grieving family members. There was only one person in there, a tall man, hardened face, and muscular. Seth had seen the man once or twice before hanging around the school, but didn't know who he was. The man got up from his seat and quickly left the room when Seth and the funeral home attendant entered.

Back inside the viewing area, people were asking who the young man was who'd cried out Sarah's name and showed such deep caring emotion. Could Sarah have had a boyfriend? Several women began gossiping, talking about Seth's show of emotion, and even more about his good looks. At sixteen, he'd just reached six feet two inches in height, and he was built like a professional football fullback.

For the last three years, Seth had lived a life of seclusion, seeing no one outside the home, except for the secret visits with Sarah. Seth's father had a rather nice weight room in the basement - one Gordon used a lot prior to his accident. Seth had taken over the weight room, using it as a means to burn off his energy, frustrations, and anger. He had lots of anger. With the help of several nutritional bodybuilding supplements, protein shakes, plus hours on end exercising and pumping iron, every muscle on his body rippled and he had remarkable strength.

Seth kept his six-pack, large guns, and other bulging muscles hidden by wearing oversized baggy clothing. Still, even at that, he could never hide his neck that looked like a tree trunk and forearms that would make Charles Atlas wince. Most boys his age worked hard to develop small bi-ceps to sport in front of the girls. Seth though, had the right genetic make-up to form hard rippling sinew with little to no effort. The girls at school, all of whom shunned him, thought he was a weirdo. Still, they found themselves feasting their eyes at him, wondering what hunk of a body lie beneath his clothes.

"Judge Boone, was that your son, Seth, over by the casket a few moments ago?" Joyce Matheny, her hairdresser asked.

"Ahmm. Yes, that was Seth," she replied, feeling her face turn red from being embarrassed.

"He's a hunk dear, and so handsome."

Janie smiled then turned away, not wanting to engage in further conversation about Seth. Gordon grinned then thanked Mrs. Matheny for her kind words.

Seth reappeared in the room after a few minutes passed. He was composed, but it was easy to see he'd been crying. He walked over and sat down in a chair, two rows behind where Janie was sitting. Gordon sat beside Janie in his wheelchair.

Janie turned in her chair and looked spitefully at Seth.

"Apparently you were more than just a friend of that girl," she said in a loud whisper with a harsh tone.

"No, we were just friends," Seth replied, looking down at the floor, still trying to hold onto his composure.

"Well, we'll talk more about this later," she said. "You can miss school and go to the funeral tomorrow, but your father and I won't be able to make it. We've both got obligations."

"Fine."

"Are you ready to go home? It's getting late and you've caused quite a stir. I hope you realize that your father and I have been embarrassed to no end here this evening!"

"Can I just like walk home?" he asked in a low voice.

Gordon looked at Janie then turned back to look at Seth. "Sure you can," he replied, not giving Janie the chance to speak further.

"We'll see you back at the house," Janie replied, with bitterness in her voice. "Since you have a long walk and a lot of fresh air ahead of you, I can only hope you'll pull yourself together by the time you get home."

Janie stood. She walked to the back of the wheelchair as Gordon released the brakes. They wasted no time leaving the funeral home. Seth sat there for a while, his elbows resting on his knees and his head cupped in his hands. Home was the last place he wanted to go. His mother was so cold and indifferent towards him. Even now, with his best friend laying in a casket a few yards away, she treated him harshly, thinking only of herself.

Turning his thoughts back to Sarah, the tears began flowing again. How was he going to make it without her? She was his rock, his foundation. She was the only thing in his world that made sense. It felt as if the weight of this cruel world now rested entirely on his shoulders, a weight he couldn't bear.

Several adults approached him, trying to drum up conversation. He knew their true interest wasn't about him when they patted him on the back, asking if he were okay. Their real interest was in how he knew Sarah, how close they were. They wanted information they could use in gossip. They would have loved Seth pouring his soul out to them, but that wasn't going to happen. He didn't like to engage with people, and certainly not this crowd. No, he didn't want to hear their questions, much less answer them. If for no other reason, he was afraid they could somehow read his mind, and see the truth – the truth about him and his family.

Since age thirteen, there had been little engagement with people at school as well. Seth had withdrawn from the other kids, pulled away, befriending no one, and only talking to the students or teachers when he had no choice. Most of the students at school thought he was strange. The others thought he was just stuck up, conceited because his mom was a judge.

On a daily basis, he heard them talking about him openly, and the upperclassmen often approached him, calling him Weird Ass Seth. The boys dared not get too close though or go too far. They could see past the baggy clothing covering Seth's bulging muscles. They only wanted to make sport of him, not fight him. Keeping their distance, the boys feared Seth might explode, take them down, and make mincemeat of their face. If that happened, they'd never live it down with their classmates.

2

Taking slow deliberate steps, Seth left the funeral home and started walking home. A kaleidoscope of thoughts rolled about in his mind. Sarah - running away - having to deal with his parents once he got home. The approaching darkness, plus a carload of teens driving by shouting obscenities caused him to snap out of his profound flood of thoughts. He hesitantly picked up the pace. As he turned the corner onto Huff Creek Road, there it was ahead – home, the place where evil dwelt. Seeing the house, his steps slowed again. The dread of another night with his parents pushed all other thoughts aside.

Walking up the driveway, he looked at the upstairs windows. Light was shining from his mother and father's bedroom, as well as Julian's room. Downstairs, light poured from the large living room window, even though the drapes were drawn closed. The light pushed back the darkness around the azalea bushes, creating strange shadows across the lawn. He slipped past the garage and walked around the house. After crossing the spacious redwood deck, he entered the back door. The light over the range was on, allowing him to walk through the kitchen without flipping on a switch. He wanted to go downstairs, use the weights for a bit before heading to bed. A workout would burn off energy and help him sleep.

As he entered the hallway by the spiral staircase, he placed his hand on the knob of the door leading to the basement. His father's voice called out to him from the living room. He let go of the door, turned, and went in that direction. There in the corner was his father, in his pajamas. His wheelchair was sitting in front of the big recliner he'd learned to maneuver into by himself. His pipe was in his mouth, and a large plume of blue smoke hung near the ceiling, indicating he'd just lit up.

"Sit down for a minute. I'd like to talk to you."

Seth took a seat on the sofa, sitting on the edge, hoping this wouldn't take long. He dreaded what was going to come next. His father never spoke much to him these days, other than to tell him what his duties were and how it would ruin the family if their secret ever got out. He used to describe how he and Janie would go to jail if word ever leaked out, and how Julian would end up in an orphanage somewhere. It had been a while since that had been a part of the speech, but it was always the same message no matter how much the words changed.

"You looked very handsome tonight," Gordon said.

Seth wasn't used to hearing kind words from his father. It appeared for once he was proud of his son.

"I like you dressed up. Even though your dress shirt is baggy, and you haven't grown into those pants yet. Still, it's a far cry from those oversized sweatshirts you normally wear. I'd like to see you start dressing better, but that's a discussion we can take up later."

"Can I go now, Dad? I'd like to work out a bit before going to bed."

"In a minute. I know we don't talk much. I watched you this evening. I could see how much you've matured.

You're already a man. I can't believe how fast you've grown."

Seth would like to have smiled. He would have liked being able to give his dad a hug and tell him how much he loved him, be he couldn't. He knew what was coming next, and he didn't want to hear it.

"Your mother noticed how handsome you were tonight too. She needs you son. Go ahead and do your workout, then get a shower and come upstairs. Don't forget your medicine. Your mother placed a new prescription on your bathroom sink."

"Oh God, not tonight, please! I'm hurting tonight Dad. Sarah was my friend, and now she's dead. I need some time to think, to mourn."

Gordon was in no mood for excuses. His face was stern and his voice demanding. "You need to take care of your mother. Don't argue with me. It's your duty!"

Seth stood. He was angry, reeling, his face blood red.

"NO. I'm not doing it anymore, Dad. I refuse. Don't try making me."

Seth's voice was breaking up. He'd never talked back to his father before. In addition to that, he was standing before him with clinched fists.

"I was in love with Sarah. We were going to run away. We were going to run away from you and the devil upstairs you worship. Damn you."

Seth began crying. He had never denied his father or mother's request. It was new ground, and although he was horrified about what might happen, it felt good to stand there in defiance.

"I love you both, but it's wrong, Dad. I can't do that anymore. Please!"

He was hoping using the words 'love and please' would soften the blow of his defiance. Gordon Boone was not a man to say no to, no matter who you were.

"Sit down," Gordon said calmly. "I hope you don't mean any of that. What has gotten into you? Where did this love thing with Sarah come from? Gees, I had no idea you were out sneaking around."

Seth didn't move. He'd crossed a line, was in new territory, and didn't know what would happen next. More than anything, he was sorry he'd mentioned Sarah.

"Go ahead and do your workout son. I'll speak with your mother, and I think under the circumstances she'll understand, just this once. I know you're upset, but I want you to think long and hard about your words and the anger you've just displayed. That's not how a man in control acts. Remember, you owe the family, and we all depend on you to do your part. The best thing for you to do is get over Sarah and whatever the hell you two had going on. The sooner the better. By the way, you're grounded until further notice."

There was silence as Gordon stared Seth down with his deep penetrating eyes. The silence was deafening. Seth felt his anger dissipate, then his knees getting weak. He'd expected his father to punish him physically for his outburst and harsh words. Perhaps his father had seen how he was at the funeral home and how troubled he was. *Maybe he remembers what it's like to be young and lose someone*, Seth thought.

"I'm sorry," Seth said. "May I go work out now?""

"Get on out of here. I'll talk to your mother. I'll tell her you're sick, running a fever." Gordon drew a long breath and exhaled. "I never want to hear Sarah's name mentioned again in this house. You know your obligation to this family, son. I don't like this arrangement any better than you do. Do you think I like being a cripple, unable to take care of your mother? Damn you - instead of me!" Gordon took another deep breath, still staring intently at Seth. "You know Julian is a man now. Although he's got a child's mind, he's got a man's body."

Seth was livid. His father's words caused his blood to drain to his feet. Gordon might as well have thrown a brick and hit him in the face. The result would have been the same.

"No," Seth said lowly, almost whispering. He meant for the words to come out loudly, indicating a demand, but they didn't. "Don't ever try that Dad. Please, don't ever...." He wanted to say more, wanted to lash out, but his stomach was churning. He rushed out of the room and down to the basement. Barely making it into the bathroom downstairs, he hurled himself toward the commode, the contents of his stomach already in his throat.

Minutes later, Seth stumbled out of the bathroom, weak, barely able to walk. He managed to reach the workout bench and he laid down. Two-hundred pounds of weights rested on the bar over his head, the amount he had been starting his workouts with as of late, before moving on to the big stuff. A new flood of thoughts flowed through his mind, and a range of new emotions unmasked themselves. It was raw emotion, far too much of it to think clearly. As bad as things were with Sarah dying, his father's words had compounded the situation exponentially. He strained to understand how his parents could be so cold, so abusive, and so cruel to their children.

He'd lost his innocence three years ago, only days after his father had gotten out of the rehabilitation center and come home. It was a day forever embedded in his mind, a day that changed his world, who he was, or would ever be. No one ever deserved what had happened to him - and now his father had threatened to let it happen to Julian. He'd never let that happen. He'd go on being the whipping boy, the slave, the chained dog. He'd do anything they wanted as long as they left Julian alone.

Gordon's words played over and over in Seth's head. He lay there on the bench staring at the ceiling. The horrible taste in his mouth from his upchuck didn't taste as bad as the words his father had spoken.

"Dad was merely making a threat. It wasn't something he and mom would ever carry out," he whispered in the darkness. "Besides, there's no way Julian with Downs Syndrome could do that anyway."

Seth stood up. He had to clear his mind of those thoughts. He wanted to think of something else. The sights and thoughts of Julian being abused were making him sick again. He turned his thoughts back to Sarah as tears gathering in the corners of his eyes.

He walked out of the weight room and into the den where a large-screen television hung on the wall. The joysticks of the game system, which he seldom touched, were stretched out across the floor. Julian had been there earlier in the evening playing a game, likely while he and his parents had been at the funeral home.

Opening a cabinet underneath the dry sink, Seth reached in the back and removed his dad's bottle of scotch whiskey. He'd removed it before, occasionally taking a sip then putting it away once the liquor began burning his lips, throat, and stomach. Tonight was different. He pulled the cork, turned the bottle up and took a large gulp. The liquor immediately burned his lips, as it always had, but he managed to swallow. The strong drink set his throat ablaze as it moved downward then he felt the warmth as it hit his stomach. The taste from his upchucking was gone. He was thankful for that. He took the bottle, sat down on the soft sofa, and in the darkness, took another swallow.

For a sixteen-year-old with little drinking experience, it was only a few minutes before the alcohol took effect. He felt relaxed for the first time since he'd crawled out of bed fifteen hours earlier.

§

Seth's mind raced back three years, to when the trouble at home first started. His father had gotten home from rehab the day before. It was near bedtime when his father came into his room. Gordon had tears in his eyes, and his voice shook as he spoke to Seth about man things - things he wasn't ready to hear. He told Seth how the accident had rendered him incapable of ever having sex again. Next, he explained that his mother was a woman who needed sex, a need that was almost uncontrollable. It embarrassed Seth greatly and he'd wondered why his father was telling him those things. He was thirteen, and clueless about many of the things he was hearing.

He remembered sitting up in bed as he listened, his father sitting beside the bed in his wheelchair. He remembered every word his father spoke, as if it were yesterday.

"Your mother works hard for this family, Seth. As a judge, her behavior is constantly being monitored, and it is required of her to be seen as a model citizen. She's held to a higher standard, one miscue and her job could be in jeopardy. Therefore, she must be careful about everything she does and says."

Seth sat there silently, taking in everything, but confused as to why he was hearing all that.

"Your mother - she needs to have sex. If she were to go outside the home – well, there's too great a danger of it being found out. If that were to happen, she'd lose her job and we'd be poor, living like the Stotesbury and Nimitz families across the tracks from the fire station."

Seth was familiar with the area his father was speaking of - it was the poorest section of town. Some of the houses there didn't have running water. One of the Stotesbury girls, named Helen, was in his class. When she came to school, she always wore the same dirty clothes. She was always hungry, taking any food that others were willing to give her. Her teeth were rotten, and she didn't smell good.

"I don't understand." Seth had said, looking toward his father for answers.

"This is our family Seth, and we all love one another. We have to stick together – do our part, helping in any way possible." There was a short silence, then – "Your mother wants to lay with you."

Seth's eyes widened. He was only thirteen, but knew what 'lay with you' meant. Did he hear his dad correctly? No, he couldn't do that. He didn't know the right words for that, or how to describe it - but he knew it was wrong. The thoughts of doing that made him feel physically sick. He'd been looking at Playboy magazines over at his friend Simon's house. They'd talked about sex and girls at school who were supposedly 'putting out', and that seemed normal. Not this though, this wasn't good - it was unnatural - strictly forbidden. What his own father had just proposed sounded like the most horrible thing a person could do.

Gordon continued talking, telling him how important it was for the family. He even cried. At some point, Janie entered the room, dimmed the lights, and sat down on the bed beside him. She talked sweetly, stroked his hair, and told him how much she loved him. Seth was tense, confused, and afraid.

With her long silk like fingers, she caressed his arms and legs then moved to his inner thigh. He had an erection, although he tried his best not to. She talked about being a judge, how the public looked at her, just as his father had already told him. She told him about her inner desires. She kept telling him how he had to be the man of the house, how he had to take care of her with things his father could no longer do.

Janie told Seth she would never cheat on his father and how being faithful and keeping things in the family were important. She told him how he could help the family - how it would be a special gift to her. She asked if he wanted to keep on living in their nice house, have nice things, nice toys. She spoke soothing words making it sound like participating in sex with her would be one of the best thing he could ever do for his parents.

"But why can't you just take care of yourself?" Seth asked. "I don't know a lot about it, but I saw women toys in a magazine, and they were guaranteed to satisfy your desires as much as a man could."

He remembered the heat on his face as he'd said that, openly admitting he'd been looking at sex magazines. He was afraid his mother and father would be upset with him for doing that, but they said nothing about it. Instead of being upset, his mother's words were sweet and softly spoken.

"Oh sweetie, it's not the same as having a man," she replied. "I know this may seem wrong to you, but under these circumstances, it's not. We can't ever tell anyone. No one would understand, but it's not wrong. Your father can't help me anymore, but you can. You can take his place and be the man of the house."

She kept caressing him, telling him how he owed the family and had to be the man in place of his father in bedroom matters. Seth couldn't believe he was having the conversation with not one but both of his parents. He'd been expecting his dad to give him 'The Sex Talk', but never would he had dreamed this would ever happen. He felt like a tremendous amount of responsibility had just been placed on his shoulders, one he didn't know if he could bear. He felt a thick darkness take over, a darkness so thick an axe couldn't cut through it.

He didn't know if he could actually have sex with a girl his age, much less his own mother. Janie was an attractive woman, and could easily have beaten out those models he'd seen posing in his friend Simon's magazines, but still - she was his mother. The talk continued about how the family needed him to step up, how he owed it to them, and what would happen to them if he didn't.

He pleaded, but his parents assured him that under the circumstances, it was the right thing to do. They said it was part of a boy growing into a man. Janie slipped her hand inside her son's pajamas. She told him to hold the headboard and relax - she would do the rest. Both Janie and Gordon kept telling him this was his duty. He was horrified, and knew it was in sharp contrast to anything decent or moral.

She stroked him gently. His male member had risen with all the stiffness and vigor of a young man. He tried not to have the erection, but it was as if he had no control over his own body. Gordon released the brakes on his wheelchair, rolled himself over to the door, turned off the lights, and left the room, closing the door behind him.

It was a clear night outside. A quarter moon shone through the window, dimly lighting the room. Seth could see the shadow of his mother as she lifted her nightgown and climbed on top of him. He placed his hands back and grabbed hold of the headboard, as she'd requested. Within seconds, he felt the warm sensation. He knew she'd slipped him inside of her. She rolled back and forth. It was over quickly, Seth exploding, unable to control his own body. He tried not to moan, but knew he had. Janie breathed hard and squeezed her legs against his as she shivered.

She quickly got off the bed and went to his bathroom, returning with a warm wet washcloth to clean him. The sensation was very satisfying, but the thoughts of what had happened made him sick, both physically and mentally. Janie kissed him on the cheek, and stroked his hair. She told him how precious he was, and thanked him for what he had done.

It was the wee hours of the morning before he fell asleep. When he awakened, he realized something sinister had taken place. He felt dirty. The act that had taken place was taboo, immoral, unnatural - an abomination. He wanted to take a long shower, but knew nothing could wash away the sin of that night. His body could be washed, but a filthy film that nothing could cleanse had crawled inside him and permeated his entire body. His world would never be the same.

At breakfast, Janie and Gordon acted as if nothing had happened. Everything in Seth's life had changed however. Loneliness, withdrawal, a lack of self-worth - suddenly became his world.

In the days following, she came to his room every night. It was the same routine night after night as his mother climbed on top of him and took control of his male member that acted on its own, standing voluntarily erect. She sometimes faced him, other times she turned in the other direction.

No matter which way she faced, she always held tight and dug into his skin with her fingernails when she climaxed. It hurt when she dug in, and he would wince. It seemed to please Janie, knowing she was in charge and had the ability to inflict pain. Although he wanted to badly, he never screamed. She would have like that, but he was determined not to give her that satisfaction. The abuse left cuts and bruises on his arms, legs, and torso. That was another reason he always wore pants and long-sleeve shirts, even in summer.

Once a month, when Janie was having her menstrual cycle, she'd leave him alone. He was thankful for those times, and he prayed every night that she'd bleed to death. The worst times were when she returned from a work-related trip or a small vacation with Gordon. From the moment she arrived back home he could see the want in her eyes. He knew that night would be more violent, more digging in with her claws. He loathed at the sight of her, and a deep hatred toward his mother grew stronger day by day.

Seth soon reached a point he would block it out. He would put his mind somewhere else when it was happening.

He'd read how fathers had raped their daughters. He didn't think it was possible for a mother to rape her son, yet it was happening to him time and time again. The shame and guilt were overwhelming, and it changed him. He withdrew from anyone outside the home, even his best friend Simon. It wasn't long before he'd lost all his friends.

He thought he'd die of guilt and shame. He never told anyone, until he and Sarah became close. How could he tell anyone? No one would believe he was being continually raped by his mother. No one thought a man, even a young one could get an erection without wanting to, but it was happening. That caused him think even more so that something was wrong with him. After a while, he was able to control his body, and sometimes he'd go limp. That's when Janie began forcing him to take an erectile dysfunction drug. The prescription bottles had Gordon's name on them.

Seth learned to block it out when they were having sex. He'd put his mind in another world, thinking about riding his bicycle across the country, climbing a high mountain, or flying an airplane.

Not thinking it was possible for a female to rape a male, he found himself at the library conducting researching. Little was found on the subject, and what he did find was controversial, doctors having opinions that went both ways. He felt the rapes were his fault, that he'd done something wrong. Even worse, he thought perhaps he was born with some genetic disorder that sent subliminal messages to his mother, making her want him. He wondered if that genetic defect had been passed down from generation to generation. He wondered if inbreeding was why Julian had Downs Syndrome. The shame and guilt continued to eat at him like a fast-spreading cancer.

One of the teachers at school, noting Seth's change of behavior, became suspicious. Something was wrong, but Seth being a boy, and knowing his father was in a wheelchair, never expected sexual abuse. Besides, his mother was a federal judge.

At a parent teacher meeting, Janie assured the teacher Seth was just being rebellious, and his behavior change was mainly because of medication doctors had given him. That seemingly satisfied the teacher and over time, everyone forgot how the once outgoing and popular Seth was now severely withdrawn. Helping ease concerns was the fact that his grades never dropped. Seth was the brightest of students, and aced every test. He even had an uncanny ability to walk into a room, take a quick look around and describe everything in detail. His reading comprehension scores were nearly perfect and when it came to math and science, it was clear to see he was gifted.

After the meeting at school, Janie told Seth that if he ever told anyone about what was going on she would say he was the one raping her, and have him put away in prison for the remainder of his life. She had put the fear of God into him. Seth knew she was manipulative, and as a federal judge, she had the ways and means to carry out her threat.

Withdrawn, having no friends, and little contact with anyone outside the school setting, Seth turned to reading. He also discovered weightlifting. A considerable amount of time each day was spent in the basement, using his father's free weights and other workout equipment. It burned off excessive energy, and helped disperse his anger. It was therapeutic.

Many of the books he read were on bodybuilding. His vigorous workouts began to show. The muscles in his arms, legs, and back began to bulge. Janie noticed but never said anything about him becoming bigger and more rigid. It was a turn-on to her. If Seth had realized that, he would have stopped lifting weights immediately.

Seth found muscle building to be easy. He had the right chemistry, the right genetic makeup to build muscle, to bulk-up. By age fifteen, he could have grabbed Janie with one hand and easily have choked the life out of her. Thoughts like that entered his mind on occasion, but he quickly suppressed them. No matter how badly she treated him, no matter how many times she raped him, she was his mother and he loved her. It was so strange that he could love her but also hate her. He hated what she was, but loved her for who she was – his mother.

Nearly two years after that first nightmarish event with his mother, he met Sarah. She was withdrawn, just as he was. They were forced to work together on a science project at school since no one else picked either of them as a partner. In casual conversations with Sarah, little things were said which made him suspect she was being abused by her father. He began asking her simple questions about her home life, all in a manner so she wouldn't suspect he was probing. It wasn't long before she began asking him questions as well.

He felt a connection with Sarah, so he opened up to her. Soon enough, they both confessed to each other about being raped by their parents. Sarah couldn't believe it, Seth being raped by his mother. At first, he had a hard time convincing her it was real, but he was always honest with her, and she quickly realized he was being truthful. Being able to share their horrors of home life was like a great weight being lifted from them. They had each other to confide in. They had someone who cared.

Sarah was gone now - forever. Seth was alone in the world again, still a teenage sex slave to his federal judge mother with a depraved mind.

He wanted to escape, but he didn't know how. He had been led to believe servicing his mother was his duty, something he owed the family, and without him doing so they all would suffer greatly, even Julian. Although he hated what was happening, he would die before seeing Julian suffer from the same abuse. He loved his big brother and hoped to someday become a doctor and find a cure for the awful defect from which Julian suffered. Janie's words about what would happen if the family fell apart played in Seth's mind every day. No one wanted a child, actually a man, with Downs Syndrome. Julian could possibly end up in an orphanage, and likely would suffer many forms of abuse.

It was a similar story for Sarah. She had been convinced by her father that if she ever told, the family would be destroyed. She had an older sister who had left home and never came back to visit. Sarah suspected her sister had been abused also. The sex abuse at Sarah's house was different from what Seth experienced. Often, her mother would join in, making it a threesome.

When Seth and Sarah could find a place and time to be alone, they always held each other and often cried. Their abusive parents had stolen their childhood, their innocence, and all but destroyed them. Their parents were mentally ill, committing sick loathsome acts of violence on their own children. Seth and Sarah were caught in a dragnet, being raked across the bottom of a river, unable to breathe, unable to escape. Sarah had escaped however. She no longer would suffer the abuse, the torture, the rapes – Sarah was dead.

3

Seth was asleep, but awakened when he fell over on the couch. The scotch bottle hit the floor, but luckily, he had placed the cork back in the bottle. Looking at his watch, he saw it was nearly 11 p.m. As he stood to put the bottle back in the cabinet where he'd found it, he realized he was still feeling the effects from the alcohol.

After putting the bottle away, he walked toward the stairwell and turned off the lights in the den as he left. He crept up the stairs to the main floor. The living room was dark. He proceeded up the spiral staircase toward his bedroom, taking gentle steps, hoping not to awaken his parents.

Tiptoeing past his parent's bedroom, he noticed the door was half-open. It was dark inside the room. He dared not look in. All he wanted to do was reach his own bedroom, unnoticed. As he slid past Julian's room, he noticed a small amount of light coming from beneath the door. He gave that no thought, Julian was scared of the dark, and often slept with a light on.

Finally reaching his own room, he eased inside and gently shut the door. He walked into his bathroom, wanting to relieve himself and brush his teeth before getting into bed. Sitting on the granite top of his bathroom sink was the prescription bottle his father had mentioned. He hated taking the erectile dysfunction medication. It kept his penis hard long beyond the four hours they talked about on television, and often it hurt for hours after the erection had finally gone away. There was no way he could seek medical treatment though, no way he could complain, no way he could do anything except suck it up and continue being his mother's sex slave.

The cap was off the medicine bottle, which puzzled him. *Why would Dad leave the cap off a new medicine bottle?* He thought.

He placed the cap back on the bottle, relieved himself, and after his hands were washed, reached for his toothbrush. After applying a generous amount of toothpaste, he began brushing. Trying to go over each molar and incisor properly, like the dental hygienist had shown him, Seth worked the brush with effort. All the while, he was still wondering about the medication. After rinsing and placing the toothbrush back in its holder, he picked up the prescription bottle.

Walking into the bedroom, he turned on the lamp sitting on the stand beside his bed. He poured the pills onto the nightstand then counting each tablet put them back in the bottle. He counted 19. He poured the pills out again, recounting as he placed each one back inside the plastic container. He arrived at the same number, 19. He read from the label on the side of the bottle, 'Quantity – 20'.

A horrible and sickening thought hit him. It couldn't be true, but he knew he had to check it out - otherwise he'd not sleep that night. Tiptoeing back out of his bedroom and down the hall, he eased up to Julian's door. There were muffled voices inside.

He slowly turned the doorknob and eased the door open far enough to stick his head inside. Julian's bathroom door was ajar and a light was on inside, spreading enough light to dimly illuminate the bedroom.

With his eyes adjusting to the light, Seth saw something that would be impressed on his mind for the rest of his life. His jaw dropped, and his eyes widened. His stomach began to churn again, and he felt his knees weaken. Gordon was at the head of the bed, sitting in his wheelchair, stroking Julian's hair. Julian was sucking his thumb. He could hear Gordon speaking lowly, telling Julian he was a good boy, that he was doing fine, and that everything was going to be great.

Janie was on the bed, her thin nightgown hiked up around her waist. She was straddling Julian, with her head toward his feet. She had her claws dug deep into Julian's knees and was rocking violently back and forth, making deep moaning sounds.

Seth snapped. He was overcome with more anger and rage then he'd felt in his entire life. He was out of control, out of his head.

It all happened so fast. He barely remembered opening the door, grabbing Julian's baseball bat propped against his dresser, and racing toward the bed.

The first swing hit Janie in the back of the head. The velocity of the bat being swung by Seth's powerful arms was akin to that of a major-league slugger. Her head sounded like a hard nut being cracked by a hammer, followed by a gushing noise. Gordon let go of Julian and was turning to face Seth when the bat hit him squarely on the bridge of his nose. The blow was powerful. Gordon's wheelchair reared and sent him tumbling backward onto the floor beside the bed. Janie fell off the bed on the opposite side from Seth. Hitting the floor, her limp body made a loud thump.

Already horrified by what his parents were doing to him, Julian watched his brother unleash his rage. Julian began crying uncontrollably. Seth dropped the bat, grabbed Julian, pulled him out of his bed, and held him closely, just as he'd done many times before when Julian was upset. With his arms wrapped around Julian, Seth led him back to his own bedroom and closed the door, locking it behind him.

Julian climbed into Seth's bed and scooted up against the headboard, pulling the covers over his head. It was something Julian had done many times over the years. Seth sat down next to Julian, cradled him, and held him tightly. Seth said nothing - he didn't have to. Julian thought of his younger brother as his protector. Being there with Seth was all he needed. He felt safe now, and was soon asleep. Seth sat there in the darkness, expecting Gordon and Janie to come pounding on his door at any moment, madder than hell and ready to give him the worst whipping of his entire life - but he didn't care. He couldn't believe they would actually take advantage of Julian, the sweetest and most innocent person in the entire world.

After an hour had passed and still no knock at the door, Seth slipped Julian's head off his lap and gently placed a pillow beneath him. He walked across the room in the dark, eased the door open, and stepped into the hallway. The house was dark and still. The dim light coming from the open doorway inside Julian's room shone into the hallway, providing enough light for Seth to make his way there without stumbling.

Standing in the doorway of Julian's room, the smell of blood and feces penetrated Seth's nostrils. Something was terribly wrong. He flipped on the light switch and saw Gordon, still on the floor, his wheelchair laying on top of him. He walked far enough into the room to see Janie lying on the floor across from the bed. There was blood everywhere, and a long red smear on the hardwood floor indicated she had scooted a few feet toward the bathroom before she'd stopped breathing.

Seth became scared. He backed toward the door, turned off the light, covering his parent's bodies with darkness, and raced back to his bedroom. He grabbed his cordless phone and ran back to the bed. After jumping in, he placed his back against the headboard. He lifted Julian's head from the pillow and placed it back in his lap as before. He then punched 911 on the phone.

A female voice answered and asked what the emergency was. Seth didn't answer. He let go of the phone, allowing it to fall to the floor. Sitting there in the darkness cuddling his older brother, a thousand thoughts went through his mind, each passing quickly as a parade of others entered. Seth lacked two months of reaching his seventeenth birthday on July 1st. His parents were no doubt dead. He knew he was going to be arrested, likely tried as an adult, and could even face the death penalty. Thinking like a child, he told himself it didn't matter because he would be free of his parent's bonds. There was a flood of emotions, he felt like he was drowning. When he hit his parents, it was only to make them stop doing to Julian what they had done to him.

It was only days ago that he and Sarah had a dream. In that dream, there was freedom. He and Sarah would run away, leave Abingdon and their parents behind. That dream had crashed and burned when Sarah died. Sitting in the bed cuddling Julian, Seth knew he'd gained his own freedom that evening as well, but it had come in a much different way, and at a very high cost. Things had turned out differently and far worse than he, or anyone else, could imagine. The book of his life had begun a new chapter and nothing would ever again be good.

The voice of the 911 operator could still be heard on the phone, trying to get a response. Seth picked the phone up off the floor and put it to his ear.

"There's been an accident," he said. "I think I killed my parents."

4

Ten minutes after speaking with the 911 operator, Seth saw streaks of blue and red light penetrating through the shades covering his bedroom windows. He heard faint voices outside, then hard bangs on the front door. Next, he heard loud banging that shook the walls. The police were using a battering ram to breech the door.

When the front door flung open, the alarm system in the house went off. The high-pitched wailing siren awakened Julian, and he began whimpering. Seth held him close and whispered to him that everything was fine. Julian put his head on Seth's chest and closed his eyes again. A few seconds passed then the alarm system became silent.

It sounded like an army had invaded the downstairs. Men were screaming orders as they rushed in. It was a S.W.A.T. team, wearing assault gear and armed to the teeth. A systematic search took place of the ground floor then the troops began climbing the spiral stairway. The lights on the men's headgear were shining about, along with red lasers bouncing off the walls and furniture, creating a scary light show.

When they reached Gordon and Janie's bedroom, everything was found in order. The bed covers were in place, having never been turned down for the night. The dress Janie had worn to the wake lay stretched across the king-sized bed.

There was a lot of commotion when the men reached Julian's room. They were shouting, calling for an ambulance while more men rushed up the stairway. Seconds later, Seth's bedroom door flew open. Bright lights and men screaming commands filled the room instantly.

Seth couldn't remember what happened for the few minutes after that. His next memory was he and Julian huddled together on the couch in the living room. There were seven, maybe eight officers in the room. A detective handed them cans of cold Coke from the refrigerator.

"Did you smell that boy?" Seth heard a uniformed officer across the room ask a man wearing a suit. "He reeks of whiskey."

An officer had already made Seth blow hard into some sort of tube. He expected it was a breath-analyzer.

The assault team, familiar with crime scene procedures, backed out of Julian's room as soon as they determined Gordon and Janie Boone were dead.

One of the officers who had burst into Seth's room was interviewed by a detective just arriving at the scene.

"They looked like two scared little boys," the officer said. "Both were huddled together at the head of the bed. They looked like they'd just emerged from the gates of hell."

Two seasoned homicide detectives were assigned to the case and showed up soon after the house had been searched and declared safe by the assault unit. Both were Virginia State Police officers, with many years of experience. Glen Rodgers, one of the officers, had forty years with the State Police. The other detective, Bradley Mullens had been in police work for thirty-seven years with over twenty-five of those as a detective. Between the two of them, they'd seen everything imaginable, but neither had seen two people with their heads bashed open like smashed pumpkins.

"I'll be curious to see the coroner's report on these two," Rodger's said to Mullens. "Appears the only injury is a blow to each victim's head with the baseball bat we found lying in the floor. Damn near took their heads off."

"Shocking but not surprising really," Mullens replied. "Did you get a look at the guns on that kid sitting down in the living room? He's just a kid, but he's built like the Incredible Hulk."

"I saw him. He's a kid by age, but little doubt, he's a man," Rodgers said. "Hopefully, our boys downstairs will get something out of him before he gets all lawyered up."

"Fat chance," Mullens said. "He's a juvenile, and one of the victims is Judge Boone, the kid's mother for crying out loud. Odds are a dozen lawyers will be swooping down on this place before we're finished up here."

"Yeah, you're probably right, plus a dozen feds since she's one of their clan," Mullens added.

"Did you know her? I mean, did you ever meet the judge?" Rodgers asked.

"Met her two or three times," Mullens replied. "It was at social events. Damn hot body. She always dressed sexy. Most men in the room, me included, couldn't keep their eyes off her. Too much beauty for a judge, that's for sure. She had a hot body and beautiful face. What a shame, she looks like shit now, ruins my memories of her."

Rodgers opened a large plastic bag and placed the baseball bat inside. It would be sent to the lab for analysis.

In machine gun fashion, Rodgers and Mullens began rapid firing comments into their hand-held recorders. It would all be transcribed to notes later. They took hundreds of photos and measurements. After that, they turned the scene over to the forensic team to do their thing.

Abingdon averages two murders per year, usually drug related or some jealous husband coming home from work early and finding John Doe in bed with his wife. This was much different. A popular 'hometown girl' and her husband had been brutally murdered, and their son was the prime suspect. The mother happened to be a well-known and well-liked federal judge. By morning, every coffee shop, schoolroom, office, and curbside conversation in town would be bustling with rumors and self-made explanations about what had happened.

On the street, there'd be hundreds of stories about what made the Boone kid, known in school as 'Weird Ass Seth', go crazy and do it. This wasn't just local news – this was big time. A federal judge being murdered by her teenage son would draw nationwide attention. All the big networks, and of course a dozen or more tabloids, would rush to Abingdon, wanting to interview anyone willing to speak into a microphone. The bloodthirsty reporters would never let the truth stand in the way of a good story that would sell papers.

The police would have a drug test conducted on Seth, which would come back negative. They'd already done a breathalyzer test, and although it indicated his blood-alcohol level was within the legal limit, the fact remained - he had been drinking and he was under age. If Seth never confessed, never uttered a word, the evidence found at the crime scene strongly suggested he was in serious trouble. To Rodgers and Mullens, this was pretty much a cut-and-dried case.

However, there were still questions that remained unanswered. What was the motive? Why would a teenage boy in an upper-middle-class home, who'd never been in trouble, suddenly turn on both his parents and beat them to death with a baseball bat?

The officer in the living room downstairs had cleared everyone out of the room, except for his partner and two FBI agents who had just arrived. Seth either couldn't or wouldn't answer even their most basic questions. He was pale, motionless, appearing to be in a state of shock. Julian was there, still wrapped up in his brother's arms. Julian was looking down at the floor while sucking his left thumb. Tears were flowing down his cheeks.

"Did you hurt your parents, son?" A detective, in front of Seth down and on one knee, asked.

Seth looked blankly at the detective with distant eyes then slowly nodded his head up and down.

"Why were your parents in Julian's bedroom? Was there a fight or argument going on?"

Seth continued staring at the officer. He didn't respond to this or other questions the detective kept asking. He'd heard his mother talk many times over the years about how stupid those accused of crimes were, too often confessing their wrong doing to the police – an act that would later come back to haunt them.

He wasn't about to tell the police anything. He had to protect the family, and above all, he had to protect Julian. He knew he'd have to make up a story, lie about what really happened. No one was to know the truth, ever.

After a while, the detectives were taking turns asking the questions, becoming more frustrated that Seth wouldn't answer. They knew he'd attacked and killed his parents, and he knew that they knew. In his mind, there was no use asking a ton of questions, there was enough evidence to finger him for the crimes and lock him away forever, so why bother. The police wanted answers though. They wanted to know the entire story, what had taken place minute by minute, but he refused to talk.

The kind spoken officer who had asked most of the questions was becoming frustrated. "We think Julian did this - and you're covering for him."

Seth locked in on the officer's eyes, licked his lips mildly, and produced a tired grin that was construed to be a smirk.

"I've had enough of this cold-hearted bastard," the detective said, turning to look at the other detectives.

The others nodded, giving confirmation that they too, were done with Seth.

"Alright," one of the FBI agents said with a cold voice. "Let's get him down to the station."

Two uniformed officers, one male and one female, were summoned to the room. They were instructed to take Julian to a hospital in Bristol to be checked out.

Seth didn't want to be separated from his brother. Julian was already frightened enough and Seth knew Julian wouldn't do well with strangers.

As soon as they tried prying Julian away from Seth, a fight broke out. Seth jumped from the couch and hit the male officer, a man over six feet tall. The punch hit the man squarely in the nose. The blow sent the officer flying backward, stumbling a few steps before hitting the floor flat on his back. Over the next two minutes, it took the four detectives in the room, plus two more rushing in, to pin Seth down and get him handcuffed. When it was over, Seth was the only one not breathing laboriously. Two of the officers had to sit down on the couch. They were attended by a paramedic, who had witnessed the scuffle from a distance.

An ambulance driver and a paramedic worked for fifteen minutes with the downed officer. He was out cold and once they got him awakened with ammonia inhalants, he went out on them a second time. The officer had to be transported to the hospital by ambulance. Before the night was over, he underwent surgery to repair a fractured cheekbone. He also had a broken nose and a concussion.

5

Seth was led out of the house. He took a deep breath, allowing the crisp night air to fill his lungs. It seemed to clear his head. He wished he could pull away, break free, and run off into the night. He would find his way to the abandoned house a half-mile down the road at the end of a dead-end street. That was where he and Sarah always met. It was their secret meeting place. If he could get there, he could rest while devising a plan to get Julian away from the police. There was no breaking free though, he was being held captive by two police officers with guns and he was bound by tight handcuffs. Seth had been a prisoner for several years in his own home, now he was a prisoner of the state.

Outside the house, there were hundreds of lights - floodlights, flashlights, red ambulance lights, blue police lights, streetlights, and every house on the block had lights on. The entire neighborhood seemed to be under siege by lights. The streets were lined with dozens of city, county and state police cars. Six ambulances were parked along the curb, plus two in the driveway. A dozen police officers were on the sidewalk. More were scattered across the lawn.

Wide red ribbons that said 'Police Line – Do not cross' were wrapped around traffic cones, creating a temporary fence across the front lawn. Behind the tapeline lay the street, where still more police officers leaned against their cars, talking, and pouring coffee from Thermos bottles. Beyond that was a crowd of local citizens, talking among themselves, already putting their own version of a story together. They were inching past the invisible line the police had drawn across the street with their cruisers. Behind the first wave of nosey neighbors were more people, on their tiptoes. They were craning their necks, wanting to get a glimpse of the action.

Seth squinted, looking past the bright lights toward the crowd, recognizing a few faces, his closest neighbors. They were the easy ones to pick out. They were wearing robes or pajamas.

As he was led down the walk toward an awaiting police car, news reporters suddenly appeared out of nowhere. They had crossed the police line, were rapidly snapping photos, and screaming questions toward him. The event in front of the Boone house was bigger than anything that had ever happened in Abingdon. It was bigger than the annual Fourth of July celebration. It was even bigger than the Christmas and Homecoming parades.

Down the street beyond the police cars, were several vans sporting television station letters and photos of the news teams plastered on the side. Past the television vans were cars parked haphazardly, abandoned by their occupants who had come running toward the Boone house to see it all happening live instead of reading about it in a newspaper.

As the officers pushed Seth along, he looked toward the awaiting police car. It seemed as if it were a thousand yards away. He felt like he was having an out of body experience, seeing himself from the sky as the police led him away from the house.

The handcuffs were too tight, and the officers were handling him roughly. Once he'd punched the officer in the face, the rules changed. At the end of the long walk, a huge hand clamped down on top of Seth's head and pushed downward as another hand shoved him into the back of the squad car.

"Where are you taking me, and where are you taking Julian?" Seth demanded.

The female officer who had been in the living room and witnessed Seth's act of violence was driving the car.

"Your brother is going to Baptist Hospital to be examined by a doctor. He'll be fine," she answered. "As for you, you're going downtown to be questioned. Let me give you some advice before we get there, kid. I wouldn't be putting up resistance like you did back there at the house. You're a tough kid, but no match for angry cops with nightsticks."

"Why does Julian need to see a doctor?" Seth asked, leaning toward the wire cage, nearly breathing on the officer's neck.

There was no reply.

"Am I being arrested?"

"Yep."

"What for?"

"Right now for assaulting a police officer, but it's more likely than not, a long list of charges will follow," she said, smiling in the mirror.

"That was my partner back there, the one you sucker punched. He's a good man, got a family, two little girls, not that you'd give a rat's ass I suppose. If it weren't for a parade of hungry news reporters following us to city hall I'd pull over and beat the shit out of you with my own stick."

"I've got nothing else to say," Seth said, falling back in the seat. "I want a lawyer."

"Yeah, you're gonna need one - a good one at that."

"Ya'll better not hurt Julian!" Seth said, turning his thoughts back to his brother.

"Well, if you ain't gonna say another word, I suggest you shut your pie-hole. You just added another charge - uttering."

It was unlike Seth to be disrespectful or disobedient. He'd never spoken like this before. He'd never been in trouble in his entire life. Even when he was teased at school and called bad names, he'd always sucked it up and kept silent. Seeing what his parents were doing to Julian, something inside his head snapped.

He wasn't thinking about what he had done to his parents. At that moment, his concern was Julian. He was worried about his brother. The officers who took him were strangers, and Julian didn't do well with strangers. He could only imagine how scared his brother was. He tried to work free from the handcuffs, but each time he tried, it seemed they only got tighter.

At the police station, there was no more questioning. It was nearly 3 a.m. and the detectives decided rest was needed to clear their own heads.

After snipping off a segment of Seth's hair for drug testing, a lab technician headed to Bristol with the sample for analysis. No one thought Seth was suicidal, but to protect him, it was decided to put him in a straitjacket and a padded

51

cell. That meant transferring him from the local police station to the county jail, located in the basement of the courthouse.

At the jail, Seth put up some resistance, but the officers knew what they were doing. It was only a few seconds before his arms were immobilized by the straitjacket. Inside the cell, he fought hard to free himself from the vest that had him bound tight. He quickly tired out, worked his way through the darkness to a corner, laid down, and fell into a restless sleep.

Soon after the first glimmer of light shone through the small rectangular window, high on the wall of the padded cell, Seth awakened. He had a terrible headache. He wondered if the scotch he'd drank was the cause, or perhaps it was his ordeal with the police, thoughts of what he'd done to his parents, or the irregular padded floor he'd slept on. He decided it was a combination of all.

Working like an inchworm, he managed to make his way to the wall and get into a halfway sitting position. He propped his head against the padded wall. The straitjacket worked against him. It was hot, tight, and extremely uncomfortable. It seemed like hours as he sat there in silence, painting scenes in his mind about what would happen next. He wondered if he would he be tried for murder? He was still angry at his parents for what they had done to Julian, and wasn't feeling remorseful about striking them. The night before was like a bad dream, one from which he'd not yet awakened.

He wasn't sorry he had hit his parents, but was sorry he'd killed them. The full effect of his actions still hadn't taken hold, but he knew he was in trouble, serious trouble. He was only trying to protect Julian, but he couldn't tell the police that story - at least not why Julian needed rescued.

That would mean telling the truth and exposing what had been going on for the last three years.

He was struggling to fabricate a story about what had happened. It had to be a story that would leave out what his mother and father were doing when he'd attacked them. He'd never tell anyone the truth about his parents, what they had done, the kind of hell he lived through each night. No one would understand. No one would believe the truth, even if he did tell it. Telling the truth wasn't an option.

Trying to come up with a story that would be believable, Seth's mind kept slipping back to when he was swinging the bat. He couldn't focus. All he could think of was telling his story the way it really happened, but no, he couldn't do that. He knew without a doubt murder charges were pending. Janie often spoke at the dinner table about law, both civil and criminal. It frightened him to think juveniles could be tried as adults. He could even get the death penalty.

"I don't care if they kill me," he said foolishly to himself. He thought about his mother, how her sick sexual desires had been the beginning of it all. She had set the events in motion, leading up to where he was now. Thinking of how he had been raped for three years was bad enough, but what they had done to Julian, in his mind, was far worse. He hated that he'd killed his parents, but was happy the abuse he'd endured at home for so long was over.

6

It was 10 a.m. before the cell door opened, filling the small space with light. Two uniformed male officers walked in. The padding beneath their feet sounded like they were walking on a giant wet sponge. Seth was lifted to his feet. The headache had disappeared, but returned the instant he stood. The out-of-body feeling from last night was gone. Seth was cooperative, no longer combative. It was best to listen and keep his lips sealed. The men weren't carrying firearms, but metal loops attached to their belts held nightsticks.

They led him to a regular jail cell just down the hall. Inside the cell sat a card table and a metal folding chair. At the far end of the cell was an open filthy commode and a washbasin, every bit as dirty.

"I'm going to cut you loose," an officer said. "You even think about putting up a fight and we'll gladly beat the living hell out of you, boy."

Seth said nothing. He stood there motionless, allowing the men to remove the straitjacket. Another officer appeared in the cell, carrying a glass of orange juice and a small bowl of thick oatmeal. He placed the food on the table then quickly left.

"Use the pisser and eat," the officer who had been doing the talking said. "Someone will be coming for you shortly."

The officers left, slamming the self-locking metal door behind them.

After thirty minutes, two different officers appeared. They handcuffed him then led him up a flight of steps and down a long hallway. He was shoved into a twelve by twelve room painted a dingy yellow.

A square wooden table sat in the middle of the room, surrounded by four wooden chairs. Just like on television, a large rectangular mirror hung on the wall near the door. In the high ceiling above was a bright, intense light. Heat radiated down from the light, making the table warm to the touch. The interrogation was about to begin. He expected a man in a suit, maybe two, would walk in and tell him to sit at the table. They'd blow cigarette smoke in his face and shout questions. The mirror was two-way, and a dozen or more cops would be behind it - listening, watching, and recording every word spoken.

To Seth's surprise, the handcuffs were removed by the officers before they left the room. He walked over to the corner and stood, rubbing his wrist and stretching his back. It was hurting due to the way he'd slept in the straitjacket on the uneven floor. Those behind the mirror raised their eyebrows when they saw Seth's rippling muscles. They were the muscles of a well-developed man, not the kind ordinarily seen on sixteen-year-old boys.

The psychologist had asked that Seth not be handcuffed and that his leg-irons be removed. The officers behind the glass had been hesitant to grant that request but had done as asked. They were worried more now, seeing Seth in person and viewing his bulging muscles. They already had one cop in the hospital because of Seth's angry outburst. The psychologist wanted Seth to feel free however, hoping it would make him more willing to be cooperative and answer questions.

When the door opened, Seth was stunned. There weren't one or two square jawed, stern faced detectives in suits standing there, sporting flattop hairstyles, and carrying small notepads. Instead, it was a woman. She was beautiful, late twenties, flowing blonde hair with natural curls. She was tall and slender. Her vermilion colored cotton summer dress showed the undeniable curves of a woman who could make a living modeling.

Seth was reading her. He observed the way she walked, her gestures, looking for clues that would tell who she was, what she was, and why she was here. He gathered that she was intelligent, professional, and he liked the way she carried herself. Her smile was breathtaking. She was classy, and she was stunning. He could smell her perfume and thought how well it accented her beauty.

"Good morning Seth," she said smiling.

Her voice was soothing. It sounded like what he imagined the voice of an angel would sound.

"I'm Rita Logan," she said. "Please, sit down."

Rita took a seat, with the mirror behind her, just as it was supposed to be done. Seth walked over to the table, pulled out the chair across from Rita, and sat down facing her.

"Are you a cop?" Seth asked.

"No, Seth. I'm a psychologist. I work for the Commonwealth of Virginia."

"Whose side are you on?"

"Well, presently I'm neutral. I'm here to talk with you and gather facts."

Seth expected she was telling the truth, but wondered why they would send a psychologist to talk to him instead of police detectives. He wondered what her real purpose was for being here.

He noticed that Rita wore no makeup, aside from a trace of eyeliner. Her lips were peach colored and her eyes were dreamy. He knew not to stare at her for too long. He could get lost in her eyes, allowing her to hypnotize him then force him to tell all his secrets. He felt guilty for looking at Rita in a desiring way, especially under the circumstances and in an interrogation room. She was so beautiful though. She was the most beautiful woman he'd ever laid his eyes on. He had to keep reminding himself that she wasn't there to help him.

"Do you know why I'm here?" she asked. Her smooth, sexy voice was too irresistible not to answer.

Seth shrugged his shoulders. She'd read his face, and knew he wanted to know why she was sitting there with him instead of a police detective. That's why she'd asked him.

He was studying Rita as hard as she was studying him. They were checking each other out, watching the other's eye movements, body language, and facial gestures. Rita had been trained in these things, but they came naturally to Seth. Rita would soon realize that Seth was much better at this than she would ever be, no matter how much training she could receive.

In the first few minutes, Rita had already determined Seth wasn't any ordinary sixteen year old. He was intelligent, a bit cunning, and someone not easily fooled. Before arriving, she'd expected to face a 'teen-gone-bad', a young person strung out on drugs. Seth's lab results turned out negative though, except for traces of chemicals found in erectile dysfunction drugs. A prescription bottle containing that type of medicine was found at the crime scene, on Seth's bathroom sink. That puzzled her.

Seth expected Rita would lay down a few traps, hoping he would become caught in her snares - after all, she was a professional. He'd have to be on top of his game to avoid her snares. He wanted to make sure he thought about each question a few seconds before giving an answer, even the simple questions. No matter how classy, sexy, and charming she was, she already said she wasn't on his side - not that it mattered overall. Still, he would be on guard to make sure he didn't say too much, and absolutely nothing about family matters.

He took his eyes off Rita briefly and looked in the mirror, seeing the back of her head and his own face. He knew to be careful about what he said, not only because of the beautiful woman sitting across from him, but for another reason as well. Even if this gorgeous woman wasn't there to cause him harm, the people behind the mirror most certainly were.

Nothing could be said about his mother, father, or Julian. He would refuse to answer those questions, divulging no information. He'd say nothing about the abuse he suffered constantly. He most certainly would never reveal what his parents had done to Julian. It sickened him to think about that. He hoped that over time he'd be able to erase from his mind what he saw when he'd opened the door to Julian's room.

He knew the police had to go through this routine questioning. It didn't matter to him, but it was a waste of time. He'd already told the cops he'd killed him mother and father, so what was the point? His parents were dead, and he was going to jail.

"Tell me what happened last night, Seth. Take your time, I won't press you."

He studied Rita as she watched him. She would know if he was telling the truth or not.

"I killed my mother and father," Seth answered.

There was a small amount of sadness in his answer, and he couldn't maintain eye contact.

"Why don't you start from the beginning," she suggested. "Start with when you were at Sarah's wake."

Seth became alarmed. This woman had conducted a lot of research in a short amount of time, but how could she have possibly known he was at Sarah's wake last evening? He wondered who her sources were. He had to be extra cautious. This woman was dangerous.

Seth's voice grew in volume. He became defensive. "What do you know about Sarah?" he fired back. "She has nothing to do with why we are here. I don't want you to ask questions about her."

He had asked for his attorney last night, but still hadn't heard from him. He was close to making that demand a second time.

Rita made a mental note about Seth's reaction to the question. She would visit this again later, but for now, she was trying to make Seth feel comfortable around her. Her goal was to make him feel she was a friend, someone he could trust. She knew it was the only way to get the truth. She wanted the truth and she wanted the entire story.

Arriving in Bristol earlier that morning from Roanoke, she'd been handed several pages of notes, one of which mentioned Seth being at the wake of his friend the evening before, along with his parents. She had assumed Sarah was a friend, perhaps an acquaintance of the entire family. She now knew it was much more than that. Seth was wrong too. Rita knew that Sarah was a part of this - Seth just hadn't told her how it all fit together.

"Did you hit your parents with the baseball bat that the police found lying on the floor of Julian's bedroom?"

There was a nod, up and down. "Yes," he said quietly, almost whispering.

"Were you angry at them? Is that why you hit them?"

Seth was looking away. He turned his head toward her and they locked on. Rita could see his eyes glazing over.

"Yes, I was angry. I didn't mean to kill them."

The glazing eyes turned to tears. He used his shirt to wipe them away.

Behind the two-way mirror, two State Police detectives, two FBI agents, and the county sheriff stood watching. One of the FBI agents rolled his eyes and looked at his partner.

"How pathetic," he said. "This kid's a real cool cucumber. He's a damn good actor."

"Just chill," a State Police detective said. "She's getting a pretty good confession out of him. His words speak louder than those fake puppy-dog tears. Rita's smart, I've worked with her before, she can see past his acting."

"Where did you find the baseball bat? Rita asked.

"It's Julian's. It was leaning against the dresser in his bedroom."

Rita had been to the crime scene just before coming to the courthouse for the interview. She'd seen Julian's baseball and glove lying on the floor by the dresser, situated to the left of the doorway a few feet. She'd also noticed a small round depression in the carpet, beside the baseball glove. It was an imprint, left from where the bat had been standing.

"Had you been in Julian's room for a while before the accident happened?

"No, I'd just walked in," Seth answered. "Don't play word games with me, please. It wasn't an accident. I meant to hit them. I just didn't mean to kill them."

"Were you angry at Julian as well? She asked, speaking slowly.

"NO," Seth answered instantly and loudly. "I'm Julian's protector. I'm all he's got. I've never been angry at Julian, even when he spills things or messes up my room."

He had answered too quickly. He reminded himself to slow down, and not show so much emotion.

"Where is Julian?" he asked at normal volume, but in a demanding tone. "Julian doesn't like strangers, they scare him. I need to see Julian, tell him everything's going to be fine."

"Julian is okay, Seth, I promise. Don't worry about your brother. I'll try to make arrangements for you to see him soon."

Seth leaned back in his chair, locked his hands behind his neck, and looked up at the ceiling. He took a deep breath and sighed as he exhaled.

"Have you ever threatened to or actually hit your parents before, Seth?"

"No. My mother would tear me apart limb by limb for such behavior. Then, my dad would beat me to death with his belt, even though he's in a wheelchair."

Seth was speaking as if his parents were still alive. Rita knew he was somewhat confused, or maybe it hadn't sunk in yet that he had killed his parents and they weren't coming back.

Rita's eyebrows raised slightly as she looked Seth over. She'd viewed several family photos on the walls inside the Boone house, plus several more framed photos sitting on shelves and tables. Janie Boone was a beautiful woman, petite and small boned. Rita expected that as far as physical strength went, Janie wasn't strong enough to rip three sheets of paper placed together. Seth, on the other hand, looked as if he could rip a person's head off their shoulders with two fingers. There was a police officer in the hospital that very morning that had just came out of surgery. He could testify to the strength of Seth Boone. Still, she knew what Seth was saying. Parents don't have to be the strong ones physically to scare the living daylights out of you. Seth was a respectable sort of kid. He feared his mother and father.

"So, you weren't angry with Julian at all, but he was in the room, right?" Rita asked, shrugging her shoulders, and pursing her lips. "Was Julian causing a problem?"

"No, no, no." Seth said. "I was trying to make them stop hurting....never mind."

Seth was angry with himself. He didn't know if he'd stepped into a trap or created one himself. He was trying to convince himself to stop, declare the meeting over - but he liked Rita. There was something far beyond her beauty. There was something else - something he couldn't put his finger on. She seemed genuine, so unlike most people he knew. He was wishing he could talk to her alone, but expected that wasn't possible.

Rita didn't want to push him. She had learned a lot already, and expected there was a long story here with some deep dark secrets. She knew it would take time, but time was something she didn't have. She was hoping to convince her boss that she needed to stay with the case for a while, even though her caseload at the office was stacked high. Rita had been assigned to this case because she was good at her job, some would say the best that had ever been.

Her supervisor, Rayburn Mason, called her at 4 a.m., getting her out of bed. This was a big case. The governor had contacted Mason about the alleged murders. That's why he'd sent Rita.

"Were you angry at both of your parents, or just one of them?"
"Both."

"Do you know how much money your parents have? Do you know about a trust fund for you or Julian? Or, do you know how much the house is worth?"

Seth tilted his head sideways and gave a half smile, but didn't answer. He knew Rita was asking this 'rubber-stamp' question to see if it was a motive. It was a prelude to dropping some sort of bomb, so he was ready – or at least he thought so.

"Were your parents arguing?"

"NO, to all of those questions," Seth retorted.

"So you were just standing in the door, became angry, picked up Julian's baseball bat, and hit your parents?"

"I wasn't standing in the door. I peeked in. That's when...." Seth clammed up, not finishing his answer.

Rita did something uncharacteristic, something against her style, something she had not intended to do. She became frustrated. Seth had pushed her button. It wasn't that Seth's answers were upsetting her. It was more the way he studied her. He was playing her while her intentions were to help him. She was the psychologist, not him. She was supposed to be playing him, not the other way around. She leaned across the table and stared squarely at Seth.

"You're about to be charged with capital murder, Seth," she said sternly, setting Seth back in his seat. "You need to know what that means. If you don't help yourself, there's a good chance you could get the death penalty – and die in the gas chamber!"

Rita's style was to remain in control, and be a smooth talker. She never became angry, never used harsh words or scare tactics. She couldn't believe how she was acting. It disturbed her and Seth knew it. She wasn't in control, and it was troublesome.

"I don't care if I die," Seth said, shrugging his shoulders. His answer sounded childish. Until now, his answers had sounded like those of a mature adult.

"Oh come on now!" she said, throwing herself back in her chair, acting childish herself.

Next came the bomb. Seth thought he was prepared, but he wasn't. Rita had now found his button.

"Was there some sort of sex act going on in Julian's room when you opened that door?" Rita asked boldly.

"NO!" Seth cried out.

"I don't believe you, Seth."

Seth's face was blood red. He stood up and kicked the chair back with his right foot. It slammed violently into the wall.

"I'm done here. I want my lawyer!" He screamed.

Rita quickly rose to her feet. The door buzzed, and she hurried out of the room. Seth found his way to the corner where he'd been when Rita had come in. He slumped down in the corner, placed his head in his hands, and began sobbing.

7

Seth was placed in a cell by himself. Since they hadn't officially charged him with anything, they'd soon have to book him or let him go. Prisoners were no longer housed at the courthouse, so if he were to be charged with a crime, he'd be moved to another location.

Unable to go to Sarah's funeral made his miserable situation worse. He wanted to be there and say goodbye before they lowered her body into the cold damp grave. She was gone, and so were his parents. Nothing in his life could compare to the events of these last few days. He'd gone from putting together a plan to run away with a teenage girl from school, to crying over her lifeless body at a funeral home. A few hours later, he'd lost all control and slammed a baseball bat into the heads of his parents, killing them both.

Seth had played 'Mr. Tough Guy' during the interview. Now he sat in the corner of his cell wailing loudly. Sarah was gone. His parents were gone. He was in serious trouble. Although he'd wished at times his mother and father were dead, deep down - he'd not meant it. Regardless of how he felt, they were dead now. They were dead because he had killed them. Sitting there, crying, thinking of Julian, thinking of Sarah, thinking of his parents – he felt more alone then anytime in his life.

Near the room where Seth had been questioned, a meeting was taking place. Twelve law enforcement personnel were in the room sitting around a large oval cherry table. Eleven of the twelve already had their minds made up. They were convinced they had the right suspect - Seth Boone was guilty of murdering his parents. They were discussing how easy this case was. They hoped the District Attorney would push for capital murder, making it possible for Seth to be given the death penalty.

Rita, knew Seth had killed his parents, he'd said so himself. Still, she didn't think it was murder in the first degree. Perhaps it was manslaughter. He'd told her that he didn't mean to kill them. She wasn't ready to lock him up and throw away the key yet. She needed more time with him, time to earn his trust and allow him to open up. She wondered if there was some justification for the killings. If so, it would call for a lesser charge than capital murder. After meeting with the young man, she felt this was the case. Unless some mitigating circumstances were discovered however, she was sure the DA would play hardball with the defense. If nothing changed, Seth might die at a young age, by lethal injection.

The detectives were ready to call the District Attorney's office and get the paperwork rolling. To them this was a cut and dried case, a premeditated double-murder charge was pending. Rita pleaded with them to give her another chance, allowing her to speak to Seth alone. They dismissed her idea, said it was suicidal. As the meeting lagged on, they began shutting Rita out of the conversation. She felt as if she'd suddenly become invisible.

With the forensic evidence from the crime scene, plus Seth's willingness to admit to the killings, there was little doubt he was guilty. The only question on the detectives' minds was why he did it.

§

The Boone family attorney was a man named Gary McDowell, III. Gary was 76 years old and had been practicing law in southwest Virginia for fifty years.

The firm 'McDowell, Tucker, and Berkley' was formed back in the depression era by Gary McDowell, Sr. and two other men, Thomas Tucker and Arden Berkley. It was a rocky beginning for the three young lawyers, all who'd just passed the bar exam. McDowell was from Abingdon, the other two men from Wise, Virginia. McDowell's deceased father, a retired railroad worker, left him five-hundred dollars in his will. There was one stipulation to the will, that McDowell finish college, which he did. The money was more than enough to pay fees, rent an office, and get the business rolling.

A year and a half after opening the firm, the three young attorneys were broke and ready to close shop - then their luck changed. A bootlegger named Cameron Marshall, out of Jolo, West Virginia, was arrested in Abingdon with a truckload of illegal whiskey. It was the days of prohibition, and the Virginia governor of that time was a supporter of a liquor free state. No one was willing to take the case, except McDowell, Tucker, and Berkley. Facing bankruptcy, they would have defended the Jews who killed Jesus if it meant getting a paycheck.

The judge overseeing the case had a taste for the illegal corn liquor himself, and had been a customer of Marshall's for quite some time. When it was all said and done, Marshall was fined twenty-five dollars, and his sentence was time already served. McDowell, Tucker, and Berkley, having done little, received all the glory.

Shortly afterward, every moonshiner, horse thief, and drunkard in a five-county area was running to the firm when arrested. The mediocre lawyers lost a few battles, but a little bribery money went a long way with the corrupt circuit-court judges of that day. That was the preferred way of doing business, any cases not requiring a jury were won hands-down. In some instances, even when there was a jury. McDowell, Tucker, and Berkley weren't bashful about buying a few votes of the good outstanding citizens sitting in the jury box. Those not willing to be bought off were threatened by a crooked deputy sheriff on the firm's payroll. The deputy had an uncanny way of persuading people to change their minds.

By the time McDowell, Jr., obtained his license to practice, the firm was splitting up. Times were changing. Several corrupt lawyers and judges around the state ended up behind bars themselves. McDowell, Sr. saw the writing on the wall. It was either change the way of doing business or get out of it all together. The firm split, and a new one was born with McDowell, Sr. the Captain, and Junior at the helm. McDowell and Son, Attorneys at Law, took on a different kind of cliental, shifting from blue-collar thugs to mostly white-collar crooks. McDowell had been around long enough and had won enough cases to attract those with old money, the rich of Abingdon.

When Gary McDowell, III was born, he had a silver spoon in his mouth. When he passed the bar and joined his father and grandfather's practice, he didn't have to go through the struggles they'd endured. He already knew most of the clients, having grown up under his father's wing. He'd been properly mentored for years. He was a slick negotiator and of course, he was the sole heir to the business.

Gary McDowell, III soon began taking over the bulk of the work at the firm and became best friends with one of the clients, Denver Preston, Janie Preston Boone's father, and Seth's grandfather. Gary McDowell, III handled all of Preston's legal affairs. Anytime there was a social event or dinner, you would see McDowell and Preston together. Janie spent as much time during Christmas holidays at the McDowell's cabin on Smith Mountain Lake as she did her own stately home in Abingdon.

When Preston and his wife died in the parasailing accident, and Janie discovered the estate was nearly broke, she was devastated. Only after her father was in the grave did she find out about the debt he had amassed. McDowell worked feverishly to keep the IRS's fingers out of the pot, but to no avail.

Using his charm, McDowell convinced Janie she was lucky to get what little inheritance that was salvaged. Janie was angry toward her father for the financial mess he'd gotten into. She showed gratitude to McDowell however. She was grateful McDowell could manage to save at least a small percentage of the family fortune. Janie was clueless, however, that McDowell had swindled more from the estate than she'd received. He charged more than double his normal rate and added a bonus for himself on top of that. He robbed her blind and she thought he was the most wonderful friend the family could ever have. Afterward, he continued to handle all of her and Gordon's legal matters plus their financial affairs.

§

One of the detectives who had been behind the two-way mirror in the interrogation room walked up to the cell bars and addressed Seth. Seth walked over the bars to face the man.

"We're moving you to the Juvenile Center in Damascus," the detective stated. "You're being charged with murder, Seth."

Seth didn't flinch. It was what he'd been expecting.

"So when do I get to talk to my attorney?"

"Maybe tomorrow. The state has just been contacted. They will provide you with legal council."

"The state," Seth said, showing concern. "Our family attorney is Gary McDowell. I want to talk to him."

"I've spoken to Mr. McDowell myself," the officer said. "Seth, he refuses to represent you. He said he hoped you burned in hell for killing your mother and father. I can't make him talk to you. He has control over the family funds. You have no money available for representation. Unless McDowell changes his mind, you'll have to accept whoever the state offers to represent you."

Seth couldn't believe what he'd just heard. He stepped back, walked to the corner, and slumped down.

"They will be coming for you soon," the detective said before leaving.

8

Rayburn Mason, Rita Logan's supervisor, had called her twice since the interview with Seth. He'd spoken with Governor Lewis again. The governor was deeply concerned about the Boone murders and wanted to know what was going on. The story was big news. A federal judge had been beaten to death with a baseball bat. Early reports suggested her teenage son had committed the atrocious crime.

The Washington Post, New York Times, and many other newspapers were on the scene. Topping that off was a dozen tabloid reporters who'd already called the governor's office, wanting information on the killings. Two reporters had asked if Judge Boone was a target of organized crime. The major networks already had camera crews in Abingdon – and they were all giving assorted versions about what had taken place.

With hopes of re-election next year, and having to deal with an approval rating that had been steadily declining, the Governor wanted to make darn sure someone competent was down there to represent his office. The last thing he needed was some major screw up by a state official. Stories of a federal judge and her husband being killed were big news and not only in Virginia. This was getting national news coverage.

The governor had personally requested Rita Logan be there. He didn't have a good contact source in Abingdon and needed someone there he could trust. The governor had often been accused of neglecting that part of the state and had few friends west of Roanoke. He was well aware that Rita was no criminal investigator, but she was nosey, a good shrink, could be trusted, and she often used her good looks to open doors that had been locked tight. The feds would be working this from all angles, and they often failed to share information with his people. He detested the way the feds always tried to make the state workers look incompetent. Rita however, would shed good light on his office.

"Keep her pretty little ass there as long as she's needed," the governor had told Mason.

Rita wasn't thrilled when Mason had called so early, awakening her two hours before her clock said it was time to rise and shine. When he told her the governor had ask for her specifically, her attitude suddenly changed. She was elated not only be a part of the investigation, but that the governor thought so highly of her.

When Rita learned that Gary McDowell III, the Boone family attorney, had refused to represent Seth, it puzzled her. McDowell not only refused to represent Seth, but through some not so ethical channels, froze the family assets as well. That action blocked Seth's opportunity to hire someone else. It would be up to the District Attorney's office to provide Seth with council. The boy was in serious trouble and needed a good lawyer. She didn't know why she wanted to help this kid, but she did.

After a shower and a quick breakfast in the hotel restaurant, Rita was off to the courthouse. Avoiding the hordes of reporters and camera crews set up on the courthouse lawn, she went to the back of the building. After flashing her badge and smiling at the guard, she was in the door.

The entire third floor was dedicated to the District Attorney's offices. Rita thought that was strange, since most of the offices there were empty while the first and second floors were overcrowded. Making her way through a maze of cubicles, she worked her way toward the District Attorney's lavish abode. His office was the only room on that floor that didn't have ancient paint peeling from the walls and stained ceiling tiles.

The District Attorney had a limited staff, and assigning a public defender to someone who couldn't afford their own lawyer normally went to the greenest lawyer on the team. Tax dollars to be spent on these cases were few. The young attorneys working there hated it. They wanted to be prosecutors, not assigned to cases as defenders where resources were limited, and their clients were more often than not, guilty as hell.

In Abingdon, the District Attorney was no different from anywhere else. He was notorious for assigning the greenhorns fresh out of law school to these kinds of cases. The fact was, even the overzealous ones willing to accept this kind of work lacked the learned skills to defend someone. They'd be lucky to win a fender bender in a parking lot case, much less a capital murder trial.

Rita knew most of the young lawyers working there were just happy to have landed a job in a country overrun with attorneys. After a couple of years working for peanuts, any lawyer with ambition and not wanting their income supplemented with food stamps, moved on. To them, the DA's office in a small town was just a stepping-stone to getting their foot in someone else's door.

Walton Roane, the District Attorney, was more than happy to let Rita look over the resumes and court history of his staff of six. He'd gotten a call from the Governor's office himself. By allowing Rita to select which one of his staff would represent Seth, the monkey was off his back. No matter which way the case turned out, his hands would be clean. Besides all that, his divorce had been finalized three months earlier and he wanted to check out the gorgeous honey that had just stepped foot into his domain. She was wearing a snug fitting bright lemon-yellow dress and a smile that would turn any man's heart to mush, single or otherwise.

It didn't take Rita long to make her selection from the six choices. Only one of the candidates, Arthur Grant, had actually tried a murder case. Arthur had two murder trials under his belt, winning one and losing one. Both were as a prosecutor though, not a defense attorney.

Arthur Grant was a twenty-seven-year-old Yankee from the Pittsburgh area. Accepting a job in southwest Virginia to begin his career in law, he'd fallen in love with the charming southern town named Abingdon. Despite the less than lucrative pay, he was still hanging on three years after landing his first job in the judicial system.

Roane wasn't thrilled with Rita's choice, only because Grant was also a single man and all the girls thought he was a real looker. The fact that Rita had just turned down Roane's dinner invitation didn't help matters.

Rita had already made up her mind. She was going to spend a considerable amount of time with this Arthur Grant, whether he liked it or not. At the time, she didn't know if Grant was single or married. If married, the wife would just have to suck it up and endure her husband spending time with her on the case. She was interested in getting Seth's full story, but she needed help. Arthur Grant held her meal ticket.

Rita Logan was good at getting what she wanted. She'd team up with Grant, and if he didn't like it, he'd have to take it up with the governor's office.

Roane reluctantly called Grant's office, down at the end of the hall. Unlike Roane's office, Grant's looked like it should have a condemned sign on the door, if for no other reason because of the black mold growing on the ceiling tiles.

Roane informed Grant he'd been selected to be the public defender in the Boone murder case. Grant immediately began to protest. He wanted one of the young punk attorneys, as he called them, to have this one. He claimed he was already overloaded and didn't need the work, especially as a public defender. It was all to no avail. Roane filled Grant in on how the selection was made, and sent Rita on her way to find him.

Arthur, after demonstrating his displeasure, hung up the phone. He was upset, and everyone in the cramped cubicles outside his office knew it. He didn't want another case. Besides, he liked working with his own two staff assistants. He didn't need some shrink from the governor's office involved in his work. He changed his mind the instant Rita walked in the door. Seeing Rita, Arthur's frown quickly turned to a smile.

Rita had read Arthur's work history back in Roane's office. Since coming to work for the D.A.'s office, he'd been reasonably successful. He was highly regarded by the staff and even Roane had boasted about Arthur having ambition and being a hard worker. Chances were he'd work hard on this case as well. Together they would try to solve this mystery and determine why Seth killed his parents. Arthur winning the one murder case was remarkable, considering the time and resources he'd been given to prepare for trial.

She predicted Arthur was one to do his homework and fight feverishly to see justice was served. Seeing Arthur in person, there was going to be a bonus to this job. She couldn't help but notice no wedding ring on his hand. He was tall, well-built, thick black hair combed to the side, and he had soothing chocolate-colored eyes. As handsome as he was, she knew to act with caution. She'd dated many men over the years. None had captured her heart however, basically, because they were all interested in sex and nothing else.

Arthur stood and came around the desk to greet Rita. The lingering handshake and intense look they gave each other created an awkward moment. They both knew the handshake had set a partnership into motion. Rita had always been professional, making sure business and pleasure didn't mix, but knew if he asked her out, she'd accept.

"I'm flattered you're on the case with me," he said.

"Oh really," she replied sheepishly. "Before that call five minutes ago from the D.A., you never knew I existed."

Rita gained satisfaction from seeing Arthur blush. He was lost for words for a few seconds then asked Rita if she'd like a cup of coffee. She accepted.

Arthur left the room and headed to the coffee pot. He heard whispering coming from every cubicle he passed by. He returned to his office with two steaming cups of coffee and using his foot, closed the door behind him. Rita sat in a chair by the desk. Arthur was on the same side of the desk as her, sitting on the edge. After a few sips from her cup, Rita filled Arthur in on all she'd learned about Seth thus far.

"Dang. It sounds like 'Mission Impossible' if we're going to get this kid off the hook," he said, worriedly.

"It's likely we won't," she replied. "I'm not sure that's the way we should proceed. He killed his parents, that's a given. I just don't know why. I want to know what the motive was. I believe a lesser charge than capital murder is appropriate. I think we'll have to fight to get it though. It's only fair to tell you - I may have to jump ship early. I think the only reason I'm here is to help the Governor's image. Once things cool down, I could be whisked away."

"Oh," Arthur said, surprised. "I must have misunderstood. I thought we were teamed up, ready to defend this boy, you being here to help me through all nine innings."

"My supervisor will be in close contact with the governor on this one Arthur. I feel certain politics will determine how long I can hang with you and lend support. I'm hoping I'll be beside you to the bitter end though," she said with a smile that made Arthur's heart begin to race.

"Yeah, me too," Arthur said, smiling back at her. "May I offer a toast? Here's to the bitter end."

They both laughed like children and clanged their mugs together. The conversation turned toward a 'get to know you' inquiry that lasted nearly an hour. Rita accepted Arthur's offer to dinner, then begged him not to tell Roane, because she'd turned him down earlier.

"Things are already complicated," he said. "Don't worry about me telling Roane. In case you've forgotten, he's my boss, and I've got to live with him."

9

There were only a few restaurants in Abingdon that offered full-course meals. Without reservations, Arthur and Rita were turned away from them all. The town was bursting at the seams with hungry news crews from around the country. Feeling hunger pangs, Arthur and Rita resorted to ordering a pizza back at Arthur's small apartment. As they sat at the tiny kitchen table, indulging themselves with a pepperoni and mushroom pizza smothered with extra cheese, the conversation was surprisingly all about Seth.

"Do you think the kid is in his right mind?" Arthur asked.

"Not only do I think he's sane, I think he's extraordinarily bright," Rita replied. "I've not told you everything. I'm suspicious about something. I think there may have been a sex act of some sort going on. There's something about the bedroom where the parents were killed that isn't right."

"Hmm," Arthur replied, wrinkling his forehead. "Very interesting twist I do say, Holmes." Arthur was doing his best impression of Watson, Sherlock Holmes' assistant.

Rita giggled. She thought it was a relatively good impression.

"You're way off base though," Arthur said. "I read Gordon and Janie's medical records today after you left my office. You've missed the boat on this one –"

"How'd you get them?" Rita interrupted.

"I was about to tell you!"

"Oh. Sorry."

"As soon as the coroner declares someone dead, the police have access to medical records if they suspect foul play. Some doctors have protested, but to no avail. I flashed my credentials and two minutes later, I had the files. Anyway, from what I read, Gordon Boone wasn't capable of sex. The surgery following his car crash a few years back took care of that."

A thought crossed Rita's mind. "Oh-my-lord!"

"What is it?" Arthur asked with a puzzled look on his face.

"There was a prescription bottle at the crime scene," Rita said. "It was sitting on the sink in Seth's bathroom. I thought it was a bit odd. It had Gordon Boone's name on the bottle. I asked Seth about it. That's was when he blew his top."

"What was in the bottle?"

"It was an erectile dysfunction medication, filled yesterday, the same day of the killings. I wonder why it would be prescribed to Gordon Boone? And, why would it be in Seth's bathroom?"

"Are you sure about the drug?" Arthur asked. "I'm quite certain after reading the medical records that Gordon was NOT capable of having sex. Trust me on this!"

"I'm positive. It was an erectile dysfunction drug and prescribed to Gordon."

Rita was looking away from Arthur, deep in thought.

"I think Seth may have been sexually involved with his mother," she blurted out.

"Seriously, Rita!" Arthur replied. "I didn't know Janie Boone personally, but I'd met her a few times. She was a nice lady, very professional, sweet, kind, gentle. Heck, she was a federal judge for crying out loud. No offense but that's a pretty sick theory you have going on in that pretty head of yours. I think you're way off base."

Arthur thought for a few seconds. "Besides, and you best believe what I'm about to say is true, a sixteen-year-old boy doesn't need erectile dysfunction medicine. I'll bet you a hundred bucks when he gets out of bed in the mornings he has to push that tool down to keep from pissing in his face!"

"Gee whiz Arthur. That's a bit too much information!"

Rita shook her head then they both laughed.

"Maybe it has something to do with the other kid, Julian," Rita blurted out.

"Rita Logan!" Arthur said loudly. "You really are sick! I don't know what caused Seth Boone to snap, but you're leading yourself down the wrong road. We'll get to the bottom of all this, but you –"

"Okay, think about it for a minute," Rita interrupted, again, her eyes focused on the ceiling as she concentrated. "They were all gathered in Julian's room. We have a bottle of old man sex pills in Seth's bathroom - prescribed to a man who you say is incapable of having sex." Rita threw her hands up. "So what do you think? Am I supposed to believe they were playing dominos, Seth lost then decided, OH, I'm going to kill everyone?"

"Calm down," Arthur said smiling. "Boy, you sure are a feisty one. Okay, let's go with your theory then. Why don't you talk to the detectives, get their take on this?"

"I'll talk to them tomorrow," Rita said, less defensive and smiling back. "I'll try using a little charm on them - maybe it will work."

"I feel certain that your charm and good looks could get the Pope to confess to the murders," Arthur said, still smiling.

Rita giggled like a girl then reached for another slice of pizza.

"Seth's hiding something. Something sinister," Rita said, wiping the sauce from her chin. "He's protecting someone, maybe the entire family."

Arthur shook his head. "I'm telling you, this weird, sick angle you've taken about mother and son sex is wrong. You'll have another chance to spend time with Seth. If you're right, you can get him to tell us where they hid the chains and whip!" he said sarcastically.

Rita picked a piece of pepperoni from her pizza and slung it toward Arthur. He dodged, but it caught him in the face and landed across his eye like an eye patch. They both laughed hard.

"You're not only feisty, you're mean!" he said.

"Yeah. Growing up with five brothers, I learned at a young age to defend myself."

"Big family," Arthur replied.

"Yes, but that's a talk for another time," she replied. "Back to the murders - I've got to spend some time with Seth, convince him that I can be trusted."

"Can you - be trusted that is?"

Rita tilted her head to the side. "Keep it up and you'll need a real patch over that eye!"

10

The next morning, Rita caught up with three of the detectives working the case. After pleading and putting on her best act, showing more of her sexy legs than usual, she got nowhere. She tried contacting the doctor who had prescribed the pills to Gordon, but he refused to talk to her. She thought about going to the pharmacy where the medication had been purchased, but expected her credentials wouldn't get her anywhere. Using her batting eyes and killer smile, she was able to convince another detective, one who wasn't even on the case, to go to the pharmacy instead.

Her scheme worked. The detective came back glistening with pride. He'd found the mother lode. The erectile dysfunction medication had been refilled every thirty days for the last twenty-seven months. Janie was always the one who came in and picked up the medicine. Her signature was on every refill.

Thrilled with what she had learned, Rita headed over to Arthur's office.

"I've got bad news," Arthur said when Rita entered, taking the wind out of her sails. "Somehow, and don't ask how, but somehow a grand jury was quickly put together and they've ruled on Seth's case. They found substantial evidence to charge Seth and send him to trial. He's being arraigned this morning – two counts of murder one."

"I don't know how all that works, but something seems amiss," Rita replied. "Wasn't that a bit swift? I mean, well - well none of that makes sense to me. Weren't you supposed to be there?"

"I most certainly think so, but guess what? My sneaky little boss, Walton Roane, he was there instead. The entire thing smells."

Rita looked troubled.

"OK, so we're looking at worse-case scenario it seems. Do you think the D.A. will budge if we find some mitigating circumstances during discovery?" she asked. "I may have something already, from the pharmacy down on 3rd. Avenue."

"You'll have to tell me all about it later," Arthur replied. "First, I've got to tell you the rest of the bad news. They're bringing in a prosecutor from the 7th District, in Norfolk. He'll represent the Commonwealth of Virginia."

"Is that normal? Can they do that - and if so, why? I'm becoming more confused by the minute."

"It's far from normal, but yes, they can and will do it. I think it has something to do with the feds. It's all political. Uncle Sam will be out to show the world you don't mess with one of their own."

"So what kind of position does that leave us in?" Rita asked.

"Not a very good one, I'm afraid. You can bet your last penny the feds will lend the prosecutor every resource they have to see Seth gets the needle. Dang it! We don't stand a chance."

"Don't give up just yet. I need to talk with Seth and convince him to open up to me. He killed his parents, but if he comes clean, perhaps we can get this down to a manslaughter charge."

"Sounds wonderful Rita, but I don't think the feds will budge. I think we're on a sinking ship, and we're a long way from reaching a harbor."

Rita threw her hands in the air, in frustration.

"So how did this happen? Let's go upstairs and talk to your boss, Roane."

"That won't do any good. I spoke to him about this mess about an hour ago. He's tight lipped. The man's a worm. He'd sell his own mother out. He let them snatch this case right out of his hands and give it to their big shot scumbag in Norfolk."

"Did Roane seem upset at all?"

"Upset! Walton Roane isn't upset about the turn of events – he's pleased! Roane likes sitting up there doing nothing, staying out of the spotlight. This case is hot, bringing tons of heat and lots of publicity. Roane doesn't want or need publicity, good or bad. He just wants to bide his time and keep his job. They probably promised him a raise or a golf club membership."

"Unbelievable," Rita said, flopping into a chair.

"I think you're right, Rita. You need to spend time with this kid. It's vital we get down to the bottom of why he killed his parents. If we can't come up with something substantial to get the charges reduced, our boy likely won't see his twenty-first birthday. He's just a kid, but they're going to try him as an adult."

"When can I see him?" she asked.

"They took him over to juvenile this morning, in Damascus. I've already called the warden and made arrangements. We can see him at four this afternoon."

Arthur and Rita rode together to Damascus. A room had been reserved, awaiting their arrival. They waited in the room fifteen minutes before a guard finally appeared with Seth in handcuffs. Rita noticed that the boy had on the same clothes as the day before. Sadly enough, he had no one to bring him fresh clothes. She made note of this and planned to go by the Boone house and gather things he needed.

Arthur watched as Seth entered the room. He was young, had a youthful face, but that was the only childish thing about his appearance. The boy was ripped with muscles. Large veins popped out everywhere. This kid looked like he could take a run and bust through a brick wall.

Seth seemed a bit shy. He sat down across from Rita and Arthur. Rita asked the guard if the handcuffs could be removed. He looked Rita over for a minute then produced a key and unlocked the cuffs.

"I'll have to remain in the room since he's not cuffed," the officer said smugly.

"I'll sign any form you need, but we want to talk to our client free from handcuffs – and in private," Arthur said sternly.

"Suits the crap out of me," the guard said, holding up his hands. "I'll get the form."

The guard left, leaving the door standing open.

Arthur looked at Seth again. He had dark eyes, the kind women think are mysterious and dreamy, but they were red around the edges, as if he'd been crying. Beyond his eyes, Arthur saw a young man who had spent his youth in a war zone. He determined the kid was carrying a heavy burden and looked as if he'd not been shown a lot of love. Just like Rita, Arthur found himself wondering what deep secrets were shoved away in the boys mind. It was just as Rita had said - he looked like he'd been to hell and back.

The guard returned and shoved a form in front of Arthur, which he quickly read and signed. The guard took the paper, then without saying a word walked out, shutting the door behind him.

"Seth, this is Arthur Grant," Rita said. "He's been appointed by the D.A.'s office to represent you."

"I'm glad you came to see me," Seth said, looking at Rita. "I apologize for my anger during our last talk. I had no right to lash out at you. I know you're just doing your job."

Rita was pleased. The meeting had just begun, and they were already moving in the right direction.

Arthur was wondering if Seth had been given a sedative. The way Rita had described her previous meeting with Seth he was expecting to face an angry young man. Instead, Seth was calm. He seemed like a nice kid, not some hotheaded, disobedient brat.

On the way to Damascus, Rita and Author had discussed how to conduct the meeting. Rita would do most of the talking, and ask most of the questions. Arthur would watch, listen, and take notes.

"I'd like to hear more of your story," Rita said softly.

"I killed my mother and father. Everybody knows that," Seth replied. "That's about it."

Rita was hoping the meeting would continue to be positive. She desperately wanted to find a way to unlock Seth's tightly sealed doors.

"Yes, Seth, you told me the last time we talked that you killed them, but you never told me why."

Seth was silent.

"When you walked into Julian's room, were you already searching for the baseball bat?"

"No, I just happened to see it as I entered."

"Thank you, Seth. Thank you for being honest, and thank you for sharing that with me. Were your mother and father surprised to see you coming at them with the bat?"

"I hit my mother first. I don't think she ever saw me. My father looked surprised. It all happened so fast."

"It's about twelve feet from the door to Julian's bed. Is that where your mother was, on the bed?"

"Yes," Seth replied, looking down at the table, not making eye contact.

"Was Julian on the bed also?"

"Yes."

"Was Julian talking with your parents?"

"No."

"And what about you? Did you say anything when you entered the room?"

"I don't remember. I may have shouted something. I'm not sure."

"I want you to trust me, Seth. I've spoken with my supervisor. The first time we met, I didn't know where I stood on this case, now it's clear. I'm on your side. I'll be with you all the way through this. I can help you."

Arthur raised his eyebrows slightly. If Rita wanted to gain the boy's trust, she should be truthful with him. The fact was that she had no idea how long she would remain on the case.

"I'm glad you're here," Seth said, looking up at Rita. "I like talking with you. I feel you're trustworthy."

Seth had a sad look on his face. Rita felt sorry for him, wanted to give him a big hug and let him know everything was fine. Things weren't fine though, and she didn't want to lie to him about that. She felt as if she was making progress and gaining Seth's trust. She needed to take things at a slow pace. However, there wasn't a great deal of time to spare.

"I don't think you can help me," Seth said, his voice low.

Rita tilted her head a little to the side and spoke with a sweet low voice. "Why do you say that, Seth? Why do you think I can't help you?"

"Because I'm guilty. Because my mother was a federal judge. Because I know what that means. The FBI wants me dead. I overheard them talking about it at the courthouse."

"I'll be honest with you, Seth. They will try their best to do what you said. It doesn't have to be that way though. I think you had a justifiable reason for hitting your mother and father. You told me last time we talked that you didn't mean to kill them."

Tears began flowing down Seth's face.

"Did you ever take any of the pills found on your bathroom sink?" Rita asked.

Seth got a worried look on his face. He'd forgotten about the pills. He'd even forgotten that after he had counted them twice he'd placed the bottle back in the bathroom. That was just before he slipped down the hall, toward Julian's bedroom. The look on his face spoke the truth. He couldn't hide it, so he didn't.

"Yes, I've taken them before," he answered, hanging his head low again.

"How often?

Seth humped his shoulders. "I don't know, pretty often."

She was pushing the limit and it was time to switch directions. She didn't want Seth to feel too uncomfortable and clam up on her. Arthur couldn't believe Rita had not only asked the question about the pills, but had gotten an answer. He was beginning to believe Rita's sick theory that something sinister had been going on inside the Boone house. Rita had suggested there was a great deal more to this story. Now, his own curiosity level was rising.

Rita wanted to ask just one more question regarding the erectile dysfunction medication. She hoped she wasn't looking a gift horse in the mouth.

"You do know those were your father's pills, don't you."

"Yes," Seth replied lowly then looked up at Rita ever so sadly.

It was time to move on. She felt Seth was about to shut down.

"I think before we're done, I'll be able to help Mr. Grant here put together a solid self-defense case," Rita said smiling.

"My mother was constantly talking about the law," Seth said. "She talked a lot about corporate bankruptcy, the kind of stuff she dealt with, but she also loved talking about criminal law. My parents weren't yielding weapons, so I know this can't be a self-defense case."

"Not necessarily," Arthur said, speaking for the first time.

"How do you get that?" Seth asked, taking his eyes off Rita briefly.

"If you were under duress, scared for your safety, or the safety of someone else - that could be grounds for self-defense."

"Were your parents hurting Julian?" Rita asked.

Seth looked down again, and didn't answer the question.

"I know I have to stand trial, but will I be able to go home until then?" Seth asked, picking his head back up to look Rita in the eyes. "I need to check on Julian. When can I see him?"

Arthur could tell Rita was struggling to answer the question. He addressed Seth, and although he wanted to apologize for not being the one who'd acted for him at the arraignment, he stopped short. His boss, Roane, had bypassed him for some unknown reason. He'd deal with Roane about that later, but it was already water under the bridge in Seth's case.

"Mr. McDowell has the family assets frozen," Arthur said bluntly. There's no money or property available for collateral, and that means no bail."

Seth had already considered that, but was hoping something else could be done. The meeting lasted an hour, but they didn't get any more information. Seth was polite. It was evident he liked talking with Rita. Still, Seth wasn't fully convinced he could trust her, much less Arthur. They were the only two people in his corner though. He'd have to allow them on the inside eventually. The thought of telling his secrets scared him though. He didn't want anyone to know what had been going on at home - especially what his mother had done to Julian.

Seth asked about seeing Julian during the meeting. Rita didn't know what to tell him. Julian had been placed in a foster home temporarily and was doing fine. Before they left, he pleaded earnestly with Rita to bring Julian by the jail so he could see him. Arthur didn't think that would be allowed, but promised he'd check and see if it could be arranged.

Rita promised Seth she would bring him some fresh clothes. She reiterated that at the end of the meeting. As she and Arthur stood to leave, Seth got that scared look on his face again. Rita could tell he didn't want them to go. There would be no family or friends coming to visit. She felt sad for him, and wanted to become a friend. He needed help, and she could provide that. She felt drawn to this young man, but couldn't explain why. It was a strange feeling. Seth was crying out for help, and she wanted to do all she could. He had no one - he was alone in the world, facing the unimaginable.

Rita knew Seth's only hope of living beyond his teen years was in her and Arthur's hands. That was a heavy burden, and she didn't know if she could handle that kind of stress. She also knew that unless Seth opened up and gave them something significant to work with, what little hope of survival he had would soon vanish.

11

The next morning Rita did as she had promised. The Boone house had been locked up tight, so she had to go through one of the detectives on the case to get inside. The detective stayed with her stride by stride, but watched her skirt instead of what she was doing. She grabbed a clean pair of jeans, one of Seth's oversized sweatshirts, and two pair of underwear. Later that evening, she went to visit him. He was happy to get the fresh clothes. It was a pleasant meeting. Even though she didn't learn anything more than the day before, a relationship was beginning to form.

Over the next two weeks, Rita met Seth daily, with Arthur present every other day. They both learned that they liked Seth. The meetings turned out to be fruitless however, regarding the upcoming trial. Seth still refused to tell his story. Rita knew it was because he was protecting family members, not himself.

She hadn't given up on her sex theory. If her hunch happened to be correct, finding out Seth had been abused would greatly increase his chance to have the charges reduced. Pushing him too hard was dangerous though. If she didn't proceed with caution, he might never reveal the truth. She needed to know all the details and Seth was the only one who could provide that information. Gaining total trust was going to be the only way he'd open that door. Developing that trust however was taking a lot of time, something neither of them had much of.

Rita went to the foster home to speak with Julian. She was hoping he could fill in some of the gaps. Julian had the mentality of a four-year-old and was of no help. She never got past, where do you live, and can you tell me about games you play when you are at home. The meeting was a total waste of precious time. Something had happened to the boy, but it was locked inside him tight as a drum. There was little doubt Julian saw his mother and father get their heads bashed in with a baseball bat. On top of that, he had been whisked away from everything in his life that was familiar and made sense. The fact was - Julian was going to be of no use to his brother.

Arthur was frustrated and discouraged. He was ready to go to Roane. He would plead with his supervisor to give the case to someone else. He dreaded going up against Mercer as the prosecuting attorney. Mercer was a cold uncaring individual who would step on anyone to advance his career. His win record was impressive, and it showed in his degree of cockiness. The man was clever and devious. He was underhanded, and thrived on throwing curve balls, catching his opponent off guard. He was a ruthless hunter and once the prey stepped on one of his rusty steel traps, there was no escape.

The governor had played a part in calling on Mercer as the prosecutor. It was puzzling why he was leaving Rita on the case working the other side. She felt betrayed, was being played a fool, and she failed to understand why. She asked her supervisor about what was going on, but he had no answers. She was told to just continue what she was doing and see how the politics played out. His answer did nothing but infuriate her. It only made her more determined to worker harder on the case. She wanted to see justice served - not politicians.

Unless the defense could dig up something to help Seth, Mercer would have no trouble getting a conviction. A rookie in his first year of law school could convince a jury the boy was guilty. Arthur could only imagine what the FBI was doing behind the scenes. It was evident, they wanted to see Seth burn.

Mercer didn't need the FBI's help in this case, but he wasn't opposed to the aces they were placing in his poker hand. He'd already sent Arthur a long list of potential experts to testify on the prosecutions behalf, and the list was still growing.

Mercer knew Arthur would want to depose all the experts slated to testify. In the end, Mercer would only pick one or two from the group to sit on the stand. Arthur would have no way of knowing who they would be though. He'd have no choice but to waste precious time sifting through thousands of pages of useless information given by Mercer's pro line up during depositions. Arthur had been given only one staff assistant to help on this case, the workload was unbearable. Mercer, on the other hand, had twelve assistants at his disposal, more if needed.

Three more weeks went by without any new development. Seth continued being stubborn as a mule. Rita's supervisor suggested she wrap things up and return to Roanoke. She'd left a pile of work on her desk before being called to Abingdon and the pile had only grown larger. She was figuring it out now. The governor had been using her to distract Arthur. In the beginning, she'd been told to stay in Abingdon as long as she felt she was needed. Now, that had changed. She was the only expert Arthur had managed to get thus far. Rita didn't want to leave. She was convinced Seth had been sexually abused by his parents, even though he hadn't confessed to that, yet. If that proved to be true, Arthur would need her to help put the evidence together in an effort to get the charges reduced. Pulling away now would only hurt Seth's fragile case.

Arthur considered calling in experts on the subject of rape. They could testify about how a woman can rape a man. He tossed that idea out though when he discovered there were more experts to dispute that claim then there were to support it. There was little doubt if the defense had two experts to testify a man could be raped, Mercer would have double that or more to dispute it. Arthur was outgunned and outnumbered.

Arthur hated the thought of having Rita testify, knowing Mercer would do everything possible to destroy her credibility. They would attack her from all angles. Still, she was a convincing psychologist. The fact she was female could even have greater persuasion with the jury. His fear was that the governor would whisk her away at the last moment, leaving him with nothing.

Not helping matters was finding out the coroner hadn't conducted any form of testing. Once the coroner determined the cause of death was severe brain trauma caused by a blow to the head, it was a shut case. He rushed to get Janie and Gordon cremated. Two days after being pronounced dead, the bodies were in a fiery furnace and reduced to ashes.

The way things were going, if Seth spilled his guts and gave every detail, it likely wasn't going to be of any help. It would be his word against his dead parents, plus a team of detectives and forensic experts. That plus a power-hungry prosecuting attorney eager to pull any number of rabbits out of his hat in order to get another notch etched into his pistol grips.

Arthur and Rita's relationship had remained professional, although Arthur wanted it to be much more than that. Rita had quickly become the mother figure, treating Seth as if he was her child. As Rita and Seth spent more time together, the relationship changed. Seth was in love, a love like he'd never known. He was smitten with her. Rita could think of nothing more each day, than getting to Damascus to spend time with him. He had captured her heart as well, but she was blinded to it.

Arthur could see it happening but had said nothing. However, as he witnessed Rita's affection toward Seth grow, he became angry. He was appalled that Rita had seemed to forget Seth was a client, a prisoner, a teenage boy. She hadn't really done anything wrong, but he saw how she seemed to swoon whenever she was in Seth's presence. She was acting unprofessionally, and walking on dangerous ground.

The trial was coming up in a few months. Arthur knew that if Seth walked into the courtroom making google eyes at Rita, the jury would label him guilty before he had a chance to make an opening statement. There was only one way to say it – this puppy love stuff had to stop. He tried telling himself this trial was lost and whatever Seth and Rita had going on was nothing to him. His reputation was on the line though, so yes, their actions did concern him.

Arthur and Rita walked out of the courthouse in Abingdon one afternoon. As they descended the steps leading to the street, Arthur pointed to a bench at the bottom. He suggested they sit for a few moments and talk. Rita had just been deposed by Mercer and expected Arthur had a few comments. She thought the deposition had gone better than expected and was feeling good about the answers to questions she had provided.

"The kids in love with you Rita," Arthur said, catching her off guard. Perhaps its best you stop arguing with your supervisor and get on back to Roanoke."

"Are you talking about Seth?" she asked, a bit drawn back.

"Of course I'm talking about Seth," Arthur replied with anger in his voice. "Who else would I be talking about?"

"Oh, nonsense," Rita replied, her face starting to redden. "Why is it I feel you are angry? You and I are all the boy has, Arthur. He needs us, both of us. Gees! Are you jealous?"

"You're in love with him as well," Arthur said, looking directly at Rita. "It's true. You're just afraid to admit it."

Rita's face was completely flushed with redness. Her mouth was partially open. She couldn't believe the things Arthur was saying and the way he was acting.

"You want him, Rita. If Seth was out of jail you'd be all over him, even though he's a juvenile."

"You're insane!" she fired back.

Arthur rolled his eyes toward the sky. "Unbelievable. Why me, Lord? I'm neck deep in this hopeless case with an unprofessional, blind assistant! You've gone astray, Rita. What you're doing is dangerous!"

Rita's face turned from blushing to a crimson red with outrage. "Good grief!" She shouted, surprised and utterly shocked by Arthur's words and gestures. "How dare you attack me! I've done nothing more than try to help Seth. You on the other hand, are a total failure. If you were to stop whining and start digging, you might find something useful to help us get his charges reduced. Right now you're no more prepared than the day you started."

Arthur and Rita rose from the concrete bench. Their angry words grew in volume as they lashed out at each other. Several people Arthur knew passed by, looking curiously in his direction. It embarrassed him.

"I don't have anything to work with, because you've not given me anything!" Arthur said with all the indignation he could muster. "All I have is that freaky kid's story – which you've not been able to get! I'll give you two days. I have my own career to think of. If you can't get Seth's story, I'm walking away, calling it quits. TWO DAYS," he shouted. "If nothing by then, I'll plead with Roane to take me off the case. Since I'm such a failure - try working with one of Roane's wide-eyed rookies fresh out of law school."

Arthur stormed off, leaving Rita standing there with her mouth hung open. She wanted to get the last word in but she was hurt, stunned, and unable to speak.

12

Seth had been evaluated and considered sane. He would be tried as an adult. If he were found guilty, Mercer would press the jury go for the death penalty. Between Arthur and Rita, they had interviewed everyone in Abingdon who knew Seth or his parents. The interviews led to two conclusions. According to town folks – Seth was a weirdo, and Janie was perfect. Little was discovered about Gordon Boone. He was a hard-working and successful real estate agent. He'd nearly ended his life three years ago when he wrecked his car while drunk, leaving him crippled.

Deep down, Rita knew Arthur was right. Seth was overly fond of her, and she'd not done enough to get him to open up. Seth's case was pretty much a lost cause, but if he had a sliver of a chance, she wanted to help. As weak as the case was, Arthur was good at his job and Seth's only ray of hope. Roane's pool of young lawyers from which to choose a replacement would be far worse. She had to do something to keep Arthur on the case. His resignation would eliminate what little hope there was of Seth ever walking the streets again. Arthur had given her an ultimatum. The gloves had to come off. She had to convince Seth to give up his secrets.

The world didn't give a crap about Seth Boone. Still, he deserved a fighting chance. In Rita's eyes, he was still innocent until proven guilty by a jury of his peers. What did that mean anyway? A jury of his peers! A peer was supposed to be one of equal standing. At trial time, Seth would be seventeen years old. The jury box would be filled with men and women much different from Seth, and they would be twice, maybe three times his age.

Rita didn't go visit Seth that day. She left him alone, worrying where she was, why she didn't show. She was hoping perhaps it would be a wake-up call, but then she worried it would only send him deeper inside his shell.

A surprise came the next morning. Mercer called an important meeting with Arthur and Judge Wirt, who'd be hearing the case. The meeting was set to take place in the judge's chambers.

Arthur had been considering a plea to the judge for a change in venue. The trial was to take place in Abingdon, but Arthur didn't think Seth couldn't get a fair trial there in Washington County.

Arthur quickly discovered why Mercer had called the meeting. Mercer pleaded with the judge himself for a change in venue. Arthur was surprised at first and overly delighted, but then thought about the consequences. If Seth was found guilty in Washington County, there might be grounds for a mistrial. If things turned out that way, it would be a year or longer before another trial was set somewhere else in the state. In a year, perhaps two, the feds might back off and Mercer might move on, climb further up the ladder and be off the case. That would give Seth a better chance to beat this rap. On the other hand, if the trial was moved and Seth was found guilty, the chance of a mistrial based on an unfair jury would be pretty much dashed against the rocks.

Judge Wirt looked amused when Mercer popped the question about a change of venue. His look went from being amused to a state of utter shock when Arthur protested.

"I've been sitting on the bench for thirty-two years," Wirt said. "This is a first. The prosecuting attorney wants a change of venue so the accused can get a fair trial, but the defense attorney is flat out against it. Unbelievable."

Godfrey Mercer and Arthur Grant both looked intently at the judge, waiting for him to say more. The judge looked toward the ceiling. He was in deep thought. After nearly two minutes, he looked down, crossed his hands, and leaned forward, within inches of the two attorneys across from his desk.

"I don't like giving up cases. As a matter-of-fact, in thirty-two years, I've only given up one! You two might think it's a pride thing and perhaps that's partly true. Bowing out makes me look weak. It makes it look like I can't do my job. In addition to all that, it creates a tremendous pile of paperwork, and I sure as sure as hell don't need any more of that! Then there's the vultures of the press to deal with. Mercer - you have a lot of nerve calling this meeting and presenting such a thing."

Arthur felt a smirk trying to spread across his face, and he was doing all he could to suppress it.

"However," the judge said, turning his gaze to Arthur. "Mercer has a good point."

Arthur's heart nearly stopped, and the forming smirk quickly turned to a frown.

"I don't see how we could find an unbiased jury in this county," the judge said. "With all the national publicity in the papers about Judge Boone, we'll be damn lucky to find someone in Nome, Alaska who hasn't heard about the murders. I rule to have the trial moved. You'll have the location, date, and all the paperwork on your desks by this afternoon."

Arthur's mouth opened and he was about to speak, but Judge Wirt held his left hand up and cut him off.

"Mr. Grant, please don't open your pie-hole and cause me to find you in contempt."

The judge stared Arthur down then slammed his open right palm down on his desk, making a sound every bit as loud as his gavel in the courtroom.

"That will be all gentlemen."

13

The next morning, Rita went to visit Seth. He was excited and said he'd been worried something might have happened to her. Rita didn't kiss him on the cheek that morning as she'd done the last few meetings. Seth liked it when she was close and had always commented about the wonderful aroma of her perfume. That morning, however, she kept her distance, denying him that pleasure. Seth was worried he'd upset her, and concerned that she didn't want to be close to him.

Rita explained what had taken place on the courthouse steps with Arthur, then about the meeting with Judge Wirt and his decision to move the trial.

"So what are we going to do?" he asked.

"I'm not going to do anything – unless you continue refusing to tell me your story," Rita said in a soft but stern voice.

She cleared her throat, took a deep breath, then walked over and sat by Seth. She placed her trembling hand in his. Her voice was shaking.

"I've been lying to myself, Seth. I love you. I love you, but I can't continue as things are. Arthur is right. If you aren't willing to help, our time is being wasted and I need to move on. Please help me to help you. I want to get see you walk away from this. That may not happen, but still, if we get the charges reduced, you could still be free in a few years. I can't believe I'm telling you this, but I can't deny it any longer. Oh God Seth, I'm so much in love with you. I don't want to lose you now."

Rita had tears in her eyes. Seth's heart began pounding in his chest when Rita said she loved him. It was the most wonderful thing he'd ever heard. The way she said it, the way her words flowed. He'd loved Sarah but very differently. They were best of friends. His love for Rita was more than friendship. He desired to hold her, kiss her, tasting the sweetness of her lips. After everything that had happened to him, he never thought he could love a woman this way.

His heart pounded even harder and louder when Rita said she would leave him if he didn't help her. He had always wanted to tell her his story but that meant confessing everything - going against what his parents had beat into his head. Although he hated what they had done to him, he respected them as his parents. He'd been taught that dishonoring them would be the worst sin he could ever commit. It was time to tell Rita everything though, but it scared him now more than ever. He was scared it would drive her away but knew not confessing would surely do so.

Seth had read all the lies in the newspapers. It was time he set the story straight, to get everything out in the open. He feared the media would twist the truth even further than the lies they'd already printed, especially the part of his mother having sex with Julian. Telling his story however was the only chance of getting the charges reduced. He expected he'd go to prison no matter what, but if he were free in a few years, he could be with Rita. That thought trumped all others.

It was an unbelievable meeting. Seth broke down, lowered his shield, and told Rita everything. It was like a dam bursting. The story poured out of him. It was like a volcano erupting deep inside his soul. As each bit of information spewed out, he felt lighter. A burden was lifting off his shoulders.

It took over two hours to tell her everything, stopping often to wipe tears and take long deep breaths. Along with the feeling of having shed a heavy load, a strong sense of guilt swept over him. He was telling the family secrets, disgracing everyone.

He felt like a traitor. He'd been programmed to protect the family no matter what, good or bad, and he'd failed miserably. He didn't want it to come out in court, but knew it must. He kept looking at Rita, expecting her to bolt out the door, especially when he gave the details about how his mother had used him. Spilling his guts was the hardest thing he'd ever done.

Instead of bolting for the door, Rita stayed by his side. She was thrilled. She'd broken through Seth's barrier, something she'd all but deemed impossible to do. As Seth told the story about how he was abused by Janie and how his father played along, a raging sea of emotions rolled back and forth in her heart. She felt so sorry for him, all the while horrified by the things he was saying.

When it came to telling about the night of the killings, he could hardly describe the scene. As he spoke in broken sentences, telling what he saw when he entered the room and saw Janie on top of Julian, he slumped forward, unable to make eye contact. Rita found herself cradling him in her arms, his head lying on her chest. She stroked his hair while kissing his head. Tears flowed from both of them like a river, soaking their shirts.

Seth shook as he continued telling all that had taken place on that horrible night. He described picking up the bat, hitting Janie then quickly turning the bat on his father. He remembered the look on Gordon's face. Seth said he'd been having reoccurring nightmares - seeing his father's eyes looking at him, awakening when the baseball bat cracked open his skull.

It was an hour after Seth stopped talking before Rita pulled away. They had cried more than either could ever remember, and they were drained of energy.

Late that evening in Arthur's office, Rita played the long tape. She made him listen to it all to the very end. He felt relieved that Seth had finally found the courage to tell what had really taken place. Arthur sat behind his desk listening, dumbfounded. Several times, he wiped tears from the corners of his own eyes, and shook his head back and forth while saying, "D-A-M-N." When the tape stopped, Arthur and Rita sat there for a long while, saying nothing. Both had suspected Seth had been abused. His story was more than shocking. It was more than sickening. It was beyond one's scope of imagination.

Seth sat in his cell that evening thinking. He dreaded facing people in court and the way they would look at him. He had been held and loved by Rita, and it was a wonderful feeling. He had dishonored his parents. He was worried about Julian. He was in love with Rita, and she'd confessed her love to him as well. The good and bad collided, waging war in his mind.

Arthur managed to set up a meeting the next morning with three of the detectives assigned to the case. He played parts of the tape for the detectives and afterwards asked them to consider this new discovery. He asked if they would go with him to meet Mercer, and support his effort to get the charges reduced. There was no doubt in his mind Seth had been under a great amount of duress when he walked into Julian's room. Seth had gotten angry when he saw what his parents were doing so he hit them, but it wasn't a premeditated plot to kill.

The confession had revealed a lot of mitigating circumstances. Arthur knew he didn't have a chance of getting Seth off the hook by claiming it was self-defense. However, he felt Seth's story left considerable wiggle room for plea bargaining and getting the charges dropped to manslaughter. What he needed now was a little help from the detectives.

"Find out if the coroner made any notes he didn't include as part of the official record," Arthur said. "Re-interview some people, look for evidence in the house," he pleaded. "Perhaps Janie kept a diary hidden somewhere. There has to be more. This abuse went on for three years. Who knows, maybe Gordon kept some sort of diary himself."

Two of the detectives laughed. The third shook his head and said, "After all these weeks, you now come up with this shit!"

Arthur sat there speechless. He was stunned.

"Oh, the kid does a good cry, and even sounds a little convincing, but damn. You want us to believe Judge Boone was raping the kid? Hell, a woman can't rape a man!"

One of the other detectives sobered up from his hard laugh and said, "Unfriggin-believable!"

"Yeah, you gotta be nuts, Grant!" The third detective added.

The meeting was fruitless. Arthur was furious and stormed out. The detectives thought Rita had worked with Seth to produce a staged tape.

Arthur called Rita and asked her to meet him for lunch at the Martha Washington Inn. He walked in with a worried look on his face.

"It was useless meeting with those Neanderthals," he told her as soon as they were seated. "The cops won't help us."

"What else can we do?" Rita asked, concerned. "There has to be something or someone who can help us with this."

Arthur ran his hands through his hair. "I don't know. I need more time to think. We need some solid evidence. Right now, it's Seth's word against everyone in the Commonwealth of Virginia. We got a boatload of people ready to say how wonderful Judge Boone was, but not a soul willing to take the stand on Seth's behalf."

"You heard him on the tape, Arthur. He's telling the truth. Put Seth on the stand."

"Oh Lord, Rita," Arthur said loudly, drawing attention from the tables around them. He lowered his voice and craned his neck toward her. "Mercer would eat the kid alive!"

"Seth's a bright kid," Rita replied. "He can handle Mercer."

"Think, Rita," Arthur said. "Seth also has a few buttons that can be pushed, making him ape crazy. Don't think for one instant Mercer won't find those buttons. All he'd have to do is start talking about Julian!"

Rita sighed. "You're right. Dang it!"

A light came on in Rita's head. It took her the next two days to convince Arthur to help, but he finally caved and said he would.

It was just after dusk when Arthur and Rita broke a glass pane out of the back door window, unlocked the door, and walked inside the Boone house. Arthur had tried to get one of the detectives to take him there, saying he was still gathering evidence, but he'd been denied. The police supposedly had gone over every inch of the house, and now it would take a judge's order to get back in. He tried that, pleading with Judge Wirt. Arthur left the judge's chambers in the same manner he had the last time, ready to explode.

Using penlight flashlights, Arthur and Rita went over every inch of Janie and Gordon's bedroom, looking in closets, shoeboxes, even behind pictures on the walls. They pilfered the study, opening every book. They examined Seth's room, the living room, the den downstairs, with a fine-toothed comb. Four hours later, their hearts pumping as fast as the moment they'd broken in, they left. They'd found no diary, not photos - nothing.

Late the next day, Rita caught up with one of Seth's teachers whom she'd missed interviewing. Her name was Dorothy Hamlin. It was the last day of school, so they spoke as the teacher packed things away for the summer break. Rita asked leading questions, hoping to get something positive, but came away empty.

Dorothy's story was no different from the other teachers. Seth was extraordinarily bright, was once outgoing, and then about three years ago began to withdraw, befriending no one after that. Rita asked if she'd be willing to testify to that. It would be of little help, but it was still something. Dorothy became defensive, and said she'd not only have to get a subpoena, but they'd also have to drag her into court.

14

In the juvenile detention center a week earlier, Seth got into a fight with a bully who'd been extorting money from other boys. The bully was sent to the hospital with a broken jaw, bruised ribs, and a right eye that would take several weeks before the swelling went down completely. Although Seth didn't start the fight, it was another mark against him and Mercer no doubt was taking notes. Seth was placed in a cell by himself after the fight.

The warden requested that Seth be sent to the Regional Jail until ready to stand trial, but the request was denied. Judge Wirt didn't want to throw a sixteen-year-old boy into the general population of adult inmates. It was ironic, considering Seth was going to be tried as an adult.

On July 1st, Seth spent his seventeenth birthday alone in his cell. Rita had to make a trip to Roanoke that day and didn't get back until late in the evening, long after hours of visitation.

Seth received a birthday surprise that afternoon, but it wasn't anything he would have ever expected or wanted. A freelance reporter bribed a guard with fifty dollars and got a close-up photo of Seth behind bars. Seth was stretched out on his bunk, his hands behind his head as he stared at the ceiling, daydreaming of being with Rita.

The photo was shocking. Seth was wearing nothing but a pair of white cotton gym shorts with a red stripe running down the side. It was the perfect shot, showing his thick muscular legs, six-pack stomach, high-rising rippling chest, and his bulging biceps. It looked like he was posing for a muscle magazine. Seth was unaware however that the reporter had stepped up to the bars with his 35mm camera. The photo was a sure sell to the tabloids, as well as many of the story hungry newspapers all across Virginia.

Just after Janie and Gordon had been killed, the trash newspapers had given Seth the name 'Batboy'. Eleven tabloids showed Seth's jail cell photo posted on their front page. One heading read, 'No More Sweet-Sixteen – Batboy Flexes Muscles While Spending Birthday In Jail'. Another read, 'Slugger Turns Seventeen Behind Bars – Parents Wish Him A Ghostly Happy Birthday'. Underneath Seth's photo was a picture of tombstones.

Rita was livid. She tried calling several tabloids but was able to speak with no one. Arthur asked the DA to conduct an investigation and demanded the guard at the juvenile center be fired. He was also planning a civil suit for defamation of character, among other claims. The guard got three days off with pay, further infuriating Rita and Arthur.

§

Judge Wirt arranged for the trial to be moved to Spotsylvania County. The feds were pushing their weight and pulling strings. They wanted Seth to get the needle for murdering a federal judge. The trial would take place in the Fredericksburg Federal Courthouse. It was just another blow to Arthur's frail case. After hearing the news, Arthur went to a convenience store and purchased a lottery ticket, expecting his chances of winning the multi-million dollar top prize had better odds than getting Seth Boone a not-guilty verdict.

A week before trial, Seth was transferred to Spotsylvania and placed in the county jail. The day after, Rita packed her bags and followed.

Back in Damascus, Rita and Seth's meetings were always private. Rita had broken through the walls that held Seth captive. When she'd first learned the truth of what had been going on in the Boone home, her intent was to help Seth recover from that horrible ordeal. He'd gone through three years of unthinkable abuse, but he was salvageable. She knew that he was still capable of living a normal life, able to love the way God intended a man and woman to love each other. Seth had told his story, and both had confessed they loved each other. After that, the daily meetings in a private room eventually blossomed into a jailhouse petting parlor.

Seth and Rita spent much of their time talking in the beginning, with Rita carefully explaining human behavior, and ridding Seth's mind from the mountain of guilt he was carrying. She walked him through the steps of a healthy and meaningful relationship. They were open and honest with each other, never holding back questions, never afraid to express their true feelings. Neither could explain how it happened, but at some point, the talks gave way to hours of kissing and fondling. Rita looked beyond the surface of rippling hardened muscles and found a gentle giant that possessed a caring heart. Seth had a temper, but it only surfaced when his defense mechanism kicked in.

Rita questioned herself about what she was doing. She'd broken all the rules. Seth was a minor. If a guard had walked in and found her lying back in his arms, her bra unsnapped and Seth's hands inside her blouse caressing her breasts, she'd not only lose her job, but likely would have been brought up on charges. Fortunately, that never happened. Seth was a client - a patient - a subject she was studying. He wasn't just any client - he was in jail and charged with murdering his parents. To the rest of the world, Seth was a lost cause, a seventeen-year-old boy who likely would never see his twenty-first birthday and deservedly so.

At times, Rita felt as much a pervert as Seth's mother, Janie, had been. She wondered if a mother figure was how Seth actually viewed her. When alone, she tried convincing herself to break the love affair off, but she couldn't. She'd let her heart do the thinking instead of her head. Thoughts of turning back were useless, her heart was in control, and she wanted it that way.

Seth was a boy and she was a twenty-eight-year-old woman, a professional counselor, with a career on the line. She couldn't believe the direction this had gone, yet she couldn't deny the strength of the love she had for him. She loved his muscular build, but she also loved his intelligence. He was charming, witty, and his love for her was genuine, something she'd never experienced. Most men she knew wanted nothing more than to get inside her pants. They were only interested in a romp in the hay, not a relationship with substance.

Seth sat in his cell day after day dreaming of being with Rita. He loved her beyond measure. He couldn't understand how she could love him though. He'd killed his parents, and was staring a death sentence in the face. Rita had a career, an entire life in front of her. She was beautiful both inside and out, and deserved someone so much better than him.

He had confessed to Rita everything that happened over the last three years. She amazingly understood, and was helping him deal with that. He knew the truth also had to come out in court. He dreaded seeing that day come. So much had happened. He thought about his parents. He'd killed them! It didn't seem real. It was like a bad dream. Every night he relived it all. He wished he could break out of jail. He could take Rita and Julian and run away, just as he'd plan to do with Sarah before she was killed.

A month before Seth was sent to Spotsylvania County, things had taken another turn south. Rita had been pulled off his case. She didn't want him to know, so she never told him. The governor, satisfied Seth was guilty, had turned to Mercer, the prosecutor. To the governor, it was all about his image. He wanted to be on the winning side. He'd not received any bad publicity on the way the investigation had been handled. A meeting with Mercer had convinced the governor that Rita remaining in Abingdon served no good purpose and could possibly hurt the case.

Rayburn Mason, Rita's supervisor, as well as Governor Lewis himself, was shocked when Rita resigned and left without a proper notice. The governor, although not pleased with her decision said nothing. Mason, however, took her resignation personally. He swore to do everything in his power to ensure that Rita never worked in a public office in Virginia again.

Rita was unaware of the Mason's outrage, but it made no difference, she'd already decided herself that she was through with politics. Once the trial was over, she would open a private practice somewhere and be her own boss. If Seth were to be found guilty and sent to prison, she'd open shop in the town where he was incarcerated. If declared innocent, they would move away and start a new life together in Colorado where her youngest brother lived, or maybe California, or Washington State, anywhere but Virginia. She loved Virginia, but knew they'd never find peace there.

Rita's parents had died a few years back, and she still had most of the fifty-thousand dollars she'd received from their estate. She'd live on that money until it ran out. It would allow her to devote all her time to Seth.

Being Arthur's only expert slated to testify, Rita was worried. She loved Seth with all her heart. It was a love she never expected to find. It was a once in a lifetime love. If Seth went to prison, she wasn't sure she could go on without him. What time she wasn't with him, she spent going over the case, which was weak. On the other hand, the prosecutor had few worries. His quiver was full of poisonous arrows - experts supplied by the feds. Mercer was anxious to get the show started.

Rita was confident Arthur would do his best, but how she wished someone with more experienced was handling the case. She considered hiring someone herself, but it was too late now. To hire a law firm with the resources needed to do Seth justice would cost far more than the savings she had in the bank. Besides, the trial was set to start. Without good cause, there was no way the judge would delay the trial while she searched for a firm willing to take Seth's case.

Arthur arrived in Fredericksburg two days after Rita left Abingdon. As they entered the court the next morning for jury selection, she met the prosecutor, Godfrey Mercer, for the second time.

Mercer was the size of a refrigerator. He stood six-feet-four, had a large, rounded belly, flabby jaws, and slicked back thinning hair. Whenever he spoke, his foul smelling breath filled the air around him. He dressed and carried himself like a gangster.

For the next two days, Arthur and Rita sat in the courtroom battling Mercer's team. Six men and three women sat directly behind the railing at Mercer's back. They were well dressed, looking like they were ready to go on stage for a presidential debate. They constantly handed notes to Mercer with personal information they'd dug up on each potential juror. Arthur and Rita knew Mercer's team wasn't from the D.A.'s office. There was little doubt - their paychecks came from the Department of Justice, not the Commonwealth of Virginia.

The pool of seventy-five candidates for the jury was whittled down to twelve. In the end, the jury consisted of two male African-Americans, an Asian American female, four white males, and five white females. One juror was in his early sixties. Eight were in their fifties, two in their forties, and one of the black males was in his late twenties. Arthur couldn't determine if this was good or bad, but he was relying on the 'with age comes wisdom' concept. He could only hope the older jurors would be wise and listen to the evidence, his in particular. He had to somehow plant reasonable doubt in their minds and hope for a hung jury. It was a daunting task.

15

Every newspaper or magazine Rita looked at on the newsstand had an article about the trial. Seth had been made out to be a sex-crazed teen out of control. It infuriated Rita. Someone had given the media information that was supposed to have been sealed tight. Arthur hadn't said anything to anyone about there being any sexual impropriety, taking place in the Boone house. Mercer, although he'd gotten wind of Seth's sex abuse story through discovery hadn't said anything as well.

The leak had to be one of the detectives they'd turned to after Seth had told his story. Instead of helping, they'd spread the story to the trashy tabloids. Now every news team in the land had picked-up on the Seth's story, except it was flipped around, making Seth the rapist. Rita expected everyone in the Commonwealth of Virginia had read the poison. In reality, Seth couldn't get a fair trial in Abingdon, Fredericksburg, or Timbuktu.

The judge, knowing the publicity on the case, decided to sequester the jury from the start. He was the honorable Harlin S. Doddridge, an old school, grumpy, old goat, who should have retired twenty years ago. He was loud, obnoxious ninety-percent of the time, and made sure everyone knew the courtroom belonged to him - literally.

Arthur had fought feverishly over the last month to strike a deal with the prosecution. If they reduced the charges of murder in the first degree, Seth would plead no-contest to voluntary manslaughter. Mercer's team laughed at the proposal. Arthur then tried for a no-contest plea to murder in the second-degree. Mercer balked at that proposal as well. Mercer felt he had the case won, so he wasn't willing to consider anything Arthur had to offer.

The trial began on Monday, December 3rd. It was a cold blustery day with gray skies that threatened snow. Seven news crew vans sat on the streets with engines running. Steam from their exhaust pipes hovered close to the ground, giving the appearance of Hollywood smoke. Cameras were everywhere. Near every camera were young female reporters with pretty faces, wearing bright lipstick, wrapped in long wool coats, and scarves around their necks.

Inside the courthouse, the jurors filed in one by one. Most didn't want to be there. They had their own lives and busy ones at that. Christmas shopping was on their minds. They had their fingers crossed, hoping things would move swiftly and by weeks end, it would all be over.

When the trial started, Mercer wasted no time. His opening statement was powerful and convincing. He made Seth look every bit as bad as Osama Bin Laden.

Photographs of Gordon and Janie with open skulls, lying in a pool of blood on Julian's bedroom floor, were passed around the jury box as soon as things got underway. The photos were damaging. Rita and Arthur watched the faces of the jurors. Most turned their heads away quickly, passing the photos on to the next person as fast as they could.

The county coroner gave his report, including the expected cause of death. Arthur questioned him about why he never tested to see if Janie had sex before she was killed. He indicated he'd found no cause to do such an evaluation.

"Besides, we quickly determined that Gordon wasn't capable," the coroner added.

Arthur also asked why the bodies were so quickly cremated knowing Seth had been accused of murder, and the investigation was barely underway. He gave no reason, only to say the cause of death had been determined and there was no reason to deny family and friends some degree of closure.

Mercer reiterated again and again how this was such a heinous and no doubt, planned crime. He claimed Seth had been planning the murders for a long time, hoping to inherit the estate. Arthur stood up and objected. He shouted at the judge, saying there was no evidence or merit whatsoever to what Mercer was saying. He wanted to make it clear how stupid it was to think this was in any way a planned crime. There was no cover up, nothing hidden, nothing done to make it look like some intruder broke into the house and killed the Boones.

"Just a simple, objection, is all that's necessary, Mr. Grant," the judge reprimanded.

Mercer was all too happy to put a busload of experts on the stand - compliments of his new friends - the FBI.

A forensic expert from L.A.P.D. spoke in such technical terms that Arthur couldn't figure out what the answers to his questions actually meant. Then there was the expert from Scotland Yard, who went over the crime scene bit by bit, as if he'd been there. He described the angle of the bat coming down on each victim, and the amount of force that had been exerted. He gave mathematical models depicting the height and weight of the assailant. There was no reason for Arthur to dispute this claim, he had nothing to use against it.

It was standing room only in the courtroom. A mob of hungry reporters was outside. Camera crews were scattered all over the courtyard. A dozen sketch artists were busy with their pencils, sketching away to make drawings of Seth, the jury, and Mercer with his red pompous face and waving arms. Seth scanned the crowd. A man he'd seen before was in the back. He recognized the hardened face. It was the muscular stranger he'd seen at the funeral home the night of Sarah's wake. He wondered who the man was and why he was there.

Arthur tried planting a few seeds with the jury. He hoped to raise doubt, and at the very least, get a hung jury. He knew, however, with Mercer and his army fighting against him, it was comparable to trying to grow watermelons at the North Pole. His attempt proved to be quite pitiful. Rita thought Arthur was a good attorney, but he had dug up nothing to dispute the evidence presented, and no way to provide his own evidence to prove the killings had gone any way other than what Mercer was telling the jury. Arthur was no match for the articulate and crafty Mercer.

It was agonizing to Seth, sitting there for hours listening to everyone talk about him, comparing him to the devil himself. He had confessed to killing his parents, but claimed it wasn't planned, and that he hadn't meant to kill them. Seth saw the Boone family attorney Gary McDowell, III, in the court sitting on the side of the prosecution. McDowell had an uncontrollable smirk on his face. Seth knew that if he were convicted, McDowell would somehow end up with the house plus whatever money his parents had accumulated. He'd also figure out a way to collect the payoff from life insurance policies.

When the first day of the trial ended, Arthur looked like he'd been run over by a truck. Mercer, on the other hand, was mingling with his group of experts as they prepared to leave the courtroom, laughing and making dinner plans. Seth knew this would be hard, but it was more agonizing than he could have ever imagined. It was painful sitting there, taking the blows delivered by the audacious prosecutor. The fiery darts flying from the juror's eyes, however, were worse than the loudest, disdainful accusations from Mercer. He expected they couldn't wait to mark 'GUILTY AS CHARGED' on their ballot sheet.

The actual charges were two counts of capital murder. The jury couldn't find Seth guilty of a lesser charge, they could only vote guilty or not guilty on the charges that had been made. They would either put him away for life, or set him free. Those were their only choices. There was always the possibility for a hung jury, but that was about as likely as the sun rising from the west tomorrow morning.

Rita got a call that evening from Detective Madison in Abingdon. She nearly fainted. She fell into the chair in her hotel room and flung her head back. The call was about Julian.

It was hard to find a good foster home for the boy. He was almost nineteen years old, and suffered from Downs Syndrome. A little more than a month ago, he had been placed with Dailey and Beverly Randolph, a couple who lived back in the sticks.

Twice in the past, the couple had been accused of abuse, but nothing had been proven and no charges had ever been filed. Everyone seemed to turn a blind eye toward the foster parents. Rita had suspected from the beginning that the couple's only interest was the money the county provided for Julian's care.

County services had been out to the Randolph house two weeks ago, and found Julian knee-deep in mud, feeding hogs and cleaning their sty. Randolph claimed the boy had just wandered off.

"The boy came up missing a few times," he said. "We'd go lookin, and sure nough, he'd be out yonder with those stinkin' hogs. Likes hogs fer sum reason - go figure."

Detective Madison told Rita that County Services were out at the Randolph place again yesterday, along with the police. Julian was found face down in the pigsty - he was dead. They found a heavily soiled blanket in the pig house. It appeared the foster parents had made Julian live there with the animals. Sometime yesterday, maybe the day before, Julian had fallen and been trampled by a group of three-hundred pound swine.

Rita sat there in the chair with her hand over her mouth. She couldn't believe the news. There was no way she could tell Seth, at least not now. She'd have to tell him, he had every right to know, but telling Seth now could cause him to come unglued. She had no idea how he would react or what he might do.

She called Arthur and he agreed, Seth shouldn't be told yet. There wasn't anything Seth or anyone else could do. Seth wouldn't even be allowed to go to the funeral. With McDowell having the family money tied up in a legal quagmire, the state would have to fork over the money to give the kid a decent burial. It was another catastrophe, throwing tons more weight on the already broken-down wagon. Rita just hoped Seth didn't get word from someone else about Julian before the right opportunity to tell him presented itself.

Five days had been set aside for the trial. Arthur took little time with the experts Mercer called to the stand, so things were moving much faster than expected. By noon on the second day, the jury had listened to all the prosecution's experts. The judge called it a day, declaring recess. The trial would reconvene the next morning at 9 a.m.

It was time for the defense to present their witnesses and experts. Arthur didn't have any witnesses and only one expert to call. He was concerned, and with good cause. As the proceedings began the next morning, Arthur was nervous.

"The defense calls Rita Logan," Arthur bellowed out, his voice a bit shaky.

Arthur may have been nervous, but Rita was confident. She threw a curve ball to the jury, but not Mercer, he was ready. Rita told how Seth had been abused. She described the rapes by his mother, and told how his impotent father had collaborated. There were a few jeers in the courtroom, and Judge Doddridge had to pound his gavel twice, calling for order. When she told the story of how Janie raped Julian, the courtroom erupted loudly. It took Doddridge several attempts to get order restored.

Seth made more eye contact with the jury than the day before. He saw faces filled with anger, revulsion, and downright hatred toward him. They weren't buying the truth. He feared what Rita told them, although it was true and accurate, would only serve to further the damage. Still, it was the truth and everyone needed to know. Arthur had his fingers crossed. All he needed for now was one juror to doubt Mercer's claims of cold-blooded murder.

Rita described the hell Seth had been through, how he had withdrawn from society and how he felt compelled to protect the family from the crimes being committed almost daily by Gordon and Janie. She spoke about the pills, and described how Seth had been forced to take the medication, guaranteeing Janie that Seth would be able to service her perverted sexual desire. She testified that Gordon was incapable of having sex and that the medicine had been prescribed unlawfully.

Arthur had considered subpoenaing the doctor that had prescribed the medication, but didn't think his testimony would be helpful. He'd also considered subpoenaing the teachers at school who'd noticed the changes in Seth when the abuse started. After speaking with the detective who had interviewed them, he decided the teachers' testimonies would be of no help. The one teacher Rita had interviewed was considered, but dragging her into court could help Mercer more than Seth.

While Rita was on the stand, Arthur asked her to describe how a woman could rape a man, or boy in Seth's case. She rattled off several studies by university doctors, describing how a young man could easily be stimulated and perform a sexual act unwillingly. She also quoted two studies conducted on drugs such as the one Seth had been given, proving a male even under duress could still get an erection that would last for hours.

Mercer surprised everyone. He didn't dispute Rita's story, or even talk about it. He'd read the jury. They'd not bought into Rita's disgraceful, tasteless claim. Instead of disputing Rita's story, Mercer attacked her credibility. He asked a multitude of questions about her former job, the one from which she'd recently resigned. It was a good attempt to discredit her character, make her look unreliable, and perhaps untruthful.

Seth was surprised. He didn't know Rita had quit her job.

Rita explained how her supervisor had been contacted by the governor, and that she'd been told to stay on the case as long as needed. Mercer asked questions about her resignation and about her relationship with Seth. Mercer didn't know anything about what had been going on between her and Seth, but had suspicions. The color and expression on Rita's face told it all.

It was three 3 p.m. when Rita stepped down from the witness stand and took her seat beside of Seth. She was exhausted, feeling like she'd spent hours churning in a meat grinder.

The judge declared it was too late in the day to start closing arguments. He called for recess until 9 a.m. Thursday morning.

16

Mercer was smart, determined, and had done his homework. He was also a slithering snake. Arthur had a degree of respect for the man, but it was small. Still, Arthur didn't blame Mercer for putting on a show. Mercer was a man moving up the ladder, and what better way than being the prosecutor in a big trial with national media attention. It helped having the FBI on his side. The resources they provided would only serve to sway the jury against Seth.

Arthur blamed the detectives back in Abingdon for the way things were going. They were the ones who were eager to declare the investigation closed, practically before it got started. The coroner was to blame too. He had his torch ready to turn Janie and Gordon to ashes the day after they were killed. If Seth had cried foul in the beginning and told his story, it may have given him a chance. Arthur was afraid the jury wasn't buying into the story of Seth being raped by his mother. Like everyone else, he could see it on the jurors' faces. They didn't believe a thing Rita had said.

Arthur was tired, ready to get this trial over with and move on. For months, it had been like swimming upstream with his arms bound. Now it was nearly over. He'd take his losing record home and hope for a better day tomorrow. He had been considering moving on, hoping to find someone willing to take on a junior associate. He loved Abingdon, which is why he'd stayed in the low paying thankless job, but this case changed everything. He didn't know if he could go back. Like Mercer, Arthur was also getting a lot of publicity from the press. He was destined to come out the loser, however. Being the loser in a high-profile case would hurt his career, or at the very least diminish his chances of landing a better job.

Arthur's seven minute long closing statement seemed to confuse the jury. He talked in circles and never completely finished any statement before moving in another direction, clarifying nothing. Even the judge wrinkled his brow and produced a puzzled look as he tried to follow. Rita was a bit taken aback, thinking Arthur wasn't at all prepared, but then again, there was really nothing to be offered. Seth sat there motionless. He expected a guilty verdict because he was guilty. He just wanted to get this over with and start his sentence. At least in prison critical eyes wouldn't be constantly upon him.

Arthur thought he'd done a decent job, even though his closing speech had been rather short. He would be given a chance to take the floor again once Mercer had his shot. He didn't think the slick prosecuting attorney would throw any blindsided punches this late in the game, but he was wrong.

Mercer not disputing the 'rape theory' when Rita was on the stand had surprised the jury and even more so the defense. Arthur thought long and hard about that. He felt it was a mistake on Mercer's part. There was a chance the jurors would mull over the rape claim and perhaps at least one of the twelve would have doubts about a guilty verdict. Arthur was shocked, however, by what happened next. Mercer opened his mouth and the floodgates opened full stream.

"We've listened for the past several days about what took place that night in the Boone house - the night Gordon and Janie lost their lives," Mercer said loudly and boldly.

"The evidence found at the house points to one person being responsible for the deaths of Gordon and Janie Boone - the accused, Seth Boone. He brutally murdered his parents, striking them forcefully and purposely with a baseball bat. You've heard all the evidence. It's overwhelming, isn't it? You and I have heard nothing at all to dispute the state's claim of Seth murdering his marvelous parents. That's because the evidence is so strong, so damaging, leading to only one conclusion. We've even seen a signed confession by Seth Boone, saying he did it!"

Mercer walked back to his table, picked up the confession signed by Seth the same night he'd killed his parents, and waved it before the jury.

"Seth Boone had been drinking," Mercer bellowed out, his voice echoing in the courtroom. "It was stolen liquor from his father's stash. The breathalyzer taken by a police officer at the house only minutes after the murders showed Seth had indeed had a couple of drinks. The underage drinker, Seth Boone, ladies and gentlemen, had been drinking whiskey! He wasn't intoxicated, however - he was legally sober and aware of his actions. Later that same evening, a drug test was conducted by the police. The results were negative – proving Seth wasn't on drugs. Further testing proved that Seth Boone is in his right mind. We'll likely never know the real reason why Seth picked up that baseball bat and beat the brains out of his precious mommy and daddy. WHY he did it is a mystery - IF he did it, isn't!"

Mercer lowered his voice, and a sad look appeared on his face.

"Ladies and gentlemen of the jury, as you go to deliberate this case, I ask that you look over the evidence one more time. Go over the evidence piece by piece as it was presented to you in this very courtroom. It isn't hard to piece together what took place that night when Janie and Gordon Boone's lives ended. The facts don't lie."

The big man took a long deep breath, paused then continued.

"As you study the facts, you'll notice that not one piece of evidence or testimony given would indicate why Seth did this horrible thing. That is, unless you believe this nonsense about poor little Seth being raped!"

There was a pause as Mercer turned from the jury and looked toward the defense table. Seth was in his now usual position - arms draped by his side and his head down.

"Take a good look at the accused," Mercer said, his voice gaining volume again.

Mercer threw his hands up then looked slightly toward Seth. His voice returned to full volume, bouncing off the courtroom walls. He pointed at Seth, using his left index finger.

"I don't see a young wimpy boy sitting there, helpless, unable to fend off a petite woman trying to rape him! Do you? You have eyes - take a good, long look for yourself. I see a man. I see a man well over six feet tall, and built like a brick shithouse."

The courtroom erupted. The judged pounded with his gavel and called for order. It took several minutes to get the crowd settled down. Judge Doddridge peered down over his reading glasses at Mercer.

"Council, I find you in contempt of this court. How dare you to use such language, knowing as well as anyone else in this room how I feel about such things." The judge's face was blood red. "I'm going to fine you five-hundred dollars. Even though we are nearing the end of this trial, if I hear anything else foul come forth from your lips, I'll throw you out of my court and you'll never come back. Understood?"

It was so quiet in the courtroom everyone could hear Mercer's labored breathing. Everyone was frozen. No one was stirring, not even the reporters standing in the back.

"I sincerely apologize," Mercer said, in a low almost whimpering voice while looking at the judge. "I assure you it will not happen again."

Mercer turned to look at Seth, then turned back to look at the jury.

"Ladies and gentlemen of the jury, I'd like to apologize to you as well for my poorly chosen words. I made a mistake, and the judge is going to see that I pay for that mistake. My apology is sincere, and I will not make that mistake again."

The jury had their eyes locked in on Mercer. He was putting on the show of a lifetime, and the jury was sucking it down like a glass of cold lemonade on a hot summer day.

"What about Seth? What about the horrible act he committed, taking the lives of two individuals. Not just some strangers on the street mind you, although that too would be a tragedy, but his own mother and father. Did Seth mean to do it? Did he mean to kill them? Well, he didn't hit them over the head with a Nerf Football!"

Someone in the back of the court laughed, but quickly quieted back down.

"I acted foolishly a few moments ago," Mercer said. "The judge lashed out at me – and rightfully so!" Mercer's eyes were bulging. He was only a few feet away from the jury box. "I made a mistake, but the judge wasn't out of control, was he? He didn't throw me out of the courtroom, although he has the authority to do so. He didn't take a baseball bat and hit me forcefully over the head."

Mercer pointed toward the judge.

"Instead, the Honorable Harlin S. Doddridge, acted with restraint. He's a judge and knows the law. He's an upstanding citizen of the community, held to a higher degree – as judges are."

There was a slight pause.

"Janie Boone was a judge! Janie Boone was a caring mother! Gordon Boone was a caring father! They were loving parents who used restraint. They never attacked Seth, Julian, or anyone else for that matter. Heck, my guess is if a bug crawled into the house, they'd scoot it out the door instead of stepping on it."

Mercer scanned the jury box, making eye contact with each juror. He had them all on his side. Not only did he know that, Seth did as well. With a quick glance at the jurors before looking down again, Seth read their faces and body language. There was no chance of being found innocent, and that would mean no future for him and Rita.

"During your own childhood, did you ever get angry at your parents?" Mercer asked. "When your parents made you angry, did you ever pick up a knife, a gun, a baseball bat, and try to kill them? Did you ever rush at your loving parents in a moment of rage, prepared to do them bodily harm? I think each of you can answer those questions with a simple – no. Oh, I bet you got angry at times. I feel certain about that. All teens are disobedient at times. I'm sure Seth was too on occasion. This wasn't some mild act of disobedience though. Seth Boone swung a baseball bat like a

135

major-league slugger and nearly took his parent's heads off! AND, he did it deliberately!"

Judge Doddridge was boiling, but could do nothing but sit there and listen. Mercer had used him to play the jury. It was working, but it was a crucial mistake. You don't play with Judge Doddridge, because he doesn't play games.

The young lawyer, about to win a big trial and thrust himself into the big league, had made a critical error. He didn't know it at the time, but after this trial, he would never again appear in Judge Doddridge's court. Furthermore, instead of climbing the ladder of success, Mercer's career with the D.A.'s Office had just turned south. Mercer didn't care though. This trial was going to get him job offers in places he never knew existed.

"I want you all to take another look at Seth Boone," Mercer continued. "Have you seen any evidence or heard any solid testimony that would indicate this big and powerful man was abused at home? He's over six feet tall, still growing, and he can bench press five-hundred pounds. He's got the kind of body that would make Mr. Universe envious."

Mercer looked down and shook his head.

"So the defense wants you to believe this man was repeatedly raped by his slender, one-hundred and thirty pound, five-feet six inch tall, mother. Well, I'm amused! I'm stunned! It's quite a story. More than anything else, I'm hurt, because like you, my intelligence has been insulted by this unbelievable cockamamie hogwash!"

Mercer took another deep breath and let out a long sigh.

"Coming into this trial, I would have expected a plea of temporary insanity, or perhaps hear that Seth was suffering from a brain tumor. Maybe he should have claimed he was possessed by demons. Maybe he should have claimed evil spirits made him pick up a baseball bat and beat his parent's brains out. Yeah, remember that ole saying 'The Devil Made Me Do It'? That would have been more believable! Instead, the defense has presented a different reason for Seth killing his petite small framed lightweight mother and his wheelchair-bound father with no legs. We've been told it was because his mother was raping him and had been doing so for years!"

Mercer shook his head back and forth, his floppy jaws flowing like waves.

"Well," he said. "I've got to give the defense credit for having a high degree of creativity. How do you, the jury, feel about their bizarre story?"

Mercer went into a long dissertation about Janie Boone. By the time he was done, Janie looked like the next Sister Theresa.

"Janie Boone grew up in Abingdon, was a member of her church, a model citizen, a pillar of the community, someone who worked hard to feed her family. She did volunteer work, helped the needy, went through all the legal hoops and background checks it takes to become a federal judge, and to top all that – she was a good mother! NO - they say. NO - she was a rapist!"

There was a pause as Mercer sighed deeply and loudly.

"How do you think Janie Boone became a judge? I can tell you. In a male-dominated world, it took courage, perseverance, dedication, and hard work. Janie broke through the ranks of old school hard-knockers who still think a woman's place is pregnant, barefooted, and sitting on the front porch stringing beans."

The judge had a scornful look in his face. His dislike for Mercer was growing by the minute. Mercer was hoping to gain ground with the six females sitting in the jury box. He didn't know it, but they were on his side before the trial had ever started.

"No one knows what went on inside Charles Manson's brain, causing him to want a racial war, and causing him to brainwash his followers to commit cold-blooded murder. We know Manson committed the crimes he was accused of though."

There was a moment of silence. Everyone was paying attention, wondering where Mercer was going. Wondering what would come out of the big man's mouth next.

"No one knows why Al Capone decided to live a life of crime, committing violent acts, avoid paying income tax, and gun down anyone who opposed, him - but we know he did those things. No one knows the mind of Adolph Hitler, but millions upon millions of innocent men, women, and children died at his hands, and we know he was guilty of those horrendous crimes against mankind."

Mercer had been talking for over twenty minutes, yet no one seemed to be tiring from hearing him speak.

"Thank God the percentage of madmen like that is very low. What about Seth Boone? Don't you think he fits the profile of men I've described? Maybe not exactly, but don't you see and feel the evil connection here? Don't you see the potential for this man to go out and kill more people?"

Mercer clapped his hands together.

"Seth Boone sits before you, accused of brutally murdering two caring individuals. He comes from a good home where he lacked for nothing. Look at him now. I don't see any signs of remorse for those horrible acts. He shows little emotion. He didn't take the witness stand, and at the very least say – I'm sorry! Do you want this man to go free? Would you want him to hang around the playground where your kids swing and play hopscotch? You have the power to send a message. You have the power to make our community a safer place to live. I ask you to deliver justice, convict this killer!"

Mercer hesitated, walked over to the prosecutors' table, and took a long drink of water from a glass. He then walked back toward the jury box.

"If I'm supposed to believe the reason Seth Boone murdered his mother and father is because his mother, Judge Boone, was raping him – then I'm the biggest fool on planet earth."

Mercer raised his hands high into the air, as if he were speaking to God. Everyone thought he was winding it down, ready to take his seat and let Arthur take his last shot at this, but that wasn't the case. Mercer loved attention and he had a captive audience, so he wasn't quite ready to give up the floor just yet.

"Nineteen years ago last month, Janie Boone gave birth to a 7 pound 2 ounce bouncing baby boy. She and Gordon named him Julian."

Seth looked up at Mercer. Rita and Arthur didn't know what Mercer was about to do. They only hoped it wasn't something that might cause Seth to lose control. Mercer knew Seth had buttons that could be pushed. Seth felt like he was Julian's protector, and if anything set him off, it was saying or doing something negative about Julian.

God only knows what Seth will do if Mercer tells him about Julian's death, Rita thought. She was praying he wouldn't do that. She was praying Mercer hadn't heard about Julian dying.

"As soon as Julian was born his parents knew something was horribly wrong," Mercer continued. "Before they brought Julian home from the hospital, he was diagnosed with Downs Syndrome. Now I happen to know that shortly after they were married, Gordon and Janie discussed having a family. They wanted to have two children. After Julian came along, they were afraid of having another child. They loved Julian, their precious little boy, but were fearful if Janie became pregnant again the results could be the same, another child with this dreadful disorder."

Mercer was talking low and had on a sad face. The females in the jury all had the look of concerned mothers on their faces. Arthur and Rita were wondering where this was going. They weren't ready for the bomb that Mercer dropped next.

"Janie was worried sick, thinking she was the cause of Julian's condition. Gordon began talking about getting a vasectomy, but Janie wouldn't hear of it. She told Gordon she would get her tubes tied instead. Then, if something were ever to happen to her, Gordon could still have children. That was the kind loving mother and wife Janie Boone was."

Arthur and Rita's heads were spinning as Mercer unraveled this information. They wanted to disbelieve it all. They had no idea where Mercer had obtained such information but he had to be telling the truth. Anything he presented was subject to verification. If it were discovered Mercer swayed the jury with a pack of lies, it could be grounds for a mistrial. Mercer was a bottom-dwelling parasite, but he wasn't stupid.

"Mr. and Mrs. Boone didn't give up on having two children. They began looking at adoption options and fourteen months after Julian was born - Seth, only five days old, was brought into their home."

Seth stood up. "That's a lie!"

Arthur stood and tried to get Seth to sit back down. Rita was as much in shock as Seth was. Arthur would have been in shock himself if not having to try to calm Seth down."

"He's nothing but a liar!" Seth screamed toward Mercer.

"Order!" Doddridge demanded, banging his gavel down hard.

Arthur was able to get Seth to sit down, but wasn't too sure he wouldn't be back on his feet again in the next few seconds. Thankfully, Seth remained seated and silent. His face was red, and the veins in his thick neck were standing out.

"That will be all from you, Mr. Boone," Judge Doddridge said. "Any more outbursts and I'll have the bailiff remove you from this courtroom!"

Doddridge was wondering himself where this was going and would have liked telling Mercer to wrap it up. He couldn't, however. He had to let each party go on as long as they wished. A young man's life was at stake here and Doddridge didn't want to be accused of not giving both sides all the time they needed to present their closing statements.

Mercer loved the way things were turning out. He folded his hands and looked at Seth. In a low voice, he gave an insincere apology.

"I'm sorry Seth. I assumed you knew you were adopted," Mercer said smugly.

Seth propped his elbows up on the table and clapped his hands over his ears. He gave Mercer a look that could kill. Seth thought Mercer was telling the biggest lie that had ever been fabricated.

"Seth hadn't yet been given a name when Janie and Gordon brought him home," Mercer continued, turning back to the jury. "His biological mother, Delphi, was a heroin junkie. She died giving birth to Seth. A nun at the Saint Vincent Church in Houston took Seth when he was three days.

When the Boone's first brought Seth home, he needed special care. He had to be constantly watched and given medication to wean him off drugs. Janie and Gordon did that. That's the kind of people Gordon and Janie Boone were – caring, compassionate and loving. They were willing to take a needy child with no hope into their home and give him a fighting chance."

Arthur was taking notes, even though the court recorder was taking it all down. He was wondering how Mercer would have obtained such knowledge, and why he wasn't given this information as part of discovery. He suspected the FBI had been hard at work. No way could Mercer have pieced this together on his own. Arthur planned to protest. This wasn't right. It was unjust. It was outrageous.

"Seth's real mother had a conjugal visit with her incarcerated husband, Arden Nicholas. He impregnated her with Seth. You see, Arden was in a Texas prison on death row. Arden took a tire iron and beat a police officer to death. He was executed one month before Seth came into this world.

Is there a heredity thing going on here? Genetics are strong – very strong. I suppose we could have a group of experts testify either way."

Mercer was slick. He had put a tall pitcher of poison in front of the jurors, and they were gulping it down. Seth was still staring at Mercer. Tears streamed down both sides of his face. Arthur should have been standing on his feet, objecting to the relevance of what Mercer was saying, demanding it be stricken. Instead, he was busy taking notes. Rita looked pale, as if she'd seen a ghost. There was silence in the courtroom. Mercer took a white handkerchief from his jacket pocket and wiped his sweat drenched face.

Mercer's large flabby face was red, and his hair was messy from where he'd been running his hands through it as he orated. The looks on the faces of the jury spoke volumes. They had followed Mercer like sheep being led to slaughter. Seth's biological father had been a killer, just as he was. Moving close to the jury box, Mercer pointed a finger back at Seth, who was still locked on to Mercer's eyes.

There was utter silence as Mercer took another deep breath. Everyone in the courtroom could hear the air leave his lungs when he exhaled. Mercer lowered his shoulders. He slumped over and shook his head back and forth, his flabby jaws bouncing. He raised back up and looked toward the jury. He lowered his voice to a normal tone as he continued. It was a voice of concern and pleading.

"My friends, I thank you for listening to my long oration. I'm exhausted. I could have made my speech a lot shorter, but what Seth Boone did has infuriated me, and I'm a zealot for justice. The souls of Janie and Gordon Boone cry out from the grave."

The jury had taken their eyes off Mercer only a few times during his prolonged speech, only to stare at Seth. As much as Arthur was despising the man, he had to admit, Mercer had the gift to do what he was doing.

"Janie and Gordon Boone were good decent Americans," Mercer said. "They cared for their children, provided a grand house for them to live in, volunteered in their community, and you won't find a soul anywhere in Abingdon, Virginia to dispute that. Gordon Boone was a man who loved his family. He was a man who lost his legs in a tragic accident, was confined to a wheelchair, yet he worked to bring a paycheck home to support his children, wanting nothing more than to give them a better life than he had. Janie Boone, the rapist, they say – I think not! As a judge, Janie stood for what is right in this country, liberty, and justice for all. I ask you - please give Gordon and Janie Boone the justice they deserve by rendering a guilty verdict. Please remove this killer from the streets, putting him away in prison before he kills someone else. Thank you so much for your precious time."

Mercer returned to his seat, flopped down in the chair and downed a full glass of water while wiping his sweat drenched face with his handkerchief.

Arthur nervously stood to make his rebuttal. Mercer had attacked from his flank, shooting a barrage of exploding cannonballs. He was on a sinking ship and had no bucket to bail water. As he'd done earlier, Arthur fumbled and stumbled, talking in circles. All twelve jurors strained and struggled to find meaning in his words.

The jury went into deliberation that afternoon. Surprising no one - they were back in the courtroom with a decision in little more than two hours.

Judge Doddridge looked at the verdict then handed it back to the bailiff, who walked it over to the jury box.

"Has the jury made their decision?"

"We have, Your Honor." the foreman said.

"On the count of murder in the first degree of Gordon Boone, how do you find?"

"The jury finds the defendant, Seth Boone - guilty."

"On the count of murder in the first degree of Janie Boone, how do you find?"

"The jury finds the defendant, Seth Boone - guilty."

The courtroom exploded. Reporters rushed for the door.

The judge pounded his gavel, bringing order back to the courtroom.

The judge wanted to wrap things up. Since the courtroom was reserved for one more day, and with the jury sequestered, he pushed to hold everyone over and conduct sentencing the following day.

On the morning of Friday, December 7th, the judge asked the jury how they'd slept and if they'd gotten a good breakfast. He then instructed them about their duties regarding sentencing. If Seth received concurrent sentences, he would serve a maximum of twenty years. With good behavior, it would be much less. If given consecutive sentences, he would be incarcerated a minimum of forty years but with good behavior would walk after that. The jury had one other choice. They could deliver the death sentence. In that case, there would be no chance for parole in Seth's future. There would only be the long wait on death row until his number was called for execution.

It took a little over two hours for the jury to convict Seth, but they deliberated six hours on his sentence. Arthur stood beside Seth as the judge read the sentence.

"Seth Boone, the jury of this court, a jury of your peers, has found you guilty on two counts of capital murder. They have also this very day rendered a decision about your sentence. Your judgment is twenty years on each count, to be served consecutively."

Judge Doddridge quickly pounded his gavel, dismissed the jury, and disappeared through a door. Rita had a few precious moments to hug Seth before an officer placed the cuffs back on him and led him away.

Seth had been spared the death penalty. There was a chance that someday, far in the future, Seth Boone would walk out of prison and be free. Arthur and Rita had been fearful the death penalty would be handed down. As it turned out, a few of the jurors just weren't going to have it on their conscience that they'd killed a teenage boy with their vote.

It had been touch and go for a while with the jurors. Two of the men were standing firm that Seth should die. When they saw they weren't going to get their way, they finally caved in and voted with the other ten to put Seth away for life, even though 'life' didn't actually mean life.

17

That evening, Rita went to the Spotsylvania County Courthouse jail to visit Seth. He would be transferred to Radford Maximum Security Prison the next morning. She knew it would be a few days at best before she could visit. She wanted to spend as much time as she could with him, even though it would be a dreadful evening.

Seth was in a quiet mood, very subdued. He told Rita he loved her, but that he didn't want her to visit him at Radford. He wanted her to go back to work and get her life in order. He hoped she would find a free man to love her as much as he did. His plea was coming from his heart. He loved her enough to want her to have a good man and a good life. He couldn't give her the life she deserved.

They both cried. They looked at each other through the glass partition with puffy eyes and sullen faces. Rita did the majority of the talking while Seth listened.

Seth learned during the trail that he was adopted. The hurt and mixed emotions resulting from hearing that news would have been enough, but he'd also been convicted of capital murder only hours later. At first he thought hearing Janie wasn't his biological mother would help ease the pain of knowing he'd had sex with her for three years, but it didn't. The pain and scars remained, not reduced by even the smallest amount.

Now he'd been sentenced to life in prison. Even worse was that he and Rita couldn't be together. His hope of ever being free and able to have a normal relationship with Rita had been dashed against the rocks. With a chance of parole coming in his late fifties, Rita would be pushing seventy.

Rita told Seth how much she loved him, and it didn't matter to her if he was in prison. She still wanted to come visit him, write letters, and call on the phone when possible. Seth wanted this too, but she had so much life to live, so much ahead of her. Holding on to him was a false hope. It was love, but an unhealthy kind of love. No matter what, sooner, or later, she would meet someone and he didn't want to be standing in the way of something good. He wanted good things for her. He wasn't it. Pushing her away was killing him, but he knew it was best.

Rita had no doubts about Seth's love for her. It was an unconditional love. They knew from the first moment they touched it would be short-lived. They knew that in all likelihood Seth would be convicted. Now that day had come. Still, she was happy for the precious time they'd spent together. She would go on with her life eventually, just as Seth had asked. Still, she'd never love anyone as much as she loved him. Of all the men she'd met and dated, she'd never met anyone who touched her heart the way he did.

Reading Rita's face and emotions, Seth suspected something else was wrong. Rita wanted to tell him something, but didn't know how. Finally, he asked her.

"Something else is wrong," Seth said. "Tell me what is bothering you."

She looked at Seth and shook her head. From the first time she'd met the boy in the interrogation room back in Abingdon, she'd been amazed at his ability to read people.

She had to tell him about Julian. It would be easy to let someone else do it, but she loved him and wanted him to hear it from her, not some stranger, and certainly not from some newspaper or tabloid. As much as he was going to be hurt, she had to tell him.

She didn't know how to begin. Seth had already gotten so much bad news, now she was about to lay even more on his troubled heart. She stumbled over her words, but finally told him what had happened. On the other side of the glass, Seth stared straight ahead. He had an expressionless face, a distant look in his eyes. Rita saw the tears begin to form, then the trickle running down both his cheeks. He rocked back and forth, agonizing over the news. Rita's heart was breaking. Tears dripped from her chin into her lap. Just as Rita was finishing the story about Julian, a guard came for Seth.

Seth lifted his head and caught Rita's eyes.

"When I draw my last breath, I'll still be loving you," he said to her as the guard led him away.

Until that moment, aside from her heart breaking and the tears flowing, Rita had managed to hold herself together. She ran out of the building, got into her car, and rested her head on the steering wheel. Her tears soaked the steering wheel, and her loud wails of despair were heard all over the parking lot. The world no longer made sense to her. Nothing seemed to matter anymore.

Seth wanted her to move on with her life, but she couldn't. The love was too strong. She felt like she couldn't live without him, yet she couldn't be with him. She would honor Seth's request and not come visit or write. At least she would try. Having a competitive spirit, she'd fought hard all her life, climbed the ladder of success, and excelled in every challenge that had ever been laid before her. Not now though. Now, she felt defeated, broken, and she'd never felt so alone.

The next morning Arthur went to visit Seth before he was transported to Radford Penitentiary. He apologized that he'd not done a better job. Seth acknowledged that Arthur had only so much to work with, and Mercer had been well supported by his friends at the FBI.

Arthur told Seth he was going to file for an appeal. Seth asked him not to. He expected the result would be the same, and the likelihood a new trial would be granted was slim to none. He was a broken young man. Over the last 24 hours, his spirit to continue fighting had vanished.

Seth looked like he'd been crying all night. Arthur told him he was sorry about Julian. Arthur was right, he'd cried all night, but not only for his brother. He'd lost his freedom, lost his brother, and he'd lost the only woman he'd ever love.

"I know Rita came to see you yesterday," Arthur said. "It took a lot of courage for her to face you and break the news about Julian."

"I know," Seth replied. "She's an angel."

"She's deeply in love with you," Arthur said.

Seth nodded. His heart was breaking over being convicted, even though it was expected. His heart was breaking over Julian. If he hadn't killed his parents, chances are, Julian would still be alive. The full impact of Julian's death hadn't yet hit home. Seth's heart was broken into a million pieces from having to tell Rita goodbye. As much as he hated doing that, it was the best thing for her. At that moment, if a guard approached to take him to the death chamber, he wouldn't have put up fight. He was done. It was all over.

"Thank you for everything," Seth said as Arthur was leaving. "I know you tried."

Seth had lived through hell in his own home for over three years. Now he was about to discover a different kind of hell - maximum-security prison.

18

The guards put leg irons and handcuffs on Seth. Two state troopers led him through a side door to an awaiting police cruiser. The troopers spoke to each other, but not to Seth. To them, he was an object, not a person. No longer accused, he was convicted. He would be treated as a subject, a prisoner with a number – a man with few rights.

It was a long but short three-hour ride to Radford. The handcuffs hurt Seth's wrists, and the leg irons cut into the skin on his legs. This was the beginning of the end. Adding to his heavy heart was a feeling of impending doom. Julian, the one he'd tried to save was gone, so was Rita, the woman he loved. It was a sunny day, but a dark cloud hung over his head.

Looking out the window, he watched as the trees, houses, and mountains went by. He was seventeen, headed for a prison chocked full of hardened criminals. The view out the window was the last glimpse of beautiful landscape he'd see for a very long time. When he walked out of jail a free man, the saplings along the side the road would be tall mature trees. He had many regrets about his past and many doubts about his future.

After going through the security gates at Radford, he was placed in a fenced area, along with seven other new arrivals. He took a good look around. There were dull brown buildings, two guard towers, and a never-ending jungle of fence covered in thick circular tunnels of razor wire. Seth and the other arrivals were herded inside one of the buildings. They passed through several steel doors, everyone's chains beating the concrete floor, creating a machine-like sound.

They were led to a large room with bright lights. Six guards circled the inmates as two more guards entered, pushing a metal cart. One of the guards pushing the cart stopped, looked everyone over and said, "Welcome to hell's basement, girls."

The outside had its laws and regulations. At Radford, there were other laws, those of the warden. He was a man that ruled with an iron fist. He was king of this chessboard, and the prisoners were his pawns.

One of the new arrivals was standing beside Seth. He looked to be forty or older. He had long salt and pepper hair tied back in a ponytail. His arms, neck, and even his face, was covered in tattoos. He was a mean looking character. He looked like someone who'd lived on the streets for a long time. "SCREW YOU!" The man shouted at the guard who had spoken.

Out of nowhere, a baton caught the back of the man's knees, sending him instantly to the hard concrete floor in pain. Seth was close enough to feel the air movement created from the baton as it barely missed his own legs.

"Lesson number one, chumps," the guard with the baton said. "Any wisecracks and you'll get a dose, same as the idiot on the floor."

Seth took a good look at the rest of the prisoners. They were years older. He guessed they were in their late twenties, thirties, and the man on the floor looked to be the oldest of this group. He was a seventeen-year-old boy, thrown into a maximum-security prison with older hardened criminals who cared for no one - not even their own life. There was little doubt they'd all lived hard lives. Most, if not all, had committed numerous crimes, and there was a long record bearing testimony to their lawless deeds.

The men sported tattoos on their arms, and their faces had that tough-guy street look about them. Seth could feel their stares. They viewed him as a rich kid who had been born with a silver spoon in his mouth. To them, he was fresh meat and they were hungry.

"Step forward, girls." the guard who pushed the cart in yelled out.

As Seth stepped closer, he noticed that the cart was actually a laundry basket on wheels.

"Strip down, assholes," the same guard yelled loudly.

All but two of the guards in the room were black men. The other two were Hispanic. Seth and the man still groaning from being struck by the baton were white. The other six inmates were black. Seth watched and sheepishly did as the other prisoners were doing. He removed his clothes. He was embarrassed, hoping no one would notice his blushing face. He thought by staying in the middle of group, he'd blend in with the crowd and not be noticed. Several prisoners acted as if they'd done this before. It gave credence to Seth's suspicion that this wasn't their first time inside prison walls.

If there was anything good about this situation, it was that the leg irons and handcuffs had been removed. Seth's wrist and ankles were still burning from where the tight metal straps had cut into his skin.

As Seth stepped forward to throw his clothes into the cart, two of the black guards noticed him. In unison, they said, "Damn!" The remark drew the attention of everyone else. Everybody stopped what they were doing and looked at Seth. His muscular body was snow white and in stark contrast to theirs. There was more though. His bulging muscles seemed to capture the light. His chest, arms and leg muscles rippled like waves in the ocean as he slowly walked back from the cart to rejoin the group.

"Shit! Somebody caught Hercules and threw his white ass in prison," one of the guards shouted.

The remark started everyone laughing, except Seth. His face turned blood red, causing him to look even stranger.

"Now he looks like vanilla ice cream with a cherry on top," another guard cried out.

"Looks like you boys got yourself a virgin to play with," another guard shouted.

Seth had just arrived, and already things were looking bad. He would have to play the part of a tough-guy if he were to survive in this place. He really wasn't a tough-guy though. He was a nice and polite, and just wanted to do his time. All he really wanted was to be left alone.

"Form a line across the room three feet apart," a guard standing at the cart shouted.

The name on the guard's shirt was a nickname, 'Paw Paw'.

"Spread your feet shoulder width apart, hands locked together on top of your head," Paw Paw shouted.

Two guards wearing latex gloves ran their fingers through each man's hair, under their arms, and all around their crotch.

"You're a friggin animal," the guard examining Seth said.

Paw Paw stepped forward with a handful of tongue suppressors and a flashlight. He examined everyone's mouth and ears. Seth was fourth in line. Paw Paw stuck a tongue suppressor into Seth's mouth, purposely ramming it to the back of his throat. His gag reflex kicked in, causing him to jerk back violently, stumbling into a guard standing behind him. The guard instantly pulled his baton from his belt and struck Seth's left calve. Seth slumped to the floor, groaning loudly, but refusing to cry.

"Anybody else want a piece of this action?" Paw Paw cried out before moving on to the next prisoner.

After recovering from the blow, Seth stood back up. His throat was hurting and his leg was throbbing with pain. As bad as things were, it was about to get worse. Paw Paw finished examining the last prisoner and everyone was told to regroup into a single line.

One by one, the prisoners were led up to the cart and forced to bend over, exposing their buttocks to the others. A guard produced a cigar-shaped tool with a cord attached. It was to be inserted each prisoners' anus. They were looking for drugs, or something that could be smuggled into the prison to be used as a weapon. Between each prisoner, the probe was dipped into a bucket containing a liquid, which Seth expected was a strong bleach cleanser. No matter, there was no way that could be sanitary, and he didn't want the probe stuck up his rectum.

"There's got to be something different you can do," Seth said as he was pushed forward by a guard.

In a split second, four guards had hold of Seth and forced him over the cart. He reared back, spreading his arms and throwing all four guards backwards. In the next second, the probe from a stun gun hit him in the back. The 25,000 volt gun produces only 5 milliamps of current, but that's plenty enough to get your attention. Seth fell to the floor. He was about to jump to his feet when the guard hit the trigger again. The large bulging muscles of Seth's body contracted then went into spasms once the juice was turned off.

Seth was lifted to his feet and slammed over the cart. The probe was rammed into his rectum, just as it had been with the five men in front of him. It hurt all the way up to his teeth. If the guard had left the probe in there a few seconds longer, he would have passed out.

"There goes my virgin," one of the prisoners said.

The prisoner was either stupid or loved pain, maybe both. The words had barely left his mouth when a baton slapped across the back of his head. He fell hard to the concrete, barely able to stick his hands out in time to protect his head from the hard floor.

Seth awkwardly walked to the back of the line, joining those who'd already been probed. His mind was reeling. He was already thinking of how he might be able to dig a tunnel or jump a wall and escape the hell where he'd been sent to live. He hadn't gotten inside the prison yet, and already he'd been tortured and abused.

"You got a little tense when they stuck that probe up your ass," a guard behind Seth said. "I couldn't tell when your big guns twitched the most - from the stun gun or the probe."

All the guards laughed but not a single prisoner so much as grinned. Nobody there wanted a taste of the guards' batons.

The prisoners were ordered to form a tight single line. Next, they were marched naked down a long corridor to a shower area. Two prison guards were in the shower waiting for them. They were wearing rubber suits, rubber boots, and had rubber hoods and masks over their faces. Each guard held a long plastic hose, connected to a foam machine filled with an antibacterial soap.

"Close your eyes, girls," one of the guards shouted.

A second later, the foam machines were turned on. Every prisoner was coated from head to toe with the thick foamy spray. The foam reeked of a strong chemical smell. Everyone was gagging. Once the machines were turned off, the prisoners were ordered to remain standing as they were for five minutes, soaking in the mountain of foam. The soap was caustic. Everyone was complaining not just because of the odor – but because it was burning their skin.

Suddenly, out of nowhere, two high-pressure fire hoses began washing the prisoners down. As soon as the water began hitting the prisoners, their hands quickly went from covering their eyes to being cupped over their scrotums, protecting the family jewels. Two of the prisoners fell down. The guards swore, and demanded they get back on their feet or face the entire process all over again.

When the water finally stopped, the prisoners were immediately rushed from the shower area to a hallway where two large fans were set up to blow them dry. At this point, everyone was too exhausted and scared to trash talk the guards or even the other prisoners. After ten minutes in front of the fans, they were led to another room where three laundry carts were piled high with wadded up prison clothing, all bright orange in color.

"You got three minutes, girls. Get your asses dressed," a guard barked.

The only clothing Seth could find in extra-large was a pair of coveralls. He was hoping they would not only fit, but would also be loose. He quickly determined the coveralls were mislabeled. It was tight on his muscular thighs, and the zipper wouldn't pull up over his huge chest. He started digging in a basket again when everyone was ordered to move out.

"I'll see if prison laundry can round you up something that fits," one of the guards said.

It almost sounded kind, causing Seth to look toward him. He'd not noticed this guard before, and wondered if there might be at least one working at this prison who had an ounce of compassion.

Seth didn't realize it, but the other prisoners had sized him up and determined he wasn't someone they wanted to tangle with. Seth had looked them over as well. Although most of the men were either scrawny or sporting large beer bellies, he had no desire to tangle with any of them.

The guards had already given Seth a new nickname, 'Pretty Boy'. They'd decided if he even looked like he was going to step out of line, they'd take pleasure in giving him a good beating.

Once dressed, the prisoners were led to a room containing nothing but twenty folding chairs and a wooden podium. They were ordered to find a chair but remain standing until the warden entered and gave them permission to sit.

Seth was in the front row. The warden appeared and told everyone to be seated. He immediately began going over his rules. He was a hard looking man, mid-forties, thinning blonde hair in a crewcut style. He didn't appear to be a man who hit the gym very often. His six-foot frame was carrying an extra fifty pounds. His face was heavily pock marked, and he had the red nose of a hard drinker. He had squinting eyes and his voice was deep like someone who smoked. Nonetheless, he spoke with authority and his cocky swagger indicated he was the man. He was the warden, and both the guards and prisoners knew it.

The warden's name was Franklin Pendleton. Pendleton had been born into a wealthy family in Richmond, who had what southerners call 'old money'. Wanting nothing to do with the family string of donut shops and convenience stores, he became a state trooper for a short stint. He left the police force and introduced himself to the correctional facility at Radford where he became a warden's assistant at age twenty-three. That was made possible through his father's political connections, who pulled some strings with Davey Welch, governor at that time. Three years later, Pendleton was given the kingdom of Radford Prison. He was the new warden, and could run the prison as he pleased. Seth guessed Pendleton was a cruel man. He'd later find this to be true.

The warden told the prisoners they'd be assigned a job. The pay was three dollars a day, no matter where you worked and what the job involved. He made the prison system seem simplistic. Keep your nose clean, show up for work, and never get into a fight. He made it clear - strike a guard and you'd live to regret it.

"I won't stand here and tell you what solitary confinement at Radford is like," he said. "You'll either hear it from the inmates, or soon enough experience yourself. The prisoners refer to it as 'The Hole'."

When the warden was through talking, he asked if there were any questions. The idiot who yelled 'Screw You' to one of the guards earlier, getting him a baton to the legs, couldn't pass up a golden opportunity to speak again. Seth remembered a saying from the Bible. He couldn't remember exactly how it went, but it was somewhere along the lines of 'better to be thought of as a fool than to open your mouth and remove all doubt'.

"Has anybody ever broken out of this piss-hole?" the man yelled, addressing the warden.

"Three have tried," the warden replied, smiling. "They're all buried in the cemetery beyond the West Gate. So - I guess you could say they made it. Guards, please give that man a day in the hole for presenting such a great question."

As the warden was about to leave, he looked at Seth.

"I know what you've done and what you're capable of doing, Boone," he said. "I'll be watching you closely. By the way, your girlfriend has asked the governor that you be enrolled in our GED program. I don't know why she would want you educated. It's not as if you're going somewhere. Anyway, the governor has honored her request. She must be something in bed - the governor charges a high price for such favors."

Seth was far from stupid, unlike the man in the back who was already on his way to solitary confinement. He wasn't going to fall for the warden's little game, lashing out and end up in the hole as well. He didn't know exactly what the hole was, but he wanted no part of it. He was thrilled just knowing Rita had thought of him. She would honor his request not to visit, but she was still reaching out, showing her love for him as no one ever had. He smiled at the warden then hung his head low.

The warden left the room. The prisoners were ordered to form a single line again. They were led into 'C' block, their new home. As they marched through the corridor with cells lining each side, prisoners put their hands through the bars and tried to grab anyone they could. They shouted profanity toward the prisoners and several held out condoms, offering them to the new arrivals.

"Take one, put it in your pocket," one shouted. "Offer it to your new boyfriend here in 'C' block."

Seth was the last in line. As they neared the end of one row of cells, a guard grabbed him by the shoulder and ordered him to stop. The guard held his radio up to his face, pushed the talk button and said, "Pretty Boy - Seth Boone, C302."

19

The cell door opened and Seth was pushed inside. The door closed then the guard moved on. The prison cell was seven feet wide by twelve feet deep. There was a set of bunk beds on the left wall, a sink behind the beds, and in the far right corner was a commode. Two posters sporting Bruce Lee hung on the right wall. Two other posters were on the wall at the bottom bunk. They didn't have photographs, just lines of oriental writing.

There were other items laying around with oriental symbols on them. Whoever was residing there was Asian, or deeply interested in the culture. A bar of soap, a clean hand towel, razor, and a can of shaving cream sat on the edge of the sink. Seth wondered when he would be given his own razor and shaving cream. He thought perhaps the guard that had promised him larger clothes might bring them by.

The bottom bunk was made. A set of heavily stained sheets and a tattered blanket were folded and lying on the top bunk. Seth unfolded the sheets and made the bed. As he worked, he was curious about who the character was that would be his cellmate. After making the bed, he climbed up and laid down.

So this is it, he thought. *This is the place I'll spend most of my life*. He was already beginning to understand how someone in prison could commit suicide, ending the everlasting misery. He'd lost his parents, his precious brother Julian, and his home. He'd lost the love of his life, Rita. She was gone forever. His memory of her would fade over time, but for now, everything about her was fresh in his mind. He wanted to hold on to that as long as possible.

Seth had lost his freedom and was condemned to prison for a very long time. He didn't think he could live like this, facing danger from other prisoners each day, and bowing down to guards who would beat him just for looking their way. It meant having to deal with the warden, and bow at his command as well. Warden Pendleton was the king, and he ruled the place as he pleased. There was no hope. Everything was lost. It seemed there was nothing to live for.

He was nearly asleep when the cell door opened. An oriental man entered the cell, and the door closed behind him. Seth jumped down from the bunk to greet his cellmate. The man was five-feet five, about a hundred and thirty pounds, shaven head and appeared to be around fifty years old. He had squinty eyes and high cheekbones. He was staring at Seth, as if he were trying to look into his soul.

"I'm Seth," Seth said, holding his hand out to shake.

The oriental man was six feet away. He didn't extend his hand. He gave a small bow instead, never taking his eyes off Seth.

"I know who you are, Boone," the man said.

His voice was deep, and had a harshness to. It reminded Seth of the Japanese generals he'd seen in WWII movies when they gave orders.

The two men continued looking at each other for a few awkward seconds, sizing one another up then the man spoke again.

"I am Shanghai," he said. "You need to know no more - just call me Shanghai."

"How did you know my name?" Seth felt compelled to ask.

"Everybody here know your name. Your case high profile. I see article in trash tabloid. Shanghai must say, picture in jail cell with all muscles don't do Seth justice. You more bigger and intimidating in person."

Seth raised his eyebrows slightly.

"I see you're a Bruce Lee fan," Seth said, trying to drum up conversation in such an awkward moment.

"Ah," he replied, sounding almost like a grunt. "Bruce Lee more big shot TV star than fighter. Inmates see Bruce Lee and it plant image in mind, they leave Shanghai alone. This place all about image and deception."

"So you don't know martial arts then. It's just a front?"

"Seth no move, Shanghai no hurt you."

Seth heard Shanghai, but didn't understand what he was saying. As quick as a cat, Shanghai jumped forward, planted his right foot on the floor while turning his body sideways. His left foot was extended toward Seth. Shanghai stopped only centimeters from Seth's nose. Both men froze then Shanghai returned his left foot to the floor.

"If Shanghai want, you be on floor. Yes, Shanghai know martial arts, but Bruce Lee posters plant bigger picture in prisoners mind. No pretend to know martial arts, still, poster reminder to leave Shanghai be. You young, got much to learn, and very long time to do so." Shanghai said then chuckled.

"Can you teach me martial arts?" Seth asked.

"Shanghai like to keep cell clean. You do likewise and we get along. Shanghai no like loud mouth either, so no talk so much. One thing - Shanghai no babysitter and Shanghai no teacher. You really big boy, you have great muscle, Seth do okay for himself. I give you one lesson, not on martial arts – but on prison life. Most prisoner size you up and say, no mess with Seth. Then there always been what you call 'Billy Badass' who like to fight and think they tough. That the one you avoid. Do not provoke, they no fight fair. Second tip. They have gang in prison but Seth no join. Gang be trouble, no want to die or end up in warden's hole."

Seth thought he understood most of that, even if Shanghai's one point was actually two.

"What about this 'hole', what exactly is that?"

"Me say this then done talking. Hole is solitary confinement. Small dark cell, no light at all. Food, when they decide to feed you, is slop. You mind go crazy in there and you body deteriorate. Too much time in hole and prisoner go crazy. Plus, guards harsher there. They play tricks on you, cause warden want that. They puppets of warden, be bad men."

"Have you ever been there, the hole that is?" Seth just had to ask.

"Shanghai be there two times, one for two days, one for four. Shanghai no can take any more hole. You no talk now, Shanghai going to rest."

Shanghai climbed into his bed and closed his eyes. Seth climbed back in the top bunk and did the same. He wanted to close his eyes, go to sleep, and wake up in a different place. That didn't happen. Sleep wasn't going to come easy for a while. He was in a world only those who have been there can accurately describe. He was scared and depressed. He had to learn quickly and make adjustments if he was going to survive in this harsh, unforgiving environment.

The prison had four main buildings or wings, blocks A through D, facing north, east, south, and west. The entire prison complex was a rectangle. In the middle of the complex was the chow hall, library, theatre, laundry and other departments. There were smaller buildings situated here and there, one of which was set up for solitary confinement. No one seemed to know anything about the remaining buildings. On the outside perimeter were basketball courts, a weight lifting area, and a walking track. Each wing was separate as if it were four prisons instead of one. Each wing ate at a different time. The only time prisoners from one wing mixed with others, was during work hours.

At exactly 5 a.m. the next morning, the cell doors on C block all opened. Seth saw men filing into the hallway. He climbed down from his bunk. Shanghai was already up and out the door as soon as it opened. It was chow time for C block. Seth hadn't been given supper the evening before, and he was starving. He left the cell and followed the crowd toward the mess hall.

The prisoners were mouthy and loud. Every time an inmate opened his mouth, a flood of profanity poured forth. Seth wondered if they had the capability of speaking without using foul language. It had become so routine they didn't even realize what they were saying. He was determined he wouldn't allow himself to stoop down to that level. He'd been taught to be respectful and never to use bad language, although he'd done so a few times, mostly when angry.

Seth went through the line as food was slapped onto his plate. It was greasy scrambled eggs, a white gravy that closely resembled watered-down milk, and a biscuit that could double as a hockey puck. At the end of the line, he picked up a glass of orange juice that looked more like urine.

Looking around, Seth saw somewhere in the neighborhood of two hundred loud mouth men in the room. He felt like all eyes were cast upon him. He scanned the room quickly but didn't see Shanghai. At the far left wall were two empty tables. He headed that way and sat down, facing the wall.

On the way to the table, he noticed that everyone hunkered down over their plates, their arms spread wide, eating as fast as they could. He'd witnessed this on a lesser scale back in the juvenile center in Damascus. Prisoners were like animals, hovering over their food to protect it and eating fast before someone else had a chance to grab their grub.

The food was nasty, but it was edible. Seth did as the others did. He sat down and within two minutes, his plate was empty. Just as he was finishing the last bite, he felt the presence of someone. Five mean looking black men came up behind him and stopped. One man stuck his crotch in the back of Seth's head. He rubbed himself hard against Seth's head then backed away. Seth turned his head and looked up to the man's face. All five inmates had hardened faces, and their arms and necks sported tattoos that were far from professionally done. He determined they must use whatever means they could find to do their own tattoos here in prison.

"How you doing, Pretty Boy?" the one who'd rubbed against Seth asked.

"They call me 'Dagger', but you can call me 'Daddy'. I'm going to be your daddy."

Dagger's friends laughed.

"I'll be your daddy, and you'll be my bitch. You and I are going to have some fun times. I got hard as soon as I laid eyes on you."

"That's right, bitch. Me too," Tyrone, one of Dagger's gang said.

"Hush, man," Dagger said. "This ho's mine, we done discussed it."

Seth was bewildered.

"Yo know what, Pretty Boy, you be sitting at the brothers' table. I'll let it slide today, but don't ever sit here again after today. You be my bitch, but you ain't no brother."

"That's right," another of the men, nicknamed Fat Man, said. "I'm gonna watch when Dagger reams yo ass. You never be the same after that. As they say, you go black, you don't go back!"

The men laughed then gave each other weird handshakes where they did a series of different moves with their fingers. It reminded Seth of the game, rock, paper, and scissors. Dagger rubbed Seth on the head then the five men moved on.

§

The prisoners had an hour and a half to spend outside their cell before they were locked in for the night. Seth skipped going out. He didn't want to mingle and most of all he didn't want to take a chance of running into Dagger and his gang again. He went back to his cell, climbed into his bunk and laid there. His heart was beating fast. He hated this place. He hated the people. He hated that he was going to have to pretend to be something he wasn't in order to survive. He liked peace, quiet, everyone getting along, but this place wasn't anything like that. Every day was going be a survival of the fittest.

He expected that he'd encounter Dagger and his boys again. He'd already decided though - he wasn't going to back away from them. There was nowhere to hide here, nowhere to run away. He would have to be strong, stand his ground. If he didn't, he'd end up just as Dagger said - his bitch.

When Shanghai showed up in the cell, Seth was hoping he might want to talk, but he didn't. Shanghai laid down in his bunk. Within a few seconds, Seth could hear his breathing change. Shanghai was asleep.

The next morning at 5 a.m., the cell doors opened as they had the day before. Shanghai was up and out of the cell before Seth could reach the floor. Seth jumped down from the bunk and joined the crowd, heading to mess hall for breakfast. A piece of toast was slapped on his plate followed by a large spoon of soupy oatmeal. Next, he was given a boiled egg and a banana. For a drink, he had a choice of either the urine colored orange juice or watered down milk, but not both.

He marched past the tables full of men and sat down in the exact spot he had the day before, the two empty tables by the far left wall. He quickly ate his food and gulped down his milk. Expecting Dagger and his friends to show up, he wasn't disappointed. As they approached, Seth stood up and faced them. As they marched toward him, Dagger was yelling, which drew the attention of everyone in the room.

"I told you yesterday, BITCH. You don't sit at the brothers' table."

Dagger threw a punch when he was within reach, but Seth moved his head enough to make the blow miss. Seth came around with a powerful closed fist and caught Dagger's left eye. Even though Dagger's momentum was forward, Seth's blow sent him flying backward and into two of his friends. Seth's action caught them all off guard. It sent all three men stumbling back and falling over a table where other black men sat watching.

Several more black men were up from the table and ready to come at Seth, standing there with a red face, and his fists clinched. When Seth pulled his arms back, ready to take on the crowd, the undersized and dry rotted cotton coveralls he was wearing couldn't bare the stress. The seams at the zipper in the chest ripped open, and the short sleeves split apart. The sound of the ripping fabric was loud enough to be heard by anyone within twenty feet of his position.

The men ready to take Seth on froze in place. He looked like the Incredible Hulk, his thick hard muscles rippling as he breathed deeply.

Three guards came running toward the crowd. A whistle blew and the black men scattered, except for Dagger - he was lying on the floor, out cold. Seth intertwined his fingers and locked his hands on top of his head. When he raised his arms, the back of his coverall and the remainder of the zipper in the front ripped open.

Seth offered no resistance. The guards cuffed him and led him away. It was Seth's second day in prison and he was already heading for the hole. He felt satisfied though. He had stood up to Dagger and his gang, making a statement that he wasn't a pushover. Little did he know - he'd made Dagger's most-wanted list. Dagger wanted to kill Seth, but first he wanted to rape him. Afterward, he would cut Seth up, and watch him slowly bleed to death.

After a ten-minute talk with the C-block commander, Seth was given five days in the hole. Although Dagger had thrown the first punch, Seth had promoted the action by purposely invading Dagger's declared territory.

"If I can't sit anywhere I want, why aren't signs posted?" Seth protested. "Five days is excessive seeing I didn't start the fight. I didn't even know I was doing anything wrong, still don't."

"Shut your ass up or I'll double it and give you ten days," the commander yelled.

The commander was black, and a friend to Dagger and his gang. It was already becoming clear that a lot of prejudice existed in the prison. Seth had noticed in the mess hall that the blacks congregated together. The white skinheads sat together, the Latinos had their space, and even the Asians had a small group that hung tight. There wasn't a table in the entire place with a mixed-race group.

As he was being cuffed in the mess hall, Seth spotted Shanghai, sitting with the Asian group. One of the keys to survival was learning the unspoken rules, but thus far, no one seemed willing to educate him, other than Dagger. He was hoping Shanghai would be willing to teach him. Otherwise, his education was going to be entirely at the school of hard-knocks.

20

After being led out of C-block to one of the smaller buildings, the guard opened the door to one of the four isolated cells called 'the hole'. He informed Seth that he had one minute to look around inside before he closed the door. It was evident there were no windows or lights in the hole.

The guard removed the handcuffs and shoved Seth through the door. He nearly gagged. The place reeked of urine. The only light was what was coming through the door. It took thirty-seconds of Seth's allotted minute before his eyes adjusted to the darkness inside the concrete cell.

He estimated the cell was ten feet wide by ten feet long. It was more spacious then the cell he and Shanghai shared, but that was the only positive difference. In the back left corner a worn-out mattress the color of dirt lay on the concrete. In the back right corner was a commode with no lid and no cover over the tank. To the right of the commode, he could see the outline on the wall where a sink was once mounted. He imagined it had been purposely removed. There were no towels, no toilet paper, and no sheets on the mattress. The mattress and commode were the entire contents of the cell. The mattress, like the concrete floor was filthy. Nothing appeared to have been cleaned in years.

The ceiling was nine feet high. Running across the center was a two-inch diameter iron pipe. The pipe came in through the wall to the left and exited on the right, hanging two feet down from the ceiling. It was supported by heavy duty hangers spaced three feet apart. Too small for a sewage pipe, Seth thought it might be a main waterline. It seemed odd though, a water pipe running across the cell.

He walked over to the commode and looked inside. It hadn't been cleaned in eons. The bowl was heavily stained, and the tank was no different. Seth's gag reflex kicked in. He had to back away or else lose his breakfast. Suddenly, the door slammed closed. Seth was in total darkness. He held his hand directly in front of his face. He could feel the presence of his hand but could see nothing.

This was the hole. This was the prisons' solitary confinement. It was a place of harsh punishment. The hole was the place every inmate feared the most.

§

Dagger received a concussion when Seth's powerful fist slammed into his thick skull. He also had a chipped cheekbone and was going to have a shiner that would last for a month. He was taken to a local hospital to have his head x-rayed. He was kept overnight for observation then returned to the prison the next day.

The gang was already plotting on how to get even. All over C-block, as well as the rest of the prison, everyone was talking about Pretty Boy. No one could believe he'd knocked Dagger out cold. Most prisoners were elated, even the majority of the black prisoners, although they'd never let it be known. Dagger had been at Radford for nine years and had been in dozens of fights, never losing one until Seth's single punch sent him flying to the floor. Dagger was a bully. He and his gang members were labeled as troublemakers. Aiding them were several black guards who looked the other way when Dagger and his gang did something wrong.

Unknown to Seth, his action gained him a few new friends as well as a host of enemies. It also gained him a high degree of respect. On Seth's second day in prison, he had already proven that he wasn't a whipping boy. He was a man who stood up for himself, and he was to be feared.

§

Seth thought he could keep track of time in the hole, but within a few hours, he was already confused. Lunch wasn't served. When supper came, he thought it was already the next morning. The guard opened the door just long enough to place a paper plate of food on the concrete floor. The light that poured into the cell was blinding. It was a couple of minutes before he regained his senses and once again adjusted to being in total darkness.

Crawling across the floor, Seth located the food by smell. He felt the plate then stuck his dirty fingers into the food. His meal was a half-baked potato with no seasoning or butter and three thin slices of what he thought was Spam. It didn't matter. The food tasted delicious.

Once he was through eating, Seth licked the plate then tore it into tiny shreds, which he also ate. If he was only going to get small portions of food, he was willing to eat all they gave him, even the plate. The only way to keep himself hydrated was to dip his cupped hands into the commode tank and pulled the water toward his face. The water tasted as nasty as the tank had appeared. The first few drinks were the worst. His taste buds were destroyed after that. He resorted to holding his nose with one hand while dipping with the other. It made it easier to swallow the foul-smelling water. So far, hell was everything he'd imagine it would be.

Every minute that passed seemed an hour long, and every hour felt like a day. He could have never imagined how the darkness and isolation from human contact messed with his mind. He thought about prisoners of war in foreign lands. The treatment they received by America's enemies was no worse than the way he was being treated here in the motherland. His human rights were being violated, but there was no one to complain to about it. He was the warden's slave now, and he'd have to bow down to his new king and follow his rules or else he'd not survive. Still, he had to make a stand for himself with the inmates. Otherwise, he'd be enslaved to them as well.

By the end of the second day, Seth could have sworn he had been there at least a week and wondered if he would ever get out. He guessed it had been days since he'd been fed, and his hunger reminded him every minute how he was growing weaker. The guards decided when and if Seth would be fed. As it turned out, there would only be one measly meal a day, delivered whenever the guards chose to feed their animals.

He thought a lot about Rita, missing her horribly. He could picture her in his mind and feel her touch as she placed her hands in his. He could smell her perfume and ached to see her one more time.

Seth gulped down his second meal since being in the hole. It was the same as the previous meal, a half-baked potato and three thin slices of the salty processed meat. As he'd done after the previous meal, he ate the paper plate. He then crawled back to his filthy bed and laid down. He screamed, but there was no one to hear his cries. He screamed again, but it only served to make his throat sore. Then, he began to cry and felt sorry for himself, knowing he had every right to.

He wished a thousand times over that he'd not lost his temper and hit his parents. He could have shoved them out of the way, grabbed Julian, and the two of them could have run away. If he'd done that, Julian would still be alive, and he wouldn't be in this dungeon. They would have been free from everyone's bonds, free men to roam the country and do as they wished.

Something positive had to be done to pass the time. Otherwise, he was going to go insane. Seth could feel his body deteriorating fast. He had to exercise or his muscles would waste away. He refused to lay there on the nasty mattress and rot. He was determined not to let the warden or the guards win.

He began doing sit-ups, running in place, push-ups, and using the iron pipe overhead as a chin-up bar. Finally, he was exhausted and slept well for the first time since being there.

Between exercise sessions, Seth paced back and forth in the darkness. In his mind, he wanted to build a cabin to pass the time. He began clearing a piece of land in the mountains near Abingdon. The only tools were an axe, a bow saw, a wood chisel, a hammer, and a file. He fell some trees then dragged them to a clearing. Using his basic tools, he hewed logs in the fashion of the Lincoln Logs he had played with as a child and began the construction. The cabin would be spacious, with a wooden door, and two windows, one on each side of the door. It would also have a large porch that ran across the front. Rocks from a nearby stream were used to build the chimney, and clay mixed with water was used for mortar. Everything was done with meticulous care and precision. The work was exhausting but satisfying.

After a while, he couldn't wait to complete his exercises and get back to building his mountain home. Once completed, he would leave to find Rita, then bring her there, back to the place where they would spend the rest of their lives. The valley below would be filled with the echoes of laughter from their children, who would never doubt they were loved.

When the cell door opened and remained so, Seth was ordered out. He thought he'd been in the dark cell for at least six months. He had a stupefied look on his face when the guard announced his five days were up. *Yeah right. Five days my ass.* Seth swore beneath his breath.

The light outside the cell was bright. Seth squinted and held his hands over his eyes. Two guards marched him down a short hallway. One of the guards unlocked a door leading to the outside of the building where there was a small concrete pad. Seth was ordered to strip. He didn't hesitate to remove what little was left of the ragged coveralls he was wearing. No sooner had he gotten his left foot out of the rags, he was hit with water from a high-pressure fire hose. He fell then rolled around on the concrete, trying to protect himself from the sting of the water. After a few minutes, the water finally stopped. A guard ordered him to his feet. It took what little strength he had left to follow the command.

"That was just to get the major filth off you," a guard said.

Seth was led to a shower and ordered to clean up. A bar of soap and a clean towel were sitting on a folding chair to the right of the shower entrance. He walked over to a showerhead and turned the water on. The water was cold, but not as cold as the water from the fire hose. After a minute, he retrieved the soap and returned to the shower stall. The water had warmed. He lathered himself then rinsed.

The shower was invigorating. Getting the dirt off his body felt wonderful. When he returned to the chair, someone had placed a pair of bright orange prison issue pants and a shirt beside the towel. Surprisingly - the pants and shirt both fit. A guard approached and handed him a pair of black flip-flops.

"Put the shoes on and follow me," the guard commanded.

Seth was led to the warden's office without being handcuffed, which surprised him. The warden sat behind his oversized walnut desk in a high-back leather chair, smoking a pipe. Four guards were in the office, aside from the one who'd brought him there. The guards had their batons in their hands, just to let Seth know there would be no nonsense or trouble. He stood in front of the warden's desk at attention, and decided it would be best to speak only when asked a question. There was no sense in giving the guards a reason to use their favorite toys.

"Well, I'll be damned," the warden said. "You don't look as if the hole wore you down one bit. Would you like a few more days in there?"

"No sir," Seth answered politely.

The warden laid his pipe on the desk and stood.

"Most men can't take more than three days down in the hole. You lasted five and look fit as a fiddle. Maybe it's because you're just young and dumb, not even realizing where you were."

"Yes sir," Seth replied, standing erect as a soldier addressing his commanding officer.

"Alright, I'm not going to give you a long speech," the warden said. "I hope you've learned a lesson about fighting in my prison."

The warden sat back down, grabbed his pipe, and took a few puffs. He stared intently at Seth for a few seconds, studying his face.

"Williamson. Take ole Pretty Boy here down to the mess hall and get him some food," the warden commanded. "After that, take him to the storehouse and see if he can afford a pair of shoes and a razor."

A guard walked over to Seth, poked him with his baton and motioned toward the door.

"Wait a minute," the warden said harshly, making Seth's heart almost stop. "You've not been assigned a job yet, Pretty Boy. Everybody in my prison works. You don't work you don't make money, and you don't eat."

Seth turned back around to face the warden. He expected he was going to be assigned to the kitchen where he'd work in the back cleaning pots and pans all day. If not that, some other undesirable job like cleaning toilets or the showers.

"Spencer Buckhannon in B-block died last week," the warden said. "He'd been the prison librarian for forty-two years. Me being the kind person I am, I asked several inmates if they wanted the job, but they all turned me down. I don't think any of the assholes can read! Seems no one here on the inside is much interested in books. I'm assigning you the job of prison librarian on a trial basis. The place is a mess, but if you can clean it up and keep your ass out of trouble, it'll be your job permanently. That's all. Now get this tick turd out of my sight."

Seth kept a straight face. Inside, he was jumping for joy. He had no idea what the library looked like, but even if it was a disaster, that had to be one of the best jobs in the prison. For the first time since arriving at Radford, he felt something positive.

§

It was just before noon. C-block was in the mess hall. The men had eaten and were sitting at their tables jaw jacking. When Seth walked in, everyone stood and clapped. It was the way they welcomed someone back from the hole. Even the blacks stood and clapped, except for Dagger and his gang.

There wasn't much food left, but inmates working the chow line scraped the pans and filled Seth's plate high. He couldn't help but smile. Everyone sat back down as Seth went down the line. The inmates were back to their private conversations. When Seth reached the end of the line and turned to find a table, one of the skinheads nicknamed Frost was standing there.

Seth would later learn that Frost's real name was James Lane. He had been convicted of three murders. He had removed his victim's vital organs and was attempting to sell them on the black market. When Lane's house was raided by police, they found him hiding in the deep freezer in his garage. He'd been in there long enough that his beard was covered with frost. Lane's cousin was also an inmate at Radford. He gave Frost the nickname, and it stuck.

"Why don't you come sit at our table," Frost said to Seth.

"Sure, why not."

Seth followed Frost to the area where the skinheads had claimed as their territory. Dagger's right eye followed Seth every step of the way. His left eye was still nearly swollen shut.

"You're still a kid, but one hell of a man," Frost said after introducing Seth to his friends.

Seth grinned and began shoveling the food into his mouth like there was no tomorrow. He never imagined prison food could taste so good. A minute later, the guard appeared.

"Let's go, Pretty Boy. Gotta get you down to the store. You heard the warden's orders."

"Hey, the man just got here, let him finish his food first," Frost said, addressing the guard.

Williamson shoved his baton under Frost's nose. "Don't make me get ugly so early in the day," he said.

"I'm done," Seth said with his mouth full. He thanked Frost for the hospitality and left with Williamson. They walked to the prison storehouse so Seth could buy the things he needed. The only problem was - he had no money. He expected he would be given a line of credit until he was able to start earning a wage as the new librarian.

The prison storehouse consisted of a long glass counter where things were displayed for sale, plus a wall behind the counter where a variety of items hung by hooks on pegboard. Seth could hardly believe the prices. A twenty-nine cent disposable razor was four dollars. A can of shaving cream was seven dollars and a bar of ordinary soap was five. He didn't smoke but couldn't help notice cigarettes were fifteen dollars a pack. He would find out later, the warden's family kept the storehouse stocked and reaped the enormous profits from sales.

The way the process worked was, you told the clerk working the counter what you wanted and he would figure the bill. Your account was checked for funds, and if you had the money, the items were bagged.

"I need a pair of shoes and some personal hygiene items," Seth told the man.

"Personal hygiene items!" the clerk laughed heartily. "What the hell kind of talk is that?"

"Just a bar of soap and a razor," Seth replied, trying to be nice. "Do I get a line of credit?"

"A line of credit! Hell no, you don't get no credit here, dumbass. This ain't no bank where you get a loan, you ignorant bastard."

Seth felt his temper trying to flare, but he kept his cool. "Hey, I'm new here, man. I'm just trying to learn the rules, so how about you giving me a break?"

"It's all cool, asshole, don't get upset or something, gees! What's your name?"

"Seth. Seth Boone."

"Ah. Pretty Boy, I thought you looked real badass. You the one knocked Dagger on his big black ass, cool man. Let me check the records here."

The man typed Seth's name into the computer. "Damn man! You got a thousand dollars in here. How's that for instant credit?"

Seth's eyes widened. "I don't understand."

"Let me see here," the clerk said, then continued punching keys on the keyboard. "Says here you had a thousand dollars put in your account six days ago. Deposited by somebody named Logan."

Seth was speechless. Rita had put the money into his account. She'd not just deposited a few dollars, she'd put in a thousand dollars. He couldn't believe it.

"Hey, you want a carton of Camels, man? You carry that out of here and you'll make a lot of new friends."

Seth snapped out of his deep state of thought and answered. "No, thank you. I only need a razor, a bar of soap, a toothbrush, and toothpaste. Oh, how much is a pair of shoes, I wear a twelve?"

"Only thing I got in your size is a pair of New Balance tennis jammers man, they be one-ninety-five buck-a-roos."

Seth couldn't believe the price. Thankfully, he had the money, so he took the shoes. No way could he get around in prison wearing flip-flops. He could see now why prisoners relied so heavily on family coming to visit and bringing them things. Seth would have no visitors ever, so he would have to work and pay the outrageous prices at the prison store for everything he needed.

On the walk back to his cell, Rita was all he could think of. He loved her. He loved her more than life itself. Although they had promised no contact, he felt compelled to write her a letter and thank her for such a generous, unselfish gift. The problem was he didn't have her address.

The cell was empty when Seth got there. He placed his expensive razor and soap on the opposite side of the sink from Shanghai's things. After putting his outrageously priced shoes beneath the bed, he climbed into his bunk. It felt wonderful laying there on a stained clean sheet and soft mattress. He felt clean, and his stomach was full for the first time in days. He was out of the hole, had on clean clothes that fit, and he'd gotten a warm reception in the mess hall. More than anything, he had been blessed by Rita's love and generosity. He knew that she loved him as much as he loved her. He wished there was some way he could repay her the money. *If only I could be with her*, he thought. *If only.*

Shanghai appeared in the cell and the door closed then locked behind him.

"SETH," he said with the deep harsh oriental accent. "Come down here. Let Shanghai get a look at you."

Seth climbed down from his bunk as a wide grin spread across his face. "Ahhh, haha," Shanghai said. "You no wear for worse!"

"It's worse for wear," Seth replied.

"Shanghai still get some phrase backward, you get jest though. You survived five days in hole but look great!"

Seth kept smiling.

"Sit down on Shanghai's bed, we have long talk now."

He couldn't believe it. Shanghai was friendly and talkative.

Seth learned that only a few prisoners had ever gotten five days in the hole. Others who had spent five days in that dungeon came out weak and sickly. Shanghai kept talking about how strong Seth was. He'd not only survived the five days in the hole but had walked out healthy. They chatted for over two hours. Shanghai told him everything he could think of regarding the prison and how everything worked. Several things Seth learned weren't pleasing, but it was good to know the rules, especially the things he could do in order to stay clear of trouble.

"You don't have to answer if you don't want, but why shave your head?" Seth asked. "I thought oriental men liked long hair. Isn't it a thing of honor or something to have long hair?"

"Many year ago when Shanghai was free man, he had long hair kept in ponytail. Chinese women love man with long locks. Shanghai's hair touched his ass. Shanghai was much loved. No more long hair though."

"Why is that?" Seth felt compelled to ask.

"In prison, no woman to love," Shanghai said with a big smile. "In here, man with long hair get in fight, it not good with ponytail. Opponent grab hold of long hair, he may as well have Shanghai by balls!"

Shanghai and Seth laughed.

"Shanghai see you hit Dagger. Shanghai happy and impressed. How they say, you cold-cock him uh knock him out. Seth mighty strong, but maybe stupid."

Seth didn't reply. He just sat there listening.

"Dagger and African-American friends, they have it out for Seth now. You avoid them. You watch your back every minute outside of cell."

"Why did you call his friends African-Americans? Everyone else in here, including the blacks themselves use that 'N' word."

"Shanghai find no pleasure or benefit in calling black man that name or any bad name. Same go for white man or any other. Black or white, harsh word provoke anger. Shanghai no need to make man angry, enough of that in prison already. We all men just trying to do our time."

Seth nodded in agreement. Shanghai was very wise. He was glad Shanghai was going to be his cellmate.

"Shanghai no like gangs. Shanghai also no like prisoners grouping together by race or country of origin, that no good - but that the way it be. Learn to accept that, do not invade the black man or Latino's space, it only cause Seth trouble. Much hate in prison, but hate only eat, Seth - do best to live and let live. Shanghai tired now he rest."

Seth got off Shanghai's bed and was ready to climb into his own bunk.

"Thank you, Shanghai. I'm happy you took time to talk with me. You're right about everything."

"Shanghai think Seth good boy, just have string of bad luck. Thing get better for you though if you make best of situation."

"Yeah, you're right again," Seth replied.

"You should sit at table with Shanghai in mess hall. Seth no hang out with shaved head white men, them make much trouble. Seth involved with gang, he be in trouble also."

"Are you serious? You don't mind?"

"Shanghai be honored," he said smiling. "One more thing. Shanghai no babysitter, but he think much about what Seth say on first day. Shanghai teach Seth martial arts if interested."

"Holy cow!" Seth said. "Are you serious?"

"Why Seth ask Shanghai if serious? Shanghai always serious. You get rest, we talk more later."

Seth was exhausted but too excited to sleep. It had been a great day. After an hour of his mind replaying the events of that day, he finally fell asleep. The next morning when the cell doors opened, Shanghai waited for him. They walked to the mess hall together. The other prisoners watched as Seth took a seat at the table claimed by the Orientals. Never before had an outsider joined their ranks.

Dagger only thought he was the most feared man on C-block, but it was Shanghai that everyone feared the most. Seth had already gained a lot of respect, and many of the inmates feared him. Being associated with Shanghai, no one would dare to touch him.

21

After breakfast at Shanghai's table that morning, Seth was shown the library where he would work. The old librarian who died hadn't left the place in a mess as the warden had described - it was a total disaster. The books that lined the fifteen tall shelves weren't in any kind of order. In one corner, there were boxes of donated books piled almost to the ceiling. There were no computers. Everything was supposed to have been organized with the old card file system. From what Seth could gather though, nothing had been logged in or categorized in the last twenty years and the Dewey Decimal System had never been heard of.

For the most part, the only prisoners who frequented the library came for one of the three newspapers arriving on an irregular basis. The Washington Post, The Radford Daily Press, and a weekly-published trash filled tabloid, which happened to be most favored.

By the end of day three, Seth had removed every book from the shelves and had begun cataloging each one. By the tenth day, he had the original books back on the shelves and was ready to dive into the boxes stacked in the corner.

Each day, a prisoner from A, B, and D-blocks showed up in the library, assigned to assist Seth. All three men were in their sixties and were more interested in playing cards than logging in books. They had been assigned there for years, playing cards every day instead of working. They saw no reason for this new young punk to change that. Seth didn't mind. He let the old men be. It was much more work on him, but he figured he had a lifetime to get the books in order.

A journal was started from day one. He found a secret hiding place for his diary, on top of a tall bookshelf. Each day he would slide the ladder over to retrieve the book then write down events from the day before. He thought someday he might write a book about prison life, telling what took place behind bars. There were many things to pen about the warden, but he wouldn't dare to start the manuscript until Pendleton was dead and gone. Seth didn't think the warden had too many years left, judging the way the man looked.

Before writing about prison life each day, he wrote a sentence or two about Rita, describing how much he loved and missed her. He had promised never to stop loving her, and that was a promise easy to keep. The daily log of his diary would be a testimony to that. She would forever be the woman he loved but could never have.

Out in the yard, several sets of free-weights and lift benches were in place for the prisoners to use. During outside time, each gang or group shared the equipment, each taking a turn at weight lifting. No one could believe the amount of weight Seth could lift and the number of reps he could do. Even Dagger and his gang were impressed by Seth's strength.

Over the next several weeks, things on C-block were peaceful. As far as Seth knew, no fights or heated-arguments had occurred. It was almost too quiet. He didn't consider himself paranoid, but he looked back constantly anytime he was outside the cell. Dagger continually gave him evil looks in the mess hall, but there had been no trouble. Seth attributed at least part of the peacefulness to the Christmas music. Christmas songs played over the intercom throughout 'C' Block long after the holiday had come and gone. It seemed to have a calming effect on everyone. Seth wondered why they didn't play Christmas music all year long since it appeared to play a part in peacekeeping.

Shanghai hadn't mentioned martial arts training so Seth never brought it up. He guessed that Shanghai would announce when he was ready to begin and not until then. Seth began watching and listening to those around him. He determined that prisoners, for the most part, were creatures of habit. Everyone in the mess hall sat in the same seat at the same table. Out in the yard, everyone had a routine. No one ever seemed to deviate from set patterns. Shanghai was no different. Seth noticed he visited a lot of people, but always the same ones, always for less than a minute, and always looking over his shoulder.

It only took Seth a few days watching Shanghai to find out why he visited so many people. Shanghai wasn't a smoker but he always had two packs of cigarettes on his person. His new oriental friend was a smuggler. One of the afternoon shift guards was in cahoots with Shanghai. The guard was purchasing cigarettes outside the prison for $4.00 a pack. He sold the cigarettes to Shanghai for $8.00 a pack, doubling his money. The guard wasn't brave enough to sell the cigarettes himself - it was too risky. Besides, he had his job to do.

If the guard got caught smuggling goods inside the prison, at a minimum, he'd lose his job. If Shanghai were to be caught, he'd lose his contraband and get a three-to-five day stint in the hole. The guard knew Shanghai would never rat out his source, which gave him peace of mind. To Shanghai, the profits well outweighed the risk. He had a nice-sized clientele willing to purchase his smuggled goods at the discount rate of $10.00 a pack, which was a substantial saving over the prison store price.

Shanghai had been doing business with the guard nearly four years, and to date, the warden hadn't even been suspicious. With such high prices, the warden didn't sell many cigarettes in his store, but he was too greedy to drop the price. The warden saw many of inmates smoking, but had determined the inmates' families were bringing them cigarettes. As much as the warden disliked it and discouraged it, there was little he could do because it was legal.

On weekends, when fewer guards and management people were around, Shanghai's partner in crime would smuggle in a handful of marijuana cigarettes to sell. They weren't cheap but they always sold and netted a higher percentage profit than tobacco products.

§

The warden swung by the library one day unexpectedly. Seth could tell when Warden Pendleton walked in the building that the man was in a bad mood. The warden walked around, pulled a few books from the shelves, thumbed through the card files then walked over to the magazine rack.

"I must say, I'm impressed," Pendleton said as he picked up a newspaper.

He had not expected to see that Seth had done such a good job.

"I'm going to give you the librarian job full-time," the warden said. "If we can only get some of these primates in here to read, it would do well in boasting my reviews by the annual audit team. I'm sending four book carts over to you. You will work two extra hours on Monday, Wednesday, and Friday at no extra pay. I want you and these lazy asses working with you to take books by the prisoners' cells in each block on those days and offer them to inmates to read, if they can. If they can't, do what you can to teach them."

The warden walked back over to the card files, pulled out a drawer, dumped it on the floor then walked out without saying another word.

§

One day at lunch, while finishing off his peanut butter and jelly sandwich on stale bread, Shanghai looked at Seth and smiled.

"Happy Birthday, Seth," Shanghai said. "Today you eighteen. Today, you a man official."

In prison, you lose track of time, except for release dates or holidays when extra meat is served in the chow hall. Seth had forgotten it was his birthday. He was sixteen when he killed his parents and although a juvenile, he was tried as an adult. It was now official, according to manmade laws – he was a man.

"Oh gees, Shanghai," Seth said. "I forgot it was my birthday. How bad is that? Thanks man!"

"Um. Shanghai think you had time to settle into prison life. Seth official man now. If him think he ready, we begin training."

Seth's eyes got big and he almost shouted.

"Heck yes, I'm ready!" he replied with a ton of enthusiasm.

"In yard today. Seth pump iron as always, then come to corner of fence near walking track. We have lesson there."

The martial arts lessons were slow in the beginning. For the first few days all Shanghai did was talk. Seth learned what he had already surmised, that Shanghai was much more than any fighter who knew how to kick box or throw a karate chop. In his hay day, Shanghai was a professional.

Back home in Shanghai, China, before he'd gotten adventurous and wanted to see the world, particularly the United States, Shanghai was a two-time national champion. Even now, up in his years, he was an awesome fighter. In Seth's mind, he could never come close to having the knowledge and moves Shanghai possessed, but after a month of training, Shanghai thought otherwise.

Seth was a quick learner. He also had the physical ability to become a great fighter. His movements were fluid, accurate, and precise. Combining those abilities with Seth's super-human strength, Shanghai soon learned something himself - to be extra careful when sparring with Seth to avoid injury.

Dagger and his gang had been observing the lessons from afar. He wanted nothing more than to catch Seth off alone somewhere and sink a shank into his heart. He knew he'd have to be patient, wait until just the right moment. He'd pick a time and place when Shanghai wasn't around.

194

His attack would have to be a total surprise, not giving Seth time to react.

As the months passed, Shanghai trusted Seth more and more. He told Seth about his smuggling business. Shanghai worked in the license plate stamp shop and when demand was high, he had to work extra hours. Seth helped Shanghai out by running his cigarettes to various cells and collecting the money. Shanghai was grateful for a friend like Seth, and the feeling was mutual.

Seth was finally approached about entering the warden's GED class. After three days in the class, he was asked if he'd like to take the final exam and see how he would fare. The instructor was a physics teacher at a local high school. He worked part-time at the prison in the evenings. In the twelve years he'd worked there, he had never run across a student this intelligent. Seth aced the test, not missing a single question. He was awarded his GED certificate, which he proudly displayed on the wall by his bunk.

Seth had been at Radford for ten months when Shanghai got into trouble. A new prisoner had arrived, a brut of a man with a look on his face that spelled trouble. Shanghai and twelve others were in the shower when the new man walked in. He walked up to Shanghai, who was soaking under the showerhead. He rubbed his male member over Shanghai's back.

"This ain't my first rodeo," the new prisoner said. "I'm back in prison, horny, and I'm going to have me some Chink."

It was a bad mistake. The fight lasted only seconds. The big brut found himself in the hospital for two days, and Shanghai got five days in the hole.

The guard who did business with Shanghai knew Seth well by now. While Shanghai was in the hole, Seth never missed a stroke, making sure all of Shanghai's regular customers got their smokes. Using books from the library, Seth hollowed several of them out. He placed the illegal cigarettes in the books. He began pushing his book cart around every day, not just Mondays, Wednesdays, and Fridays. He'd deliver a book to a smoking customer and collected the money, taking care of business for Shanghai.

When Shanghai came out of the hole, he looked bad. He was weak, dehydrated and it took him nearly two weeks to recover. Seth kept him going and nursed him back to health. The unlikely pair had bonded, making a friendship that would last as long as they were alive.

A month after Shanghai had gotten out of the hole - Seth got his second turn in the warden's dungeon. He was heading back to the library after lunch when the warden and two guards stopped him. Warden Pendleton ordered the guards to search him, expecting they might find some form of homemade weapon. They found no weapon, but Seth had two packs of Marlboro's in his pants pockets. He was helping Shanghai by making a delivery to a customer on his way to the library.

"What's this?" the warden barked. "You don't smoke. I know that for a fact."

Seth hung his head low and didn't answer. This wasn't going to turn out well. He wasn't going to lie to the warden, but he wasn't going to tell him the truth either.

"Two packs of Marlboros. That's a value of thirty dollars in my store. Where did you get these?"

Seth didn't answer.

"You've never had a visitor, so I know a family member or friends never brought these to you. Hmmm. We don't sell this brand in the store, so where did you get them, Pretty Boy?"

Seth still never uttered a word. One of the guards drew his baton, but the warden held out his hand.

"No," the warden said. "Pretty Boy here has apparently found a way to make some extra cash. Since you don't smoke, I can only assume you're pushing contraband. I don't know where you got these, and I don't suspect you are going to tell me even if I beat you. Let's see how strong you are - Pretty Boy."

The warden laughed, snorting while he did so, sounding like the pig he was.

"Ramsey," the warden said, addressing one of the guards. "I want Pretty Boy's storehouse account dropped down to zero. He's been robbing the store of profits, so I want whatever he's got in his account to go to the store. Search his cell and confiscate additional cigarettes or money he has there as well. Let's also see how he likes being alone. Maybe time spent by himself will help him think twice about cheating me. I'm giving him a full week in the hole."

Seth's mouth dropped open. He looked up at the warden with an expression of surprise on his face. He had never heard of anyone being given seven days in the hole. The stories he'd heard were always five days max. He'd done that much time himself, and it was almost more than he could bear. Shanghai had recently returned from the hole, and five days had almost killed him.

The warden walked off, holding the cigarettes, laughing, and still snorting like a swine. The guard whipped out a set of handcuffs. He closed them tightly around Seth's wrist and led him away. As they were about to make a turn and go down the long corridor leading out to the solitary confinement building, Seth spotted Shanghai. Shanghai and three other inmates had just been released from work that evening. They were heading back to their cells.

"Pendleton gave me seven days in the hole," Seth shouted loud enough for Shanghai to hear. "He also stole my store account, took my cigarettes and all my money!"

Almost immediately, the guard's baton hit Seth hard in the back, nearly causing him to fall. Shanghai couldn't believe what he had just heard. Seven days was too much. He feared Seth would never leave the hole alive. He was angry, and it took all his inner strength not to run down the hall and attack the guard.

22

Seth was placed in the same cell he'd spent five days in on his first trip to the hole. He didn't have to familiarize himself with the cell layout. The place was forever embedded in his mind.

In the hole, there was never enough food provided. Seth was glad he'd eaten a good-sized lunch. He was hopeful it would help sustain him for a day or two. No sooner had those thoughts crossed his mind, his stomach began to churn. The dirty stinking mattress was the same one he'd slept on months earlier, and the stench of urine and feces seemed worse than ever. He became nauseated and had to rush over to the heavily stained commode. Vomiting would cause him to become weaker at a faster rate, but he couldn't hold it in. He lost his lunch. No evening meal was served, which was just as well. Seth didn't know if he could eat anything.

Just like the first time he had been in the hole, he quickly lost track of time. He was disoriented and had no idea how long he'd been there. When the cell opened the next morning, Seth's hunger pangs told him he'd been there for days already. The guard ordered him to come out, and stated his seven days were up.

As soon as Seth began crawling toward the door, it shut. He could hear the guard laughing as he walked away. Seth collapsed on the filthy concrete floor. The warden was playing with him. Since he'd been at Radford, he'd discovered that the warden abused prisoners constantly, especially those in the hole. He had been told that at least two prisoners went insane while serving time in the hole and had committed suicide. It made him wonder if the true purpose of the overhead pipe in the cell was to give inmates a mechanism from which to hang themselves.

At noon, food came. It was a piece of bread smothered with a cheese spread. As when he'd been in there before, it was served on a paper plate, which Seth ate. He felt he'd been there for at least seven days already when that meager meal arrived. Just like the first time he was there, the minutes seemed like hours, and the hours seemed like days.

In the penetrating darkness, Seth exercised, just as he had months earlier. He did pushups, sit-ups, ran in place, and used the pipe overhead to do pull-ups. He had some new exercises this time, the ones Shanghai had taught him. He also mediated, but couldn't do it for long. Too many bad thoughts were going through his head. He wanted to kill the warden.

Seth had built up his account in the warden's store plus had seventy dollars hidden in his cell. He wanted to buy nice sheets for both his and Shanghai's bed, and give Shanghai a subscription to a martial arts magazine for Christmas. The guard who smuggled in the cigarettes was going to make the arrangements. It was going to cost Seth a pretty penny. It didn't matter now because it was all gone. The warden had stolen all his money. Seth could think of nothing more except placing his fingers around the warden's throat and choking him to death as he did his little pig snort thing.

200

Seth knew he had to change his attitude and begin thinking about positive things. He remembered what Shanghai had said about hate eating at someone. The hatred was hurting him, not Warden Pendleton.

He began to construct the mountain cabin in his mind again, just as he had when he'd been in the hole before. This time he expanded his mountain mansion, making it four rooms instead of one. He allowed himself to have more tools and supplies. His new cabin would have electricity and running water.

He made every attempt to keep his mind occupied and did his best to keep his muscles toned by exercising. Still, he could tell his mind was slipping and he was getting weaker. Food was coming once a day and what little was on the plate wasn't enough. His mind and body told him he'd been in the hole for two weeks or longer. In actuality, it had been three days.

An hour, maybe twelve, after his meal on the third day, the door opened again, and a box was slide inside the cell.

What is that? Seth thought, seeing the silhouette of something similar to a shoebox sliding across the cell floor. He crawled across the floor to the box. He felt its size and shape. It was indeed a shoebox. It felt light though, appearing to be empty. He carefully pulled the lid off.

In the pitch-black darkness, he stuck his hand inside the box to feel around, to see if anything was inside. His hand and arm immediately began to burn. He could feel something crawling up his arm. The box was full of red ants. They were biting his arm, and he could feel hundreds, maybe thousands, crawling on his legs. He threw the box into the corner and slapped his arms, legs, and torso, screaming, desperately trying to sling the ants away or kill the creatures. He hurriedly crawled back toward the filthy mattress. He spent hours raking his hands over his body each time an ant found him and sank what felt like sharp teeth into his skin.

Seth stood and found the pipe overhead, using it as a guide, and providing orientation. He then stepped forward then, toward the shoebox. For a long while, he stomped the concrete, hoping to kill the remaining insects. He was thankful that his feet were protected by the expensive shoes he'd purchased from the storehouse.

Sleep didn't come easy. He was constantly rubbing his head, feet, arms, chest, thinking he felt the biting insects. Many of the swats and slaps to his body were because his mind was playing tricks on him. It felt like ants were crawling all over him, but he didn't know if it were true or just his imagination.

The anger kept building. Seth wasn't about to let the warden win. He would overcome anything the warden tried. He would survive and someday – someday – even if it were far into the future, he'd find a way to get even. His attempt to be a model prisoner had fallen by the wayside when he began helping Shanghai sell the cigarettes. Still, he didn't think that action warranted such severe punishment.

Why should I try? He thought. *I work my butt off in here for three dollars a day then the warden comes along and steals my money. I trust the other prisoners more than I do him. He's evil, scum, nothing more than a louse!*

Seth decided he would report what the warden was doing - but to whom?

He couldn't mail anything out of the prison without it being censored. He could talk to Shanghai's guard friend about mailing a letter addressed to the prison commission, but he was doubtful the man would agree to do so. The last thing the guard wanted was someone to start an investigation. There was too great a chance someone would discover his lucrative smuggling business. He'd not only lose the income being earned on contraband, but likely his job as well. He could even end up living in the prison instead of working there.

Seth slapped, scratched, stomped, and swatted for the next four days, thinking he'd missed killing some of the ants. It was driving him crazy. After the shoebox of ants had been put in his cell, he tensed up every time the cell door opened. Fortunately, the guards and the warden hadn't played any more games.

When his seven days were finally up, Seth could hardly walk. He realized that many religious people fasted for longer periods then seven days, but expected they still took vitamins and drank something with nutrients to keep their strength. Fasting wasn't his gig though. He needed protein and a certain amount of carbohydrates to keep him going. The little food the guards had served him was barely enough to keep him alive. The mental stress while in the hole had far more effect than the lack of food. Far more than the solitude, the darkness had put Seth on edge insanity. The absence of light for such a long period was almost unbearable.

Out of the hole, Seth went through the same routine as the first time he'd been there. He was washed down with a fire hose outside the building. It was an unusually cold day for mid-November. The thermometer had dropped down to 25 degrees and a stiff wind was blowing. When the water hit Seth, it felt like a sheet of ice. Before the dousing was over, his entire body was numb and he had to be helped to his feet.

After being dragged back inside the building, the guard let him go. He fell to the floor then tried to get up but his legs felt like lead. The guards began kicking him, and shouting commands for him to get to his feet. The punishment seemed to give him the motivation and energy he needed to get his blood flowing again. He was able to crawl toward the shower room. A guard followed, kicking him in the buttocks as he struggle to move forward.

The water coming from the showerhead wasn't hot but it was warm. After a few minutes, Seth was able to stand. Although still numb, he could feel his fingers again. He stood beneath the showerhead until one of the guards appeared, ordering him to get dressed.

Clean clothes were sitting on a folding chair nearby. He got dressed, but couldn't find his shoes. The guards had taken his only pair of shoes and tossed them in the trash along with his soiled prison clothing. He began protesting, but after a baton slapped hard against his right thigh, he quickly closed his mouth and said nothing more.

He had pretty much worn the shoes out over the months, even more so scooting around on the floor inside the hole. Still, they were his and the guards didn't have the right to throw them away. With no money in his account, there wasn't a way to buy a new pair of shoes. He wasn't even offered a pair of flip-flops this time around, leaving him no choice but to walk around barefoot in November.

Seth was weak and weary looking. The prisoners were astonished he'd survived. No one in C-block ever recalled someone being in the hole for seven days. He had crossed a mountain that no one thought possible to climb. It gained him even more respect from the other prisoners. He was only a few months past his eighteenth birthday, but he was a man among men, both respected and feared by the prisoners.

The inmates were highly upset at the treatment Seth had received. Seven days in the warden's hole was bad enough, but Seth's story about the ants and his shoes made it ten times worse. The prisoners feared Pendleton would begin giving everyone extended periods in the hole.

There was talk of a riot, but it was more talk than action. Most inmates feared what would happen afterward, knowing how cruel Warden Pendleton could be. Just because Seth had been treated inhumanly, they weren't ready to carry his cross and take a chance on the warden treating them harshly as well. After a couple of days, Shanghai and Seth were the only ones still talking about rioting. The prisoners were not unlike most Americans outside those walls. They were unwilling to take a stand on anything if there was a chance the end-result could cause them discomfort.

The warden got word of the riot talk. He was thankful when the rumors settled. A riot would bring reporters and investigators. The last thing he wanted was a bunch of suits from Richmond snooping around. Radford was his kingdom. Even when auditors came on their annual visit, Warden Pendleton would treat them harshly. Most rushed through the books and their inspections, completing the audit days ahead of schedule. They were in the utmost hurry to get away from Pendleton's house of hell. A riot would give them cause to come back, seeking revenge for the way they'd been treated.

Afraid things could get out of control Pendleton decided to back off for a while. He didn't show his face for a few weeks, and the guards appeared to be less strict. The inmates took notice and felt like they had scored a victory.

Shanghai and his oriental friends pitched in and bought Seth a new pair of shoes. He would be eternally grateful for their generosity. He promised to pay them back so he worked out a plan with Shanghai to expand the business. Seth was becoming a rule breaker instead of a rule follower. Prison was changing him, but not for the better.

Seth convinced the three old men who worked for him in the library to start selling contraband in their perspective blocks of the prison. The old men agreed to a 60/40 deal, with Seth getting the sixty. The guard who did the smuggling was more than happy to supply the extra contraband. Having hopes of retiring within five years, the profits from his illicit dealings were being shoveled into an IRA. It would help to supplement the meager pension he'd get from the prison system.

Using book carts as a front, the four library workers delivered smokes to all four blocks, A-D. If an inmate had money, smuggled cigarettes were available. The marijuana business doubled. Seth was finally able to get Shanghai the martial arts magazines. Every evening his oriental friend could be found stretched out on his bunk, reading every article and every ad in the magazine.

As the months passed, Shanghai turned Seth into a fearless fighting machine. Seth wasn't just good - he was awesome. The guards, as well as the prisoners watched Seth develop and hone his skills. Although the guards tried not to show it when around him, they were frightened of Seth, and always had their batons in their hand when they approached him. Dagger and his gang seemed to have moved on. They found some newly arrived, puny prisoners, to pick on.

Counting his time at Damascus, Seth had already spent over two years of his life behind bars. It was June and outside the prison walls people were getting ready for the approaching summer. Seth had grown accustomed to prison life but still yearned dearly to be among those roaming about freely on the outside world. He'd run a few prison-break schemes through his head but quickly dismissed them, knowing they'd never work.

He wondered where Rita was these days and if she was happy. In another month, he would be nineteen. Rita, being twelve years older was thirty-one. She had talked about wanting to get married, and raise a family. Seth expected she'd done that by now, at least the getting married part.

He closed his eyes and imagined how it would feel to touch her lips again with his. He could feel the softness of her skin as they held each other close. Back in Damascus, he could smell her perfume on his clothing long after she left each day. He would sit in his cell and take long whiffs of his shirt. The only scent on his shirt now was that of his own sweat.

§

Shanghai had been working late the last two evenings. A press in the license plate shop broke down earlier in the week, putting production behind. Bradshaw, one of the old men who helped in the library approached Seth as he was leaving. He said he desperately needed two packs of cigarettes that evening. It was getting late, but Bradshaw insisted he needed to get the contraband delivered before lock-up, taking place in about an hour. Seth told him to wait there and he'd see what he could do. He walked back inside C-block, past three guards along the way, and entered his cell. Shanghai had a stash of cigarettes hidden away in a secret place for emergency situations. Seth considered Bradshaw's dilemma was close enough to an emergency.

With two packs of Salem Lights stuffed inside his shirt, Seth headed back to the outside door. As he stepped out, a stiff cold wind hit him. For the last three days, it had been extraordinarily cold for that time of the year. Darkness was approaching, and the wind brought a chill to the air. He rushed down the sidewalk leading to the library.

The library had been in shambles all week due to a waterline that had burst. Contractors had been in and out, tracking mud all over the place. The bottom section of the left wall had been ripped out, and a trench stretched from there into the bathroom some forty feet away. Two bookcases had to be emptied and moved out of the way. Concrete dust particles, created by jackhammers cutting out the floor, had left the entire place with a white coating.

When Seth arrived back at the library, the lights were off. He called out to Bradshaw but got no answer. Bradshaw had Crohn's disease so Seth figured he was in the bathroom, the one that looked like a war zone. The circuit breaker panel was on the wall just past the construction mess. It wasn't at all uncommon for the lights to go off in the library. The electrical system was in dire need of being upgraded. Using a variety of power tools, all at the same time, the contractors had tripped the circuit breaker nearly a dozen times that day because of an overload.

The warden wasn't going to spend any of his precious budget money on upgrades for the prison library though. He wouldn't have fixed the burst water pipe if it had not been absolutely necessary. The warden's office was getting a full makeover however. Most of the budget dollars slated for the prison that fiscal year was being spent on upgrades to either Warden Pendleton's already fine abode, or the break room where guards hung out.

There was enough natural light shining inside the library windows for Seth to find his way to the circuit breaker box. As soon as he flipped the switch, the lights came back on.

A second later, Dagger had slipped up behind him. At the same time, four of his goons stepped out from behind a bookshelf. Dagger was wielding a long butcher knife stolen from the mess hall kitchen. He had his arm around Seth, with a razor-sharp edge pressed against his throat. Seth had grown in height since he'd entered Radford. He now stood six feet four inches tall. Dagger at five eleven had to hold the knife high, causing him to put more pressure than intended against Seth's throat. Seth stiffened, afraid to move.

"How you doing, Pretty Boy?" Dagger said, so excited his voiced shook.

Seth remained frozen. He could feel the sharp blade against his skin. One slight mishap and he would be lying on the floor in a pool of blood.

"Now this is how it's gonna work, Pretty Boy. You be real nice and I might just let you live. You try any of that fancy hand and footwork that 'ole slant eyes been teaching you and I'll slice your jugular open and watch you die."

Seth didn't try to talk. He just stood still, and tried his best to breathe normal.

Dagger's gang was well known for their homosexual lifestyle. Two of Dagger's gang, nicknamed Sig and Zag were standing close by.

"Shit. I'm too excited. I can't wait any longer," Sig said.

Sig dropped his pants, and Zag did likewise. Sig dropped to his hands and knees, and Zag got behind him.

Seth saw them performing their sick sex act out of the corner of his eye. He focused his eyes back to center facing Tyrone, another one of Dagger's men. Tyrone was a big man, as tall as Seth, but weighing nearly twice as much.

Dagger had his left hand on Seth's shoulder. He was yielding the knife with his right hand. It was a bad situation, and Seth didn't think he would get out of this alive.

"You're gonna give me a good head job," Dagger said, ever more excited. It was something he'd dreamed of for months, waiting patiently until the opportune time. Now that time was here.

"While you're doing me, and it better be damn good, Tyrone here is going to use his big stick and take away your virginity, Pretty Boy."

Dagger was chuckling, which caused the knife to dig deeper into Seth's skin. Another ounce of pressure and Seth would be bleeding uncontrollably.

The other member of Dagger's gang was a huge round man they called, Fat Man. He had unzipped his pants and was stroking himself as he watched Sig and Zag down on the floor. Seth couldn't believe he had been so stupid and had fallen into the trap set by these depraved men.

Turning his eyes downward, Seth saw that Tyrone had unfastened his belt, allowing his pants to fall to his knees. Just then, Seth felt the sharp blade ease from his skin.

"Get on your knees, Pretty Boy, then turn to face me," Dagger demanded. "You better do it right and it better be good. You bite me and I promise you, asshole, it will be the last thing you taste."

Tyrone and Fat Man both chuckled.

210

"Hold the knife," Dagger said to Tyrone. "I'm about to probe ole Pretty Boy's tonsils."

Seth knew it was now or never. He had to act and act fast. There would be no second chances. In his mind, he had already picked his targets. It was a rule that Shanghai had pounded into his head from day one of the martial arts training. There was no way Dagger would let him walk out of that building alive. He'd seen the intent to kill in Dagger's eyes ever since the day he punched him in the mess hall.

With the quickness of a cat, Seth's left hand came around and grabbed the knife just as the exchange from Dagger to Tyrone was taking place. In an instant, he thrust the long blade deep into Tyrone's chest. At the same time, Seth's right elbow came back sharply. Dagger had started to move, but wasn't quick enough. Seth's powerful blow caught Dagger's right eye, the same one he'd blackened with his fist months earlier.

He pulled the knife out of Tyrone's chest and swung it around in a wild circular arc. Fat Man had turned his eyes back to watching Sig and Zag on the floor. He looked up and saw the knife blade coming in his direction. He instinctively started to turn and fall back, but it was too late. The end of the blade raked across the side of Fat Man's throat, slicing through his carotid artery. A stream of bright-red blood shot out, spraying Seth, Dagger and the wall.

Seth wheeled around to face Dagger, who had just regained his faculties. Dagger took a swing at Seth with a clenched right fist. The blow was easily deflected, swept away by Seth's big powerful arm. In one quick step forward, Seth thrust the knife straight into Dagger's heart. He twisted it twice then withdrew the blade. A grimacing look instantly came over Dagger's face, and his eyes were already going dim.

With his adrenaline level through the roof, Seth was out of control. His danger meter was pegged, and his fight or flight button was stuck on fight. Everything happened fast. Seth swung the blade and made a deep cut into Tyrone's throat, even though the man had already fallen back into the bookcase and was on his way to the floor. Fat Man fell directly on top of the two men on the floor having sex, who had just realized things had gone south. Seth dove into the pile and began stabbing all three men repeatedly.

Thirty seconds later, Seth finally came to his senses and stopped. Zag, the last of Dagger's gang still alive, gasped for air and stopped breathing.

Seth sat there in the middle of a pile of dead men who looked like they'd gone through a meat grinder. It was over. Blood was everywhere. Seth was covered from head to toe. His heart was trying to pound out of his chest. His breathing was fast and hard. He dropped the knife, pushed himself away from Fat Man and stood to his feet.

Stumbling as he walked toward the library entrance, Seth put out a blood-covered hand and pushed the door open. He stepped out into the cool evening air. Little more than a minute ago, Dagger and his men had him trapped. He never thought he'd walk out of there alive.

Seth bent over and threw up. He took a few steps back then bent over again, placing his hands on his knees. He was still breathing hard, and his heart was still pounding. The cool air felt good to his lungs.

Just then, two guards were coming down the sidewalk talking about the chill in the night air. They were heading to the library to make sure it was clear before locking the doors for the night.

One of the guards spotted Seth and screamed out. "WHAT THE HELL?"

The light shining from atop the library doorway created a shadow where Seth was standing. His breath was creating steam, and being covered in blood, he looked like a creature from a zombie movie. When the guard yelled, Seth went to his knees and locked his bloody fingers behind his head.

Less than two minutes later, sirens were sounding loudly and the prison was in lock-down.

When Shanghai got to the cell, Seth wasn't there. The sirens were blaring and as soon as he stepped in, the door closed and locked behind him. He feared the worst. He expected something had happened to Seth. When the lights went out later that evening, Shanghai still didn't know what had taken place, nor did any of the other inmates.

Seth was handcuffed and led straight to the hole. It was the same cell again. The guards didn't ask if he was hurt or needed to see a doctor. They didn't even ask him what had happened.

When he walked into the cell, the guards never uttered a word, leaving him with no clue about how long he'd be in the hole. The blood that covered him from head to toe wasn't his, but the guards didn't know that. All they knew was that one man walked out of the library, and five didn't. For all the guards knew he could have been stabbed and was bleeding to death. It angered him that they never checked him over for injury. With his adrenaline still rushing like a river, he felt his throat and ran his hands over his body. He wondered if he was hurt, bleeding and just hadn't realized it yet.

Seth paced back and forth in the darkness. It was a long time before his heartbeat returned to normal. The sticky blood that covered him was beginning to dry. He stripped down and spent the next thirty minutes dipping water from the commode tank, splashing his body, trying to wash the blood off his skin.

The next morning, the cell doors on C-block opened as normal. It was time for breakfast. Seth hadn't come back to his cell during the night. Shanghai was worried. Prisoners were chattering about the sirens and lockdown last night, but no one knew a thing. After everyone had gone through the chow line and sat down, the inmates finally got a clue as to what may have happened. Dagger, the four members of his gang, and Seth, were missing. One of the guards informed Shanghai what had transpired.

23

Seth paced back and forth in the darkness of the small cell for hours before lying down. He was exhausted, but his mind wouldn't rest. He had killed Dagger and his entire gang. He didn't know what was going to happen next, but it couldn't be good.

As other times when in the hole, he quickly lost track of time. He became confused as to whether it was day or night. A guard finally opened the door and slid in a plate containing two cold hotdog wieners and a slice of white bread. Seth could have sworn he'd been there a week or longer. In actuality, it was fourteen hours.

After eating the food, he laid down. Next came two hours of tossing and turning before he finally went to sleep. He awakened with a horrible headache, one that lasted for hours. He was in serious trouble. He feared that killing those men, even though it was self-defense, could get him the death penalty. The warden, nor anyone else, would buy his story of self-defense, especially since he'd killed five men.

Exercising vigorously to relieve tension, Seth pushed himself to the limit doing pull-ups, using the overhead pipe. The exercising relieved some of his tension, but it did little to clear his mind. He could only imagine what was going on in the prison office. Certainly, the Governor's office would investigate. He feared what that would bring on him, but he feared the warden the most. He suspected the warden might have him killed. A guard might shoot him in the back, claiming he'd tried to escape. All hope was lost.

Even if his life were spared by the warden, he'd have to be on guard against an attack from one of the black gangs. It was a given, they would seek revenge for the killing of their brothers. If the gangs didn't kill him and the warden spared his life, he still had to face the fact that he'd never leave Radford. The chance of someday being paroled had left the moment he grabbed the knife out of Dagger's hand. If he were fortunate enough to remain alive, he'd die an old man, still behind bars.

There would be no more library work, no time to write about Rita every day and make notes in his journal about prison life. The most undesirable job in Radford Prison would be his for many years to come. *Perhaps being shot in the back wouldn't be so bad*, he thought. *It would be quick, ending my misery.*

It was a week later when the guards opened the cell door and ordered Seth to step out. He had spent almost nine full days in the hole. No one had ever spent that much time in the dungeon. Although he had survived, Seth was worse for wear. He was weak from hunger and sick from worry.

The guard's eyes widened as they got their first look at Seth. He had the appearance of a creature that had been dug out of an ancient grave. His hair was matted, and his skin was a ghostly white. His eyes were sunken, with large dark circles underneath. Seth stumbled about like an old man. He walked humped over, and it was clear to see he was disoriented.

The guards led him outside where the fire hose lay on the ground, ready to give him the normal high-pressure bath. As he exited the building, Seth tilted his head back and inhaled, taking in several deep breaths of fresh air.

It was the ninth day of June. The scents of flowers and new growth of trees were being blown in from afar and entering the courtyard. The clean air was invigorating to his lungs. The air in the hole had been stale and foul smelling. The fresh air with the fragrance of late spring gave Seth a small boost of energy. It was enough to help him stand upright, just in time to receive more punishment.

When the first blast of water from the firehouse hit, it propelled him backwards ten feet, and he fell to the ground. He curled up into a ball, his legs drawn in tight to protect his manhood. His hands came up to protect his face from the sting of the water exiting the fire hose with tremendous force. The guard laughed as he swept the spray back and forth. It was painful and Seth wanted to scream, but that would have taken energy he didn't have to spare so he resisted.

"That's to get the bugs and major stuff off," one of the officers said.

Seth knew the drill. He'd heard that familiar line before. The guards were new and didn't know this wasn't Seth's first time in the hole. After his outside torture bath, Seth was led back into the building to a shower area. After being told to strip down, the guard pointed to a chair where soap and a towel awaited him.

The fire hose dousing had zapped Seth's remaining strength. He had to be helped to the shower. Using the wall for support, he eased along until reaching the showerhead. He placed his back against the wall and waited until the water was lukewarm before stepping beneath it. The guard had already stuck his head in and told him to hurry up, but Seth was in no hurry. *What else can they possibly do to me for taking an extra minute?* He thought.

Fresh prison clothing was sitting on a bench near the shower entrance. Seth got dressed, expecting to be taken before the warden, and the guards didn't disappoint him. As the guards dragged him along, handcuffed and chains binding his legs together, each step brought on more dread of what he was about to face.

The warden was sitting behind his oversized walnut desk. He was quick to get the meeting started, not wasting time with pleasantries. He told Seth the State Committee on Criminal Affairs had met to discuss what should become of him. It was as Seth had expected, he wouldn't be given a chance to explain what had happened. His plea of self-defense would never be heard.

Since Seth had killed inmates, this was a prison issue, which fell outside the court. The warden wasn't interested in what had happened. Warden Pendleton's only concern was himself. Five inmates had been killed on his watch, bringing a lot of heat on him and his kingdom.

Seth's rights had been stripped when he was convicted of capital murder. The warden was now at liberty to do pretty much as he wished with Seth Boone. The warden explained that a briefing would take place soon with the governor, who had the power to invoke the death penalty. There would be no trial. There wouldn't be lawyers present, no judge, or a jury to hear what had taken place. Seth's fate lay in two people's hands, Warden Pendleton, and the governor of Virginia.

"The best you can do is have your sentence extended 100 years, 20 years for each inmate you murdered," the warden said, staring directly into Seth's eyes. "Worst case, the one I plan to vote for, is strapping you to a gurney and sticking a needle full of poison in your veins!"

Seth was too weak to fight, but he had something he wanted to say. As he started to open his mouth, the guard to his right slammed his left elbow into Seth's temple. Seth winced in pain.

Warden Pendleton and the governor would decide his fate, and their decision would be final. There could be no argument, no appeal to a higher authority. Seth's previous thought about never getting out of Radford was the least of his worries now. The warden wanted him dead, and there was little cause for the governor to go against his wishes.

When Seth first arrived at Radford, he didn't care if they killed him or not, but he had changed his mind over time. He wanted to live, and had hopes of one day walking out of prison. He'd be old when he walked away, but he'd be free. That hope had vanished now, like a fleeing vapor, gone forever.

As normal for Seth, he'd scoped out the warden's office when the guards dragged him in. Shanghai had trained him to always check the scene, determining who was around and look for an escape route. He noticed a man standing in the shadows of the back corner, to the left of the warden. The man was well over six feet tall, dark hair, muscular. He wasn't dressed like the guards. He was wearing dress slacks and a black polo shirt. It was the mystery man, the one Seth had seen before. He seemed out of place. He just stood there taking notes.

Seth wanted to know who the man was, and why he always seemed to be around. The man was always behind the scene, lurking in the shadows. He remembered seeing the man at school a few times, but always at a distance. Then, he was in the funeral parlor the night of Sarah's wake. The man jumped up and left the room as soon as Seth and the funeral home attendant entered. At the trial each day when Seth scanned the courtroom, there he was, always in the back, hidden in the crowd.

The stranger's hair was shorter than at the trial. Still, Seth knew without a doubt, it was the same man. He noticed how lean and muscular the man was. He estimated the man was twice his age, yet he was built every bit as well as him.

He couldn't help but notice that the man had a look of worry on his face. Seth wondered why, he was the one in trouble here, not this stranger. There was something about the mystery man's face and eyes, something that drew Seth toward him. He looked like a man who was dangerous, not in a careless way, but in a deliberate one. He questioned himself why he had an interest in this person, especially today when he was standing before the warden under these circumstances.

The warden's harshly spoken words snapped Seth out of his state of profound thoughts with the mystery man. His voice was loud and full of anger. An inmate dying always brought a bit of heat, but now the kitchen was on fire. The warden would have to address local reporters and those special interest groups who claimed to be for human rights. In this case, it had been five inmates dying, and the national media was still set up outside the prison walls, hounding the guards as they came and went.

The governor had called for a face-to-face meeting with the warden. He was due to arrive tomorrow. The feds, who provided a lot of grant money to the prison, were in the middle of conducting their own investigation. They had already interviewed most of the guards and a few of the inmates. It was a total disaster for the warden. As soon as he got things back under control, Seth was a dead man, one way or another.

The warden's secretary paged him over the telephone intercom.

"I told you to hold all calls Sandy," the warden spoke harshly as he answered. "Damn it. I'm in an important meeting here."

"I'm sorry Mr. Pendleton. It's Senator Sutton on the line. He says it's about the audit he discussed with you yesterday."

"Ah, shit! Alright, hold him off for one minute."

"Yes sir."

"Get this worthless piece of human garbage out of my sight," the warden said, motioning toward the guards. "Get his ugly ass some food, but not in the mess hall. I'll decide shortly what to do with the bastard."

The warden didn't want Seth in the mess hall where he'd mingle with other prisoners. Afraid Seth would cause a riot, the warden didn't want him back in the general prison population - period.

Seth was led to a private room where a large tray of roast beef with a savory gravy, cubed potatoes, carrots, and what looked to be homemade yeast rolls, sat on a small table. There was even a large slab of pound cake in a dish to the side. It was all Seth could do, holding back until the guard announced the delicious meal was for him and he was allowed to eat. This had to be what they fed the guards. He'd not seen this kind of food from the time he'd arrived at the prison. His mind was spinning, hoping this wasn't another of the Pendleton's games, dangling food in front of him, only to be denied the tasty meat and vegetables.

"Are you going to eat, or just look at the food?" the guard yelped.

Paying no attention to the utensils on the side of the overfilled tray, Seth used his fingers to stuff food into his mouth. He was still gorging himself when another guard entered and announced the warden was sending Seth back to solitary confinement. Seth's knees felt like melting wax. He had spent more time in the hole than anyone before him, and it had left him weaker than he could ever remember. He didn't think he could survive another day in the warden's dungeon, but the choice wasn't his.

The call with Senator Sutton hadn't gone well. The senator was head of a committee overseeing federal funding for state prisons. He wanted an audit conducted at Radford, which would likely bring about changes to the way the warden conducted business. After the call ended, Pendleton went into a rage, pacing back and forth in his office, cursing anything and everything, but most of all, Seth Boone.

The guard sitting across the room watching Seth eat wasn't pleased with the news. He had compassion for Seth, and felt he'd been mistreated. Still, he had his orders. He had no choice but to take Seth back to the cold damp darkness from which he'd just been released. Turning his back, the guard pretended not to see Seth fill his pockets with the food left on the tray. Later, Seth would remove his pants after the last morsel of mixed food was dug out of his pockets. He'd lick the fabric until all he could taste was polyester and cotton.

The food Seth had eaten, and the extra he had stowed away in his pockets, was enough to sustain him for the next three days while living like a caged animal in the warden's torture chamber. When the three days were up, he was led back out of his dungeon once again. It was the same routine, washed down by fire hoses, then led to a shower. This time though, he wasn't taken to the warden's office, but a small private room instead. The room was dimly lit with nothing on the walls. The only furniture was a small square table and two chairs.

The handcuffs and leg irons were removed. Seth sat down at the table and began eating an apple the guard had graciously handed him. He was surprised by what happened next. The mystery man walked in and sat down across from him.

Seth was confused. He was confused about why he had been led to this room. He wondered who this man was and why he was there.

"My name is Foreman," the man spoke softly, just above a whisper.

"I've seen you around a lot, at my school, and you were at my trial. Who are you?"

"That's not important right now. What's important is that you listen to what I have to say."

"OK. I'm all ears," Seth said smugly.

"You're most assuredly headed to death row. If not, then you'll be killed by a guard or inmate. I'm sure you've already given that some thought. It's highly likely the governor will get your paperwork for execution pushed to the top of the stack. If so, you have a year to live, two years tops. You can fight and try to get your case reviewed, and maybe if you're lucky, the governor will grant you a stay and delay your death. That would only happen though if you have a good lawyer fighting your case, which you don't. Your future isn't very bright, is it?"

Seth had a trainload of questions to ask, but remained silent. He wanted to hear every word the mystery man had to say. There was something strange going on. This meeting was far from normal. He wondered if this was some cruel joke being put together by the warden. He'd seen this mystery man several times in the past though, long before being put in prison. No way could he be associated with the warden. Still, here he was.

"The warden has to put you back in the prison population sooner or later, Seth. You have enemies there. They won't approach you in the manner their friends in the library did. Instead, they'll ram a shank in your back when you least expect it, and when you turn to address your assailant, there won't be anyone there. If that doesn't kill you, they'll send someone else. When they decide you're dead, you're dead. As I said, your future is pretty bleak."

Seth listened and watched. He knew what the man was saying was true. He'd already figured that much out himself. *So, why bother telling me all this? Why is this meeting taking place?*

"How would you like to avoid all that?" Foreman asked. "Avoid death row. Avoid being killed by lethal injection while the warden and a group of politicians sit in front of you and stare as you take your last breath. How would you like to avoid the gangs, the prison walls, the prison guards and the prison food? Even if you avoid the death chamber and the prisoners wanting to kill you, you'll be in prison when the last hair falls off your head. How would you like to be free instead?"

Foreman certainly had Seth's attention. He was still confused though. He knew only God could save him from these prison walls, and this man wasn't God nor one of God's angels.

"When they lead you to the chair and strap you in, the governor, the warden, old man McDowell, and a host of others will be there to watch. You've been getting screwed since Janie Boone first jumped into your bed, Seth, no pun intended."

The remark angered Seth. The mystery man had been at the trial, had heard about how he'd been raped by who he thought at the time was his mother. It was a touchy subject - one Seth didn't like to think about - much less talk about. *Why is this Forman guy here, and why is he throwing that hellish memory into my face?*

He studied Foreman, trying to put the pieces of this jagged jigsaw puzzle together. Foreman stopped talking. He was silent as he and Seth stared into each other's eyes. An awkward minute elapsed, which seemed like an hour. The thought crossed Seth's mind again that this man might somehow be part of one of the Warden Pendleton's cruel and senseless jokes. Seth had spent an unbelievable amount of time in the hole. He was weak, exhausted, and wasn't thinking clearly. The warden was known for playing games, doing all sorts of crazy things to prisoners, torturing them, both physically and mentally.

"I'm the key to changing your luck, Seth," Foreman said. "I can make all of this go away."

Foreman's word struck Seth as being funny. He couldn't help but chuckle.

"I suppose you're going to bust me out of here and make me a secret agent," Seth said, amused. "Let me guess.

You're CIA and want me to be an underworld spy. Maybe you want to put me on a mountain in Afghanistan to try to infiltrate a group of terrorist and spoil their plans to kill Americans. Perhaps you want me to be part of some secret drug experiment, a human lab rat. You'll make me into a modern day Frankenstein. Maybe I'll break out and terrorize New York City, and they'll make a movie or something."

"I understand your skepticism, Seth, but this is serious business," Foreman said sternly. "You're smart, but you're wrong about why you think we're having this meeting. You're thinking this is one of the warden's mind games, but it's not. You've been selected to become a part of my team – for a multitude of reasons. You have nothing to lose, and you have the brains and brawn I need. We aren't CIA or FBI related – it's far beyond that. I need your youth, your intelligence, physical abilities, and above all, your killing skills."

Seth looked intently at the man, his mind twirling. He studied the man's face, trying to determine if he was being truthful. As far as Seth could discern, he was.

"Tell me more," Seth said, playing along.

"That's it," Foreman replied. "I can't tell you anything else. Either you're in or you're out. Being in, means you get out. It means you don't continue to wither away in Radford or head off to death row. It means freedom - except you'll belong to me. That choice means you do as I say, no questions asked - ever! You mess up, you don't come back here - you'll no longer exist."

"You want to use me as an assassin, don't you?"

Foreman stood up and walked toward the door. He turned back to look at Seth, smiling.

"See, you are a smart man. You figure things out quickly. The guards will take you back to your solitary cell now. You have two hours to think – to make up your mind."

Seth's head was spinning. *Could this be real?* He still didn't know if it was real, or if it was the warden messing with his head. He'd heard the stories about how the warden had driven prisoners insane with mind games. He'd even experience some of the cruel treatment himself. Still, he had nothing to lose by saying yes to Foreman. He didn't need two hours to give his answer. He didn't need two minutes.

If there was even the slightest chance Foreman was for real, he didn't want to miss the chance to live outside of these God forsaken prison walls. He had no desire to sit in a cell on death row, counting the days until his execution date arrived. There were no resources to hire an attorney to fight for him. Even if he did, there was no way he'd ever be granted a new trial, much less the governor of Virginia ever granting him a stay of execution while his case was being reviewed. Chances were - the governor was working feverishly to get him to death row. He didn't want another day of prison life. If this were real, he'd be more than willing to do any job Foreman could think of. Seth felt as if he'd never really lived, and still a teenager, he had a lot of living he wanted to do.

Oh please let this be real, he thought. *If it isn't – I'll figure out a way to kill the warden for toying with me and giving me false hope.*

"I'll take your offer, Mr. Foreman!" Seth cried out just as the door was closing.

Foreman didn't respond. He acted as if he didn't hear Seth's answer, although Seth knew he had.

24

Seth was led back to the hole. He wanted to resist but was too weak. He feared he was going to die there in the darkness.

"I've had enough," Seth screamed at the guard. "Tell the warden I'll do anything he wants, anything! Don't you care that my human rights are being violated."

He was still pleading with the guard as the large metal door creaked and closed. He continued ranting for a minute then found his corner, slumped down, and sat there in the darkness. He was exhausted, both mentally and physically. He lay there on the filthy, rank smelling mattress, rewinding the meeting with Foreman in his mind. It had to be a sick mind game being played by the warden. The warden had won, succeeding in driving him to the brink of insanity.

Seth had maintained a positive attitude in prison. He'd kept himself toned and in good physical condition, keeping up the appearance needed to help him survive in the penitentiary. Now it seemed all for naught. He'd reached the bottom of the pit of despair.

If only what this Foreman guy said had been true. He lay there wallowing in his misery. He had the killing skills the stranger had mentioned, never giving that any thought until now. At age eighteen, he'd killed seven people. *They all deserved to die*, he thought, *even my parents*. All he could think of now was killing again - killing Warden Pendleton.

In the darkness, with nothing more to do than exercise or think, Seth wondered if he truly had gotten killer genes from his father. *I think I really could be an assassin. Could I possibly walk up to a total stranger though, put a gun to their head and pull the trigger? What if I was ordered to kill a child - I couldn't do that! Perhaps killing a stranger would be easier than fighting someone you know, someone who's hurt you or trying to hurt you. There would be no emotions tying me to the person. I would think of them as an object, not a human with feelings, friends or family.*

Those thoughts, plus a raging river of others, swept back and forth inside Seth's head. He couldn't stop thinking about life as an assassin. He wasn't proud of having killed seven people. Killing Dagger and his gang was justified though, so were the death of his parents. Faced with a similar situation, he knew he'd not act any differently. Although killing people was easy, living with what he'd done ate at him like a cancer. Still, if it meant getting out of prison, he'd be willing to kill again.

Seth had already endured more time in the hole than anyone had imagined possible. The guards, who had worked at the prison for years, were amazed. The young man had not only survived, it appeared he was still sane. They had never witnessed anyone so strong and with such determination to survive.

Another day passed. Seth imaged it had been a week. Sleep evaded him. He was consumed with an evil plot. Once out of the hole, he'd try to arrange a meeting with the warden. He'd figure out a way to have his hands free during the meeting. There would be a half-dozen guards standing by, but perhaps he could convince them the cuffs weren't necessary. He didn't need a weapon, no knife, no sharp-pointed object. Seth would leap forward and grab the warden. He'd kill the miscreant with his bare hands.

The more Seth tried to remove the evil thoughts of killing the warden from his mind, the more it plagued him. The more he refined his scheme, the more he knew he could do it. He was troubled by his thoughts. It bothered him that the thought of killing someone seemed to come natural. It seemed demonic. He'd shockingly discovered during his murder trial about the adoption. His biological father was a murderer. Without a doubt, he'd gotten some radical genes from his father, making him a born killer as well. He was possessed by the devil.

Seth shook his head, trying to clear it of such thoughts. He was on the edge of a cliff called insanity and his feet were telling him to jump. He went so far as to place his shirt over the iron pipe and twist it into a rope. Fortunately, the shirt wasn't large enough to make a noose.

The next morning, Seth's breakfast came with a small piece of paper lying on top of the soupy grits. He removed the note from the plate and opened it, but there was no light in the cell to reveal what it said.

He had the note ready and was standing by the cell door that evening. He'd been there for hours but it had seemed like days, anticipating the door swinging open. When the guard opened the door to deliver Seth's measly supper, there were a few seconds when light entered the cell. He struggled to adjust his eyes to the light. Just as the door was about to close and the light vanish, his eyes adjusted and he saw the writing clearly. The note simply read 'Tomorrow'.

The next day came and went. The warden had planted another seed, wanting to give Seth the slightest hope that what Foreman promised was real. It made him angrier, and even more determined to find a way to kill the warden. All he needed was a few seconds. That would be long enough to place his hands on the warden and watch him die.

In that dream, his hands were around the warden's throat, choking the life out of him. Their eyes would be locked. The warden would struggle for air, finding none. The six guards would be working frantically to get Seth's hands torn away but he would have already crushed the warden's larynx. As the guards fought to separate the two men, he would snap the warden's neck, ensuring Warden Pendleton's death.

Seth considered that one of the guards would pull his gun and shoot him before he could finish his vengeful deed. With this new thought in mind, he refined the plan. As soon as he grabbed the warden, he would turn the lowlife miscreant toward his men, but that would mean not getting to look into the warden's eyes. The plot to murder the warden continued scrolling through his mind with one refinement after another. There was no way to turn it off.

As time in the dark, rank smelling cell continued slipping by, various versions of the same murderous act consumed his every thought. He remembered reading in the Bible where it spoke about a man lying in his bed plotting evil. It was sinful, wrong in every way, but the demons inside Seth's head wouldn't let go. Mercer had been right, when he'd pointed toward him in the courtroom and boldly stated he was possessed with evil spirits.

The next day was worse. The half cooked, watered down slime Seth expected for breakfast never came. A guard had approached the solid steel door as usual, knocked then walked away laughing. He had lost many of his rights when he'd entered the prison, but this went beyond cruel and unusual punishment. Third world countries were often accused by the United States government as violating the human rights of their people, but the politicians turned a blind eye to what was going on right here in America.

Seth didn't think his anger could grow any stronger, but it did. Every day in the hole had made his body weaker and his mind more corrupt. Even though he exercised, without proper nourishment his muscles were losing strength - strength he needed to face the warden in order to carry out his plan. He ran his hands over his torso. He could feel his ribs. He had to get out of there and get some food. He didn't think he'd last much longer.

"How can they get away with this?" he cried out in the darkness.

Seth had long ago lost track of time. In his mind, it was an hour, maybe five, maybe it had been days, but someone approached the cell door again. He sat in the corner waiting to hear the knock followed by laughter. He listened as the keys rattled, the lock clicked, and the cell door opened.

"Boone," a rough voice called out. "Put your hands on top of your head and come out. You know the routine."

Seth was blinded by the light pouring into the cell. Slowly moving toward the door, he saw two guards standing outside waiting. One guard grabbed him from behind while the other clapped his hands against Seth's ears. Instant pain and ringing ensued. Seth could barely hear the guard say, "Maybe that will clean your damn ears out so you can hear and obey, boy."

With his ears ringing, barely able to see, and only able to walk in a stoop, Seth was led through a familiar door to the courtyard where the fire hose awaited. He stumbled forward in the bright sunlight. The cold water came with tremendous force knocking him down. It was painful. The water was cold, but it wasn't icy as it had been other times. It was June 18th. The cold spell had passed days ago. Today the temperature outside was 76 degrees.

The guards laughed heartily as they watched Seth roll around on the concrete, trying to dodge the force from the spray. After a two minute dousing, the water stopped. Seth had to be lifted to his feet. The ringing in his ears had stopped, and his eyes had adjusted to the light, but he was weak. He tried standing twice, but fell each time.

The two guards smoked cigarettes, allowing Seth time to gather his faculties and rest. They punched him in the back with their batons as he stumbled back inside the building. He staggered about aimlessly. A guard grabbed him, shoving him forward, toward the doors leading to the showers. Inside the shower area, the guard shoved Seth in the back of the head, sending him flying. He nearly fell, but caught himself just before slamming into the wall.

It was no different from other times when he'd arrived in the familiar shower area - soap and a towel were sitting nearby in a folding chair. A clean pressed set of hunter-orange prison clothes were underneath the towel. He wanted to lash out, scream at the guards, but resisted. He detested everything about them, their lives, the jobs they did every day. He was smart enough though to know any backtalk would bring more pain, and on that day, he couldn't have survived being beaten by the guards.

"You've got five minutes," a guard grunted. "Wash the rest of the stink off your ugly ass and get dressed."

Seth moved slowly toward the showerhead. He lathered his body with soap and rinsed. The clean feeling was therapeutic. He was weak, but felt a bit rejuvenated. He tilted his head back and allowed the wonderful stream of lukewarm water to flow over his face and down his torso.

"Hurry it up in there," Seth heard one of the officers yell.

Seth turned the water off and walked over to the chair. Once dry, he slowly dressed himself, holding to the back of the chair with one hand for support due to his weakened state. He was hoping the next move would be a trip to the warden's office. Although he was very weak, he knew he could muster up enough strength to carry out the plot that had consumed his every thought. He might die during the struggle, but not before choking the life out of Warden Pendleton. *Yes! Finally! The warden is about to die!*

The guards returned, and the handcuffs went back on Seth's wrists. He protested, claiming he was so weak the handcuffs weren't necessary, but to no avail. They led him down the long corridor back to the main building housing the general population, but they turned toward 'D' block. Seth was confused. This was unusual, something he'd not expected. He'd already figured out they weren't going to the warden's office – but why 'D' Block?

"I want to see the warden," Seth cried out. "Please stop. I don't know where we are going, but I really need to see the warden! I want to see the warden!"

His pleading with the guards only got him two strikes in the back from a baton.

Seth continued mumbling about seeing the warden as they led him down 'D' block on the East Wing of the building.

He'd never been in 'D' block. It appeared no different than 'C' block, where he'd lived in the tiny cell with Shanghai. They passed by the cells lined on each side of the walkway. Prisoners jeered and shouted profane remarks. Seth paid them no mind. His thoughts were consumed with Warden Pendleton. It wasn't supposed to be like this. This wasn't right. They were supposed to take him before the warden. Little did he know, the warden didn't want to see him, nor did he want him back in 'C' Block with his friend Shanghai.

Near the end of 'D' block, they stopped. The door on an empty cell to the left was open. The mattresses on both bunks were rolled up, indicating no one was occupying the cell. At least for now, Seth would have a cell all to himself.

One of the guards removed the handcuffs then shoved Seth into the small cell. Looking up to the overhead camera, the guard gave thumbs up and the cell door closed shut, making a loud clang as metal engaged metal and the lock activated. After that, the guards turned to walk away, saying nothing.

Seth turned and grabbed hold of the bars, pressing his face between two of the bars as if he were going to squeeze through.

"Hey, don't I get fed today?" he yelled back at the guards.

One of the guards returned briefly. He stopped close to the bars and looked inside, staring at Seth, only a foot away.

"Your ugly ass is being transferred out of here tomorrow morning. You can eat at your new home when you get there."

"TRANSFERRED!" Seth yelled out, surprised. "Transferred to where?"

"Your lucky little ass is headed to Leavenworth Supermax."

The guard loved the surprised look on Seth's face. He turned and walked away, laughing.

"Damn man," an inmate across the aisle from Seth's cell said. "Leavenworth Supermax is reserved for the bad-asses of the bad-asses."

After pacing back and forth in the tiny cell all evening, Seth laid down to rest. The clean bed was soothing, but it brought little comfort. He'd heard nothing but horror stories about Leavenworth Supermax, a prison within a prison at Leavenworth, Kansas.

The Supermax side of Leavenworth Prison was added twenty years ago. Its purpose was to house the most violent criminals in the country. Leavenworth was a Federal Prison. Seth wondered if the feds had made the decision to send him there.

State Prisons on occasion transfer prisoners to Leavenworth Supermax for execution. If a prisoner had no one fighting for them through the judicial system, it was a way for the States to rid themselves of scum quickly. Those sent to Leavenworth Supermax were executed within a few months, a year tops. They were lost causes, all but forgotten by those outside the prison walls. The executions at Leavenworth Supermax were never publicized. There were no television reports, nothing in the newspapers. It was all done quietly, behind the scenes without the media present. Once a prisoner was sent to the Supermax, they were never heard from again.

Warden Pendleton didn't have any trouble convincing the governor to order Seth's transfer and execution. Seth had killed his parents, plus five inmates at the prison. If they continued to house this cold-blooded killer, it would only be a matter of time before someone else died. Chances are it could be a guard next time.

Seth had no money, no family, no attorney, no one willing to help him. Every day Seth Boone lived, it cost the Commonwealth of Virginia hundreds of dollars. Over time, the housing, food, and medical care, would grow into a fortune, all spent to keep a hardened criminal alive. It was time to rid the State, and all of society, of this worthless human.

Seth's ravenous hunger and thoughts of placing his hands around the warden's neck ruined any chance of him sleeping. He would have eaten a rat if one had been unfortunate enough to enter his cell. Laying on the bed, staring at the concrete ceiling, he pushed his hunger pangs away as he thought about Warden Pendleton.

He expected the warden wouldn't transfer him before they had a meeting. Pendleton would want to take his last stab, rubbing salt into his wounds. He'd want to tell Seth all about Leavenworth Supermax and what was in store for him once he arrived there. That's when Seth would make his move. If he could get his hands free of cuffs, he'd carry out his plan to kill the man with his bare hands. The guards would kill him, he was certain of that now. Seth decided that wouldn't be a bad thing though. It would end his misery and it would do so without him going to Kansas, only to suffer more before getting the needle.

Seth looked forward to breakfast the next morning. He needed food to gain the strength he was going to need. After that, he was certain the guards would come for him, taking him to the warden's office for a good tongue-lashing.

The warden doesn't know it, but his tongue will be hanging out his mouth like a dead animal when I'm done.

25

Seth never got the opportunity to eat breakfast. Minutes before it was time for the cell doors to open that morning, two plain-clothes officers bearing side arms came to his cell. He was handcuffed and placed in leg irons with a short chain between them. As the officers marched him down the corridor, he had to take short choppy steps to keep up with their pace.

A plain white, passenger van, was sitting just outside of 'D' block, in the grass, close to the basketball courts. The officers grabbed Seth's arms and lifted him into the van through the open side door. As they buckled him in, Seth looked around, still expecting to see the warden. Pendleton would want to get the last word in. No one was there, however.

The meeting with the warden never materialized. The door slammed closed, and the two men climbed into the front. A minute later, they were outside the prison gates and on their way.

Seth was upset. He'd been planning his attack on the warden for days. His hands were aching to reach out and grab the man by the throat and watch him struggle for air, finding none. All the dreams, all the planning, it was all to no avail. He was free of Radford and the warden, but on his way to a far worse place, if that were possible.

Seth's thoughts soon turned to other things. It had been a long time since he'd ridden in a vehicle and a long time since he'd seen scenery from outside the prison walls. He wondered what route they would take, and how long it would be before they got to Kansas. It was nice seeing cars go by, and houses along the roadway, but Seth's mind wouldn't allow him to really enjoy the view. He began thinking about Leavenworth Supermax. It caused his empty stomach to twist into a bundle of knots.

The officers were silent, saying nothing. Seth remained quiet as well. He'd learned that unless you were spoken to, it was best to keep your lips zipped. Prisoners who opened their mouths to talk when the guards hadn't asked a question were normally hit with batons, or they might get a fist or elbow up the side of their head.

Seth had studied an atlas at the prison library many times in the past. He liked geography and had often dreamed of traveling the country once he'd served his sentence and gained his freedom. He was traveling now, but he wasn't free, not now, not ever. Freedom, precious freedom, was something he'd never know again.

There was a map lying on top the console, with a route marked in red. The part of the map Seth could see showed a route going north of Interstate 81 then west on Interstate 64. He determined from the map that he wouldn't be flying to Kansas. He supposed a private flight was too expensive, and someone dressed in prison clothing with handcuffs and leg irons would be too unsettling to passengers on a commercial flight.

He predicted it was an hour's drive to Interstate 64, then across West Virginia, Kentucky, and on westward until reaching Kansas. It was a good fifteen to eighteen-hour drive to Leavenworth. He was hoping his escorts wouldn't take turns at the wheel and drive without stopping overnight. Seth was in no hurry to arrive in Kansas. Besides, if he were in a hotel somewhere overnight, an opportunity of escape might present itself. If it failed and he was shot, it would only mean dying a few months earlier than scheduled.

The driver took the route Seth expected, heading west on interstate 64. He watched the scenery go by, enthralled by the colorful folds of the mountains and the lush green fields of the valleys. He wondered what it would be like to be there hiking along those blue ridges, free from the bonds that man had placed on him. Although escape to that place was unlikely, he dreamed of it. He would rush toward those grandly carved mountains and disappear forever, living off the land. Perhaps he could build the cabin he'd constructed over and again while serving time in the hole.

A few hours passed before arriving in Beckley, West Virginia. The driver took an exit off the interstate and headed west on State Route 3. Seth was hoping they were headed to some out of the way mom & pop restaurant favored by the officers. He was salivating at the thought of a blimp-sized juicy cheeseburger. After ten minutes on the curvy road, at a speed well above the limit, Seth became concerned that something else was taking place. He broke the silence.

"Where are we going, Sirs?" Seth asked cautiously and politely.

The officer sitting in the front passenger seat turned to look at Seth.

"Shut the hell up," he replied.

Seth pulled his head back as his eyes widened. He was in no position to argue with the man. Continued questioning would only cause his face to become swollen. He sat silently, watching the road, trying to determine why they were off the beaten path. He could feel perspiration running down his back and trickling down the side of his face. He was genuinely scared. He was wondering if the two men who'd taken him from the prison were going to kill him and dump his body somewhere. *This is something the warden planned! He's going to meet us somewhere and kill me himself!*

Twenty minutes passed. They drove through a community called Glen Daniels. They left State Route 3 at that point and continued west on State Route 99. After another twenty minutes, they began climbing a ten-mile long curvy mountain range. After reaching the top, they descended a few miles before Route 99 ended at State Route 85. Just before reaching the intersection, the driver pulled over at a wide spot on the right shoulder. The officer on the passenger side got out. The driver unfastened his seatbelt and turned around to face Seth - with his pistol drawn. Seth froze. This was the end. *The warden has won again. These men are going to say I tried to escape, and they had to shoot me in the back!*

The officer fired nine shots in Seth's direction. The sound of the gun being fired was deafening. Other than the initial flinch, Seth remained motionless. He was numb. He sat there as if frozen in a block of ice. He knew he was dead.

As the smoke cleared, he waited for the searing sensation of pain to rock his body and to see blood flowing from his torso like a rapid moving river. The officer seemed disappointed that Seth hadn't screamed and cried for mercy. The shots had hit the van roof, the back window, and both sides of the bench seat where Seth was sitting. The odor of gunpowder, plastic, and seared fabric filled the air. A million dust particles floated about, swarming like a hive of bees that had just witnessed their nest being destroyed.

The side door of the van suddenly slid opened and the officer who'd been occupying the passenger side of the van climbed in and sat down beside him.

"Well I'll be damned. You do have ice water running through your veins!" the officer said to Seth.

Seth, realizing that he'd not been hit, shot a look of pure undefiled hatred at the officer. If this was some sort of joke, it was the sickest of them all.

The driver got out of the van. The officer beside Seth then drew a pistol and began firing toward the front of the van, shattering the windshield, hitting the seats, and ripping apart the dashboard. Seth sat there watching, wide eyed, bewildered, and trying his best to breathe.

Another van suddenly pulled in behind them. It was white also, and two plain clothes officers were inside. The officer beside Seth re-holstered his sidearm then unbuckled Seth's seatbelt. As the officer climbed out of the van, he pulled Seth along behind him.

Seth was quickly led back toward the van that had just arrived. As he was being pushed in that direction, the two men in the new van had the side door open. They pulled a man who appeared to be dead out of the van. They dragged the body past him, toward the van he'd just left, the one that looked as if it had gone through a war zone.

The officer half pushed, half threw, Seth into the side door of the second van. As soon as he landed in the seat, the officer buckled him in. Sitting there motionless, he looked forward. One of the officers drove the bullet-riddled van to the edge of the embankment. As the officer was getting out of the van, two others were ready to load the dead or unconscious man, into the driver's seat.

The fourth officer opened the back doors of the van Seth was sitting in. He retrieved two gas cans, slammed the doors closed, then quickly headed toward the others. Seth was in shock. He watched as the officer dumped gasoline inside the van, even pouring some of the gas on the man in the driver's seat.

After checking the highway for no traffic, the van was put into gear. All four officers got behind the van and pushed it to the edge of the embankment. The officer who had driven Seth to that location lit a signal flare. He opened the back door of the van and threw the flare inside just as the other three men pushed it over the embankment.

The van instantly became a fireball then disappeared as it headed downward into the gorge. Seth estimated it was a four to five hundred foot near vertical drop to the bottom. He couldn't see the van once it left the side of the mountain, but seconds later, he heard it crash. A column of smoke rising from far below slithered upward as if it were being belched out of a volcano.

The officers from the second van ran back. One jumped into the driver's seat while the other opened the back doors and threw the gas cans in. The back doors slammed shut, and a few seconds later the officer was climbing in the front passenger side. Both men were breathing heavily. Seth could smell gasoline fumes coming from the cans behind him. The men didn't look at Seth. They ignored him, as if he wasn't there. He felt like he was sitting alone in a theater, watching a movie on the big movie screen as a crime unfolded.

The officers who picked Seth up at the prison and drove him to this lofty mountain pinnacle scurried over the embankment, toward the burning van below. The driver of the van Seth was in wiped his brow with a handkerchief, started the engine, and pulled onto the highway. At the intersection, the van turned left, heading south on State Route 85. The curvy road descended steeply down the mountain to a small mining town named Oceana.

Just as the other officers had been, these two were silent, saying nothing. After what he'd just witnessed, Seth was too scared to ask questions. He sat silently, staring out the windshield, listening to his heart thump in his chest. His mind was reeling, trying to put together this gigantic puzzle, but failing to find two pieces that matched.

Arriving at Main Street in Oceana, the driver turned left, toward Pineville. Twenty minutes later, they turned off the highway onto a single-lane paved road that winded up another mountain. Seth peered out the side window. There weren't any guardrails on the narrow road. If the driver ran off the shoulder, they'd roll around, bouncing off trees like a pinball, until reaching the bottom several hundred feet below. His empty stomach of twisted knots drew even tighter.

After reaching the top of the mountain, they followed another narrow road to a small airstrip stretched out across the ridgeline. Seth's head was still spinning. He was too scared to think clearly, still expecting this was part of some evil concocted plan developed by the warden. He didn't understand what had happened back on the other mountain, the dead body, the torching of the van, being picked up by two different officers. With every heartbeat came a thousand unanswered questions.

There was no control tower at the small airstrip. The only structures were two hangers situated fifty yards from the single runway. Seth saw a twin-engine Cessna aircraft sitting in front of the first hanger with its props turning.

The van pulled up beside the aircraft, and the two officers got out. The officer who had been on the passenger side opened the side door, unbuckled Seth, and helped him out of the van. The officer was much gentler getting Seth out of the van than when he'd been thrown in. He turned Seth around then removed the leg irons and the handcuffs.

Seth wanted to stretch his arms and rub his wrists, but as soon as the cuffs came off, he was grabbed by the shoulder and led to an open door on the Cessna. He climbed into one of the rear seats, and the officer climbed in beside him. The only other person in the plane was the pilot. *How odd*, Seth thought. *Why would they go through all this to take me to Kansas? I'm missing something! Who was the dead man? Are they going to kill me? What could possibly be going on?*

The door on the jet closed. A minute later, they were at the end of the runway, turning and ready to take off. As the plane picked up speed, it zoomed past the hangers. Seth looked out the window and saw the van. It was heading back to the road leading off the mountain.

The plane shot upwards, turned, and headed west. For the first time since leaving Radford, Seth began to think he wasn't headed to Leavenworth. He began to think this was some sort of escape planned by the stranger, Foreman. He wanted to believe that was true, that this was an escape, and that he was being freed, but he was afraid to believe such a thing could actually happen. That was something only read about in books, not something that happened in real life.

Once the plane leveled off, the officer beside Seth moved forward where an ice chest was sitting. He came back with two cans of Coke and two packaged tuna salad sandwiches. He extended a can of the soda and one of the sandwiches toward Seth, who was more than willing to accept the food.

"I expect you're hungry, cowboy," the man said. They were the first words he'd had heard the man speak. "Eat up. And, welcome to your new life," the man said with a wide grin.

Seth's brain hadn't slowed down. He was weak, and felt like he might pass out. He kept waiting for the man to laugh, just like the guards outside the cell when he was in the hole. No laughter came though. The man simply opened his sandwich and took a bite.

Seth was famished. He could taste the tuna before it touched his lips. He ripped open the package and all but inhaled the sandwich. His brain, aside from trying to figure out what happening, had been crying out for food. He thought the sandwich was the best thing he'd ever eaten. The first drink of soda burned his throat, but it felt good entering his stomach.

After he was finished eating, Seth eased back in the seat and tried to relax. For the first time in well over an hour, his heart rate began slowing, returning to normal. The food gave Seth comfort from the hunger pangs, and helped him to think clearly again. The officer, or whatever he was, had welcomed him to his new life. One side of Seth's brain was telling him this was real, that he had been freed, that he had escaped prison. The other side of his brain was screaming that this new life meant Leavenworth Supermax. After all, the plane was flying in a westerly direction.

Stealthily slipping his hand down his right leg, Seth pinched himself hard, expecting he would awaken and find himself back in the hole at Radford. The questions were still mounting. He thought again about the events that had unfolded. He realized that if this were some ill devised plan dreamt up by the warden, Seth Boone would have been the one in the van that went over the mountain in flames.

This was truly an escape! The dead man in the van was supposed to be him. If they were headed to Leavenworth, he'd still be in the first van, on the Interstate, handcuffed and bound with leg irons. Instead, his hands and legs were free, and he was in a small plane, heading who knows where, but most assuredly, it wasn't Kansas.

He felt light, as if the weight of the world had been lifted off his shoulders. He was out of prison. He was away from the hundreds of inmates, many of whom would like to see him dead. More than that, he was free from Warden Pendleton. He was euphoric! He wasn't in a cold damp cell. He wasn't being watched by guards and other inmates. He wasn't thinking about death row, or how much time he'd have before the order came down for his execution.

It was all he could do to control his emotions. He wanted to lift both arms upward in the air and shake his fists in victorious exultation. He refrained, however. There was still a fraction of doubt in his head. He was also afraid any form of celebration might bring a hard swung baton down on his head or extremities.

26

The flight was excruciatingly long. There was virtually no conversation whatsoever. Seth didn't have a watch, but estimated the trip to be five to six hours in duration. The plane finally descended, and they landed on a grass airstrip by a secluded ranch. Never having traveled much, Seth didn't know where he was, but expected it was somewhere in Wyoming or perhaps the Dakotas. The sun was beginning to lay low in the sky as the plane came to a stop.

Stepping off the plane, Seth observed the land. It was flat. The high mountains in the distance provided a picturesque backdrop. It was beautiful country, and the air was fresh. He had been in prison for a long time. Being out in such an open space, he felt small, as small as an ant.

An aircraft tow vehicle came out of the half-moon shaped corrugated aluminum hanger. The tow operator was preparing to transport the plane inside the hanger. A pickup truck pulled up beside Seth and the officer. They climbed in the back seat of the extended cab truck and rode to the ranch house a mile away. The road was lined along both sides with a white wooden fence. Seth counted two dozen horses near the fence, and saw many more off in the distance. It was a beautiful site. He couldn't help but smile. Although he had a million questions, and feared what lay ahead, his insides were jumping for joy like a young boy on Christmas morning.

The two-story house was two-hundred feet across the front, and had a circular drive that led up to a large covered porch. Stately oak trees were evenly spaced across the front and back of the house. It looked like a western ranch homestead with a country charm. To the left and right of the house, a few hundred feet away, were two large barns, both freshly painted. Farming equipment was parked outside of both barns.

As soon at the truck stopped, Seth and the officer climbed out. The driver then sped off, toward the barn to the right. The officer looked at Seth, extended his hand to shake, and spoke for only the second time all day.

"Time for proper introductions," he said in a deep voice. "My name is Trainer. You and I will be spending lots of time together."

Oh great, Seth thought. *I hope he warms up if that's the case.*

Seth was wondering if everyone in this outfit had a single name. There was Foreman, and now Trainer. He expected he'd be given a single name. *If so, what will it be? Escapee, Killer, or perhaps, Assassin.*

At the door of the house, they were greeted by a small Chinese man. He was dressed in white pants, white shirt, and was wearing a white chef's hat. The man was old, had a heavily wrinkled face, and squinty eyes. His long gray hair was pulled back and tied into a braided ponytail, which hung out of the hat and down his back. The man smiled continuously and seemed to be full of life.

The man bowed then said, "Ahhh. You Seth. My name is Buffalo."

Seth couldn't help but chuckle. This man was Asian. He was small in stature, unlike the buffalo of the Great Plains. He wondered how the man got such an odd name. It was another single name too. He was hoping he'd have some say in what his own name would be. If it was to be his choice, he was going to give himself the name of 'Eagle'.

"Me take care of you," Buffalo said smiling widely, sporting two gold teeth in the center top. "You no follow me to guest room."

Seth was guessing that Buffalo's no - meant 'yes'.

Following Buffalo up the stairs to the second level, Seth was led to a spacious suite. Walking through the door, they were in the sitting room. It looked a hundred times larger than the tiny cell he'd been living in. To the right of the sitting room was an oversized bedroom with a king-sized bed. The bathroom was large enough to house four inmates. Seth smiled. He hoped he would be living here for a long time. He could hardly contain himself.

Buffalo pinched his nose with two fingers and looked closely at Seth.

"You stink. You get shower, leave clothes by door. Buffalo burn yucky prison clothes."

Buffalo smiled again, the gold teeth sparkling from the overhead lights. "New clothes for Seth in bedroom. Once dressed, you come downstairs, supper ready in thirty minute, you no be late."

Buffalo left the room quickly, closing the door behind him. Seth spent a few minutes walking around the guest suite, smelling the fresh flowers in vases, feeling the soft mattress of the king-sized bed, looking out the window at the horses trotting around the fields. He pinched himself again to see if it was a dream. He was out of prison. He thought this could never be. He was free! He wasn't in Radford, wasn't heading for the Supermax at Leavenworth, and he wasn't on death row.

Foreman was real. It hadn't been some cruel joke of the wardens. Seth didn't know what lay ahead, but it didn't matter. He would do anything they asked. He'd do anything to stay away from the hell he'd been in since that dreadful night back in Abingdon.

There was an immeasurable amount of renewed hope. Seth was excited. He felt as light as a feather in a windstorm. As he went through the bedroom, he pulled out dresser drawers and found new clothes inside each one. Each was packed with neatly folded shirts and sweaters all his size. He opened the two bedroom closets. It was the same, full of new jeans, slacks, and dress shirts. The shoe racks were full of boots, running shoes, and all sorts of casual footwear.

In the bathroom, sitting on a tall square table was a cell phone and a wallet. Seth picked the wallet up and examined it. Curious, he unfolded the wallet and peeked inside. It contained several bills, fifties and hundreds.

A VISA card was in one of the credit-card slots. In another slot, was a plastic card wrapped in a thin waxy paper. He removed the credit card. There was a decal on the back, giving an 800 number to call in order to active the card. On the front was the name 'Tyler DuPont'.

He removed the card wrapped in paper from the wallet. On the back of the paper was written 'Your new identity'. He quickly unfolded the paper and saw that it was a driver's license. He was shocked - his photo was on the upper left corner. The photo looked recent, making him wonder when and where it was taken. *It had to have been taken at Radford, but since the day I first arrived there, I don't recall ever having sat for a photo.*

The address on the license was a street in Meridian, Mississippi. Underneath the photo was the same name as the one on the credit card, 'Tyler DuPont'.

"So this is my new name," he said aloud. "I guess I get two names, not a single one like Foreman, Trainer, or Buffalo."

He thought back over the days' events. There was no more Seth Boone. He'd died in a shootout with officers after somehow obtaining one of their weapons. His body had been consumed in the burning van that plummeted over that high mountain back in West Virginia. He wondered who had really burned in that van. Was it the real Tyler DuPont, or someone else? He expected he'd never know.

A small square box sat on the table, only inches from where the wallet had been. Seth now Tyler, picked it up and opened the lid. Inside was a gold Rolex watch. He knew it was for him. "Wow," he whispered.

Stripping free from the soiled and stinky prison outfit, Tyler walked naked through the sitting room and placed the bright orange clothes by the entrance. He then headed back to the bathroom. He turned the water on and got under the showerhead.

He stood in the pulsating streams of soothing hot water, allowing it to pour over his head. "My name is Tyler DuPont," Seth said several times. Having his name changed was something he'd never given any thought to before. The more he repeated his new name, the more he liked it. He thought about the luxuries he was about to enjoy and the new identity. He truly had begun a new life.

After several minutes of scrubbing to get clean, Tyler stepped out of the shower, reached for a towel, and dried off. He walked out of the bathroom and over to the bed. He pressed down on the mattress again, imagining how good it was going to feel to sleep in a large comfortable bed.

A pair of tan Docker pants and a black Polo pullover shirt had been neatly folded and placed at the foot of the bed, along with a pair of boxer briefs. Sitting on the floor was a new pair of canvas loafers. He knew it was meant for him to wear those clothes to supper, so he put them on. It felt wonderful to have on nice comfortable clothes. He took in several deep breathes, smelling the fabric. After pinching himself once more, he looked in the dresser mirror and smiled. He repeated his new name several times then went downstairs.

Something delicious was cooking. He could smell the aroma of food as he descended the stairs. Buffalo was at the bottom of the steps waiting for him.

"I've hardly eaten at all for days," Tyler said. "Please tell me I get to partake in eating whatever is cooking."

"Ah - you hungry! That good! You eat tasty meal, Seth – Ugh, Tyler, I mean." Buffalo was again all smiles. He bowed out his chest and tried to stand tall. "You clean up good, Mr. DuPont, you fine looking young man, very strong!"

Tyler followed Buffalo down a short hallway and through a set of oak double doors to the large dining area. Inside the dining room, was a long rectangular table covered with a white cloth. Counting the ones on each end, there were eighteen chairs situated around the table, but only two were occupied. At the far end sat Trainer and Foreman, across from each other. The chair at the head of the table was vacant. The two men stood as Tyler entered.

"Welcome, Tyler," Foreman said, gesturing with his hand for Tyler to sit at the head of the table. "From here on out, you will refer to yourself as Tyler DuPont. Erase Seth Boone from your memory."

Tyler nodded then walked to the head of the table. As he sat down, so did Foreman and Trainer.

"I know you have questions, Tyler," Foreman said. "We will soon get to answering them, but right now, I'm starving, and I feel most certain you are as well."

Foreman was right. Tyler felt as if he could eat a horse, bones, and all. There were several covered dishes on the table. Buffalo removed the covers before heading off to what Tyler assumed was the kitchen.

After viewing the extravagant room upstairs, seeing all the clothes, the wallet full of money, and a Rolex, Tyler was guessing lobster and prime rib lay beneath the covers. Like so many times over the last week, he was wrong. Instead, it was golden fried chicken, mashed potatoes, white gravy, green beans, corn, and a hot steaming pone of white cornbread.

The food was well prepared, and there was plenty of it. It was much more than he was accustomed to getting. He'd survived for many days on soupy grits, watered down oatmeal or a slice of stale bread smothered in some rancid unknown sauce. Tyler looked like a finely oiled machine as he methodically loaded his fork and shoved bite after bite into his mouth. In that one sitting, he consumed more than he had eaten in the last three weeks combined. Foreman looked at Tyler and smiled.

"I suppose we'd better hold off on the peach cobbler and ice cream until you digest that freight train of food you just wolfed down," Foreman said, then laughed.

"Whew! You're right, no dessert for me," Tyler said. "Wow. I'm grateful. Thank you all so much! I'm well fed, wearing fine clothes, and I'm FREE! And, for all that, I could never thank you enough!"

Everyone arose from the table and walked out of the dining area. They entered the parlor, where a fire was burning in the open-hearth fireplace. Foreman and Tyler sat down in wing backed chairs sitting perpendicular to the fireplace. Trainer went to the liquor cabinet, retrieved a bottle of twenty-year-old scotch and three glasses. He sat down on a Victorian sofa facing Tyler and Foreman and put the bottle and glasses on a mahogany coffee table with a glass top.

"Anyone care for a drink?" Trainer asked.

"Yes, please," Foreman said.

Tyler's mind raced back. The last time his lips had touched liquor was the night he'd picked up the baseball bat in Julian's room and ended his parents' lives.

"No, thank you. I'm fine," Tyler said to Trainer.

"So, what do you think of this place?" Foreman asked proudly.

"I'm still in a bit of shock from today's events," Tyler said honestly. "I'm overwhelmed. This is more than anyone could ask for. Again, I don't know how to properly thank you."

The evening conversation turned out to be anything but a question and answer session like Tyler had expected.

They talked about football, weather, politics, and a little about the ranch and the horses.

"Tomorrow, after breakfast, we will get down to business," Foreman said as he rose from his chair, ready to turn in for the night. He opened his arms wide as he looked at Tyler. "Feel free to roam the property. Go anywhere you please."

Tyler was exhausted, and the large portions of food he'd eaten made him feel sluggish and sleepy. He left as Foreman did, climbed the stairs, and entered his bedroom. The bed felt like heaven. Never would he had ever dreamed he'd be sleeping on a comfortable bed again. He laid there thinking, but only for a minute. Tyler went out like a light being turned off.

27

The next morning at 6 a.m., Buffalo came knocking on the door.

"Tyler DuPont, this is Buffalo," he bellowed out after knocking. "Time to get up. Breakfast downstairs in thirty minute."

Tyler sat up in the bed and rubbed his eyes. He still couldn't believe he was there. He rolled over in the spacious bed. Only in his dreams did he ever think he'd sleep again on anything other than a small worn-out prison mattress.

Twenty-four hours ago, he was expecting to have breakfast in the mess hall at Radford Prison. Afterward, he imagined he'd meet with the warden and do his very best to end the man's life. Now he was somewhere great, somewhere unknown. It was as wonderful as any place he could ever imagine. He'd received new clothes, ate a great meal, slept in a comfortable bed, and he'd gotten a new identity. There were no loud inmates shouting profanity every second, no clanking of items against bars, no one barking out orders through a loudspeaker, and no guards.

Someone, likely Buffalo, had slipped a Denver newspaper beneath Tyler's door. He bent over to pick it up.

The front headline read 'Killer Prisoner Attempts Escape – Burns in Fiery Crash'.

Taking the paper and climbing back in bed, Tyler, propped his head on two pillows, crossed his feet, and read the full article. It described how Seth Boone was being transferred from Radford to Leavenworth by two guards when he broke free of his handcuffs and grabbed a gun.

…..The driver pulled off the highway, pulled his gun, and returned fire at the prisoner firing wildly in his direction. His partner opened the door and jumped out just in time. The driver then jumped out also. The convict jumped into the driver's seat, and apparently in all the excitement, put the van in drive instead of reverse. Pressing hard on the accelerator, the van, instead of backing toward the highway, plunged forward over the embankment, landing 700 feet below in a deep ravine. The gas tank, having been ruptured during the gunfight, burst into flames as it tumbled down the mountain. The two officers, although badly shaken, received only scratches during the ordeal. Boone's body was burned beyond recognition, ending the life of a disturbed young man who had brutally murdered his parents and five Radford Prison inmates.

The story was pretty much along the lines Tyler had expected. Seth Boone was dead. Reading about his own death was more disturbing than he thought it would be. Those who knew him would remember Seth Boone as a vicious killer, the boy who killed his parents with a baseball bat. Arthur and Rita would read the papers and believe the lie about his death. So would everyone else. Tyler tossed the paper aside. He wanted to read the article again later, as if he expected it would change somehow and depict Seth Boone as an innocent young man who'd been handed a raw deal and was, indeed, truly innocent of those so-called murders.

After a quick shower, Tyler put on the clothes he'd worn the night before. As soon as he opened the bedroom door, it hit him – the unmistakable aroma of bacon frying. In prison, they were never served meat for breakfast. Tyler rushed down the stairs, his mind troubled by the article, but his mouth watering with the thoughts of consuming strip after strip of perfectly fried bacon.

After breakfast, Tyler was back in the parlor sitting with Foreman and Trainer.

"I hope you slept well, Tyler," Foreman said. "Today we begin your training. This will be your home for the next twelve months. We have nearly nine-thousand acres here. Roam around as you please – you are free to do so. Smell the air, jump for joy! There are horses, dirt bikes, and four-wheel drive recreational vehicles. Everything here is at your disposal."

Tyler listened. He was still trying to wrap his head around what had happened the day prior. He had died yesterday, and today he was in paradise. He pinched his right leg lightly, still thinking he was going to awaken. There were more surprises in store, but unlike prison, he expected the surprises would be pleasant ones. This place, wherever it was, was much more than some dude ranch where everyone rode on horses all day checking fences.

"Your days will start with breakfast at half-past-six. There will always be a light lunch provided, and a full-course evening meal. If you should happen to get hungry between meals, feel free to make a run through the kitchen, there's always plenty of food in the refrigerators and cupboard. There will be three, three-hour training exercises daily, not always on the same schedule and sometimes at night. There will also be a lot of classroom and study time in addition to that. Don't worry about getting bored, that won't happen."

"Much of your time will be spent with me," Trainer pitched in. "I'll be the lead on much of the survival skill training, explosives, and firearms – plus a ton of other fun shit."

"You'll be taught a lot from the classroom, things like the court system, politics, and the stock markets. Those and many more things," Foreman added. "By the time you leave to start your mission, you'll speak Spanish, know a bit about accounting, have some engineering skills, and after studying theatre here at the Foreman school of acting, you'll be a relatively good con man. In addition to all that, you'll be an expert with firearms and explosives."

Tyler was astonished. He'd hit the lottery. He was about to become the lead actor for a new spy series, except what he was about to get into was real life spying, not moving making.

"Why Spanish and not some other language?" Tyler asked.

"It will all become clear in time, Tyler," Foreman replied. "Oh, I almost forgot. You'll be taught martial arts, fine-tuning what Shanghai taught you in prison."

Tyler wondered how Foreman knew about Shanghai. It appeared this man knew every aspect of his life. He couldn't hold back any longer. He had to get some answers to his thousands of questions.

"Okay. You busted me out of prison, brought me here to a land of paradise, and you want to train me. I feel special, and don't get me wrong, I'm very grateful. Actually, I'm ecstatic! I'm also curious though. What happens once this battery of training exercises is complete? And, why didn't you just pick some kid off the street instead of going through the extreme difficulty of breaking me out of prison?"

"You were picked because you're special, Tyler," Foreman said. "You have a brain, and not just any brain. You have a high IQ, yet you're not a nerd who can't function outside a laboratory. You have the right genetics, just look at your body. You've never been given steroids, never been in a real gym, yet your bulging muscles ripple as you breathe. You have the ability to read people. That's a special gift, one very valuable in our business. You have everything it takes for the type of work you will be doing."

"Well, what's the name of this outfit? What are you guys called?"

"We don't have a name," Trainer answered. "We aren't FBI, CIA, or any other acronym. We're just here. We never get praises when things go right, and when things go wrong, no one stands up for us. We have to clean up our own messes, so we're careful not to make any. On the bright side, we don't have to follow the rules if you know what I mean."

"But you're government funded, right?

"We get our funding from a variety of sources," Foreman answered. "We do get some government funding, but it's indirect, earmarked for things other than what we do of course. We have a group of private sponsors also, including a few politicians, and important business people in high places. They decide our work for us. They select a target, and we do the dirty work. Don't worry about who it is you work for or where the money comes from. I don't know it all myself. Just focus on your training and enjoy a second chance at life, something very few ever get. We have a nice sized budget, so you'll be able to enjoy the finer things in life."

"I don't mean to sound ungrateful," Tyler said. "But doesn't all this just make us a group of vigilantes?"

"In some ways," Foreman said. "We don't select the targets however, someone else does. Yes, you could say we are vigilantes of a higher degree perhaps. Assassins, vigilantes, hit men – no matter what you call it, people die. Think of us as doing a service to the country, taking care of business where our broken down court system has failed to do so."

Tyler wrinkled his forehead, contemplating Foreman's words.

"Allow me to preach to you for minute," Foreman said. "Do you think you were treated fairly by the American injustice system? Gary McDowell stole your family fortune. If you had been given access to that money, you could have hired a decent lawyer. Do you think if that had been the case, your trial would have turned out differently? No doubt, you should have gone to prison, but do you think you deserved two life sentences? Do you think murder-one was the right charge? What about the judge? Do you think you got a fair trial? And of course there's the jury of your peers. That was a joke. It usually is. I happen to know for a fact that one of the jurors was bought off. Juror number 7 owed the IRS quite a bit of money. That suddenly went away. Money talks and bullshit walks. Four of the jurors who convicted you had their mind made up before the trial started.

Tyler listened closely. Foreman was right. He truly believed he'd gotten a raw deal.

"Are you serious, the jury was rigged!"

"I was there. I knew some underhanded deals were in the works, but it wasn't confirmed until after you were locked away."

"I remember seeing you," Tyler said. "So, why were you there?"

"That's not important right now. What is important is that you're out of prison, and you're being given an opportunity few ever get."

"How did you arrange getting me out of there?"

"Again, that's not important right now. Focus on this instead. The justice system is broke. People who deserve to die are getting off on technicalities, never serving a day behind bars. Others are never caught and go on for a lifetime, murdering, robbing people of their pensions, and a host of other crimes. This country is run by cops on the take, low life lawyers, and crooked politicians. They're all looking out for themselves, and don't give a rat's ass who gets hurt or if justice is served. The United States has seventy-percent of the world's lawyers. They're all money hungry and a high percentage care about nothing else. It's all about money and the power it brings. The entire country is a mess. Our in-justice system is anything but what our founding fathers intended it to be.

"So where do I fit into all this? I mean, I think I know, but not totally."

"You're very strong and very smart. We will make you stronger and wiser. Once your training is over, you must repay your debt. You'll be given jobs to carry out, each target having a predetermined value, worth a given number of points. Your debt is 140 points, one for every year of prison sentence we saved you from serving. You were enslaved in your home. You were enslaved to Warden Pendleton. Now, you belong to me. You're my slave. Once you've paid your debt, you're a free man. Think about that, Tyler. For the first time in your life, you will be free. Most people take their freedom for granted. You never have, because you've never experienced it. Now you have that opportunity."

Tyler agreed. He'd been a slave to someone since age thirteen. He marveled at the thought of someday being able to come and go as he pleased, answering to no one. He thought about Rita. If he were free to come and go as he pleased, he could find her again. *It will be complicated though. I'm supposed to be dead."*

He had many questions, too many to ask in a day, or even a month. He didn't think a group of outlaw businessmen and politicians taking the law into their own hands was the solution to a corrupt and broken down court system though. On the other hand, however, they had gotten him out of prison. His life had been spared, so he wasn't complaining. The best thing to do was to play along, see how this training and life at the ranch turned out. *How bad could this be? I'm not in prison, and this place is unimaginable!*

"Today will be a fun day," Trainer said. "We'll tour the ranch and get you acquainted with the ranch-hands, facilities, and training staff.

"Aren't you afraid I'll run away?" Tyler asked.

"No. We aren't afraid of that," Foreman answered. "We could put a tracking device on you, but that isn't necessary. There's nowhere you can go to hide from us - trust me. Besides, I think you'll find the ranch to be quite enjoyable."

"Are there others being trained here, or just me?"

"For now, you are our lone trainee," Foreman replied. "We aren't a big agency like the FBI. We're a very small, tight-knit group. We're few in number, no flash, no fame, not a lot of drama - and we're very low key. Just as Trainer said, we don't exist. As far as the ranch goes, it's legit. We raise horses and livestock to be sold in various markets. It's the perfect front."

After a long tour of the ranch, Tyler was free to do as he wished for the remainder of the day. The ranch house had a huge library. Tyler spent several hours there, thumbing through books.

It was late in the afternoon when he decided to hop on a 4-wheeler and ride across the meadows, in the direction of a mountain to the south. After riding for what he thought was a few miles, he stopped by a stream. He sat on the bank for a while, enjoying the peacefulness of the place. The birds were singing, and several fish were jumping out of the water, catching insects flying close to the surface. Never would he have dreamed of being able to enjoy nature again. This place was marvelous. He was about to leave and head back when he heard a vehicle approaching.

It was Foreman, driving a pickup truck. He stopped and they talked for a long while, about the weather, the beauty of that place, and the abundance of fish. Foreman then turned to business. He got a serious look on his face.

"I've got something for you to memorize," Foreman said. "It's a set of numbers. I want you to implant them in your brain. Each day I want you to think about the numbers and repeat them to yourself."

"What are they?" Tyler asked.

"11-19-30-50, and 40. Remember them in that exact order. No one else is EVER, under any circumstances to learn of this conversation and these numbers. Do you understand that?"

"Sure. But, what do the numbers mean?"

"All I can say for now is that you and I are the only ones who know these numbers. I hope you never have to use them, but if you do, you must know them, and you must get them in the right order. I need you to trust me on this. I can't stress enough about how important this is."

"Okay," Tyler responded, uncertain why Foreman was telling him this. He expected it was some secret code.

"If you ever have to use those numbers, you will be asked what your favorite game is. The answer is 9-ball. Every time you and I are in a private setting from now until you leave the ranch, I'll ask you to repeat the numbers to me."

"Sounds easy enough. 11-19-30-50-40, and my favorite game is 9-ball."

"Great. Just don't ever let anyone else know. This could save your life someday."

§

At breakfast the next morning, the conversation was light.

"You haven't told me where we are," Tyler remarked.

"Does that matter?" Foreman asked.

"No. Not really," Tyler said. "I think I've figured it out though."

"Oh have you?" Foreman replied, somewhat amused. "So you tell me where the ranch is, and how you've come to your conclusion."

"We're somewhere in central Montana, perhaps toward the southern border of the state," Tyler replied.

Foreman looked at Trainer then at Tyler as he smiled.

"So, how did you determine this?" Trainer asked.

"I studied an astronomy book in the library yesterday, plus a guide on sailing by the stars. I did a little observation experiment. It was a beautiful clear night, with thousands of stars shining. I guess that's why they call Montana, 'Big Sky Country'. When I first got off the plane, I thought we were in Wyoming or the Dakotas. By watching the sun set over the range in the west yesterday, and by looking at the position of the stars last night, I refined my guess and came up with south-central Montana."

"You're already confirming that we made the right decision by selecting you," Foreman said, looking toward Trainer for confirmation. "That's pretty amazing. Your observation is off, but not by much. We're about a hundred miles west of where you determined we are. Still, that's extraordinary."

"He'll put us out of a job if we don't watch," Trainer added.

Tyler smiled, pleased that he had been able to determine where the ranch was located, but more pleased that he'd impressed Foreman and Trainer.

Shortly after breakfast, Trainer took Tyler to the rifle range. They spent the majority of three hours looking at handguns. Trainer started with the basics of handling, aiming, loading, and cleaning. They ended the last hour talking about cartridge sizes and ballistics. They covered pistols ranging from a .22 caliber to a big .45 auto. In the afternoon, Tyler spent three hours of vigorous martial arts training with an instructor who went by the name of 'Surveyor'.

Tyler wondered why he had such an odd name. He presumed that Surveyor must be someone who scoped things out. *He must be a lookout or something else besides just an instructor. What an odd group of men. I can't get over these names, like Buffalo and Surveyor.*

Surveyor was impressed by how much Tyler already knew. He asked questions about who had trained him. Shanghai had taught Tyler well. He soon discovered that Surveyor, at least an equal to Shanghai, had moves and technique's Shanghai didn't. He imagined what he learned from this man would further advance his skills and was excited about spending time with him.

From 6 p.m. to 9 p.m., it was three hours of study time with Foreman and Trainer. They went over handgun ballistics again, hand to hand combat, plus types of explosives and their characteristics. They also covered basic military tactics. Foreman informed Tyler that he'd go through many tests, both written and hands on. He would be required to master every level of the training before he was declared suitable for the field.

As the first few days passed, it was more training, demonstrations, and study time in the library. Tyler had no trouble sleeping at night. At the end of each day, he was exhausted. He was advancing at a faster pace than anyone had expected, pleasing everyone, especially Tyler.

On the first Friday after arriving at the ranch, Foreman, Trainer, Surveyor, and Tyler loaded into a Cadillac Escalade that afternoon and drove ninety miles to Sheridan. They ate dinner at a steakhouse then attended a high-school rodeo. Tyler was elated. It was the first time since being at Sarah's wake that he'd been in a public place. Unlike that dreadful evening, the hours spent at the rodeo was a time of celebration. It was fantastic.

Foreman was right. There was no way he would want to run away. He was living a dream life. The only thing missing was Rita. He still thought of her multiple times each day. He wondered where she was, how her life was, if she'd met someone. He wished he could see her, but knew that would never be possible. Seth, the boy she'd fallen in love with, had died.

He was Tyler DuPont now, a new person, being trained for one purpose only, to take human life. He'd been given a second chance to live. He would be forever grateful, but he still lacked something - something essential. He lacked being by the side of the woman who had captured his heart and still had it in her hands. He ached to see Rita.

On Saturday, Trainer took Tyler to an abandoned silver mine site. They spent the day setting off several small explosive charges. Trainer demonstrated proper handling and placement of explosives and detonators. By the end of the day, Tyler was relatively proficient in the use of nitro based dynamite, detonation cord, and C4 plastic explosives. There would be more training later, including creating larger explosions using ammonium nitrate and fuel oil, commonly known as ANFO.

On July 1st, a surprise birthday dinner was held at the ranch. It was Tyler's nineteenth birthday. He welled up with emotion and could hardly speak. The men at the ranch were his new family. He'd never been treated so well in his entire life. He was beside himself. When asked to make a wish and blow out the nineteen candles on the German chocolate cake Buffalo had made from scratch, Tyler closed his eyes and blew hard. Thoughts of being with Rita Logan flashed through his mind.

The birthday bash was one of the happiest evenings Tyler could ever remember. Life had changed so much, in a most unexpected way. Gone were the days of abuse in the Boone house back in Abingdon, and the dreadful days of prison. He was happy there on the ranch, among new friends. Janie and Gordon Boone were gone, so was Julian, but he had a new family now, one who cared about his well-being.

A few days later, Foreman didn't have much to say during breakfast. He had a worried look on his face. After eating, Tyler and Foreman walked out to the front porch of the ranch house and sat down in two of the oversized rockers.

"I've got some news I need to tell you, Tyler," Foreman said. "After I tell you, I want you to take the day off. Rest, go horseback riding, do anything you want. We won't work you today."

Tyler wondered what could possibly be wrong.

"It's Shanghai," Foreman said. "He's dead."

"NO," Tyler yelled out. "How?"

"You'll never read in the papers about what really happened. He was poisoned."

"POISONED!" Tyler said, staring wide-eyed at Foreman.

"The warden put him in the hole after busting up his cigarette smuggling ring. A day or two after Shanghai was in the hole, the warden had a guard slide a plate of raw pork into the cell. In the dark cell, unable to see what it was, Shanghai ate it. A short time later, he was deathly ill. Two

271

more days passed, and no one checked on him. Then they dragged him out of the hole and never offered him medical attention. Unable to walk, they carried him back to 'C' Block. The next morning when the doors opened for breakfast, one of the inmates found him on the floor by his bunk, dead."

Tyler jumped out of the rocker, ran across the yard, and down the road leading toward the hanger. He kept running until his legs gave out then fell to the ground. He spent the entire day out in the fields with the horses. It had been a long time since he'd cried, but he did that day, several times.

Towards the end of the day, the racking sobs that involuntarily erupted from his shaking body eventually subsided into sighs. The horses stood around Tyler and neighed as if they understood and felt his pain. Draped over a rail fence, Tyler looked at the sky and let out a long breath. He never knew so much raw emotion and grief could be contained in a single sigh.

After darkness sat in, Tyler slowly made his way back toward the lights shining through the ranch house windows. He made a vow to himself, that if he ever were truly free again, he'd hunt Warden Pendleton down and do as he'd planned the day he left Radford. He'd kill the man with his bare hands.

In the following weeks, the training became more difficult, more intense, more challenging. Still, Tyler excelled, never having to repeat any of the exercises twice. With the early morning starts, vigorous workouts, and study periods, come bedtime Tyler fell asleep soon after his head hit the pillow. As he closed his eyes each night, he cast the excitement of the day aside and turned his thoughts to Rita. In his mind, they were together, walking along a beach or having dinner at a nice restaurant. He wondered where she was, what she was doing, and if she ever thought of him.

28

Using a computer at the ranch, Tyler researched his biological parents. Since first finding out he was adopted, he'd longed to find anything he could about their lives. His research indicated his father had lived a life of crime. He'd spent eight months in jail for a carjacking conviction, two separate twelve-month sentences for drug distribution, and several thirty to ninety-day stints in the slammer for battery. Killing a police officer ended his life of crime on the streets, and soon enough brought about his own death.

Piecing information together, Tyler determined that his father, unlike himself, wasn't a big muscular man. His father was five feet eight, compared to Tyler's six feet four. He apparently made up for his size by being a good fighter. Early in his teen years, he was often in trouble for street fighting or involved in some brawl in a pool hall. At sixteen, he was kicked out of school after beating up his history teacher who'd given him an 'F' on his report card.

Tyler didn't find any information on his mother. His research for siblings and other family members also came up empty. The obituaries for both his father and mother listed no children, leading Tyler to believe he must have been an only child. His research provided little insight on who he was, or if he had family members still living.

Finding information on Rita proved to be even more frustrating. The computer kept locking up, and he'd have to start over again once he rebooted. Becoming discouraged, he gave up, deciding the problem wasn't the computer, but someone not wanting him to find Rita.

A little more than nine months after arriving at the ranch, Tyler had completed all levels of his training, passing each physical exercise and every written test with flying colors. It was determined that Tyler didn't need the full twelve months originally set aside for his training. It was time for Tyler DuPont to start paying back his obligation.

Every day had been filled with new experiences and excitement. Tyler loved the challenges he'd faced and felt that for the first time in his life, he had accomplished something. He felt triumphant, finishing each day exhausted, only to wake up the next morning full of energy and enthusiasm. It was hard for him to believe he'd been there nearly a year. It seemed like only a few weeks.

The relationship he'd built with Foreman was excellent. Tyler enjoyed the man's company immensely. They had formed a tight bond - one he expected would continue growing long after he'd left the ranch. Foreman treated Tyler like a son. It reminded Tyler of how it was with Gordon, before the accident that changed everything in the Boone family home. It still felt odd when he thought about Gordon being his adopted father and not his natural one.

As much as Tyler enjoyed being at the ranch, the weekly trips to Sheridan on Friday or Saturday had created a longing for complete freedom. He wanted to roam about unfettered, able to do as he wished. He wanted to be on his own, be his own man. He was well trained and ready to begin his mission. There was no question in Tyler's mind about what that mission would be. He had been trained each day in combat tactics, how to blow things up, how to kill people. Tyler DuPont was about to become a killing machine.

Although he could and would carry out any job he was given, he didn't know how he would react when it came time to kill someone who'd not given him cause. All the training in the world couldn't prepare him for the feelings that would come from walking up to a total stranger placing a gun against their head and pulling the trigger. Letting the organization down however, would quickly bring about his own death. He had little choice but to follow orders.

Early one morning, Tyler and Foreman headed out from the ranch for a full day of horseback riding. Buffalo packed a box lunch in each of their saddlebags. Tyler watched as Foreman placed a manila envelope in the saddlebag, alongside his lunch. The envelope contained instructions and rules of behavior for Tyler, once he left the ranch. He would be given an opportunity to read the papers and ask questions, as many as he wished.

When they stopped for lunch, atop a high craggy hill overlooking a lush green valley below, Foreman opened the manila envelope and removed its contents. It contained two folders, which he handed to Tyler. One folder contained papers listing rules of conduct – the do's and don'ts. In bold red print at the bottom of the last sheet of paper was a stark warning of what would happen if the rules were broken.

The second folder contained papers describing where and how he would live. There was also information about the point reduction system and the debt Tyler owed. One of the pages told how he would be contacted when it was time to do a job. After Tyler had taken time and read everything thoroughly, Foreman went over them again making doubly sure all the rules were understood.

Being apprehended by the authorities would be the end of his life. Fingerprints don't lie, and his fingerprints said his name was Seth Boone. There would be no booking by the police, no interrogation, no standing before a judge to ask for bail - he'd not live to make it that far.

Tyler had been trained on how to avoid law enforcement officers. With his new identity, there was little chance a routine traffic check would be troublesome. The type of work he was about to undertake however, would summons the police, often in large numbers. It was stressed that when the police arrived, Tyler DuPont was to be miles from the scene.

He could never enter the state of Virginia ever again, even after he'd fulfilled his commitment to Foreman and become a free man. He could never contact anyone he knew from his past, especially Rita Logan.

"I know you still love her, and that you've conducted research, trying to find her," Foreman said. "I'm sure you noticed how the computer locked up when you tried gathering information. It's for your own good as well as hers. You'll be tempted to contact her once you're on your own, but don't. You have to resist. The sea is full of fish, so find yourself another one. Don't do anything to compromise yourself. I care for you. You've been given a new life, a second chance. We've put forth a lot of effort to train you properly. Don't do anything stupid and end it all chasing a piece of tail."

Tyler had suspected he was being monitored. Now it was confirmed.

Tyler cared for Foreman, and it pleased him to hear the man cared for him as well. He had become more than his instructor. He was a true friend, a father figure in his eyes.

"I've never been treated so well in my life," Tyler said.

Foreman looked at Tyler and smiled.

"If you think I'm ready to be turned loose, I'll do my very best not to disappoint you," Tyler said.

"The day after tomorrow you'll fly out of here, just like you flew in. You'll be going to your new home. Once you leave this ranch, you won't ever come back. Erase this place from your memory. You've had your share of hardship in your life. I won't lie to you, what you're about to undertake will bring about its own hardship, but once you pay your dues, you're done forever. You might like this line of work, some do. If you decide you want to stay on after you've fulfilled your obligation, I'm sure we can work something out. Either way, I want you to live to a ripe old age, so you have to do this right."

"When you say, 'new home', do you mean Mississippi, to the address on my driver's license?"

"That would be correct," Foreman said with a smile. "It's an apartment complex on 2nd Avenue in Meridian."

"Why Mississippi? Why don't operations take place from the ranch?"

"The ranch is a training ground. Forget about the ranch. Agents are independent, working on their own. The apartment doesn't have anything that will lead authorities back here. There are other reasons why the ranch isn't used as a base. I can't tell you everything and besides, there's no reason for you to know."

"So what do I do once I get to Mississippi?"

"Relax. Sit and wait," Foreman replied. "There's a pool and a gym connected to the apartment complex. You'll find a checkbook on the nightstand in your new bedroom, along with an envelope containing a substantial amount of cash. After you arrive, activate your credit card and use it as you wish. Go to an ATM machine if you need more money. Settle in and get comfortable. You'll get a call on your cell when your services are needed. When the call comes, you will be given a set of coordinates. Four hours or less - be there. You don't show - someone comes and finds you. If that happens, you're terminated. I was the one who got you out of prison, Tyler. I'll do everything I can to protect you, but I can only do so much. The rest is up to you."

"Why not just give me the details over the phone?" Tyler asked.

"A couple of reasons," Foreman replied. "You need to have some physical contact with us. That's one. The biggest reason is security. You never know who is listening."

Tyler nodded his head up and down, indicating he understood. This was serious business and there was no room for error. He knew the rules, and knew not following them would end his life.

"Why Meridian, Mississippi? Tyler asked. "Why not Omaha, or Vegas?"

"I chose the location," Foreman said. "It's a nice town, the one I grew up in."

Tyler was surprised. As much time as he'd spent with Foreman and as close as they had become, it was the first piece of personal information he'd learned about the man. Tyler suspected that Foreman had told him this for a reason, although he didn't have a clue as to why.

"Do you have family there still?"

Foreman didn't answer the question. Tyler had learned not to be persistent if a question wasn't answered, it would only be a waste of time.

"You're a cutthroat now Tyler, a killer, a highly trained assassin. At any crime scene, the police are always looking for a motive. Unless instructed to do otherwise, make it appear the motive was robbery. Never give detectives a reason to think anything else. Use your training. Wear gloves, take out any cameras in the area, and always wear disguises. Leave no clues about yourself. Always take the victim's wallet and anything of value, such as jewelry, valuable coins, or stamp collections. Dispose of it all as soon as you can, making sure no one finds it."

"How am I to go about disguising this big frame of mine?" Tyler asked.

"Do as we taught you. Use your head. Your brain is your most powerful tool. Use it!"

"Will I be seeing you in the future?" Tyler asked.

"I'll be in touch occasionally. I've got a lot invested in you," Foreman said, smiling. "I can't tell you how much I've enjoyed these last nine months, Tyler. I'm going to miss your company."

Tyler read Foreman's face. He couldn't help but notice how emotional Foreman was. He'd never seen the man like this. It served to enforce what he already knew, that underneath the surface, Foreman was a caring man. He was mysterious, cunning, lethal, and likely had killed many men himself. Still, he had a soft side, and Tyler knew that somewhere buried deep below the surface, Foreman had a big heart.

29

Tyler left the ranch on April 2nd, nine and a half months after arriving. As the twin-engine plane took off, Tyler, the only passenger, stared out the window at the ranch. It had all been like a dream, albeit a good dream. He felt a small lump in his throat. He wanted to be free, but he hated saying goodbye. He'd made friends at the ranch, something he'd had so few of in his life.

It was just before three in the afternoon when the plane landed at the Meridian, Mississippi, Municipal Airport. The pilot handed Tyler a set of car keys and pointed toward a parking area to the left of the terminal. So many things were unclear, left for him to figure out on his own. He had questions, but there was no one there to provide answers.

Foreman sent him away without a suitcase full of guns and ammunitions. He left the ranch with only the clothes on his back, nothing else. His departure from the ranch was quite similar to his arrival in that respect. It seemed a waste, leaving behind all the nice clothes and shoes. In prison, he would have loved having just one pair of nice shoes or a pair of jeans.

Tyler left the terminal and walked toward the parking area the pilot had pointed out. It was his first time in a public place without someone from the ranch present. He was excited, but also scared. A new chapter in his life was opening. He was wishing he could turn through the pages to see what was going to happen next.

The humidity of central Mississippi was ramping up, even though it was only April. It was a vast change from the dry, cool, high altitude air of western Montana. Still, Tyler thought it was wonderful. He was alive. He was out of prison. He was on his own and he felt free and as light as a feather.

He had the keys to a car, parked somewhere in the parking lot. He wanted to find the car, find the apartment, and find a local restaurant. After that, he'd go shopping at a clothing store and perhaps buy some groceries. He was nervous. He was still getting used to having a fake name, a fake identity - a fake everything. He had to be cautious of the police, or anyone who might approach him. Walking about freely would take some getting used to. He'd have to try and not look as if he were guilty of something and draw attention to himself.

Pushing the unlock button on the key fob, the taillights flashed on a vehicle ahead. It was a dark-green GMC Yukon. As he drew closer, he could tell the Yukon was new. Tyler opened the door and climbed in. The vehicle had that new car smell. He inhaled deeply, filling his nostrils with the pleasant aroma. He thought back to the days he spent in the hole at Radford and the rancid odor of that place. How different and unexpected things had turned out. He'd never darken the walls of a prison again. He'd live as a free man, or die trying. There was a new world to explore. The wonder and excitement of it all was growing by the second. He couldn't believe this was real.

Sitting in the Yukon was strange. He felt like he'd just broken into someone's car. He looked around to see if anyone was watching. Satisfied they weren't, he opened the glove compartment and looked inside. He found the owner's manual and a white envelope. He opened the envelope. It contained an insurance card and registration card. Both bore the name Tyler DuPont and a Meridian, Mississippi address.

"Wow," Tyler said. "I can't believe this new vehicle is just for me!"

He started the Yukon and turned the AC on. Removing the owner's manual, he flipped through the pages. He activated the GPS system then put in the 2nd Avenue address. A pair of expensive sunglasses was laying on the passenger seat. The tag was still attached. Tyler put them on then looked in the rearview mirror and smiled. His skin was tingling with excitement – already loving his new life.

He didn't have a lot of driving experience. Aside from a couple of times when Foreman let him drive on their weekly trip to Sheridan, he'd only driven on the dirt roads of the ranch. Even with the air conditioner running on high, there were beads of sweat on his brow.

He nervously left the airport and entered the main highway in the direction of downtown Meridian. The GPS was a wonderful tool. It led him directly to the parking area of the 'Terrace Gardens Apartments' in Meridian.

There was another key on the ring with the Yukon's remote. A number was stamped into the brass key, '307'. He climbed the open stairway to the third floor. As he rounded the first flight of stairs and turned to the second, he got a glimpse of the pool, directly behind the building.

Without counting, he estimated fifty or more people were at the pool area. At least a dozen young women were wearing bikinis. Many of the sunbathing beauties were sitting in chairs, a few rubbing sunscreen onto their already tanned, slender bodies. Several more were stretched out face down on towels by the poolside, soaking up the sun's rays with bikini tops dangling over their lounge chairs.

Less than a year ago, he was in a maximum-security prison, ready to be shipped out to Leavenworth to face death row. The only women in Radford had been a large, overweight woman who worked in the kitchen, and a black, female guard who hated men. The guard was meaner than a rattlesnake. Her language was worse than the nastiest of inmates. She was quick to pull her baton out and hit someone if not given the utmost respect she demanded. She never aimed for the limbs or torso. It was always a direct strike to the back of the head.

Standing before the door looking at a gold-colored number placed at eye level, it read '307' matching the number on the key. Tyler slid the key in, turned it, and heard the familiar click of a lock opening. Pushing the door open, the chilled air from the air conditioner rush out and touched his face.

Tyler stepped inside and closed the door behind him. He flipped the three light switches on the wall by the door, and the entire place lit up. Looking around, he was pleased with the decorations. It was manly and nicely decorated. The apartment was spacious and had quality furniture. He walked over and looked out the living room window. It was directly above the pool.

In the bedroom, Tyler found a dresser and a chest of drawers full of new clothes, all his size. When he opened the spacious closets, it was more of the same, slacks, dress shirts, and casual wear. In the bottom of the closets were a variety of new shoes - sandals, running shoes, dress shoes, and boots. It was just as it had been when he'd arrived at the ranch. It was Christmas morning all over again, and Tyler felt like Santa had given him everything in the sleigh.

In the corner of the bedroom was a metal gun safe. The lock combination was written on a sheet of paper and taped to the door. He worked the tumble then pulled the heavy metal door open. The smile already on his face, spread wider.

Inside the safe, Tyler saw a sniper rifle and five handguns. On one shelf was a large supply of ammunition. Gun cleaning kits for every caliber imaginable were stored in the bottom of the safe. As he looked down at the cleaning kits, he saw a shoebox sized wooden container. He bent down, picked it up, and unlatched two brass latches. Looking inside, he was staring at an estimated three to five pounds of C4 plastic explosives. It was enough to blow up the entire apartment complex. Taking a closer look at the shelf where the pistol and rifle cartridges were stored, he saw a box of explosive detonators behind a box of .45 auto shells. He closed the safe and spun the tumbler.

Adjacent to the bedroom was an office with a nice wooden desk, desktop computer, a printer, and sitting on the floor was a paper shredder. He looked again at the paper in his hand, showing the combination to the gun safe. He committed the combination to memory then fed the paper into the shredder.

In the kitchen, he found the cupboard to be adequately stocked, including protein shakes and other body building supplements. They were even the brands he'd used back at the ranch, the kind he liked. Opening the freezer and refrigerator doors, he noticed both compartments were packed with food. On the top shelf of the refrigerator sat a twelve pack of beer. He wondered if the person who had stocked the apartment realized he was under the legal drinking age.

He took a second look at the bottles of beer and smiled. He'd killed people, spent time in prison, and had just completed a rigorous nine months of training at a secret government sponsored camp that prepared him to kill on command. If that didn't qualify him to drink a beer, nothing did. He grabbed one of the bottles, twisted the top off, and took a long swig.

Walking into the living room, he looked out the window. Four girls had just arrived at the pool and were laying out their towels and other gear. He guessed they were college girls, about his age. It had been a long time since he'd seen that much skin.

Although the girls down by the pool were beautiful, Rita still held his heart. His mind raced back to the few private times they'd had to kiss and pet. He'd caressed her breast during those times, and her moaning had nearly aroused him to a point of climaxing. He wondered what Rita looked like in a bathing suit. He remembered Foreman's words about the sea being full of fish. He'd been warned - he could never make contact with her. Still, she was the only woman he desired, and he ached to see her, hear her sweet voice, and touch her lips to his.

Casting thoughts of Rita aside briefly, Tyler thought about his time spent in prison. He thought about the long days and nights he'd spent in the hole during those months. He felt fortunate to be where he was now. He was blessed beyond measure. Although he was Foreman's slave, this wasn't a slave's life. He thought about all the men in the world who worked hard every day, struggling to feed their families. Those men were slaves too, just of a different kind.

Tyler was grateful. He'd been given a second chance. He was living a life of luxury. Still, it was a life of discontentment. He didn't want to kill anyone else. Those he had killed ate away at his insides daily. He wondered how long this life of secrets and murderous acts would last. Would he ever actually be free?

In the days ahead, he'd be ordered to kill people, people he didn't know, people he'd never met, people who for all he knew had been handed a raw deal, just as he had. There was no real choice however, it was do as Foreman commanded or cease to exist. He wanted to be free, and he wanted to be with Rita. Those two dreams would be his motivation for moving forward, even though he realized those dreams might never materialize.

The first night in the apartment was a restless one. He wasn't used to the surroundings and the noise of cars and people outside. He dreamed of the warden. The cruel man was laughing hysterically while bending down over Shanghai's dead body. Several guards stood by, also laughing. They all had fire hoses in their hands, and began pelting Shanghai with ice cold, high-pressure water. He tried to stop them, but he was paralyzed, unable to do anything to stop the cruel act. He sat up in bed. Beads of sweat covered his face, and the back of his head was wet.

After breakfast, he went for a long run. It felt weird, being on the sidewalks of a city, running about freely. He discovered he had a bit of paranoia. He constantly turned to see if anyone was following him. He'd been trained to observe his surroundings, looking for signs of trouble, and an escape route if needed. This was different though. Tyler was expecting to see someone from the organization watching him from a distance. If not that, then perhaps some nosey cop who might think he'd committed a crime and want to take him in for questioning. He remembered what Foreman had said about being captured by the police. Being arrested, or even taken in for questioning would be as good as signing his death warrant.

Returning to the apartment complex, Tyler worked out in the gym. After a shower, he spent an hour watching news shows on television. He was used to being up early and on the go at the ranch. Here in Meridian, with little to do, he was already becoming bored. It also felt like the four walls were closing in around him. He decided to go lay by the pool and soak up some rays. The sun was rising high in the sky. It was another cloudless, Mississippi spring day. It felt better being outside, breathing fresh air. He'd spent enough of his life indoors and felt perhaps the time spent in prison was the reason he was feeling claustrophobic.

Sitting on the edge of the pool with his feet dangling in the water, he checked his phone, wanting to make sure he'd not missed a call. There were no numbers in his directory. He wasn't given an emergency number to call if he were to need help. They could call him, but he couldn't contact them. He had been completely cut off from Foreman, Trainer, and anyone else at the ranch. He'd been told to erase the ranch from his memory, but every day he'd spend there was permanently embedded in his mind. He missed the place, his instructors, Buffalo, and most of all, Foreman.

Studying the phone, Tyler was tempted to take it apart and look inside. He suspected it was bugged, so he'd have to be careful about who he called and what he said. The phone would have to go wherever he went, on his run, to the supermarket, to the bathroom. He couldn't leave it behind and take a chance the dreaded call would come. He had already become paranoid, checking the phone often to make sure it was still working.

He liked the fact that he could come and go as he wished. He had a new SUV, a new apartment, new clothes, credit cards, plenty of food, and cash. He had all he could ask for – except Rita.

Sitting by the pool, in the warm sun, with dangling his feet in the water, Tyler was surrounded by a hundred noisy people. It was strange, he'd never felt so alone. He felt guilty for feeling so sorry for himself. If not for Foreman, he might be having his last meal that very evening, just before being executed. Prison, life at the ranch, becoming an assassin, being free, being with Rita – those thoughts rolled around in his head like a tumbleweed, blown about aimlessly by the winds of the prairie.

Every female from twelve years old and up took notice of the new man sitting at the poolside. The sun reflected off Tyler's rippling muscles, making him look like a superhero who at any moment might stand, wrap his towel around his shoulder forming a cape, and fly off to save an innocent dame from the grasp of a villain.

Sitting in lounge chairs across the pool, two women had taken notice and were very interested. Their children were playing in the water a few feet away. They were having a conversation about the handsome, muscle bound man some eighty feet away. He'd moved in just yesterday. Now here he was, sitting at the edge of the pool, wearing only swimming trunks. He wasn't just handsome - he was downright gorgeous.

Tyler, peering through his sunglasses, noticed the two women staring in his direction. Having been taught the art of lip reading at the ranch, he used this new tool to eavesdrop on their conversation.

"Go on over and talk to him Jodie. Don't be such a chicken."

"Rhoda, I'm thirty-two years old, with two kids. Beside, I'm married - as you well know. I'm perfectly content to just sit here and drool."

"Oh come on, Jodie. You sacrifice everything for Henry and the kids - and what does it get you? When do you ever get to have any fun? Henry cheated on you last year with your sister, for crying out loud. Here's your chance to get even. Can't you imagine a fun night in the sack with a hunk like that? If you don't go after him, I might. Imagine how it would feel having that strong muscular chest pressing against your breasts. You should at least go invite him up to your place for a quickie. I'll watch the kids."

"Are you serious? Really! Sex with a strange man."

"Don't tell me you've never thought of wild sex with a stranger, especially someone who looks like that. It's certainly on my bucket list, darling. At least go flirt with him, it'll make you feel like a teenager again. Even after two kids you've still got that sexy, curvy body. I'm sure he'll find you hot and irresistible! If nothing else, get his number for me."

"So, tell me Rhoda. Have you ever cheated on Gilbert?"

"Oh God. Here I go with confession," Rhoda said. "I cheated on Gilbert once. Well, maybe twice, or three times. One time it was at a Christmas party with an old flame, Jerome Hodges. We had a wild and wonderful three-minute fling in a storage room. Gilbert was at a table with our friends when I came back. My face was red and dripping with sweat. Gilbert saw Jerome come by a minute later, looking the same."

Rhoda laughed heartily. "Gilbert suspected that I'd screwed him, and confronted me about it in the car. I acted hurt that he'd think such a thing. I cut him off for three weeks!"

Jodie looked at her friend, a bit stunned by what she'd just said.

"Honey, if a woman wants it, there's always a man around willing to give it to her," Rhoda said. "Just look at those muscles. Like I said, Henry cheated on you, and here's a chance for you to even the score."

Tyler was amazed by the women's conversation. He expected to hear men talk like that, but never suspected women would do the same. It saddened him that the women were in seemingly unhappy marriages and so willing to cheat on their spouses. *It would never be like that if I were with Rita.*

Tiring of the women's conversation, Tyler went to lay down on his towel. He'd just put a hand towel over his face to shade the bright sun when he sensed someone sitting beside him. He could smell suntan lotion, and a there was a slight scent of perfume. He pulled the towel slightly to the side, looking to see who it was. It was Jodie, the woman from across the pool. He removed the towel from his face and sat up.

Jodie's eyes were trained on Tyler's bulging bronzed chest muscles rippling in the sunlight. She noticed no ring on his finger. Her heart was pounding hard in her chest.

"Hi, I'm Jodie," she said nervously.

Jodie's friend was right. She was a very attractive woman with nice curves. She had a nice smile, and her bikini top left little to the imagination.

"Tyler DuPont," he said, extending his hand.

"You must be new here, haven't seen you around," Jodie said, her voice shaky.

Jodie's friend from across the pool was watching, studying them closely with tell all eyes.

"Yeah, just moved in yesterday," Tyler replied.

"Some people consider me the entertainer and greeter of the complex," Jodie said proudly. "Would it be okay if I were to prepare you a dinner and bring it over to your place this evening? I like to cook, and it would give me a chance to meet my new neighbor."

Tyler had already heard Rhoda mention that Jodie's husband worked in the oil and gas industry, and would be out of town until Friday.

"I appreciate your generosity," Tyler said, looking at her inviting blue eyes. "I don't think that would be a good idea though."

"Oh," Jodie said, a bit taken back by the rejection. "So, you have a girlfriend?"

"No, I'm single, no girlfriend. No wife."

"I promise, I won't hurt you," Jodie said, trying to sound sexy. She bravely slid her hand over and touched Tyler on the arm. "I'd like to get to know you. Perhaps we could become good friends." She said, winking. Inside, she was marveling at the amount of bravery she'd mustered up.

"Listen, Jodie," Tyler said politely. "It's not that I don't find you attractive, you're a beautiful woman."

"Then take advantage of me!"

Jodie's voice was changing, getting stronger. She couldn't believe this man was rejecting her. "You might find out you like me," she said, pressing on. "I think I could bring you a lot of pleasure!"

Tyler didn't want to play this game. Rhoda had coaxed Jodie into what was becoming an embarrassing situation for both Jodie and Tyler. Jodie's husband had cheated on her by having sex with her sister. Rhoda had convinced Jodie that cheating on her husband would somehow even the score and make things better.

"What do you tell your kids the next morning when they asked where you were all night, Jodie?" Tyler asked. "Do you lie to them? What about your husband - Henry? Do you really think having sex with me will make you feel better about what he and your sister did?"

Jodie's mouth dropped open and her face instantly turned red. She was shocked, and embarrassed.

"You know what?" Tyler continued. "If your friend over there was truly a friend, someone who cared about you, then she wouldn't give you such bad advice. I suspect that you're a decent woman, a good mother. I've done some things that messed up my life, and I regret it. Don't do something foolish to mess up your own. A roll in the hay isn't worth a lifetime of regret."

Tyler couldn't believe the words that had just left his mouth. He was a teenager, giving advice to an older married woman. He was the child here, but Jodie was the one acting like an adolescent.

Jodie hadn't anticipated being chastised by this stranger. She had approached him, practically begging for sex. She would have never guessed he would be preaching to her about morals. A myriad of emotions swept across her mind. She was stunned, confused, embarrassed. This wasn't at all what she expected to happen.

She wondered how the man who had moved in only yesterday knew so much about her. Was he a friend of Henry's? She was speechless. Her mouth was still agape as she stood and stormed off. She marched around the pool where Rhoda was, grabbed her things, gathered her two children, and left. Tyler heard Rhoda calling out to her, but Jodie never responded. Rhoda then looked indignantly toward Tyler. She gathered her things and children also and left the pool area.

The following day, Tyler sat by the pool again. Rhoda was perched in a lawn chair across the pool at the same location as the day before, but Jodie wasn't with her. Rhoda looked toward Tyler a few times. Her eyes were filled with fiery darts. If looks could kill, he would be dead.

Minutes later, Tyler watched Jodie enter the pool area. She and her children passed by the area where Rhoda was sitting and settled down at the far corner of the pool. From across the way, she looked toward Tyler and their eyes locked. She gave him a glancing half smile then turned away.

A short time later, Tyler watched as Jodie came walking toward him. She came directly at him, her head high and her steps deliberate. She had something to say to him. He was expecting a slap in the face, or perhaps a good cursing. She stopped just to the right of Tyler's chair, towering over him.

"Thank you for humiliating me yesterday," she said. "I don't know how it is you know so much about me, but that's for another time."

Tyler was surprised. Her words were far different from what he'd expected.

"I'm a decent woman," she said with a shaky voice. "I love my children, and still love my husband, although we have some serious issues we need to work through. I wanted to kick you where it hurts yesterday. You angered me. You embarrassed me. You humiliated me, and I didn't sleep well last night."

Jodie pulled her long hair back and threw it over her shoulders. Tyler noticed tears in the corners of her eyes.

"I knew you were right," Jodie continued. "I was about to do something extremely foolish. I thought about my friend last night. You were right about her too. If she were truly a friend and cared about me, she wouldn't have wanted me to do wrong by my husband. I don't know who you are, but you appear to be a decent man. You must have been raised right. You're very wise for your age, and I can tell that you have a big heart. Thank you for setting me straight."

Jodie turned and walked back to play with her children.

Tyler decided it was time to go shower and take a ride through town in his new truck. Jodie's words kept cutting through him like a knife. He wasn't a decent man. He didn't have a big heart. He was a killer, a deceiver, a criminal living with a fake identity. He was the scum of the earth, and he had no right to judge others or give advice. For the next two days, he steered away from the pool. He didn't want to be seen, or have contact with anyone. He had all the luxuries one could ask for, but he was living a lie. Nothing about his new life was right.

30

Over the next week, Tyler fell into a pattern. He slept until seven each morning. As soon as he was out of bed, he went for a 5K run. He worked out for an hour in the gym then ate a late breakfast. After a hot shower, he rode around town, getting to know his surroundings. He constantly checked his phone, making sure he hadn't missed a call. Each afternoon, he sat around the pool reading. He saw Jodie and Rhoda at the pool most days. He was happy they avoided him. They not only avoided him, they avoided each other as well.

No one else had attempted to befriend him, which he thought was good. He thought it was best not to have friends, at least for now. His last friend, Shanghai, was dead. Before that, it was Rita. She was more than a friend - she was the love of his life. She too was gone. Prior to that, his only friend was Sarah, a sweet young girl who'd been abused sexually on a daily basis by her parents. Sarah had died also. He sometimes wished it had been him hit by the drunk driver instead of Sarah.

It was becoming routine for Tyler to sit on the couch each evening, flipping through the television channels until getting sleepy, then turning in for the night. He was becoming depressed. A change of venue was needed.

He began frequenting a pool hall in mid-town Meridian. The pool hall was a rough redneck joint, but aside from a few shouting matches, he'd never seen any fights. Compared to prison, it was a calm place to hang out. He didn't want trouble and was prepared to do everything he could to avoid it. Everyone who sized Tyler up felt likewise.

One of the perks with his new identity was a conceal-carry weapons permit. He legally carried a Sig Sauer 9mm, stowed away nicely in a shoulder holster beneath his shirt. He discovered an indoor shooting range down on Cook Parkway, and went there one evening to shoot.

After shooting a few clips of ammo, he understood why Navy Seal teams had adopted the same type handgun. The pistol was accurate, never jammed, and had only a slight recoil. The grips felt as if they'd been custom made to fit his big hands. A suppressor had been provided for the Sig Sauer. Tyler was tempted to bring the silencer to the range and see how it worked, but dared not to. The firing range was a favorite of the local police force, and silencers were illegal.

He worried his phone wasn't working properly. Every day he'd call a retail store, or he'd order pizza, just to make sure the phone was functioning properly. He even had the pizza delivery boy call him back once. He wanted to make sure he could receive incoming calls. Foreman had never mentioned how active, or inactive he would be. He dreaded the call that would send him into action, but he wished Foreman would call, if for no other reason, just to say hello. He was lonely and longed for someone to talk with.

As much as Tyler tried, he couldn't get Rita off his mind. The temptation to find her and make contact was overwhelming. He wished he could call her. He wanted to hear her answer the phone with her sweet, sexy voice. He wondered where she was. Was she dating anyone? Had she gotten married? Was she happy? Did she ever think of him?

On Saturday morning, Tyler went for his usual 5K run. He had often seen three teenage nerd looking boys sitting at a table outside a coffee shop playing some sort of game with each other on their tablets, while drinking coffee and eating bagels. Seeing them there that morning, an idea popped into his head. He expected these geeks knew far more about computers than he did, and could steer him toward someone who could build him a special computer.

He stopped a few feet from the teens and greeted them. They were concentrating on their game and hardly noticed Tyler.

"Hey guys. I need some info," Tyler said.

The boys didn't reply or look up.

"I only need a minute of your time."

Tyler was wearing running shorts but no shirt. The teens looked up and noticed Tyler for the first time. They were ready to trash talk the person who'd interrupted their game.

"Holy shit! The Hulk is in the house!" one of the teens said.

Tyler looked like the poster child for a muscle-building magazine. The boys looked at him with amazement. He had their undivided attention.

"Do you guys know where I can buy a computer with some special bells and whistles?"

"Try the computer store in the mall," one of the boys replied.

"Come on guys," Tyler pleaded. "I suspect you know someone who can do some special programming for me. Something far beyond what I can get at the mall."

"You mean like something you can do some hacking with?" the same boy asked.

"Not exactly. Something along those lines though."

"Cool," the boy replied. "Two miles out of town on highway 11. Campbell's Custom Cycle. Ask for Hagel or Renee."

"I've passed by that place," Tyler replied. "I'm not looking for a motorcycle though. I need someone who can build me a special computer."

"Like I said," the boy replied. "If you want something special, see Hagel or Renee. You pronounce his name Hãy-Jûll."

Tyler thought that the boys were toying with him about the computer. He smiled, thanked them for their time, and moved on. After finishing his run, he went back to the apartment. In the shower, he was thinking. *What the heck. I've got nothing to lose. I'll check this Hãy-Jûll guy out. I know where to find those geeks if they've led me astray.*

Walking into the showroom at Campbell's Custom Cycles, Tyler couldn't help but admire a motorcycle sitting by the display window. It was chromed out, had an oversized back tire, and extended forks. The tan colored leather seat was a nice contrast to the burnt orange paint. He'd never ridden a motorcycle, but had always wanted to. He wondered what it would feel like to climb onto the motorcycle and take off riding across the country, the wind blowing in his face, being free as a bird. He considered this as something to do once he had fulfilled his obligation to The Company.

The Company, he thought. He'd been told back at the ranch that the organization didn't have a name. 'The Company' sounded appropriate. He decided that was what he would refer to it as from then on.

"You can sign the papers and ride it out the door," a loud voice roared from behind him.

The interruption to his deep thoughts startled Tyler. He instinctively found himself ready to fight. As he turned around with clinched fists, the man who had spoken to him took a step back. Tyler was wearing cowboy boots, snug jeans, and a tight T-shirt revealing the hard body beneath.

"Damn! What a man," the man shouted. "I didn't mean to startle you. Hell. You put on some leather and hop on this bike, every woman from here to Tupelo will be salivating to jump on the back with you."

The man was five-feet-ten, stocky build, and had jet-black hair. He wore glasses, and had a scruffy black beard speckled with gray. Tyler estimated the man was pushing fifty years of age.

"Hagel Campbell," the man said in a lower voice, extending his hand for a shake.

"Tyler. Tyler DuPont."

"You related to the DuPont's that live south of town?"

"No," Tyler answered. He wasn't aware there was anyone in Meridian with the last name of DuPont.

The two men shook hands.

"I like what you've got here," Tyler said. "Nice. Very nice. I might be interested in this at a later date. Right now though, I need something else. I was told you build custom computers," Tyler said, being as blunt as possible.

"Yeah, the wife does the computer stuff, I'm just a motorcycle salesman," Hagel replied. "What is it you're looking for?"

"I want a laptop that works like this," Tyler said, a distant look in his eyes as he concentrated. "It has to have WIFI. When I log on, I want the computer to indicate it's being used in another city or town. For example, if I logged on in a coffee shop in downtown Meridian, I want the internet to tell anyone watching that I'm in Los Angeles. If I log on an hour later, I want it to appear I'm logged in from Chicago, New York, and anywhere in between. In no way can the computer identify who I am or where I am. Can you do that?"

Hagel had a look of curiosity written all over his face, which Tyler naturally detected.

"Hell, the government can lock on your IP address and suck their way right into your computer man," Hagel responded, stroking his whiskers. "They can monitor every keystroke you make, if they want to. I'll have to consult with my wife, Renee. Why do you want this?"

"I want to research someone without anyone knowing about it, and I'm stressing the ANYONE part."

"You a PI or a cop?" Hagel asked sternly. His eyes were wide with a growing look of suspicion.

"Neither," Tyler replied, without hesitation.

"What you're asking for could be illegal!" Hagel said, still looking at Tyler as if horns were protruding from his forehead. "I'll have to research it a bit. But - if you're a cop you have to tell me if I ask. It's the law."

Tyler didn't think that was true.

"I am not a cop," he said smugly. "I don't work in law enforcement, and I'm not undercover for any law enforcement agency. I simply need to find someone who disappeared on me a couple of years ago. She's important to me. I work for myself, a stock trader, so I'm monitored closely by the Securities and Exchange Commission."

Tyler was amazed at what was coming out of his mouth. It was becoming more frequent that whenever his lips moved lies rolled off his tongue. It was happening without him batting an eye, and it was troublesome.

"Oh, a lady friend," Hagel replied skeptically. "Most women are whiney and carry two twelve packs of drama in their purse. Good women are a rare breed. I got lucky, Renee is a good one."

Tyler wasn't in the mood for chitchat. He was twitchy. He was there to do business, not to tell jokes or make a friend. He looked at Hagel indignantly. There was a moment of awkward silence.

"You sure you aren't into something that'll get you hurt?" Hagel asked, attempting to show concern as he dug for information. "It can be dangerous dealing with a jealous husband or boyfriend?"

Tyler knew that Hagel was working the edges, trying to gather information. He hadn't intended to let this man know it was a woman he was looking for, but it had slipped out. Speaking hastily, he felt like he'd already given away too much. It was in every way against how he'd been trained at the ranch. He realized that when it came to Rita, he quickly threw rational thinking out the window. He needed to be more careful. He remembered a verse he'd read in the Bible about thinking quickly and speaking slowly. *What kind of man am I*, he thought. *I'm a contract killer, everything in my life is a deception, I open my mouth and lies come out, and I'm think of some verse in the Bible. I'm pathetic!*

"I can't divulge any more information," Tyler replied. "Can you build the computer? I'm willing to pay top dollar."

"I don't know you," Hagel replied, squinting his eyes and again rubbing the stubble on his chin. "Nothing against you, but I don't trust anybody. Like I told you, I'll have to consult with Renee, she'll know if this is illegal or not. Hell, it might not even be possible."

"I have to be sure that no one, not even the government can tell where I am or who it is on the computer," Tyler reiterated. "If it turns out this is illegal, we'll forget the entire thing. How's that?"

Hagel wrinkled his brow as he looked out the showroom window. "You're apparently a smart young man. Stock market must be doing you right. That's a high-dollar ride you're driving."

"When can you give me an answer about the computer?" Tyler asked, not commenting on Hagel's remark about his vehicle or the stock market.

"Give me two days. I'll talk with Renee, plus, I need to check you out. If it can be done, I'm assuming this computer will be paid for with cash," Hagel said, a tinge of sarcasm in his voice.

"Of course," Tyler replied, shrugging his shoulders.

Tyler rattled off his phone number then pulled out his wallet. He handed Hagel four crisp new one-hundred-dollar bills.

"Here's a down payment," Tyler said. "I'm not a crook, but nonetheless, I want our deal kept a secret."

"What if it can't be done or if it's illegal?" Hagel asked.

"Then keep the cash for your efforts," Tyler said then walked toward the door. He turned back to look at Hagel as he pulled the door open.

"I'll see you in two days," he said, then left.

Hagel promised to check Tyler out, but that didn't concern him. It would be a litmus test to see if Foreman and his group had done their work properly. He expected Hagel's wife, Renee, was some sort of computer geek, and would conduct a thorough search on Tyler DuPont. If her research didn't turn up anything suspicious, he'd feel much better about the security of his new identity. If he could obtain the laptop he'd requested to be built, he could search for Rita without Foreman or anyone else ever knowing he'd done so. With high hopes Hagel could come through on this request, he headed back to his apartment.

Tyler had a desktop computer at the apartment. He suspected though that Foreman or one of his crew had it bugged somehow. He was a high-risk, a burdensome liability, so he understood why they would be watching his every move, monitoring every keystroke, listening to every phone call.

Everything he did was supposed to be for their benefit, not his. Not following their rules could compromise The Company. If that happened, it would end his life. It wouldn't always be this way though. Soon enough he would fulfill his obligation and be free – or would he? Would they actually let him go? Would they allow him to walk away to freedom, to live his life as he wished? He wanted desperately to think positive and believe the answer to those questions was 'yes', but he had serious reservations.

He needed to begin preparations now for the days ahead when he would say goodbye to Foreman and The Company. He hoped when he was finished with their dirty work, he could walk away – but in reality, he expected it would be a dead run. He estimated his chances of walking off to live as he wished once he fulfilled his agreement, was ten-percent or less. He knew too much. Once he'd done their dirty deeds, he'd be nothing more than a grand-scale liability. He'd likely have to slip off into the shadows, hiding from their pack of wolves. They would enjoy the challenge, hunting him down, joyfully standing over him to watch as he bled to death. After all, that's what these men did for a living.

Prison had educated him. He'd learned never to trust anyone - ever. He knew Foreman and his people were highly intelligent. They knew he was already thinking about whether they'd let him go or not. When it came time for him to depart, they would expect the unexpected - just as they'd taught him to do. It could all end with a high-speed chase as Tyler tried to get away from Foreman and his team, who loved nothing better than a good car crash.

On the way back to the apartment, Tyler stopped at a bank and used the ATM machine. Foreman had told him to do so if he needed cash. His only expenses were gasoline and food, both of which were charged to a credit card. He didn't know why Foreman had set up the seemingly unlimited bank account. Nonetheless, large sums of money were at his fingertips, with nothing to spend it on. Since arriving in Meridian, he'd been watching his on-line bank account.

Regular deposits of two grand were being added weekly. He withdrew three thousand dollars from the ATM. This new computer, if it could be built, was bound to be expensive.

As he was leaving the bank, he spotted a U-Haul rental business across the street. It gave him an idea. Aside from the airport, there wasn't anywhere in town to rent a car. He turned around and parked in the bank parking lot, then walked across the street. He suspected the Yukon had a tracking device well hidden somewhere. The Company wouldn't be suspicious of his vehicle sitting in a Meridian parking lot, but if he were driving it out on the interstate, they'd be right on top of things, monitoring where he was going.

After renting a pick-up sized moving van, Tyler headed west on interstate 20. He drove forty-five minutes, to the town of Forest, Mississippi. There, he pulled into a small, fenced storage unit facility and rented a ten-by-ten storage unit under a false name. He'd thought about renting a safe-deposit box at a bank in Meridian, or some other town. That would require paperwork though, and was easily traceable.

The clerk at the storage facility didn't ask for any identification. Tyler filled out the form using a fictitious name and paid for a full year in advance with cash. The teenage clerk didn't bat an eye. He was more interested in his cell phone than the customer he was waiting on.

Tyler took one last look inside his new secret hiding place before pulling the door down. He slapped the padlock he'd purchased from the incompetent clerk on the latch and closed the hasp. The storage space was empty inside, except for a cardboard box he'd purchased when he'd rented the truck. Inside the box was two-thousand dollars cash. Over time, he would be placing much more cash in the box. He didn't know how far in the future the day would come when he had to run, but when it happened, it was important to be ready. He wanted to have a nice little nest egg stowed away in a place no one knew about, somewhere outside of Meridian.

He had been perspiring heavily since he'd left Meridian in the van. He was expecting the phone to ring at any time, and he'd have to leave to go meet one of The Company agents. Arriving back in Meridian with the rental van, he looked at his watch. The trip to Forest, plus the time taken to rent the storage shed, was just over two hours. He thought that with a faster vehicle, minus the time spent with the sales clerk, he could make the trip in an hour and a half.

A thought crossed his mind. Perhaps he could work out a deal with Hagel and purchase a used motorcycle. Hagel might even be willing to store it for him until it was needed. If so, he could ride the motorcycle when making trips to Forest. A motorcycle would be much faster than a moving van. There was a slight problem though. He didn't know how to ride a motorcycle. *Perhaps Hagel would be willing to teach me*, he thought. *I don't have much else to do, and it would be fun.*

☐

31

On Monday morning, Tyler got out of bed at 7a.m. He drank a cup of coffee while eating two eggs over easy and a piece of wheat toast. He then got dressed for his usual 5K run. After that, he'd shower then drive down to Campbell Custom Cycles to see Hagel about the laptop.

Just as he'd walked out the door, his cell phone rang. He'd foolishly given his cell number to Hagel. The last thing he needed was for someone from The Company to investigate and find out Hagel and his wife built computers on the side. It could reveal his plan. Looking at the display on the phone, he realized, it wasn't Hagel calling, it wasn't even a Mississippi area code.

"Hello," Tyler said as he answered, shutting the apartment door behind him.

"You're about to receive a text. You have four hours."

He didn't recognize the voice, but knew it was from someone in The Company. The phone went dead.

Unlocking the apartment door, Tyler stepped back inside. Just then, the phone gave the tone indicating a text message had been received. The message was two sets of numbers, representing coordinates of where he was supposed to be within the next four hours. He opened a special application on the phone and plugged the coordinates in. A map appeared. Zooming in on the exact location, it was at a casino near De Kalb, Mississippi, about thirty miles to the north of Meridian.

This was it. He was being called to do a job. He knew this day would soon come, but somehow hoped it never would. He would be given an assignment to go somewhere and kill someone. A dread came over him, and he got a headache.

There was no clue about who would meet him at the casino, or how they would find him once he was there. All he knew was to be at the coordinates given within four hours. Back at the ranch, Foreman had explained that using computers or phones to give out an assignment was dangerous. Certain words or keystrokes alerted Homeland Security computers and for good cause. Numerous terrorist attacks were thwarted each year by Homeland Security checking our messages sent via computers and cell phones. Any information about his assignments would come through a face-to-face meeting.

Before heading out, he ran downstairs to the apartment office and gave Hagel a call. He didn't want to use his own cell phone and was regretting he'd given out his number. Hagel answered and Tyler explained that he'd been called out of town unexpectedly. Therefore, he couldn't come by the shop.

"Everything's cool," Hagel said. "Renee's working on a software program that should do what you want."

"Wonderful!" he replied. "I don't know when I'll get back, but I'll be down to see you as soon as I can."

"It's gonna cost you a pretty penny. About a grand and a half. Maybe a little more. Are you okay with that?"

"Sure. I'll bring you a thousand more when I get back and settle the bill with you once you're done. One more thing, please don't call on the number I gave you. I'll come see you as soon as I can."

"Be careful on your trip," Hagel said then hung up the phone.

Just as Tyler was about to get into his Yukon and drive to De Kalb, he heard a woman's voice call his name. He turned and saw Jodie walking toward him. Her hair was a tangled mess, and she had black circles under her red eyes.

"Can I talk to you for a few minutes?" she asked.

"I'm really busy this morning," Tyler answered. "I've got a meeting that I must attend."

"I just wanted to let you know I'm moving," Jodie said. "Turns out you were more right about Rhoda than you'd ever know. Friday night I caught her and Henry getting it on behind the equipment shed by the pool."

Jodie started crying. She walked up and hugged Tyler, her tears falling on his shoulder. She pulled backed and continued her story.

"Henry and I are getting divorced. I'm taking the kids and moving back to my folks' place down near Biloxi."

"I'm so sorry," Tyler said. His remark brought no comfort, but those were the only words he could find at that moment.

She handed Tyler a slip of paper.

"Here's the number where I'll be staying. You're a nice young man, Tyler. If you ever get lonely, or just need someone to talk to, give me a call. Perhaps we could start a friendship and do things the right way."

She kissed Tyler on the cheek, hugged him again tightly, turned, and walked away. He stood there motionless for a moment. He felt sorry for Jodie. Her life was in shambles, and he knew all too well what that felt like. He wished he could make things better for her. He wished he could make friends. He wished he could be her friend. He wished he could be in a normal relationship. He wished he were with Rita, living high up in the mountains where no one could find them. *I'm wishing my life away*, he thought, climbing into the Yukon and starting the engine. So far, the day had been all bad news, and the hours ahead didn't look any better.

If Jodie only knew what I am, he thought. *I'm about to get orders to kill someone - and she thinks I'm a nice man. I've killed people, escaped from a prison death sentence, and now I'm about to kill again. I'm alive, but this isn't living.*

§

No sooner had Tyler pulled into the parking area at the Lucky Stars Casino, he heard a tap on the passenger side door. He looked over, and saw Foreman standing there. He unlocked the door and Foreman quickly climbed in.

"Good to see you, Tyler," Foreman said, leaning over to give a hug.

"I didn't expect I'd be meeting you," Tyler said, pulling away from the awkward hug.

"I've got a lot invested in you, so I wanted to be the one delivering your orders. How the heck are you?"

Foreman was jovial, smiling, glowing with excitement. He was acting as if he'd met a lifelong friend after many years apart. Tyler was just the opposite. Although he was happy to see Foreman, he was depressed. He hated being there under these circumstances. On the way to the meeting, he kept wondering if he would be ordered to walk up to a total stranger and kill them in cold blood. He'd have to be tough, pay back his debt by doing the dirtiest deed a man could do, all for the sake of survival.

"I'm good," Tyler said in a voice of indifference. "I'm settling in, getting to know my surroundings."

"Have you been to the old hamburger joint over on 5th Street? Best burgers in the country. It's been there since the thirties and still run by the same family."

"I think I drove by the place once or twice, but I've not eaten there. Perhaps I'll give it a try."

Tyler wasn't in the mood for small talk. He wanted to get his orders and get away from there. He would have loved spending the day with Foreman as they had back on the ranch, but under these circumstances, he wished someone else had shown up. He was feeling sick at his stomach. He'd killed his parents in a moment of rage, and killed Dagger and his gang in a life or death self-defense situation. This was different. He was about to commit a cold-blooded pre-meditated murder, and he didn't know if he could do it.

"How's the apartment?" Foreman asked, looking Tyler over as the conversation continued.

"Everything is perfect," Tyler replied, staring out the windshield. "I'm blessed. I couldn't ask for anything more.

"You met any nice ladies?"

"I met a couple of married women, but that didn't turn out to be a good thing."

"Hmm," Foreman gestured. "Be careful out there, that sea full of fish also has a lot of piranhas."

Tyler forced a smile.

"You seem down, perhaps a bit depressed. Are you sure you're okay?"

"Really, I'm fine," Tyler answered, still not making eye contact.

"Okay. Down to business," Foreman said. "You've got work to do."

Tyler turned to look at Foreman. It was a look of repugnance.

"Go back to your apartment this afternoon," Foreman commanded. "Pack a light suitcase, enough for two or three days at most. Drive to Jackson and take the 6 p.m. flight to Philly. Rent a car, drive to the American Family Inn in Cherry Hill and get a room."

Foreman handed Tyler an envelope.

"Here's a new ID and three-thousand in cash. Be sure to wipe down everything you touch - the rental, the hotel room, everything. Do this every time you get out of the car or leave the hotel room. Make sure nothing can trace you back to Meridian, and certainly not to Seth Boone."

Tyler nodded, indicating he understood.

"On the corner of Broad Street and Wallace, sits the St. Peter's Church. The target is a priest."

Foreman handed Tyler a photo. The priest's name, Verner Herndon, was written on the back.

"Look the photo over, memorize the name and face, then give it back to me," Foreman said.

"So he's my target?"

"Yeah. He's your man. Over a fifteen-year period, he raped at least six boys. Two years ago, one of his victims, named Kerby Rosemont came forward. After charges were made, two more boys, adult men now, opened up and told their story. Herndon went to trial, but someone got to all three witnesses. We don't know if they were paid off, or scared off. Anyway, to make a long story short, Herndon wasn't convicted. During depositions, Rosemont fingered two more boys Herndon had raped. Both denied it, but it was written all over their faces. No doubt - it had taken place. One of those boys happens to be the nephew of a client who supports our organization. He has graciously contributed a million dollars to our budget."

"So this is how it all works," Tyler said smugly.

"Not always, but often. How'd you think targets are selected – a random drawing?"

Tyler wasn't amused, nor did he appreciate Foreman's sarcasm.

"You have any issues with taking out Mr. Herndon?"

Tyler's answer was obvious. Indicating he had issues with killing someone for The Company could be the key that unlocked the chamber to his own crypt.

"No," Tyler replied, unconvincingly.

"Good," Foreman replied. "Once the deed is done and declared successful, 10 points comes off your bill, leaving you 130 points remaining."

Tyler had hoped killing a man would be worth much more than 10 points. Still, he'd expected this, or even less. If the rate of 10 points held true for every job, he'd have to kill fourteen people before being set free.

"One of Herndon's duties at the church is to inspect the organ pipes. He does this every Wednesday. He starts around 9 a.m., and it takes about forty-five minutes to complete the task. A stairway is situated directly behind the pipes, running all the way to the top - forty feet above the mounting platform. If you time it right, you'll catch him near the top. A fall from that height will certainly be fatal."

Tyler understood. There would be no weapon, aside from his muscular hands. He was to throw Herndon from the stairs and let him fall to his death.

"It's great seeing you again," Foreman said, smiling. "You look well, fit as ever."

"So, that's it?" Tyler asked.

"That's it. Use your training, and above all, use your head. Improvise where needed. If something happens and you can't do the job on Wednesday, stay another day. Herndon won't be inspecting the pipes, but you might find him alone somewhere else. Wrap your arm around his neck and snap it in two. Just be sure it looks like an accident."

Foreman reached over and gave Tyler a second hug. It was another awkward moment for Tyler. He was glad to see Foreman, but the man was too jolly considered the orders he was there to give. He'd given the order to end a man's life.

The Company was the judge and jury, and Tyler was the executioner. Verner Herndon had attended his last mass.

"Be careful," Foreman said, as he opened the door to climb out of the Yukon.

"Yeah. I will," Tyler replied as he nodded.

"Oh, by the way," Foreman said, sticking his head back inside. "Forest is a nice little town. Next time you're over that way, check out Bubba's BBQ. Best smoked brisket you'll ever eat."

The door closed. Foreman slipped into the shadows, and was gone. Tyler was a bit dazed by Foreman's last remark. Foreman knew he'd been to Forest, but how? He'd been thinking all along that the Yukon had some sort of homing device, which most likely was true. Since he'd taken a U-Haul truck to Forest instead, the cell phone had to be the culprit. He wondered if some minute device had also been planted in his shoes, or his clothing. He didn't know if that were even possible, but wasn't willing to take any more chances. He made a mental note to go buy new clothes and shoes as soon as he returned from the trip to Philadelphia.

32

Tyler awakened on Tuesday morning confused. He had been tired when he went to bed and had dreamed all night, although he couldn't remember anything he'd dreamt. It took him a few moments before realizing he was in a hotel room in Philadelphia.

After washing his face and getting dressed, he decided to go for a run. He wanted to go by the St. Peter's church, to check things out. The priest wouldn't be conducting his examination of the organ pipes until tomorrow. That would allow time to view the area, and as he'd been trained, look for an escape route in case things went awry.

With his hoodie pulled up over his head, he walked slowly down the street. Stopping near the end of the block, just before the intersection, he looked around. The church was across the street on the corner. It was an old stone church, with large stained-glass windows and a tall bell tower. He admired the architecture and thought it was a grand and stately structure. Moving forward, he stopped again at the corner. There was a single traffic camera on a utility pole. He closely observed the other buildings and utility poles, but saw no other cameras.

Walking further down the sidewalk to avoid being seen by the camera, he crossed the street then walked back to the large entrance of the church. Pulling on one of the doors, it opened with little effort. The church was open daily from eight to eight, for anyone wishing to come in and pray or confess their sins. Tyler needed to do both, but that wasn't why he was there.

The foyer led to the large open space of the sanctuary. It was empty, except for a man and a woman sitting on the front pew. They were whispering just above the choir voices singing over the speakers hanging from supports above. In the front, far to the right of the podium, was the pipe organ. It sat a few feet higher than the stage area, on a platform. A series of huge gold colored pipes sprang upward directly behind the organ. They ended near the ceiling, varying in height from one another. To the right of the organ, just beyond the last pipe and slightly hidden, was a narrow door. It had to be the door leading to the stairway behind the pipes.

Taking a seat on the far right of the back pew, Tyler sat there quietly. After fifteen minutes had passed, the couple up front rose from the pew and left. As soon as they exited the sanctuary, Tyler moved forward. He climbed onto the stage and went for the door to the right of the organ. Just as he had suspected, it led to a narrow and steep stairway that climbed upward behind the organ pipes. Wasting no time, he retreated out of the church, and walked back across the street, again avoiding the range of the traffic camera.

The next morning at a quarter past nine, he was standing on the corner again. He was wearing navy colored dress slacks, a white dress shirt, and a tie that closely matched the slacks. Before leaving the hotel, he'd opened a hidden compartment in his suitcase and removed a wig, a pair of black-rimmed glasses, and a fake mustache. Placing the wig over his head, he'd looked in the mirror.

The black hair of the wig combed to the right. The part on the left was perfect, and the edges around the ears and neckline were impeccably trimmed. The rug fit snugly and it was as perfect a business haircut as one could imagine. He had noticed several suits on the street the day before, all sporting haircuts that closely matched the one he now wore.

The mustache was several shades lighter than the hair on the wig, so it was tossed aside. He'd placed the glasses with clear unmagnified lens on his face and looked again in the mirror. It was impressive. He could easily pass as any of the thousands of businessmen in Philadelphia heading to work for another day in their office or cubicle. The only thing he couldn't hide was his bulging muscular neck and his large powerful hands.

Entering the sanctuary, he was pleased to find the place empty. Taking the same seat on the back row as the day before, he waited. It was essential to make sure the priest had made his way to the top of the stairway before proceeding.

It was 9:20. The minutes seemed to drag by. It reminded him of how slowly time passed when he was in the hole, back at Radford. At 9:30, he could wait no longer. His palms and brow were moist with perspiration, and he was getting antsy. No one else had entered the church, but at any moment, one or a dozen people could come walking through the doors.

Hurrying to the door to the side of the organ, he pulled it open and stepped inside. The old wooden handrail of the stairway was rickety, and the wooden planks of the steps were squeaky. Choir voices were singing over the intercom again, but Tyler didn't think it was loud enough to cover the noise he was making. There was no way to climb up without being detected.

Half-way to the top of the stairs, he looked up. Small particles of cigarette ashes hit his nose. There was a platform at the top of the stairs, and a man was standing there smoking, looking down - watching Tyler as he ascended.

"Who the hell are you and what are you doing here?" the man asked with a harsh tone.

Tyler continued upward, stopping three steps before reaching the platform. He recognized the man from the photo Foreman had shown him. It was Verner Herndon, the man he'd come to kill. He needed to make certain though.

"I'm looking for Father Herndon," Tyler said.

"You're trespassing," the man said with a sharp tone. "And I'm not your damned father. You're one of those asshole reporters, aren't you?"

"I've just got a few questions for you," Tyler replied, knowing the priest was assuming he was from a newspaper or television station and not someone there to cause him harm.

The man reached into his pocket and removed a cell phone. "I'm calling the police."

Continuing forward, Tyler stopped at the edge of the platform, three feet from the man. Getting a close-up look at the man's face left no doubt - he was staring into the eyes of Verner Herndon.

"You don't talk like a priest," Tyler said.

"Oh yeah. And you don't talk like a Philly reporter either. I guess I was wrong. You sound like some ignorant backwoods hick from the south."

Herndon looked down briefly at his phone, ready to punch in 911 and summon help to remove the intruder. Just as he did, Tyler lurched forward and with his powerful arms, shoved the man toward the railing. The ancient wood railing gave way, and it, along with Herndon went into the void. Herndon's body slammed into the pipes on the way down, causing them to ring out a dull thud. A second later, the priest and railing hit the bottom below simultaneously. The crash was loud.

Tyler had slipped on a pair of thin latex gloves as he'd moved forward in the church toward the pipe organ. Descending the stairs quickly, he stopped at the bottom and hovered over Herndon's body briefly. There was no use in taking time to check for a pulse. A large pool of blood was forming around the man's head. It was evident the fall had been fatal.

Running through the sanctuary, Tyler looked around assuring himself he'd not been spotted. The sanctuary was still empty. He peeled off the gloves and stuffed them in his pocket. Using his shoulder, he pushed the church door open and stepped outside. There were only a few people on the streets, but very shortly, the area in front of the church would be packed with ambulances, police cars, and a thousand curious citizens.

Out on the street, Tyler walked half a block then jaywalked across the street. He wanted to make doubly sure the traffic camera was avoided. Walking briskly, the twenty-minute walk back to the hotel was cut in half.

The hotel room had been paid for with cash. Tyler quickly packed his suitcase, but placed the wig, moustache, glasses, and the clothes he'd worn to the church, in a plastic bag. The room had been wiped down that morning before heading to the church, but was wiped again, ensuring no fingerprints were left behind. Amazingly, nothing had gone wrong, and he wanted to keep it that way. A garbage truck was parked on the corner two blocks from the hotel. Walking past, he threw the plastic bag into the back of the truck. It blended nicely with the hundred other bags of discarded trash piled high and ready to be compacted.

After hailing a taxi and arriving at the airport, it was a two-hour wait before his flight. Finding an empty seat in the terminal, Tyler sat down and took a deep breath. It was the first moment of relaxation all day. Slumping in the chair, his body rested but not his mind.

Herndon had been mean and nasty, uncharacteristic of a priest in all respects. That had made the task easier, but still, he had killed a man. He'd killed a stranger. Even if the man deserved to die, he didn't deserve to do so by Tyler's hands. Lost in deep thought, the evil deed of that morning continued eating into his soul. Thankfully the war within was interrupted by a loud voice over the intercom system, announcing the final boarding call to his flight.

33

It was getting dark as Tyler drove from the airport in Jackson to Meridian. On Thursday, he didn't leave his apartment. Pacing back and forth, he agonized over what he'd done. When not pacing he tried watching television, but was unable to remember what he'd watched. He sat there trying to justify in his mind that what he'd done was right, but was doing a poor job. He told himself he'd rid the world of a sick and cruel man, while allowing himself to persevere. He replayed the look on Herndon's face as he broke through the railing on his way to the sting of death lying below.

On Friday morning, a text message came. It read 'Nice job. Relax now. See U soon'.

Tyler got dressed and went for a run. He ran for twelve miles, thinking the long exercise would help, but it didn't. He showered, and drove down to the pool hall. He took a seat at the end of the bar. Without asking for identification to prove he was twenty-one, the bartender said, "What are you drinking big man?"

One mug of ice-cold draft beer led to another. Tyler drank until he wasn't able to walk. The bartender opened Tyler's wallet, and still not noticing his age, looked at the address on the license. He stuffed a note into Tyler's pocket, letting him know his Yukon would be at the pool hall when he sobered up. He then turned the bar over to another worker and drove Tyler home.

An hour before daybreak on Saturday morning, Tyler woke up. He had a splitting headache and felt like he'd been beaten up. There was no memory of how he'd gotten home, but finding the note in his pocket, the pieces came together.

Later that afternoon, he took a shower then got himself dressed. It was a long twenty-five-minute walk to the bar while nursing a hangover. He thanked the bartender for what he'd done, and refused a drink on the house. He'd had all the alcohol he could stand for a very long time.

Returning to the apartment, he flopped down on the couch and turned on the television. After thirty minutes of flipping through channels, he turned the television off. He needed to get himself together and move on. Nothing could change what he'd done, and he couldn't change what he was – at least for now. He got in the Yukon and drove down to Campbell Custom Cycles.

"You look like you've been ran over by a bus," Hagel said as Tyler entered the showroom.

"Yeah, I feel like it too," Tyler replied.

Tyler pulled an envelope out of his pocket and handed it to Hagel.

"Here's the cash I promised you. Don't call me, just give me a time you think the computer might be ready and I'll come back."

"It'll be ready this evening," Hagel said. "Renee ain't no slouch. She's been working hard on this project the last couple of days. She enjoyed the challenge."

"Wow. So you think it will work the way I want it to?"

"You ain't dealing with an amateur here," Hagel said smiling. "Renee's the best. She'd be hurt if she heard you talking like that."

"Sorry," Tyler replied. "It's been a rough couple of days for me."

"I'll tell you what. Come by the house for dinner this evening. Bring me four hundred more and we'll call it even."

Tyler hesitated. He wasn't sure about the invitation. He wondered why a man he'd only met once would invite him into his home. The training at the ranch, plus prison, had taught him to be skeptical. This might be some sort of trap. Perhaps what he'd requested was illegal, and the cops would be waiting for him.

"I'll ask you, what you asked me earlier," Tyler said. "Are you a cop? If you are you have to tell me."

Hagel chuckled. "I understand. You think this is some sort of setup. Don't bring the money, just come by for dinner."

Tyler thought for a moment then out of pure curiosity, accepted the invitation.

"I don't know where you live," Tyler said as he was about to turn and leave.

"Right behind the shop," Hagel replied. "Dinner will be ready at six. You'll get to meet Renee. Besides being a computer genius, she's an excellent cook."

§

Tyler was punctual. At exactly 6 p.m. that evening, he was knocking on Hagel's front door. When the door opened, Tyler's eyes widened as big as saucers. Renee was standing there. She wasn't what he had expected. For a moment, he thought it was Rita. She was a few years older than Rita, but could easily pass for her sister.

It was an awkward moment as he stood there staring at the woman. She noticed, and it seemed to embarrass her. Her cheeks were starting to turn red.

"You're beautiful," Tyler blurted out.

"Well, thank you," she said slyly. "Maybe I can send Hagel out for some milk and we can fool around."

Tyler immediately blushed.

"Just kidding" she said then laughed hard.

"I'm. I'm sorry. I didn't mean to stare," Tyler said. "You remind me so much of someone from my past."

"Hmm," Renee replied. "Could it be the lady friend you're so anxious to find?"

Tyler pulled his head back slightly. "Ah. Actually yes," he said, still dazed.

"Dinners on the table," she said. "Get your butt in here and let's eat."

She led Tyler to the dining room, where Hagel was sitting and waiting.

"Both of you have red faces," Hagel said. "Something going on here I need to know about?"

Hagel laughed. Renee slapped him on the head as she went by.

"Sit down. Let's eat," she said, taking a seat beside Hagel.

"You're about to partake in the best five cheese, three meat, lasagna you've ever tasted," Hagel said, as he scooped out a huge pile of the pasta dish onto his plate.

As they began to stuff themselves with the lasagna and garlic bread, Tyler couldn't help but moan.

"You're right," he said. "This is the best I've EVER eaten. Umm. Are you Italian?" He asked Renee.

Using her right hand, Renee stroked through her blonde hair with her fingers.

"Now, do I look Italian?" she asked.

Everyone laughed.

It was the best meal Tyler had eaten since leaving the ranch. It felt good to sit with others and share a meal. All through dinner, he kept looking at Renee. The resemblance to Rita was remarkable.

When the meal was over, Renee cleaned up the dishes while Hagel and Tyler went to sit on the front porch.

"She really is a remarkable woman," Tyler said.

"Yep. Best there is. I'd never find another one like her."

Tyler felt more relaxed than he had been in a very long time. There was a connection with Hagel, but he couldn't explain it. All the thoughts about Hagel setting him up with the police somehow left. He felt that if given the time, he and Hagel could become friends, something he missed having.

"So, what made you decide to invite me to dinner?" Tyler asked politely.

"I don't know. Curiosity, felt sorry for you, hard to say. You just looked like a sad puppy dog this afternoon. I decided you needed something to eat and some good southern company."

"Well, whatever your reason was, I thank you," Tyler replied, as a smile crossed his face.

"So how long were you in prison?" Hagel asked.

Tyler was surprised, shocked by the question that just came out of thin air. What did Hagel know, and how did he know it? He suddenly became uptight. Hagel had checked him out and found out everything. Tyler was about to bolt for the door.

"Prison! What brought that on?" Tyler answered, unconsciously edging upwards in his seat.

"I can tell," Hagel said.

"How?"

"The way you hold your fork and the way you hover over your food. Only people who've been in prison do that."

Tyler was surprised at Hagel's observation. Mannerisms were something he'd worked hard on back at the ranch, and yes, the way he ate was one of the first things they'd attempted to change. He felt like kicking himself. *Old habits die hard*, he thought. This wise old owl, Hagel, had seen something that got his attention. Tyler was oblivious to how he'd been eating, but Hagel had zeroed in on it. He was already making mental notes to be more aware of his mannerisms in the future.

"I'm very observant, highly trained, and well educated," Hagel said proudly. "I spent five years at Mississippi State."

"Did you study criminal justice?" Tyler asked.

Hagel laughed. "Hell no. It was Mississippi State Penitentiary."

Tyler joined in Hagel's laughter and relaxed a bit. This was the connection Tyler could feel but not describe. Hagel had been in prison, just as he had been. That's why he'd noticed how Tyler was eating.

"I spent a total of 62 months of my life in that dog hole," Hagel said. "Grand theft auto. I was twenty years old when I got caught. Young and dumb as they say. Judge gave me eight to ten, but I got out early for good behavior. So how long were you in for?"

"Nineteen months," Tyler said, feeling compelled to answer and not deny he'd been in prison.

"Well, I know you don't want to talk about it, and that's fine," Hagel said. "Nineteen months wasn't too long. You're young. I bet you did your time in juvenile. You must have gone through a stupid spell and stole an 'ole ladies purse or something. You couldn't have done anything really bad."

Tyler wanted to change the subject. It was bothersome that he'd once again given this man information about himself. He thought it was funny though that Hagel thought he'd not done time as an adult. *If only he knew the truth. It would scare him to death.*

Hagel now knew he was looking for someone, a woman. Hagel also knew he'd been in prison, and on his first visit to the shop, Hagel had commented about the Yukon and the kind of work he did. Hagel was sharp and paid attention to every detail. Tyler admired that, but planned to be more careful. If an ordinary shop owner was keen enough to observe him and learn so much, how much more would a trained eye, such as a police detective see. He'd have to work hard and pay more attention to the way he walked, the way he talked, the way he did everything.

One thing was a given, Hagel was way off base. The man had no idea about the act that had landed him in prison and the events that took place during the nineteen months he was there.

Renee appeared on the porch with cups of coffee and banana pudding.

"Don't spoil the man, Renee," Hagel said. "He'll be like a stray dog, feed him once, and he's forever at our doorstep."

Everyone laughed, and Renee slapped Hagel's head again.

"You mess up my hair and it's gonna be a long night for you," Hagel said, still laughing.

The banana pudding was just as Tyler expected – delicious.

"How would you like to learn a new trade?" Hagel asked Tyler.

"What do you mean?" Tyler answered, with his own question.

"I've got a bid in to build ten custom motorcycles for a group of bikers in Illinois. I need the work so I'm bidding low. If I win the bid, I'm going to need a helper. It won't pay much but its rewarding work. You can learn how to build a motorcycle from the ground up."

"You're offering me a job?" Tyler asked. "Why?"

"That day-trading stuff can't keep you busy all day. I like you, although I don't know why. I need someone to work part-time. I need someone I can depend on, and you seem that type. You fit the bill, so, what do you say?"

"It sounds interesting, but I can't," Tyler responded, flattered by the offer. "I have another job as well as the day-trading and can be called out of town at a moment's notice."

"All I need is a part-time worker. You can set your own hours. I just need to know you can give me ten to fifteen hours a week," Hagel said.

"Let me sleep on it then," Tyler said.

"Take your time. I won't know if I've won the bid for two weeks."

As Tyler was leaving, Renee handed him a box with the laptop computer he'd asked for.

"I didn't bring the four-hundred with me," Tyler said.

"I only need three-hundred. Bring it down to the shop when it's convenient," she replied. "If nothing else, we'll take it out of your paycheck!"

She kissed Tyler on the cheek, causing him to blush again.

"Gosh you're cute when that face is red," she said, laughing.

"What about me?" Hagel blared out. "My feelings are hurt!"

"I'll take care of you after the company leaves," Renee replied, winking at Hagel.

Everyone laughed again. Tyler said goodnight and left. It had been a great evening, just what he'd needed to pull himself out of the ditch. For a few hours, he'd been able to take his mind off Herndon and enjoy himself. On the way home, he felt guilty for that.

34

Sunday morning, Tyler was at the coffee shop early. He had the laptop with him, nervous but ready to try out his new machine. After logging on, he clicked on an icon Renee had placed in the top left corner of the screen properly named 'Where am I?' The screen came alive and a note at the bottom right indicated he was in Wheeling, West Virginia. He logged off, logged back on, and hit the icon again. This time it indicated he was in Casper, Wyoming. He was elated.

"She did it!" he yelled out, drawing attention from others in the coffee shop.

Tyler overloaded his system with coffee and pastries that day while he sat punching keys for nearly six hours. He weeded through tons of unimportant information surfing dozens upon dozens of websites. At the end of the day, he'd gathered a great deal of information on Rita Logan. He felt like he'd found the mother lode.

Rita had left Virginia soon after Tyler was sent to Radford. She landed in Colorado Springs and began teaching at a small college. One day, she suddenly disappeared from Colorado. She'd packed up and moved again. Her new address was in Longview, Texas.

He looked at the date Rita terminated her employment at the college. He scratched his head, thinking there was something significant about that date. Finally, it dawned on him. Rita had resigned a week after his transfer from Radford. He'd been declared dead, after a shootout with police when he burned to death inside the van that rolled off that West Virginia mountainside. That was the day Seth Boone became Tyler DuPont.

A week after moving to Texas, she was working at a local hospital in Longview. Two months later, she purchased a two-bedroom condominium unit not far from her work. The search didn't turn up a marriage license or newspaper articles indicating Rita was engaged. As far as he could tell, she was still single.

Rita wasn't that far away, but how could he get to her? Back at the apartment, he pulled out an atlas. His best estimate was she lived 370 miles away. It would be a five and a half hour trip by car. For all practical purposes, she may as well have been living in Hawaii.

There was no way he could get to Longview. Although he'd only been called into action once in the weeks he'd been in Meridian, Murphy's Law would surely rear its ugly head. As soon as he'd get to Louisiana or maybe before then, the phone would ring. He'd be called to meet Foreman or someone else, in the opposite direction. Taking a drive to Texas was out of the question, there wasn't any feasible way he could make the trip.

He had to be patient, and think before acting. Rita thought he was dead. There had to be some way he could get to her though. He wanted her to know he was alive. He wanted her to know that he thought of her day and night. He wanted to let her know he loved her more now than ever before.

He had no idea how long it would be before his contract with The Company would end. He expected to be on the run long before then. They'd never let him rest. He'd spend the rest of his years hiding from The Company goons seeking to end his life. Even if he could reach Rita, and she agreed to go on the run with him, she deserved a much better life than that. Still, being with her was all he could think of.

§

On Monday, Tyler thought about taking another trip to Forest. He wanted to make another deposit to his nest egg laying in the box inside the storage facility. Remembering the discussion with Foreman, the decision was made not to go. He could rent a car and leave the Yukon behind, but no way could he abandon the phone. He'd have to speak with Renee and see if she could work some of her magic and fix that problem.

At noon on Tuesday, Tyler walked into the shop at Campbell Cycles. Tyler and Hagel shook hands like old friends.

"You were right. I need something to keep me busy. I'd like to take you up on your job offer," Tyler said. "I can't promise you any sort of set hours, but while I'm here, I'll work hard, and I'm a quick learner."

Hagel smiled. "Sounds great, but I won't know for a couple more weeks if I got the contract. I thought I told you that."

"You did, but I don't need paid. I'll work for free. Teach me to ride a motorcycle, that'll be my pay."

Hagel smiled again. "How could I pass up an offer like that? Renee will be happy to know the young stud she met the other night is going to be hanging around the shop. You got a deal."

"Give Renee a big kiss for me," Tyler said with a smile. "Tell her the computer works great."

"Remember what I said the other night about a stray dog? I fed you and now I can't get rid of your ass."

"You're pathetic!" Tyler said laughing.

He liked Hagel's humor. He was looking forward to spending time with the man, learning some new skills, and most of all, learning to ride a motorcycle.

"I have another request for Renee," Tyler said as he was about to leave. "Ask her if it's possible for me to leave my cell phone in my apartment, carry another phone, and if the one in the apartment rings, it will automatically transfer the call without the calling party knowing."

Hagel had a puzzled look on his face. He had a thousand questions, but didn't ask any. He nodded and told Tyler he'd consult with Renee that evening.

During the next two weeks, Tyler spent three hours each afternoon at Campbell Custom Cycles. Hagel was amazed how quickly the young man caught on to things. By the end of the first week, Tyler could tear an engine down, and with limited oversight, rebuild it.

Renee mentioned that she was working on his phone request. She didn't think it was going to do what he wanted, and if it did, it was going to be expensive. She tried explaining how his request was far different from 'call forwarding', but Tyler got lost in the jargon. He never asked about it again. She'd let him know when she'd either given up or had worked her magic.

Keeping to his word, Hagel gave Tyler a riding lesson that first evening, and every evening afterward. The first lesson included two hours of instruction. The safety training was a prerequisite before hitting the road. When it was finally time to crank up the engines, Hagel started Tyler out on a street and trail 250 cc machine. The motorcycle was lightweight, easy to handle, and perfect for a beginner. Renee was there. She and Hagel watched as Tyler mounted the motorcycle and placed the helmet on his head. They got a good laugh out of seeing the big muscular man on the small framed motorcycle. He looked like an overgrown kid on a minibike.

Tyler thoroughly enjoyed the ride. Cruising down the highway with the wind in his face was therapeutic. He wasn't a free man, but riding the motorcycle brought a feeling of freedom never before experienced. His only disappointment was when Hagel circled back through town and led them back to the motorcycle shop. Tyler could have ridden all day and into the night. He was ecstatic and couldn't wait to graduate up to a larger machine.

On four occasions during those two weeks, Hagel and Renee invited Tyler over to dinner. He accepted every time. No matter what Renee cooked, it always tasted great. During the meals, Tyler often found himself looking at Renee, thinking how much she favored Rita.

It quickly became routine for Hagel to stand up at the table and accuse the two of them of having an affair. Hagel was excellent in playing the part of a jealous husband. Tyler would act terrified. Renee would laugh until running off toward the bathroom, on one occasion, wetting her pants. The three of them would sit at the table long after the meal was gone, role playing and just simply being goofy, laughing like children until their sides hurt. Tyler couldn't remember ever laughing so hard and having so much fun. As much as he'd tried to avoid having friends, Hagel and Renee in a short time span had become very dear to him.

On Wednesday, May 5th, Tyler was walking into Campbell's Custom Cycles front door when his cell phone rang. He stepped back out the door an answered.

"Hello."

"You've got work to do."

Tyler recognized the voice. It was Foreman.

"Meet me. Same place as last time."

The phone went silent.

"Dang it!" Tyler said, shaking his head.

He walked back into the shop. It was empty. He found Hagel in the back, inside the paint room, spraying primer on a gas tank.

"I just got a call," Tyler said. "I can't stay this evening. I may be out of town for a few days."

"I thought I saw Renee packing a suitcase this morning," Hagel said, smiling. "You two have a good time."

Tyler forced a smile, then left. Hagel could tell by the look on Tyler's face, he wasn't happy about this trip."

§

Although it was good to see Foreman, Tyler hated being there. Being there meant another job - killing another human.

Foreman was cheerful and inquisitive. He asked lots of questions. He asked Tyler if he'd been exercising, eating right, and going to the firing range. Tyler gave details about his daily routine, but didn't mention Hagel, Renee, and the motorcycle shop.

Judging by Foreman's questions, The Company monitored his movements when he left Meridian only. It gave him pleasure, knowing he at least had some degree of privacy. Along those lines, Foreman took notice of Tyler's new shoes and clothing. Foreman asked why he wasn't wearing the clothing he'd been provided. After the last meeting with Foreman, Tyler had purchased an entirely new wardrobe. The clothing and shoes supplied by The Company were neatly arranged in one of the closets in Tyler's bedroom.

Tyler answered Foreman's question by stating the shoes they'd provided weren't comfortable and the clothing wasn't his style. Foreman seemed satisfied with his answers, and Tyler was pleased the subject had been brought up. Foreman's questioning gave credence to Tyler's suspicions that a bug was planted in either his shoes, his pants, or both.

It surprised Tyler to learn his next victim was a woman. Her name was Victoria Harper, a partner in a large law firm in Nashville. He was given her daily routine and told to be waiting inside her house when she arrived home from work on Friday evening. It was to look like a robbery gone bad.

Foreman didn't provide any information about what the woman had done to get targeted. Tyler asked, but didn't receive an answer. The only personal information given was that the woman was single and lived alone. Foreman pulled out a drawing showing the layout of the house. Tyler put it to memory then asked about pets. The woman didn't like animals, so there would be no dogs ready to attack an intruder. The large house had a first-class alarm system, but that was no problem. Back at the ranch, Tyler had been taught how to disable any commercial or home security system on the market.

Instead of flying, Tyler was to drive to Columbia, Tennessee, rent a car, then drive on into Nashville. He'd spend Thursday afternoon and part of the day Friday scoping out the area. As always, he'd be looking for the best means of escape in case something went wrong. Early in the afternoon on Friday, he was to be in the house, ransack the place, and wait for Ms. Harper to arrive home.

Pulling a photo of Victoria Harper out of his pocket, Foreman showed it to Tyler. She was a tall woman, overweight, and unattractive. Her very short red and orange streaked hair didn't help matters at all. She didn't look nor did she dress like someone you'd expect to see sitting in a high-rise building providing legal services for the rich, but apparently, that was the case.

Once the job was done and the death confirmed, Tyler would be awarded another ten points. That would leave him with a whopping 120 blood spilling points to go before given his freedom.

"Meet me back here Saturday at noon," Foreman said, after a few more minutes of small talk.

This is different from the last job, Tyler thought. *He's either going to want to know how the job went or he's going to want to know about my mental state. Foreman knew I was depressed for several days after the last job.*

Foreman gave Tyler a huge bear hug and a rub on the head. Next, he opened the door, and just as before, slipped quickly into the shadows.

§

The stately million-dollar home of Victoria Harper was located in a prominent gated community in the suburbs of Nashville, Tennessee. Tyler disabled the alarm without a glitch. The system was still working, but monitoring nothing. The ninety-nine dollars per month, rated No.1, Century Guard Security Company, monitored their clients' homes from a computer room in downtown Nashville. They never received a beep or a chirp on their system.

Tyler was in the house working feverishly two hours before Victoria was expected to arrive home that Friday evening. He scurried about from room to room, pulling out drawers, turning over furniture, creating a total mess. It had to look like a robbery, and it most certainly would.

Foreman had told Tyler to collect anything valuable and put it in safe keeping once he got back home. He was dumbfounded when Foreman brought up the subject of 'life after parting ways with The Company'. He'd told Tyler to save every dime he could and steal anything valuable when on an assignment. "You'll need every penny you can find to live on once you leave us," Foreman had remarked.

Tyler suspected that Foreman knew why he'd gone to Forest the day he rented the storage shed and made his first cash deposit to his nest egg account. He'd gotten three grand out of the ATM machine an hour earlier, and The Company would have known that. Why else would Foreman have mentioned it?

When Tyler came up with the idea of the out of town storage facility, it was because he expected to leave Meridian in a hurry some day in the future. He could stop along the way out of the state, collect the valuables, and keep moving.

Having his nest egg inside the Meridian city limits was risky. If he were being chased by the bad guys and in a hurry to skip town, he'd have to either take time he couldn't spare to gather his loot, or else he'd have to come back later and recover the goods. He preferred neither, and that's why Forest seemed a logical place. The storage facility was right off the interstate and easily accessible.

Discovering that out of town travel was monitored Tyler decided somewhere in Meridian would be the best place to store his loot after all. The storage shed at Forest wasn't working out. The Company was already suspicious about his trip there. He needed to bury his treasure chest somewhere only he was familiar with, somewhere Foreman nor anyone else would ever guess. If push came to shove, and he had to leave town in a hurry, he could have Hagel collect his stuff and mail it to him, but that would be his last option. No way would he involve his dear friend unless it was a critical situation.

Tyler found Victoria's treasure chest. It was a safe in the den, behind a portrait of George Washington. Getting the safe open wasn't a problem. In a drawer at Victoria's computer desk there was a manila folder with a single sheet of notebook paper inside. Written on the paper was every password the woman used for her on-line accounts, bank account numbers, credit card numbers, her social security number, and yes, even the combination to the safe. For someone so highly educated, and working in a position of such prominence, Victoria's stupidity level was amazing. He imagined that whatever she did to get herself targeted by The Company likely happened because of this sort of reckless behavior.

Tyler's eyes nearly popped out of his head when the safe door opened. There was a remarkable collection of jewelry stowed inside. He was no expert on jewelry by any stretch of the imagination, but knew the gold and sparkling diamonds sitting before him were worth a small fortune. Even at pawnshop prices, the jewelry would fetch enough money to live on for a few years. He stuffed everything into a pillowcase taken from the linen closet.

The worries about survival once away from The Company were fading fast. He hated stealing though, and was already feeling guilty. The thought of stealing paled in comparison however to what was to come next. Soon the owner and lone occupant of the house would be home. It was his job to make certain the sunset Victoria saw on her way home was her last.

Framed photos were on the mantle, on top of the computer desk, and along the wall of the stairway. Some photos included Victoria, which he recognized. Even the photos from many years in the past showed her as unattractive, overweight, and sporting the same wild colored hair in one style or another. The other people in the photographs, mostly men, were either family, friends, or perhaps partners in the law firm. There weren't any photos of children, making him think Victoria had none.

Finding nearly three-thousand dollars in cash beneath Victoria's mattress, Tyler shook his head. This woman was super-intelligent, but lacked all aspects of common sense. *She could have at least hidden the money in her safe. On second thought however, with the combination so easily found, beneath the mattress may be the better hiding place.* He stuffed the fifty and one-hundred-dollar bills into the pillowcase.

Continuing his pilferage of the bedroom, he pulled out drawers, purposely spilling the contents across the floor. He also emptied closet shelves, creating a total mess. After that, he worked his way back to the kitchen.

The last rays of natural light had just faded away and the streetlights outside flickered on. Moments later, there was the sound of a garage door opening. Tyler was waiting, standing silently inside a broom closet, located in the breezeway between the garage and kitchen.

A car door shut, and seconds later, the breezeway door creaked open. The door creaked again as it shut. A series of buttons on the alarm keypad were quickly pushed in order to avoid a siren located on the rooftop to begin blaring away. The effort was nothing more than going through the motions. Tyler's reconfiguration of the alarm system showed it was operating correctly, lights and all, but in reality, the alarm was as useless as a dead car battery on a cold winter night.

Next came heavy footsteps as Victoria Harper walked past. Tyler opened the closet door slightly and peered out. He looked toward the kitchen. The refrigerator door was open, and Victoria was bent over thumbing through cold cuts and cheeses placed in one of the storage bins.

Swinging the broom closet door open, it made just enough noise to get Victoria's attention - but it was too late. Before she could stand totally erect, Tyler raised a 9mm pistol with silencer attached and shot her in the back of the head. Victoria fell hard onto the tile floor, creating a loud thump. Blood from the exit wound splattered both inside and outside the refrigerator, on the tile floor, the small table, and everything else within a ten-foot radius. A large pool of blood gushing from Victoria's head instantly began pooling on the floor.

Tyler found the shell casing on the floor, picked it up, and stuffed it in his pants pocket. He grabbed Victoria's purse off the kitchen counter where she'd laid it, took it back into the breezeway, and dumped the contents onto the floor. He retrieved her wallet, grabbed the cash and credit cards then tossed the expensive leather wallet back onto the floor.

Not wasting time, he removed the keypad cover from the alarm system. He enabled the alarm, but left it unarmed. The pillowcase full of loot was lying inside the closet where he'd been hiding when Victoria arrived home. He grabbed the sack then headed into the garage.

He exited through the side door, locking it behind him. Using a pry-bar he'd placed outside that same door, he jammed it into the frame near the lock. Pulling hard on the pry-bar, the wood snapped, tearing off a large chunk. This was done twice more before the wood gave way around the lock and allowed the door to open. He laid the pry-bar on the concrete stoop in front of the door.

It was to look as if Victoria had arrived home and foolishly not reset her alarm. An intruder had broken in through the side door of the garage, surprised Victoria, shot her in the head, and robbed the place before leaving in a mad rush. Some of that was true, but detectives would scratch their heads for months, never finding a single fingerprint, a murder weapon, or coming up with a suspect.

Three minutes after laying the pry bar on the concrete stoop, Tyler DuPont had worked his way through the trees and crossed a drainage ditch. He was headed toward the dark parking lot of a closed laundry service where he'd left the rental car. He'd left the scene without being spotted. The only attention drawn was that of an already barking dog as he'd sped across a short stretch of open ground two doors down and behind Victoria Harper's home.

After turning in the rental car in Columbia, he got into the Yukon and headed south, toward Meridian. It was getting late, and he was tired. He could have found a hotel for the night, but wanted to get back and sleep in his own bed.

Tyler was pumped with adrenaline, wired, and thrilled that he'd been able to disarm the alarm and was able to sneak into and out of such a prestigious and well-watched neighborhood unseen.

Along the way, his mood changed. Killing the priest bothered him, but in a much different way. He wanted to know exactly what Victoria Harper had done to deserve a bullet in the back of her head. Unlike the priest, he was confident rape wasn't her crime, although if anyone knew a woman was capable of raping a man, he was. It was unlikely she'd killed anyone. Whatever she'd done, it had pissed off some client of The Company. Whoever that person was, they'd likely paid a million dollars, maybe more, for the satisfaction of seeing Victoria Harper's obituary in a Nashville Newspaper.

He wondered how many people actually worked for Foreman and The Company. Aside from him, how many more agents were out there? How many accidental falls or robberies gone bad did The Company create each year, fooling the cops, fooling all of America.

He thought back to when he was taken from Radford. The two so-called officers who led him away from the prison had to be on the payroll. Then there were the two who took him to the small airport in West Virginia, one of which turned out to be Trainer. He wondered how often The Company ordered the death of one of their own. Odds were, one day the order would come to hunt Tyler DuPont down, just like Victoria, and put a bullet in his head.

35

At ten minutes before noon the day after killing Victoria Harper, Tyler pulled into the Lucky Stars Casino parking lot. Just as other times, Foreman seemingly appeared from nowhere. He climbed into the Yukon and sat down.

Foreman looked over at Tyler then reached for his normal hug. Tyler didn't resist, but still thought it was awkward how Foreman hugged him so tightly each time they met.

"How did it go?" Foreman asked, their eyes locked together.

"I didn't have any issues," Tyler answered. "Actually, it went better than I expected."

"Good. You appear to be fine. I was really worried about you after the first job."

"I want to know what that poor woman did," Tyler demanded. "Did she sell government secrets or kidnap some Senator's daughter and cut her to pieces?"

"I told you a while back, sometimes it's good not to know."

"I remember that, but I'd like to decide for myself if it's for my own good or not."

"Calm down then. Damn if you are stubborn as a mule. I don't know what you think you'll gain by this knowledge, but since you're so damn set on it, I'll tell you!"

Tyler was fuming, and now Foreman was as well.

"She pissed in her boss's cereal, OK," Foreman said, his voice loud and bold. "The head of the law firm, a man named Duffy Guyan, was having an affair in the office. Vicky Harper somehow obtained photos of the couple stretched out on Duffy's office sofa and gave them to his wife. I guess she thought it was her moral duty to interfere, hell, I don't know. Anyway, the wife sued for divorce and walked out with six mil, about three-fourths of Duffy's worth. He got word Vicky had set him up, so he paid to have her eliminated."

"If he was head of the law firm, why didn't he just fire her?" Tyler said, his voice every bit as loud as Foreman's.

"Listen. You wanted to know, and I'm telling what I've learned. I have no idea why he didn't fire her. That wouldn't get his money back, so I can only guess he took another route. I don't have a clue. I happen to follow orders and don't ask questions. Questions can cause a man a lot of grief in our organization."

"You mean to tell me I killed a woman because she revealed that her boss was having an affair!"

"Believe it or not Tyler, men and women have been killed for lesser offences. It's not your job to decide who the target is or determine if their deeds warrant a death penalty. You wanted to know, so now you do. Suck it up. You've got a hell of a long way to go before this is over. The best thing for you to do is stop asking questions. Just do the damn job and go home. When we're done with you, then you can walk off and make your own decisions about what's right and wrong, but until then, quit whining."

Tyler was ready to fight. So was Foreman. They sat there for a long time, both looking out the windshield and not saying a word. After several minutes passed, Tyler's anger abated, and he spoke.

"I don't like this. I wish this was all over," Tyler stated lowly, his voice calm.

"That's good. I'm glad you don't enjoy it," Foreman replied, his own voice back to normal volume. "I hope you never do. I also hope you can get out soon."

"Will that happen?" Tyler asked. "If I fulfill my duty, will you really let me go?"

"You do this the right way, and yes, someday you'll be free to walk away."

Foreman's words weren't very convincing. Tyler was sorry he'd asked about what Victoria had done. Learning the truth was already bringing him more pain and anguish. He'd beaten himself up over killing the priest. Now he would do it even more so for killing Victoria, whose only sin was revealing photographs of Duffy Guyan committing adultery. Duffy ordered the contract on one of his law partners. Tyler hoped that someday Guyan would face an assassin himself for the evil thing he'd done.

The target had been taken out, as ordered. Foreman knew if Tyler had been aware of everything prior to going to Nashville, he wouldn't have killed Victoria. Not doing so would have brought about Tyler's own death. Tyler didn't know it, but Foreman hoped that someday he too could walk away and leave this life behind.

"I'm sure you read about Victoria in the paper this morning," Tyler said. "What did it say?"

"Not in the papers yet," Foreman answered. "Body might not be found until tomorrow or Monday. Vicky didn't have many friends, so she might lay there for a while."

Tyler didn't like Foreman calling Victoria, Vicky. It sounded disgraceful. The woman was dead, and that alone demanded some respect. He didn't like hearing Victoria may not have been found yet either. He was hoping she wasn't still lying in a pool of blood on the cold kitchen floor. It sickened him to think about what he'd done. Victoria was no different from the priest. Neither should have had their lives ended by the hands of an assassin. Neither should have lost their lives at the hands of Tyler DuPont.

"So tell me. Did you find anything good in the house?" Foreman asked curiously. "I know she was a wealthy woman, basically because of her inheritance. Her mother was well off. The woman lived near Santa Monica, by the coast, died three years ago, and left everything to Victoria, her only child."

Tyler recalled that some of the jewelry looked as if it was very old. He wondered if it had belonged to Victoria's mother. He'd not taken the bag of jewels into his apartment when he'd gotten home. It was still behind his seat. He reached back, grabbed the bag, and held it up to show Foreman.

"Take a look," Tyler said indifferently, offering Foreman the bag.

Foreman opened the bag wide, looked inside, then whistled.

"Nice. Very Nice!"

"How long it will take me to pay back my debt?" Tyler asked, staring out the windshield again.

"Two years. Maybe four," Foreman said, closing the bag and handing it back to Tyler.

Foreman changed the subject. He was over his spell of anger and back to the business of coaching Tyler, trying to keep him safe.

"I know - that you know - that you're being monitored," Foreman said. "I do some of the monitoring myself, but there are others too, as you would expect. It's been noted that you aren't wearing the new clothes you were provided. I'd recommend when milling around town, out for a jog, or on a job we've assigned, to wear the shoes you were provided."

Tyler was taken back. Foreman was all but admitting the shoes were bugged, just as he'd expected. But why was Foreman telling him this? Was Foreman trying to get him to trust him in order to betray him somewhere on down the road? Perhaps Foreman was genuine, a true friend who wanted to help and protect him? It was confusing.

Tyler kept silent. He would let Foreman talk, provide him information then he'd digest it all later. Foreman was an expert, with years of experience in deception. Tyler was new to this high-stakes world that had unfolded before him like a good spy novel. He had to be smart, sorting out the chess moves carefully, slowly, methodically.

"You won't be called again before Monday," Foreman said. "When you get back to Meridian go to the airport. Rent a car and leave your phone in the Yukon. Drive the rental to Forest, where I figure you're hiding your goodies. Dig up the money and find somewhere close to your apartment to hide your jewels and cash. Right now, I'm the only one who knows you were ever in Forest, but if you go there again after today - I can't guarantee others won't find out. It's dangerous. You have a four hour time to arrive at a meeting spot, so you think you can roam around within a few hours of Meridian and be fine, but don't. Don't raise suspicion. We've lost men in the past because management got nervous - worrying an agent was up to no good, perhaps ready to skip out on them. I want you safe, so do as I say, no questions asked."

Foreman's commands were harsh and stern, but absent from anger. Tyler continued to be amazed at what he was hearing. It was as if Foreman had read his mind. Foreman had suggested the very thing Tyler had been thinking – find a better place to hide the stash, somewhere close by. The thought crossed his mind that Foreman just wanted to know about where he would hide the goods, so he could drop by and steal them. If that is what Foreman wanted though, he could take them now. As good a fighter as Tyler was, he was no match for the man. If Foreman wanted him dead, he'd be dead.

There were many things about Foreman Tyler just couldn't figure out. The hardened man seemed to go out of his way to protect him, and he didn't understand why. As much as he hated what The Company stood for, he liked Foreman. It was odd. He wasn't about to put his full trust in this man, yet he considered him a friend, albeit a strange and secretive one.

Tyler's mind was already churning with something Foreman had said. It would be at least a day and a half, likely more, before his phone would ring again, sending him off on yet another killing mission. He could easily make it to Texas and back in that amount of time. He was hoping the meeting with Foreman was about over. He'd rush back to Meridian, dump the phone, rent a car, and be on his way. He marveled at his luck. In a few hours, he'd been in Longview, Texas – knocking on Rita's door.

"Well, anything you need to discuss?" Foreman asked, his voice changing and his smile returning.

"No. Nothing," Tyler replied.

"Alright. I'm leaving then."

Tyler's adrenaline was already rushing through his veins. He couldn't wait to get out of the parking lot and headed back toward Meridian. He reached toward Foreman. This time he was the one ready to initiate a hug.

Foreman opened the door and stopped just before getting out.

"I got one more question before I go," Foreman said, his voice once again changing to the deep harsh tone.

Tyler noticed that Foreman's face was turning red. Tyler stiffened, and his adrenaline seemed to come to an abrupt stop. Before Foreman left, there always seemed to be something else, something he didn't want to hear.

"You understand that our organization has to have a system of checks and balances don't you?" Foreman asked, presenting it more as a statement than a question.

"Sure," Tyler said, feeling compelled to answer.

Foreman looked Tyler directly in the eyes.

"Do you have any idea why someone in Casper, Wyoming, would be conducting internet searches on Rita Logan?"

Tyler's blood drained to his feet. The ghostly look on his face told all. Foreman shook his head.

"I can't keep covering your ass, Tyler," Foreman said sternly. "Next time, I may not be able to. I've been sticking my own neck out, taking a chance on getting in some deep shit. You've got to get your head screwed on straight. Think about this. If you were to contact that woman, it wouldn't just get you killed. It would get her killed as well. I don't think you want that – do you?"

Tyler wanted to look away, but couldn't. He wanted to run, but couldn't. He wanted to deny having done the search, but couldn't. Foreman was right - they would kill Rita as well as him. He hadn't thought of that. He was too blinded by love to consider everything.

He'd been foolish, thinking Foreman wouldn't find out about him doing the research. For an instant, he thought Renee had messed up - that her software wasn't as good as she'd claimed it to be. Then he realized - that wasn't it at all. Not only was he being monitored, Rita was being monitored as well. Of course – she would be. Of all the people in his old life - who would he try to contact? A child could have guessed right - it was Rita Logan.

"I'll destroy the computer as soon as I get back to Meridian," Tyler said, hanging his head low.

Foreman reached over and patted Tyler on the arm. He then stepped out, closed the door, and was gone.

Tyler kicked himself, all the way back to Meridian. He could have easily gotten Rita killed.

36

Following Foreman's instructions, Tyler dropped his phone off at the apartment and headed toward Forest, Mississippi. He would pick up the box sitting in the middle of the storage shed and head back to Meridian. He'd already been thinking of a safe place in Meridian to store his cash and stolen property.

As he drove, each mile brought about more anger. He was angry with himself for being so unthoughtful as to endanger Rita. He was angry with Foreman, and he was angry with anyone associated with The Company. It was one thing to monitor him, their slave, but they had no right to watch an innocent citizen who'd never done anything but help people. The Company had to have a system of checks and balances as Foreman had said, but he hated them for that as much as he hated everything else they represented.

He had to forget about Rita, and the cruel, threatening ways of The Company was his motivator. There was no way to erase her from his memory though, because he didn't want to. The thought of them someday being together is what kept him going. She was his inspiration, the only reason to go on living. He was going to figure this out, find a way to outsmart The Company goons and be with her. At that moment though, he didn't have a clue how to do so.

Foreman had mentioned this could all be over in as little as two years. He'd spent nearly that long in the nightmarish hell of Radford. Surely, he could wait two years. He was living a life of luxury aside from the times being called upon to commit murder. He didn't think he could go on with the assassinations though. The two people he'd already killed were eating away at him from the inside out. He wondered if he'd ever be able to tell Rita what he'd done. The obvious answer was - no. She would never understand - no one could. Even if she did, and even if she forgave him, he could never forgive himself.

The future was quickly becoming a tangled mess of what ifs. *What if The Company won't let me go? What if Rita gets married to someone else? What if I find her and she tells me she doesn't love me anymore? Even after my debt is paid, it's not as if I can just drop back into society. The rest of my life will be under an assumed name. I'll always be looking over my shoulder watching for the police. Not only that, but chances are I'll be hiding from a hit man sent by Foreman or someone else in this gang of thugs. Even if I find Rita and she wants to be with me, it isn't fair to her. How could I ask her to live that kind of life?*

§

On the way back from Forest, Tyler pulled off the interstate, drove two miles down a two lane road, then drove down a dirt road that appeared to head toward a farm house a mile further on. There was a dip in the road, dropping several few feet in elevation before crossing a small stream. Hidden from view of the surrounding landscape, Tyler pulled down into the swag and stopped. He got out, and using a hammer he'd brought along, smashed to bits the computer he'd purchased from Hagel and Renee. He then lit a propane torch and melted the plastic, fusing it into an ugly glob that looked like the remains of a manmade meteorite.

Back in Meridian that evening, he thought long and hard about heading down to the bar and getting soused, like he did after the Philadelphia trip. Deciding that wasn't any way to live, and knowing it most certainly didn't solve any of his problems, he put on his jogging clothes instead and went for a long run. The fresh evening air and the strenuous exercise seemed to clear his head. After a hot shower, he watched television for an hour then went to bed. It had been a long couple of days.

On Sunday, Tyler went to visit Hagel. Renee had driven to Vicksburg, Mississippi to visit her ailing sister, so Hagel was a free man until Wednesday. Hagel was about to prepare a bologna and cheese sandwich. Tyler insisted on taking him out for lunch instead, suggesting they go by motorcycle. A few minutes later, they strapped on helmets and headed off to the Blue Bend Family Restaurant on US 11, not far from the airport. It was an old dive dating back to the 1950s. The locals gave the place mixed reviews. Although Hagel had lived in the area all his life, he'd never eaten there, and they were about to understand why.

"Can I ask you something, Hagel?"

Hagel had just filled his mouth with a huge chunk of country-fried steak smothered in white gravy. He made a face at Tyler, indicating it was a bad time for a question. Tyler watched for what seemed like an hour as Hagel worked his jaw muscles up and down, chewing the not so tender steak, and using his tongue in a failing attempt to remove the stringy meat from between his teeth. Finally, Hagel gulped, took a long swig of sweet tea, and his mouth was clear of food.

"Don't catch a man with his mouth full of mystery meat and ask questions," Hagel said in a brutal voice with a half-smile. "Where's your manners? Were you raised in a barn?"

Tyler chuckled. He should have learned by now. Don't mess with Hagel while he's eating, especially when he's eating rubber steak.

"So what did you want to ask me?"

"I was just curious. Before I bought the computer, you did a search on me. Do you mind telling me what you found out?"

"Nothing," Hagel replied, working his knife hard to saw off another piece of the steak.

"Nothing?" Tyler asked.

"I didn't do a search on you," Hagel said. "Renee said what you wanted wasn't illegal, so I didn't waste my time researching your sorry ass."

That explained why Foreman had not mentioned Hagel or Renee. He felt confident now that Foreman nor anyone else in The Company was aware of his new friends. If Hagel had actually run an on-line search of Tyler DuPont, Foreman would have surely known.

"I know you have lots of questions you'd like to ask about my life," Tyler said, watching Hagel in an ill attempt to chew another bite of the steak. "I'll tell you what I can as time goes on, but there are many things about me you can't ever know."

"What are you getting to?" Hagel asked, surrendering to the steak by spitting it from his mouth into a paper napkin.

"I want you and Renee to never ever, under any circumstances, try and find out things about me on the internet."

"I told Renee you had some dark secrets," Hagel said. "You're in the Federal Protection Program, aren't you? I knew it!"

"It's far worse than that," Tyler said. "I can't tell you much, but if you use any form of electronic media to search for me, it could put you in danger."

"You're shittin me!"

"No. I'm serious," Tyler said firmly. "I work for some really bad people. I'd like nothing better than to walk away, but I can't. Please trust me - and never mention this to anyone."

"Is it the mob?" Hagel probed.

"Even worse than that," Tyler answered. "I won't come by the shop anymore unless you think its ok. I don't want to involve you with my troubles. Gees, I wish I could say more, but I can't. I can't even believe I've told you this much. You and Renee have treated me like your own child. I've never felt so wanted and never felt so loved. I just don't want anything bad to happen to either of you."

"I don't know what you've gotten mixed up in, but I don't really care, other than I want you to be safe," Hagel said. "If I can help, all you have to do is ask. Renee and I both come from a hard upbringing. We had to fight somebody every day to survive, so we don't scare easy. I'll talk to Renee about never conducting research on you, that won't be a problem. As for coming by the shop, you do what you want, but if Renee finds out you've bailed out on her – hell, it'll be worse than facing the bastards you're working for."

Tyler wanted to laugh at Hagel's remark, but all he could do was breathe a sigh of relief. He wanted to keep hanging around Hagel. Hagel and Renee were good company. He also had a desire to learn more about riding and building motorcycles.

"Alright. I'll keep hanging around then," Tyler said. "If the kitchen heats up, I'll just walk away. As I said, I don't want anything to happen to you or Renee, especially on my account."

"I wish I could pay you," Hagel said. "I didn't get the contract I was hoping for. To be quite honest, Renee and I have been struggling to keep our heads above water. Three times over the last two years, we considered closing down the business, but we somehow managed to keep it going. Right now, I think we have more debt than the Federal Government. We'll survive though, always have. I just can't afford to pay a worker for now, that's all.

"I don't want to be paid. Heck, I can pay you for teaching me a new trade. You should have let me know that you need money."

"No. No. No. I wasn't making a plea for some charity, just stating the facts. Of course, if its drug running you're into, you could cut me in on a few trips. That might help me pay down my debt."

Tyler forced a smile. He didn't think Hagel was interested in running drugs. Tyler wished drug running was his trouble. Getting away from a gang of drug dealers would pale in comparison to getting free from the grasp of The Company.

§

Over the next few days, Tyler couldn't help but replay in his mind the meeting with Foreman. Trying to reach out to Rita, he'd been playing with fire. He couldn't believe he'd been so naïve, not considering that The Company would monitor her.

As soon as the name Rita or Logan was typed into a keyboard anywhere, red flags began flying at the ranch, or some undisclosed safe house where 24-hour monitoring of agents took place. The Company had broken him out of prison and given him a second chance in life. He was thankful for that, he owed them his life, but he now had a deep hatred because of what they'd made him. Killing people was easy for Tyler DuPont. Living with it was the hard part. It was like a malignant tumor wrapped around his organs, inoperable, incurable, eating away at the flesh. The sting of its bite penetrated every nerve, every fiber of his being.

While waiting to get his haircut at a local barbershop on Wednesday morning, Tyler was thumbing through the newspaper. In the classified ads, something caught his eye. It was an advertisement for a high school alumni website. The ad asked the readers if they wanted to reconnect with old friends from their glory days of high school.

He remembered Foreman saying he'd grown up in Meridian. It gave Tyler an idea. If Foreman grew up in Meridian, there would be school records. Perhaps he could dig and find out about the man's past and who he really was.

The name, Foreman had to be a bogus name, but it was all he had to go on.

That afternoon, Tyler was in the back of the motorcycle shop. A local biker had hauled his Harley in with a broken drive belt. Tyler was helping Hagel install a new one.

Renee dropped by, curious about what her favorite two men were working on. She also wanted to invite Tyler to dinner. Tyler had learned weeks ago never to tell the beautiful woman no. Besides, he wasn't about to turn down an opportunity to eat Renee's cooking.

That evening, Tyler was smacking his lips over a steaming bowl of seafood gumbo. It was his second helping. Between bites, he commented that he'd gained five pounds since meeting Renee.

"Get out while you can then," Hagel commented. "I weighed one-o-five when I met the woman. Now look at me!"

It was another relaxing evening spent with his new friends. The Campbell house was a safe haven so to speak. Being with Hagel and Renee helped Tyler forget about the hard life he'd lived and his uncertain future.

The Campbell's had opened their home and their hearts to this troubled young man who one day walked into their lives out of nowhere. They knew little about him, but from the onset had taken a liking to him. Tyler felt likewise. On the evening Hagel had invited him to dinner for the first time, a lasting friendship had but put into motion.

The secretive, young Tyler DuPont, who looked like he could rip a house apart with his bare hands, actually had a gentle nature. It was evident to Hagel and Renee, that Tyler had been kicked around and abused all his life. He was the redheaded stepchild, a lost sheep. He needed a tremendous amount of love and guidance. He needed someone to help him, just be there, offering support as he struggled to work things out. Fortunately, for him, Hagel and Renee were suckers for lost causes.

They knew this young man was in some sort of trouble, and it was serious. They had no clue as to what he'd gotten involved with, but they were willing to help him get his life straightened out if that was possible. They'd only known Tyler for a short time, but thought of him as the son they never had but always wanted.

While the three of them sat at the table eating a slice of homemade German chocolate cake for dessert, Renee asked Tyler how his new computer was working.

"I don't have it anymore," he replied. "I destroyed it."

Hagel and Renee both looked up from their plates.

"Did you tell Renee about not researching me?" Tyler asked Hagel.

"Yes. He told me," Renee answered.

"The people I work for found out I was researching my lady friend. Your computer worked great Renee. It was awesome, and I thank you so much for what you did. The thing I didn't count on was that my friend is being monitored too. They knew someone was searching for her, and they knew that someone was me. It put her in danger, and I could kick myself from here to the coast for doing so."

"Can't you just quit?" Renee asked. "Can't you just walk away from whoever it is you're working for?"

"Not for a long time," Tyler replied. "I belong to them. They own me."

Renee seemed confused, but not Hagel. Hagel hadn't fit all the pieces together, but he'd formed the border to this puzzle. He knew from his time spent in prison how easily you could become indebted to someone and become a slave. Whatever Tyler had gotten himself into - it was very serious, more so than he'd originally thought.

"I'll explain slavery to you later," Hagel said to Renee. "It's a different kind of slavery than you've read about in history books. Right now, we just need to support Tyler and help him if we can."

Tyler was moved by Hagel's remark.

"Why have you befriended me like this?" Tyler said. "I certainly don't deserve it!"

"Everybody needs somebody," Hagel replied. "I could tell the first day we met that you were a troubled young man in search of something. I know what it is you're looking for. You're looking for peace, love, freedom. The woman you're trying to find, she's the answer."

Tyler didn't think he was so transparent, or maybe it was that Hagel had some special gift. Regardless, Hagel had looked into the windows of his eyes and seen his soul.

"I didn't exactly get myself into my present trouble," Tyler replied. "The trouble sort of found me. Listen. I love your friendship. The two of you have helped me so much. Much more than you know. I want so badly to tell you my story, but knowing that could put you in danger."

"I think Hagel made it clear," Renee said. "We care for you and want to help. You only need to tell us how to do that. If you decide to tell us more, fine, we aren't going to abandon you, and we ain't scared of this devil that's haunting you."

"All I have to do is look in the mirror," Hagel said. "Thirty years ago, I was where you are. Then I met Renee, and she saved me from myself. Just let us know what we can do to help you."

"Well, it's early but I'm tired," Renee said, rising from her chair. "You two continue this conversation over the kitchen sink while you do the dishes. I'm going to take a shower and go to bed."

The evening had turned from laughter to a somber mood. Tyler helped Hagel wash the dishes and clean up the kitchen. As they were finishing, Renee stuck her head through the kitchen doorway and observed. Her two men were struggling to find the right drawers and cabinets to put away the silverware, bowls, pots, and pans.

"Fried chicken and homemade buttermilk biscuits tomorrow evening you two," she said. "It'll be ready at six, so, don't go riding those iron horses off into the sunset and be late. Yes, that goes for you as well, DuPont! I want to see a happy face, and I want you here on time."

"You ain't the boss of me!" Tyler fired back at Renee with an ear-to-ear grin.

Renee shook her fist at him then retreated to the bedroom.

"What a mouth. No damn wonder you're in trouble," Hagel remarked. "You better get your ass out of here before she gets back with her shotgun."

Tyler ruffled Hagel's hair as he slipped past him toward the back door.

37

The next morning, Tyler walked downtown to a coffee shop. He paid twenty-five dollars for three hours use of a computer. Searching several high school alumni sites, he was hoping to find information on Foreman. He didn't have a name, but he had a face, even if it was an older face. If he could find an old photo of Foreman, he could finally find out who he was.

Tyler thought Foreman was somewhere between forty and fifty years of age. Just to be sure, he widened his search to the years 1980 to 2000. If Foreman attended high school in Meridian, it should have been during that time span. The search was fruitless. Tyler didn't find anyone pictured on an alumni site who resembled Foreman. As he walked back home, a thought occurred to him. *What a waste of time. Foreman wouldn't show up on a high school alumni website. He would never join such a thing. Even if he had, The Company would have removed it. However, if he went to high school in Meridian, the school would have a record.*

Tyler made a visit to both Meridian high schools, meeting with the principals. He expected the schools would retain copies of their yearbooks, and he was hoping to look through them.

Both school principals turned Tyler down. They said they couldn't allow him to enter the school for security

367

reasons. The last principal he met with suggested he try the local library. Tyler smiled when the man said that. If anyone should have thought of the library, it should have been him.

Tyler hit pay dirt. The Meridian Public Library was a gold mine. They had most of the two Meridian high school annuals dating back to the fifties. After two hours of thumbing through annuals from Shady Spring High School, Tyler found no one resembling Foreman. There was a couple of possibilities from the graduating class of 1986 and one from 1989, but they were stretches. Turning to the annuals for Westside High School, he gathered all the yearbooks and placed them on a table. Three were missing for the years he'd selected to research, 1980, 1982, and 1991.

He decided to look at senior photos only. The photos were larger, and the faces of seniors looked more mature than the underclassmen. Flipping to the last page of seniors for the Westside High School 1987 yearbook, he'd not seen anyone thus far that came close to resembling Foreman. On the last page however, after Butch Zimmer, was a listing of 'Those Not Pictured'. One of the names stood out, catching Tyler's eye. The name was 'Samuel DuPont'. The first day Tyler had visited the motorcycle shop, Hagel had asked if he were related to any of the DuPonts in Meridian. *That's interesting*, he thought.

Setting the annual aside, Tyler turned to the 1988 yearbook and began studying faces of the senior boys. He received another surprise when he got to the Ds. There in front of him in the senior portraits was a boy named Tyler DuPont. *My Lord, this kid has my name!* The boy in the photo had short black hair, and his eyes, yes, those eyes. They were the eyes of someone Tyler had seen before.

He quickly grabbed the 1986 yearbook and turned to the photos showing the junior class. There was a photo of Samuel DuPont. There was no doubt that Samuel and Tyler DuPont were brothers. Tyler couldn't believe what else he was seeing. Not only were the two boys brothers, he was positive that Samuel DuPont was the one and only - Foreman. The facial features and eyes were the same. It couldn't be denied. He could hardly believe it, but it was true. He was looking at a high school junior photo of Foreman.

"YES!" Tyler shouted out, forgetting he was in a library. Several patrons and workers shot hard glances toward him. Tyler put his head down, burying it into the open yearbook. It was an amazing find. He felt like he'd hit the lottery. He didn't know what else he could find out about Foreman, and didn't know what good the information would do him, but he was elated. As wonderful as the information was, it only brought about more questions. The biggest questions were - why did Foreman give him the same last name as his own - and why would his new given name be the same as Foreman's younger brother?

Turning back to the annuals, he looked at every page of the Westside High School yearbooks from the years1984 through 1988. Samuel and Tyler DuPont's names and photos were found in several places. They'd played football, basketball, ran track, and had been members of several clubs.

Satisfied that he'd seen everything available in the annuals, he placed all the books back on their proper shelves and headed to the front desk. A young girl sporting long golden blonde hair was busy typing on a computer. Tyler interrupted her work and asked to borrow a telephone book. Without saying a word, she gave him a sparkling smile that revealed a mouth full of braces, and handed him the latest telephone directory.

He took a couple of steps back then opened the telephone book to the Ds. There were two listings for DuPont - Jules A. and Edgar, both on Clearfork Valley Road. Tyler returned the directory to the young lady. She'd been watching him, admiring the hot stud ever since he'd drawn her attention by politely asking to see a telephone book. Her heart was beating fast, and her mind was wondering how it would feel if he were to hold her close and kiss her. Tyler thanked the girl, and produced a smile that made her blush. Inside, she was swooning. She watched him walk away until he was out the door and gone from sight.

Tyler decided to drive over to Clearfork Valley Road and look around. It was a narrow single-lane paved road, located three miles south of the city limit. The road cut through farm country. The houses were spaced far apart. Slowing to look for names on mailboxes as he drove past, he found what he was looking for. Promptly displayed at 8200 Clearfork Valley Road was a mailbox with the name Jules A. DuPont. The house was a short distance off the road. An old man dressed in bibbed overalls was sitting in a rocker on the front porch. He was watching Tyler, expecting some stranger from the city had lost his way.

Tyler pulled into the graveled driveway and stopped. He got out of the Yukon and walked toward the porch, addressing the man as he went.

"Good afternoon, sir. Would you happen to be Jules DuPont?"

"You a bill collector or somethin?" the man replied, looking Tyler over.

"No sir. I'm just looking for information," Tyler replied.

"Infermation bout what?" The man asked.

"I'm from up near Tupelo," Tyler said.

He'd found in prison that lying and acting were essential to survival. At the ranch, they had honed his skills for doing both. Lying and pretending to be something other than what he was, were things Tyler wasn't very proud of, but that was only the tip of the iceberg these days.

"I'm doing a college project on family history, and DuPont was one of the names I was assigned."

Tyler had moved to within ten feet of the porch before stopping. He didn't feel welcomed, so he decided he'd gotten close enough. He was looking up at the old man, who was studying this unsolicited stranger.

"Ya come a fer piece just ta git sum history," the man said gruffly.

"Are you the only DuPont living around here, sir?"

"That boy of mine lives on up da road a ways. I reckon we be da only DuPonts in these here parts. What'd ya say yo name was son?"

"Seth Campbell," Tyler replied, using his real first name and borrowing Hagel's last.

"Lot of Campbell's in this area. Ya studyin em too?"

"Yes sir, I got three names to study, my own, DuPont, and Simmons. My professor selected DuPont and Simmons."

"Well, don't know anyone called Simmons. Fraid I can't be much hep to ya sonny."

"I found two names going through records at the library, Samuel and Tyler DuPont. You know anything about them?"

"Had a cousin named Leon. They be his boys. Lived outside town on da north end."

"So they don't live there anymore?"

"Fraid not. Leon twas a widower, wife died of consumption way back. Leon be gone quite sum time himself. His ticker stopped dead whiles he workin on a tractor."

"What about the boys? Where are they?"

"Don't know bout Samuel. Not like they's close family. Don't rightly recall em ever come fer a visit. Those boys of his was sum fine football players in thar day. Both of 'em tougher en nails.

"What about Tyler?"

"The two of 'em boys joined the Marines. That younger one Tyler, he got himself killed by Noriega's troops durin da Panama Invasion. Don't have a clue bout Samuel, he mite be dead too. I really don't know, boy."

Tyler thanked the man for the information and his kindness, then left.

So Foreman named me after his kid brother who was killed in Panama, Tyler thought as he drove back toward Meridian. *Interesting. Very interesting.*

38

Over the next week, Tyler only spent a few hours at the motorcycle shop. Hagel thought it was because he needed space, but Renee suspected it was because of something else.

On Saturday afternoon, Tyler was assisting Hagel with putting a new tire on the back of a custom-built chopper, nearly ready for delivery to the president of a local biker group. Renee entered the shop and pulled up a stool. She sat down and watched the two men on their knees working beneath the motorcycle jack. After two minutes of being ignored by the men, she decided to strike up a conversation with Tyler.

"Ain't seen you around much this week," she said.

"I've been busy," Tyler answered, not taking his eyes off the tire as he and Hagel were getting it properly aligned.

"How are you two ever going to become lovers if you don't spend some time with the woman?" Hagel asked jokingly, as he reached for a screwdriver.

Tyler glanced up at Renee's beautiful face. They both chuckled.

"So this girlfriend you've been looking for, what's she like?" Renee asked.

"She's beautiful. She looks a lot like you. She's also wonderful, just like you. If I didn't know better, I'd swear she was your younger sister."

"Or my daughter!" Renee replied.

"No. Sister. She's twelve years older than me."

"See, you do like older women," Hagel said as he sat down on the floor and straddled the tire. "I think you two have been fooling around at night while I've been sleeping."

"Shut up and keep working, Hagel," Renee said. "I'm trying to find out about his girlfriend, and you keep interrupting."

"You ain't the boss of me," Hagel replied, smiling.

"Oh, so you liked that line Tyler used on me the other night. Let's see what that gets you, smart aleck."

"I should have known better," Hagel said grunting as he pushed against the tire.

Renee crossed her legs, placed her left elbow on her knee, and propped her chin in her left hand.

"So, what's the girlfriend's name?"

"Listen," Tyler replied. "You and Hagel are like family to me. I care a great deal for both of you. It's really best you don't know a whole lot. I've stopped looking for this girl. I'll find her again someday. I just have to wait and be patient."

"I think you've already found her," Hagel chimed in. "You just can't reach out to her, for whatever reason."

"I told you before, I'm closely monitored, and so is she," Tyler stressed.

"If we're like family, then we should be involved," Renee said, unwilling to drop the matter. "Hagel and I feel the same about you. We barely know you, but we think of you as our son. We see you're struggling, and want to help."

"I know you do," Tyler said, glancing at Renee. "It's just too risky."

"Bologna!" Renee replied. "Why don't you fill us in on things, then we can decide for ourselves if it's too risky. Stop avoiding us. You've not been hanging out here much this week, and it makes us sad."

Tyler was looking at Renee. She had a look of hurt on her face.

"Does she ever let up?" Tyler asked Hagel.

"Only when I beat her!" Hagel replied.

Renee laughed. "That'd be the day before your funeral."

Tyler had played along, but he was uncomfortable with Renee's persistence. He thought perhaps if he fed her tidbits of information it would satisfy her curiosity."

"Rita. Her name is Rita."

Hagel looked at Tyler, amused that he'd given in to Renee.

"That's a pretty name," Renee said. "It's not as pretty as Renee, but it's a pretty name."

"I disagree," Hagel said. "Renee is a pretty run-of-the-mill name if you ask me. I don't care much for it, never have."

Renee was within range. She kicked Hagel's right thigh hard with her foot. He rolled over on the floor, holding his leg, screaming out with pain.

"What a wimp," Tyler said, getting his own licks in on the fun.

"Let her kick you one time, Mr. Muscle Man," Hagel said, sitting back up again, suddenly pain free."

"What an actor!" Tyler remarked.

"So, where does Rita live?" Renee asked, still probing for information.

"Dang if you ain't one nosey woman," Tyler replied.

Hagel was looking for the nuts to place on the axle bolt. "Just answer her questions," Hagel said. "Trust me. Life's just easier that way. Besides, she's within kicking range of you too."

Hagel was tightening the nuts and no longer needed assistance. Tyler stood, grabbed a rag from the bench behind him, and began wiping the grime from his hands.

"I was able to find Rita's address and where she works. She's living in Longview, Texas," Tyler said to Renee.

"Longview, Texas! That's only about a six-hour drive from here. Why can't you go see her?" Renee asked.

"Listen," Tyler said, still wiping his strong hands. "I can't go to Texas. Just searching for Rita placed her in danger. I want nothing more than to see her, but for now, I can't. There are a lot of things I can't explain. I can't go anywhere without my cell phone. The people I work for have some sort of bug on my phone. They know everywhere I go. As soon as I take off toward Texas - let's just drop this. Trust me. I can't go to Texas."

Renee looked at Tyler. She had a thousand questions, and every bit of information she was able to drag out of him created a thousand more. Although many of the questions she had were about his employer, her focus was on getting Tyler and Rita together. Tyler's looks could get him any woman he wanted, but he chose not to get involved with any of them. He was deeply in love with this Rita. If there was a means of getting the two of them together, Renee wanted to be in the middle, pushing to see that it happened.

"I've not worked out your phone request yet, but I have an idea," Renee said. "Why don't you leave your phone with me and go see Rita. You can take my cell phone. If your boss calls, I'll say you are busy, out for a run, or something. I'll give you a call then you can call your boss back."

"I really appreciate you trying to help," Tyler replied. "I really do. The thing is, if you answered my phone, it would endanger both of us. It's complicated. If I get a call from my boss, I have a set time to meet him or one of his associates. I never know where the meeting will take place and the time window to get there is set in stone. If I don't show up on time – let's just say, you'll never see me again!"

Hagel stood, took the rag from Tyler's hands, and began wiping his own.

"You're a drug runner," Hagel said. "Drug mules can make a lot of money! I really do wish you'd cut me in on the action."

"No. No. I told you once before. I'm not a drug courier," Tyler protested. "I wish I was. I could walk away from that."

Renee still wasn't focusing on what Tyler did for a living, or any of his work related issues. She was zeroing in on a way to get two lovers together and nothing else. In high school, Renee was well known for her matchmaking abilities. It was common for her to act as the go between, setting up dates for all her friends, both male and female. If someone wanted to go out with a particular person, they got word to Renee and the wheels were put into motion.

"Roast beef with carrots, celery, potatoes, fried okra, homemade sourdough bread, and cherry pie for dessert," Renee announced as she stood and walked toward the door. "That's tonight's supper. Six-thirty, and don't either of you be late!"

Renee left and the conversation turned from Tyler back to the motorcycle.

An hour later, Hagel announced he was done working for the day. He threw Tyler the key to one of his three Harley Davidsons and asked if he was interested in a motorcycle ride. Tyler was elated. Hagel had promoted him up to the big class of motorcycles, and he wasn't about to pass up the chance to ride.

"Just be careful," Hagel said. "You wreck or even put a scratch on that bike and you'll wish the people you work for would come drag me off your ass!"

Tyler looked like a child on Christmas morning and was every bit as excited. They rode off with Hagel leading the way. It wasn't long before they were out of the city limits. They rolled the throttle back as the big bikes roared down the highway. Down a long stretch of highway, far above the speed limit, Tyler wondered if Foreman or some agent was monitoring his movement and wondering where the heck he was going at such a breakneck speed. If asked, he'd tell them he was in a rental car, mad because he'd lost a poker game and was blowing off some steam. It was another lie, and he knew it wasn't a very good one. At that moment, he didn't care. He was having the time of his life.

Losing track of time, it was six-twenty when Hagel and Tyler hurriedly rolled back into the garage located to the side of the motorcycle shop.

"Hurry up. We've got to get our leather off, get in the house, and wash our hands," Hagel said as he dismounted the motorcycle. "Renee will be madder than a wet hen if we're late."

As Hagel and Tyler walked through the door of the house, they both looked toward the dining room. Renee was putting the last dish on the table.

"I heard those bikes come roaring in less than five minutes ago," Renee barked out. "You two like playing with fire, don't you?"

"I took Tyler to that whore house out on route 61," Hagel said. "We didn't want to leave until we were both fully satisfied!"

"You give me the crabs again and you'll be living down at that whore house," Renee said sharply then smiled.

Tyler shook his head. If he could ever get with Rita, they could live care free, joking and teasing like Renee and Hagel did constantly. He admired the love this couple shared and wanted the same.

Renee had a plan, and she knew men are more cooperative while they're eating a good meal. She wanted to help get Tyler with Rita, but she needed more information. Tyler had suspected all along what Renee was up to, but he couldn't pass up one of Renee's home cooked meals.

Renee asked a few questions during dinner, just as Tyler had expected. He responded, but didn't give her anything constructive to work with.

"Okay. Enough questions," Hagel interrupted after Renee refused to give up her bombardment of questions.

Renee gave Hagel a hard look. He looked at her and smiled, then turned to look at Tyler.

"Renee means well, and so do I," Hagel said. "Just remember this. I don't know what you are tied up in, but if you ever need anything, anything at all, a motorcycle, money, our house, or our help, it's yours."

Tyler was moved. The generosity and kindness he'd received from this couple was sincere and never ending. They hadn't known him long, and knew very little about him. Still, they'd welcomed him into their home and were offering him anything they owned.

After dinner, everyone retreated to the front porch. Hagel and Renee sat close in an old metal glider. Tyler sat in a rocking chair to their left, rocking back and forth. They ate cherry pie and drank coffee as they watched the last rays of light disappear for the day. By the time they had finished the pie, darkness had set in. Hagel and Renee were doing most of the talking, teasing each other as they always did.

"I'll tell you my story," Tyler said somberly.

He felt that Hagel and Renee were trustworthy. If he was going to hang around, they needed and deserved to know the danger that it brought.

Renee and Hagel got quiet. They were surprised by Tyler's sudden change of heart. They were ready to listen.

"Hearing what I have to say could endanger you if any of it leaks out. Of course, after hearing my story, you may tell me to leave. You may even decide to call the police."

"I promise we won't do either," Renee said softly.

It took two hours and another pot of coffee before Tyler was finished. At times he rocked back and forth so hard Hagel was worried it would chew through the porch floor. The rocker sped up at times, slowing down at others, keeping pace as Tyler's roller coaster life was unfolded. Several times Tyler paused, wiped his eyes, then continued. Hagel and Renee were moved by some parts of the story, flabbergasted by others.

He didn't tell them everything. Some things just wouldn't come out. He didn't spend a lot of time talking about being raped by who he thought at the time was his biological mother. He provided enough detailed information to paint a good picture, even though the gory details were skipped. He told them about being in jail, meeting Rita and how they'd came to falling in love. That part touched Renee's heart as well as Hagel's. Tyler spoke about Gary McDowell and how he'd found legal ways to prevent the family money from being spent on his defense. He talked about the trial, and described how Godfrey Mercer shocked him with the news about being adopted.

When it came to the part where Tyler was sent to Radford, all the stories of the cruel treatment from warden Pendleton came out. Renee was dumbfounded, but Hagel wasn't surprised. Hagel had never experienced such treatment when he was in prison, but he'd heard enough stories from other inmates to know it went on in some places.

The biggest shocker to Hagel and Renee was the prison break. It was hard for them to grasp there was a rogue organization out there, unclaimed by the government, yet getting government funding as well as support from rich tycoons. Tyler spent little time talking about his training at the ranch, and as far as assassinations go, he gave no details at all, only saying he'd been called carry to out two jobs since arriving in Meridian.

At the end of the story, Tyler was drained physically and emotionally, but at the same time, he felt light. He felt as if a gigantic weight had been lifted off his shoulders. It felt good to tell someone what had happened to him, but it also scared him out of his wits.

Hagel and Renee were speechless. Their heads were spinning. Tyler was as strong of a man physically either of them had ever met, but he was meek as a kitten. They had both marveled over his gentle nature and his kindness. How could Tyler possibly be a killer? Learning Tyler had killed nine people gave them a sick feeling. They still felt love for this big galoot, it was unconditional, but they struggled to understand everything. It would take time to sort through all the information. It would take time to digest everything they'd just learned.

Tyler wasn't asked to leave, and no one reached for a phone to call the police. Instead, Hagel and Renee scooted apart and asked Tyler to come sit between them. Tyler sat down on the glider, placed his elbows on his knees, and his face in his hands. With Hagel on one side and Renee on the other, they hugged the giant of a man tightly as he filled his shaky hands with teardrops.

After ten minutes passed, Hagel sat up straight. "You're a hell of a man, Tyler," he said. "At the moment, I don't know how I can help you. Hell, I don't even know what to say. I need to do a lot of thinking about everything you've told us, but that doesn't lessen the fact that you're our friend. As a matter of fact, I think our friendship is stronger now than ever. We love you like a son, and I think I'm speaking for Renee as much as myself when I say, we want to help you in any way possible."

"I agree," Renee said, wiping away tears with one hand and rubbing Tyler's back with the other.

Tyler was now the speechless one.

The night air suddenly seemed to have turned cold. Everyone went back in the house. Hagel and Renee both tried to get Tyler to spend the night, sleeping on their couch. Tyler insisted on going back to his apartment. It was only a short drive. Hagel and Renee needed time to talk, and Tyler needed to be alone.

Lying in bed that night, Hagel and Renee talked about Tyler for a long time before shutting their eyes and going to sleep.

"I had a top ten list of what I thought Tyler was into," Hagel said. "An assassin was number six."

"What was number one?" Renee asked.

"I would have sworn he was tied up with the mafia and running drugs."

"Until tonight, I thought his talk about being a bad guy and being monitored and such was at least in part, something he'd fabricated," Renee responded. "Wow, was I ever wrong. He's done a lot of bad things, Hagel, but it was all in self-defense or to stay alive. I feel sorry for him, as strange as that may sound. The boy needs somebody to love him. He's never really had that."

"I agree," Hagel said. "He's never hurt anyone unless under attack. This assassin stuff is different, but if he don't do as they say, he's the one who will die."

"I can't believe we're laying here in bed trying to justify Tyler killing people," Renee said.

"I can't either," Hagel responded. "We're doing it though."

There was a moment of silence in the darkness of the bedroom then Hagel spoke again.

"I think if Tyler could get with this Rita woman and run away, he'd never hurt anyone for the rest of his life."

"I'd like to be a fly on Rita's wall for a while," Renee said. "I'd like to put a bug in her ear, no pun intended."

39

Tyler didn't go visit Hagel and Renee on Sunday. On Monday, he took a drive north. He went to the Lucky Stars casino, where he'd met Foreman twice before. He spent the day playing slot machines and drinking beer. He got a room at the casino and stayed the night. The next morning, he ate in the hotel lobby and afterward went back to playing the slots.

He was now regretting that he'd told Hagel and Renee his story. He wasn't afraid they would change their mind and report what they'd heard about the police. Instead, he was afraid of how they might now feel about him. Saturday night had been an emotional time, and they'd clearly stated they wanted him around and would do anything they could to help. Now it was Tuesday, however. They'd had time to think, to mull over his words. Would they really want him hanging around the shop? Would they want to be associated with a murderer? He thought not.

Waking up Wednesday morning in the casino hotel, Tyler was prepared to spend yet another day doing nothing but pulling handles on the one-armed-bandits downstairs. Just after nine that morning, as he sat on a stool feeding a slot machine, he heard a sound much different from the surrounding bells and whistles going off around him. He suddenly realized it was his cell phone ringing. He quickly dug the phone out of his pocket as he walked toward the hotel lobby. The lobby wasn't noise free, but it was much quieter than the endless chatter of the slot machines and the three dozen patrons already two hours into their losing streak of the day.

"Hello," Tyler shouted into the phone as he hurried along.

It was Foreman on the other end. "What the hell are you doing?"

"Nothing," Tyler replied, sounding like a child who had been caught putting his fingers in the cookie jar.

"What are you doing at the casino, and why have you been there for three days?"

Tyler didn't like the tone of Foreman's voice and him questioning why he was there.

"Hey," Tyler said. "I've been stuck in Meridian with nothing to do. Money keeps showing up in my bank account, so I wanted to spend some of it. I decided to take a vacation!"

"Well the vacations over," Foreman said. "Get back to Meridian."

"Why?" Tyler asked, his voice showing disagreement.

"Because at a casino thousands of people come and go. Although the chances of someone recognizing you are slim, the odds are much greater if you are hanging around a tourist attraction."

"I don't have anything to do in Meridian."

"Then find something. Get a hobby. Go to the pistol range and hone your shooting skills. Do something, but get the hell out of the casino!"

"Fine."

Tyler hung up the phone. He felt like a five your old that had just been called down for writing on the wall with a crayon. He stormed back to his room, packed what few things he'd brought along, and checked out. He hated that he was being monitored so closely. Just for spite, he took back roads to Meridian and stopped at a dozen gas stations along the way. It was five hours later when he finally arrived back at the apartment. He was acting like a spoiled brat, and he knew it.

He sulked for the remainder of the day, but by bedtime, he had worked through his tantrum and was back to feeling grateful for what Foreman had done for him. As much as he hated this life of lies and murders, he wasn't on death row. He was out of prison, had money, could eat any food and as much of it as he wanted, anytime he desired. He tried to call Foreman back, to apologize. He used the number that had shown up on his phone when he got the call at the casino.

"The number you have reached is no longer in service. Please check...." Tyler hung up the phone. Foreman, the ranch, The Company, they couldn't be traced. For all intent and purposes, they didn't exist.

Thursday morning Tyler did his usual run, showered, got dressed then rode down to visit Hagel. They knew he was a killer, but was still hoping somehow, they'd want him hanging around.

The shop was closed. There was a sign on the door that said they were out of town and wouldn't be open until

Tuesday. Tyler thought it was strange. Hagel nor Renee had mentioned anything about a vacation. Renee had mentioned that her sister in Vicksburg had been very sick. He wondered if her condition had worsened and they'd gone to be with her. He then had a thought much worse. *What if The Company found out about Hagel and Renee? What if they knew I had told them everything? Could both my friends be dead?* He snooped around the house then using the key Hagel had given him, entered the shop. Hagel's Road King was gone. It was a relief. He knew then that Hagel and Renee were out somewhere touring on the big bike.

Back at the apartment, he spent the day by the pool. Rhoda was there, and a man was sitting with her. He wondered if the man was her husband, or if perhaps it was Jodie's husband. He thought about Jodie and hoped she was settled in at her parents and was doing well. *What a mess this world is in. Is anybody happily married?* He thought of Hagel and Renee, they were the exception to the norm.

He relaxed, sit back and covered his face with a towel to block out the bright sunlight. For the first time that day, his mind wandered off to Rita. He'd been trying hard not to think of her, but that was impossible.

Saturday morning, he was awakened at 6 a.m. by his cell phone ringing. He answered with a sleepy morning voice.

"Hello."

A recorded voice on the other end said, "You have an incoming text."

The message ended and a second later, the tone notifying a text message had arrived chimed. Tyler looked at the text. It was a set of coordinates. He plugged them into the special app and a map appeared on his screen. He zoomed in on the satellite image. It wasn't the Lucky Star casino to the north this time. Instead, it was the parking lot of a shopping mall in Hattiesburg. Hattiesburg was south on I-59. He estimated he could drive there in about an hour and a half.

He predicted Foreman was ticked because of their last conversation, when he was 'vacationing' - as he'd described it. That had to be the reason for not meeting at the casino. It didn't matter. By doing their dirty work, he felt a little freedom and an occasional vacation were well deserved. Foreman was right though. It was stupid to be in large crowded place where tourists and tons of cameras were located. Without a disguise, he stuck out like a sore thumb. Hagel had said more than once that with his well-built muscular body, he drew more attention than a fresh pile of cow shit at a horsefly convention.

Like a spoiled child, Tyler purposely delayed his departure. He wasn't about to sail out the door without a shower or breakfast. It was an hour after the call when he started the Yukon, ready to head south to Hattiesburg.

Shortly after 8 a.m., he pulled into the parking lot. The mall wouldn't be open for a couple more hours, so the lot was practically empty. He looked through the windshield and mirrors but saw no one around. Fifteen minutes passed. He checked the app on his phone to make sure he'd gotten the right coordinates. He wasn't late, but was becoming anxious about whether or not he'd came to the right place. Panic was setting in. He regretted not leaving immediately after receiving the text. Suddenly, the passenger door opened. Tyler was startled, and liked to have jumped out of his seat. It was Foreman.

"How you doing, Big Guy?" Foreman asked.

"Where did you come from?" Tyler asked. "I just checked the entire parking lot and never saw anyone."

"Good. I guess I've still got what it takes then," Foreman replied.

The usual hug was initiated by Foreman then he looked Tyler over, checking him out from head to toe.

"You look great!"

"Yeah. You too." Tyler replied.

Foreman seemed happy. Tyler suspected Foreman was no longer angry with him, which was a relief. He'd expected to meet some other agent this time, not Foreman. He was glad it was Foreman however. It was good to see his familiar face.

"Sorry about my outburst back at the casino," Tyler said. "You were right. I shouldn't have been there."

"Forget about it," Foreman said. "Just use your head from now on. I don't want anything bad to happen. I've got a lot invested in you."

Tyler thought about how he'd been broken out of prison and the amount of planning that had been done to pull off such a stunt. He thought about the ranch and all he'd been taught there. Foreman, or someone in The Company, had spent a lot of time and money to get him where he was now. Foreman was right, they had a lot invested in him, and he owed them. He owed them big – he owed them his life.

Foreman was looking directly at Tyler, reading his face, determining his mood, trying to read his thoughts. Tyler knew that look. At the ranch, Tyler had been taught to watch for subtle facial movements, twitches, the way the head is tilted, positioning of the shoulders, and most of all, the eyes.

The eyes told everything. That's what Foreman was doing, reading his eyes. Reading a person was something Tyler had found himself doing early in life, but with the training he'd received, he'd become a master at the craft, just as Foreman was.

"I'll try to be more careful," Tyler said, looking away from Foreman. "I'm living the good life and loving it. I don't want to mess that up."

"Good. I want that for you," Foreman said.

Tyler looked back at Foreman, who was still staring at him. He smiled, so did Foreman.

"Yeah, I know - that you know - what I was doing," Foreman said, now laughing. "Alright, enough of us feeling the other out, let's get down to business. I've got to get out of here, got a meeting at six this evening in Washington."

It was information Tyler never expected to hear. He wondered if the meeting was with some senator or member of congress who derailed spending from road projects or education bills into the coffee can that funded The Company. He was certain he'd never know, but why else would Foreman have business there.

"Can I ask you something personal?" Tyler asked.

"You can ask anything you want, but that don't mean you'll always get an answer."

"You named me after your baby brother didn't you."

The expression on Foreman's face changed.

"I guess I should have expected that question," Foreman answered as he turned away. He was even more bothered by the question then he pretended to be.

"Yes, I was the one who gave you the name. Tyler and I were close. Growing up, we did everything together."

Foreman had a faraway look in his eyes. They were even becoming glassy.

"We even dated identical twin sisters for a while," Foreman said. "Sometimes we joked about whether we had spent the evening with the right one or not."

He drew in a long breath then exhaled. "We had a heated argument right before Tyler was sent to Panama. It was over something stupid. I never had a chance to set things right. It haunts me to this day."

There was silence for a long time. Tyler was glad Foreman had opened up to him, but in some ways, was sorry he'd brought the subject up.

"Thanks for sharing that with me," Tyler said. "To be quite honest, I like the name Tyler DuPont better than Seth Boone. It has a nice ring to it."

Foreman smiled then reached over and punched Tyler in the right arm.

"Alright. Back to business, I'm in a hurry. Since you feel like you need a vacation, I'm giving you one," Foreman said smugly.

"I'm taking it isn't at a casino," Tyler fired back jokingly.

Foreman laughed as he turned his head to look out the windshield again, his eyes still glazed over.

"Your target is a couple - a man and a woman. They're far from being priority targets but nonetheless, they're on our list. We aren't getting any sponsor money for this one, but I can still swing getting 5 points shaved off your bill.

"I only get 5 points for killing two people!"

"We have a green light on this couple, but it as I said, it's not sponsored. If we don't get paid, you don't either. Crap rolls down hill. I'm pushing it to get you the 5 points."

"So why do this one? Why not a higher-priority job?"

"Because I chose this one – just for you. Just because some rich tycoon or politician hasn't flagged this couple doesn't mean they aren't on our list of targets. They've done some bad things."

"Such as?"

"You don't always get the details," Foreman said, turning to look at Tyler again. "The history of your target isn't always important. Sometimes you're better off not knowing. Let's not get into that again. Trust me, these two deserve what they're about to get."

"Well, I hope you're going to provide at least some vital information!"

"Don't worry. You're going to enjoy this one. These two lucky assholes just won a cruise, all expenses paid – airfare, tips, even alcoholic drinks up to a three-hundred dollar tab."

Tyler was confused. Foreman seemed too thrilled about this low-yield job. If Foreman was changing the rules and going to start handing out this kind of work, he'd never get his debt paid off.

"The couple will be arriving in Miami tomorrow afternoon. They'll be checking into the Atlantic Breeze Suites. They need to meet you - close up and personal."

"So you've managed to send this couple on a cruise, just so I can kill them?"

"That's the beauty of this setup, Tyler," Foreman said, unable to control a smirk spreading across his face. "They really did win a cruise. It'll work perfectly. You can make it look like any ordinary robbery gone bad."

There was something amiss, something more to this story. It was useless though, trying to get Foreman to fork over more information.

Foreman removed an envelope from his jacket pocket and handed it to Tyler.

"There's a plane ticket, cash, and a key inside the envelope. Go back to Meridian and pack a light suitcase then drive to the airport in Jackson. You'll arrive in Miami around five this afternoon, a day ahead of the targets. Check into the hotel beside the Atlantic Breeze. Take a cab to the Amtrak Station and go to the lockers. The locker number is on the key. Inside the locker, you'll find your tools and instructions. Burn the instructions once you've read them."

"Don't I get photographs to look at? How am I supposed to know who to kill?"

"You'll know."

"Something about this stinks really bad!"

"I told you already - don't worry. You'll enjoy this trip."

Tyler had never been to Miami. The thought of spending a few days on a sunny south Florida beach sounded appealing.

"I have a team member ready to hack into the Atlantic Breeze Suites computer," Foreman said. "Once I get word on which room your guests are occupying, you'll get a quick phone call. Unless the plan changes, you'll be visiting your friends Sunday evening."

Foreman opened the car door and stepped out. He stuck his head back inside the car. Tyler was expecting that, it had become one of Foreman's trademarks, always sticking his head back inside to say one more thing before he vanished out of sight.

"Be careful in Miami. It's Memorial Day Weekend, and lots of visitors in town, as well as crooks - I hear it can be a dangerous place for tourists."

Foreman was chuckling. The door shut, then he disappeared. Tyler looked inside the envelope. There was a key and thirty crisp new one-hundred-dollar bills inside.

He was concerned about this job. He was being sent to a hotel room to kill two people. He was clueless about who they were or what they looked like. *What if Foreman or someone else in The Company makes a mistake and sends me to the wrong room? What if I break the door down, guns blazing, and there are more than two people inside - who would I shoot? What if this couple has children with them? What's wrong with Foreman to think I'd enjoy any part of being sent to kill someone? Why did Foreman want to meet here? If I'm going to take a plane out of Jackson, why did he make me drive all the way to Hattiesburg?*

Tyler was confused about the way The Company did business. He knew he'd never be able to figure them out.

40

Stepping outside the terminal at Miami International, Tyler hailed a taxi. He could feel the sting of the hot sun. It was a Memorial Day weekend, the official start of the summer tourist season. The airport was packed like a sardine can. Travelers rushed about, dragging suitcases on tiny wheels, roaring against the concrete, sounding as if they had their own tiny jet engines. He wished he were there for the same reason they were. He would like to explore the city then rent a car and drive down to the Keys.

He climbed inside a cab, and the driver pulled away. Two hours later, he had checked into his hotel, completed a thirty-minute workout in the weight room, showered, and shaved. He slipped into a pair of white jeans and put on a flashy Panama Jack shirt. With sandals on his feet and a straw hat on his head, he looked like the normal tourist that Floridians loved to hate. After running down another cab, he arrived at the Amtrak Station a short time later. The cabbie kept the engine running and the AC on high.

Rushing into the station, Tyler located the locker. He inserted the key and opened the door. Inside was a mid-sized brown leather suitcase. He grabbed the suitcase then without hesitation hurried back to the awaiting taxi. There was the temptation to open the suitcase in the taxi, but decided it was best to wait until he was alone, behind a locked door. Whatever was inside was for his eyes only.

Laying the suitcase on the bed, Tyler flipped the latches and watched them spring open. On top was clothing, neatly pressed. A small caliber pistol, a silencer, and a captain's hat, lay beneath the clothing. He removed a white shirt and pants from the suitcase, laid the pants on the bed, and held the shirt up for viewing. It was heavily starched, and the logo for a cruise line company was sewn onto the left pocket. The captain's hat had the same logo displayed on the front.

An envelope was lying in the bottom of the suitcase. Tyler removed the envelope, sat down in a wingback chair by the window, and opened it. A single piece of paper was inside. It was a message typed in all capital letters.

"A BOX OF CHOCOLATES AND A BOTTLE OF CHAMPAGNE WILL BE DELIVERED TO YOUR ROOM. TAKE THEM WITH YOU WHEN YOU VISIT YOUR GUESTS. THEY WILL BE EXPECTING A REPRESENTATIVE FROM THE CRUISE SHIP TO DROP BY WITH A GIFT, THUS THE SWEETS AND DRINK. GO VISIT YOUR FRIENDS TOMORROW EVENING AROUND 8 P.M. ONCE INSIDE THEIR ROOM, PRESENT THE GIFTS ON BEHALF OF THE CRUISE LINE. I'M CERTAIN YOUR FRIENDS WILL BE DEAD TIRED FROM THEIR FLIGHT, SO DON'T STAY LONG - LET THE COUPLE REST IN PEACE.

P.S. I THINK YOU WILL FIND VISITING YOUR FRIENDS MOST REWARDING AND ENJOYABLE – THIS IS A GIFT TO YOU!

Anyone with a third-grade education could have read between the lines and figured out the true message. Still,

Tyler was confused about the enjoyable part. He wished he knew what the couple had done. He thought about Victoria, the woman he'd killed in Nashville. While he wished he knew the crimes of the couple he was about to kill, he also didn't want to know.

Something weird was going on. He detested this silly 'play on word' game. Two people were about to lose their lives by his hands and The Company thought it would be cute to make up this childish letter. He was thankful for a second chance in life, being free from prison, but he detested the killing, the games, and Foreman thinking he would somehow enjoy this evil deed.

Why not just tell me who it is I'm supposed to kill, give me a time to do it, and be done with it? Why all the theatrics? Foreman and his thugs apparently enjoy these games and the killing, but I'm not like them. There is nothing right, thrilling, enjoyable, or in any way fun about any of this!

Tyler opened the patio door and stepped outside onto the balcony. Using a butane lighter, he burned the envelope and letter. Looking out at the ocean, he drew in a long, deep breath. The smell of the salt air filled his lungs. Back inside, he grabbed two shot sized bottles of Jack Daniels from the liquor cabinet, and returned to the balcony.

He spent the evening sipping whiskey on the balcony and wondering what it would be like if Rita could be there with him. They would enjoy the view, the smells, and each other's company. They would laugh and talked about everything or nothing at all. Later, they would retreat to the bedroom where they would spend hours making love until their tired bodies gave out. Then they would wrap up in each other's arms and sleep soundly all night long.

On Sunday morning, Tyler took in some of the sights of downtown Miami then returned to his hotel room in the early afternoon. Bored with television, he sat out on the balcony again. He liked looking at the ocean, and hoped someday he and Rita could have a small beach house.

A few minutes past 6 p.m., Tyler's cell phone rang and he answered.

"Room 1347," a gruff male voice said then hung up.

He sat there for a minute. The voice on the phone wasn't Foreman's. He wondered how many people were employed by The Company, if there were different units in different cities, and how many agents like him were in the field doing this kind of work. He wondered if Foreman had been a field agent at one time, then at some point moved up in the ranks until becoming a boss man. Foreman wasn't the head-cheese but he most certainly wielded a lot of power.

A minute later, there was a knock on the door. An unsuspecting delivery boy handed him a box of expensive Belgium chocolates and a bottle of champagne in a bucket.

The suitcase from the train station contained a 22-Magnum pistol with a suppressor attached. He opened the box, removed the chocolates, ate a few, and placed the remainder on the nightstand. The gun fit perfectly in the box.

Decked out in his white cruise ship outfit, Tyler used the stairway to leave his eighth-floor room at the hotel. With the candy box stuffed under his left arm, and carrying the champagne bottle with his right hand, Tyler strolled down the street toward the Atlantic Breeze. The hotel lobby was bustling with activity, tourists checking in, others sitting around waiting for their group to assemble for a night out on the town. The lobby area was loud with several dozen conversations going on at the same time. Those milling about were dressed in a variety of beach life attire. No one seemed to notice Tyler as he slipped past and entered one of the six elevators. He pushed 13, and the doors closed.

When steel construction made it possible to begin building high rises, most builders skipped floor 13, going straight from the 12th floor to the 14th floor. People were strongly superstitious in those days and 13 was considered an unlucky number. Although most superstitions today have all but been forgotten, most modern structures still don't have a 13th floor.

When the Atlantic Breeze was being built nine years ago, the owners never considered going from floor 12 to floor 14. During construction, the builder mentioned the superstition in a management meeting, but the corporate officers, most being from Generation X, did nothing more than get a good laugh at the notion of not having a 13th floor. For the first couple of years, all was well. Over the last four years, however, there have been seven drug overdoses, two suicides, and three robberies at the hotel, all taking place on the 13th floor.

When the elevator doors opened, Tyler stepped out. He looked down the long corridors on his left and right. A plaque hung on the wall with arrows pointing to room numbers. The arrow pointed to the right for rooms 1344 to 1398.

Tyler had his act together. He was cool, calm, and collected. Aside from a small trace of perspiration on the palms of his hands and the slightest tinge of nervousness, his walk down the corridor was no different from any other of the hotel guests.

He had no idea what crimes or evil deeds the couple in room 1347 had done, nor did he care. Tyler told himself that terminating this couple, meant points shaved off his bill, and that's all that really mattered. It was a lie, but it was his justification at that moment. He only hoped they'd sent him to the right room, and that the targeted couple would be there alone.

Tyler knocked three times on the door.

Having received a telephone call earlier, and expecting a management member from the cruise company to stop by with a complimentary gift, the woman inside room 1347 opened the door, but only as far as the latched chain would permit.

She saw a man in a white uniform sporting a captain's hat. He was standing erect with a smile on his face. The logo on his hat was the name of a cruise line company. It was the same company where they'd luckily won an all-expenses paid five-day cruise.

This was their first cruise and she was excited. Her husband was less thrilled. At first, he was going to stay at home and let her sister be her travel companion. The more he read the company's brochures though, the more he dreamed of hot young girls everywhere with little more than thin strings standing between them and total nakedness.

The door was quickly opened, giving her a full view of this charming man, all dressed in white. She couldn't help but smile. He was very handsome, young, and had rippling muscles. She wondered what it would feel like to have a man like that on top of her, having his way. He was holding a bottle of champagne in one arm. In his other arm, there appeared to be a box of expensive chocolate candies. She swooned and hoped he'd noticed.

The stench of cigarette smoke filled Tyler's nostrils. Although the couple was staying in a non-smoking suite, the air was filled with a cloud of choking smoke.

The woman appeared to be in her mid to upper forties. Her shoulder length, tangled, salt and pepper hair looked dried out. She had pale skin, and her face and arms were severely sunburned. He expected the couple had spent the day on the beach, having never considered an application of sunscreen. She was short, thick in the middle, and her arms were big. The legs sticking out of her dingy blue mid-length worn out nightgown were chubby and had spider web streaks from varicose veins.

The television in the spacious living room was blaring loudly. A black and white western was on, showing the scene of a posse chasing two Mexicans bandits on horseback. Tyler was sure he'd seen the movie, faintly recalling the scene but the name of the film wasn't registering at that moment.

A balding, big-bellied man was sitting on the sofa. He was drinking a beer and smoking a cigarette. There were three empties sitting on the table beside him, along with a drinking glass from the bathroom, a quarter of the way filled with cigarette butts. The man was mesmerized with the old western being shown on the big-screen television. He was wearing dirty faded jeans with the left kneecap threadbare. His nasty looking dingy white, wife-beater shirt was riddled with holes. The stubble on the man's face indicated he'd not shaven today, perhaps the last several days. He was so enthralled in the movie he never looked up to see Tyler standing at the door with a grin stretching from ear to ear.

Why this couple? Tyler thought. *Why target this pair of ratty looking humans who look more like backwoods hillbillies than white-collar criminals?*

"Good evening Ma'am," Tyler said pleasantly. "I'm First Mate Conrad from the cruise ship. May I interrupt your evening for a few moments?"

"Well, yes of course," she said, then turned her head to look at the man on the sofa. "Turn that damned thing down, we've got a visitor!" she screamed out.

The thought crossed Tyler's mind that he was most certainly in the wrong hotel room. He was about to execute two innocent souls, guilty of nothing more than being in the wrong place at the wrong time.

The woman walked toward the sofa, trying to get the man's attention. Tyler used his foot to ease the door closed then followed her. As he walked, he removed the box from under his arm, removed the gun, and allowed the candy box to drop to the floor.

"We got a guest you deaf bastard, turn that damned thing down," the woman screamed at the man. She then turned back to look at Tyler, smiling.

Tyler's gun was pointing directly toward her. The joy on her face instantly melted away. She took a step, catching her heel on the edge of the sofa. She fell on top of the man, who at that point had only begun to take his eyes off the action on the screen to look around.

The man's jaw dropped when he saw a stranger standing there. A young man was standing in front of the sofa, holding a gun with what appeared to be a silencer screwed onto the barrel. The gun didn't look real though. It was confusing. The man looked more like a Navy Seal than a representative of the cruise ship. He remembered Melissa telling him the cruise ship had called and someone would be coming by to deliver a complimentary gift. He thought that perhaps this was some sort of publicity stunt. The gun would go off and a flag would drop out saying they'd won something else besides the cruise. He didn't like their sense of humor, however.

"Is this supposed to be some funny-assed joke?" the man shouted out, loud enough to be heard over the blaring television.

The woman pushed herself off the man, straightened herself, but remained sitting by the gruff looking character. Her mouth was partly open. She looked as if she wanted to say something, but no words were coming out. The man leaned forward, straining past his beer gut to reach for the remote. Tyler expected he was going to turn the volume down on the set.

"No, no, no," Tyler said softly, but loud enough to be heard over the men and horses on the television as they crossed a river, guns blazing and smoke rising, but no one being hit.

Tyler was in a jam. If this turned out to be the wrong couple, he didn't think he could kill them. He was compromised, however. He didn't know what to do.

The man slumped back, pressing his body into the sofa. He and the woman stared at Tyler, wide-eyed and their faces growing pale. Tyler studied the couple's faces. He realized he'd seen them before. The woman's hair and sunburned face had thrown him off. He knew her though. The man was several pounds heavier, his face more puffy, and he'd lost more hair, but he recognized him as well. Tyler's mind was racing in reverse, trying to determine when and where they'd met. It only took a split second. Foreman had said he would enjoy this – it all made sense now.

This indeed was a gift. It was a gift he'd never have expected receiving. Sitting on the sofa, only a few feet away, was a couple he recognized from his past. It was a married couple who Tyler had thought of many times over the last few years, but never thought he'd see again. He'd only met them once, at the funeral home, the same evening he'd killed his parents. Sitting there on the sofa, ready to beg for their lives – was Milton and Melissa Cabell - Sarah's parents.

Tyler remembered holding Sarah while she cried and described how her father raped her over and over, while her mother watched. He remembered Sarah telling him how his mother would laugh. Sometimes her mother would join in, making it a threesome. He remembered Sarah telling him about her buttocks being burned with cigarettes and the many other types of abuse she'd endured.

"I know you," the woman said, with a frightened voice. She recognized Tyler at the same time he'd recognized her. "You were at Sarah's wake. You're the one who bent over her casket and wailed like a baby. You're that Boone kid, the one who killed his mother, the judge."

"H-O-L-Y S-H-I-T," the man said slowly, his mind racing back in time. He too recognized Tyler.

"Sarah's in heaven now," Tyler said as he pushed the gun forward and took aim at the man. "I know about everything you did to her you 'sons-of-bitches'. You two won't be joining Sarah in heaven - because both of you are about to burst the gates of hell wide open!"

The gunfight ensuing on the television set was louder than the sound produced by the 22-Magnum with the suppressor attached. The bullet hit directly in the center of the man's forehead. His eyes slowly rolled back, then his head slumped forward as a stream of blood poured out from the small but lethal entrance wound.

Sarah's mother held her right arm out, waving her hand like someone riding in a parade as she greeted those watching from the street. Her eyes were as wide as saucers and her quivering lips were fluttering, but no words were coming from her mouth. The bullet pierced her right eye. Her mouth flung open and her jaw dropped. She slumped over, her head falling onto the armrest. A stream of blood began soaking into the fabric.

Tyler killed his parents in a moment of rage and he'd instantly regretted his actions. Killing the five men in prison was an act of self-defense and he'd acted out of fear for his life. The executions he'd done for The Company were carried out only to save his own life, and he hated what he'd done. This however, this act of revenge, this was different. It was gratifying and he felt triumphant. It wouldn't bring Sarah back, and he knew it wouldn't make things right, but for the first time, he got satisfaction from ending someone's life. Later, he'd regret his actions, but for now, he was enjoying the moment. He stood there for almost a full minute, on the opposite end of his smoking gun, satisfied as he watched the blood of life flow out of this evil couple.

"As my perverted mother, the judge, used to say – justice has been served," he said with a smile.

Tyler sat the champagne bottle on the floor then removed a pair of latex gloves from his pants pocket. He continued watching the couple on the sofa as he put the gloves on. The man's wallet, a pocketknife, and a plastic room key, lay beside the empty beer bottles on the table. He opened the worn leather tri-fold, removed the cash and driver's license then dropped the wallet on the floor.

Walking into the bedroom, he spotted the woman's purse on the nightstand. He emptied the contents on the bed. Along with cash in an envelope, he found a debit card from the Big Stone National Bank of Southwest Virginia. He smiled when he saw the four-digit pin number was written on the back of the card.

The television set was still blaring away. A commercial was playing, describing an age-old brand of laundry detergent that was new and improved. Tyler picked up the champagne bottle. He desperately wanted to spit on the man and woman, but refrained, knowing it would leave his DNA. He walked back toward the door, picked up the candy box, placed the gun inside, and tucked it under his arm. Inside the elevator, the latex gloves were removed and stuffed into his jacket pocket. When the doors opened, he strolled through the busy lobby and out the front door.

Back in his room, Tyler quickly changed and headed back to the street, wearing a jogging outfit. With the hood over his head, he jogged two blocks to an ATM machine. Keeping his back to the camera located to the right of the machine, he withdrew five hundred dollars in cash using the debit card he'd stolen. A block further down the street, he walked into a jewelry store.

He picked out a pair of $1,300 diamond earrings and explained to the young female clerk that he'd been planning to purchase them for an anniversary present. Following the nicely dressed young girl to the cash register, he handed her the same debit card used moments earlier. The girl smiled and asked for an ID.

Tyler removed the Virginia drivers' license from his pocket that said his name was Milton Cabell. The girl glanced at the card, not noticing the photo of the older balding man who looked nothing like the young stud with bulging muscles she was waiting on. Tyler scratched out an unreadable name on the sales slip using his left hand, returned it to the girl, smiled, and walked out with his new purchase. He'd put the cash and earrings in his secret place once he was back in Meridian. After rubbing fingerprints from the stolen card and license, he dropped them in a trashcan on the way back to his room.

Returning to his hotel room, he walked over to the nightstand, and picked out one of the candies, a hazelnut morsel double-dipped in rich milk chocolate. As he chewed the candy, he popped the cork from the champagne bottle. He poured a small glass, and took a nice sized gulp to wash down the candy. Tyler's mouth filled with foam. He swallowed the myriad of bubbles, took another gulp of the champagne, and headed to the shower.

In his mind, he attempted to justify his work. He felt that he'd done the world a favor by popping the cap on Sarah's parents. By the time his shower was over however, the joy of his deed began to evaporate. As much as Sarah's parents deserved to die, it wasn't his place to decide when and how. He knew God would never forgive him for the wrongful acts he'd committed, but he wanted Him to.

An hour later, the suitcase was returned to the same locker in the Amtrak Station. Five minutes after that, he was in a cab, on his way to the airport. He was still 115 points away from true freedom. There was no way he could keep this up. No way could he stay with The Company long enough to see his debt drop to zero.

41

It was Rita Logan's 31st birthday. She celebrated alone in her condo with a chilled bottle of White Zinfandel, cheese, crackers, and some stuffed Spanish olives.

She was in a somber mood, and she soon found herself having a pity party instead of a birthday bash. She lived alone, had never gotten married, never had a baby, and the years were continuing to slip by. She'd met the love of her life three years ago. He was a teenager for crying out loud, a mere boy, yet he was so much of a man, much more so than any she'd ever met.

Up until then, her life seemed as if it were on track. She was a well-liked and respected psychologist. She was known in political circles, even as high as the governor's office. The boy she had met was in jail, awaiting trial for murdering his parents. Falling in love with Seth Boone was never supposed to have happened. He was her client, a teenage client, and she was twenty-eight. It wasn't supposed to have happened - but it did. As strange and unethical as it was, she couldn't help herself, and if given the chance, she knew she'd do it all over again.

She was devastated when Seth requested she not visit him in prison. Of all the boys and men she'd dated in her life, none had captured her heart like Seth Boone. She knew Seth's request to break off the romance was best, but hearing him say it was more than she could bear. Seth wanted her to move on, find someone else, someone who could share a life with her. He wanted and needed her, but having a relationship looking through a one-inch thick glass plate wasn't a relationship at all. Still all Seth had to do was say the word and she would have been there on the prison grounds anytime visitation was allowed. He didn't turn her away because he didn't love her. He turned her loose because he did.

When Seth was declared guilty, it was determined he'd be housed at Radford. Rita researched the facility. Radford Penitentiary had a nasty reputation. The warden and the guards were as hard as the iron bars in the prison walls. The prisoners themselves were no different. Warden Pendleton ran a tight ship, punishing all forms of prisoner insubordination – all within legal guidelines of course.

Aside from pants and a shirt on their back, inmates at Radford were required to purchase anything else they needed or wanted. The prison had a store where shoes, tobacco, and toiletry items could be purchased, but prices were extraordinarily inflated.

Inmates lucky enough to have family bring them such things were considered blessed. Everyone else had to pay the high prices or do without. Seth wouldn't have any friends or family to come visit and Rita knew that. She graciously and unselfishly deposited one-thousand dollars into his account. At least for a while, he'd have toothpaste and other needed items. It was her last act of kindness, her final goodbye.

Seth entered the prison as a minor. He was twelve years Rita's junior. When and if he ever walked away from the high walls and razor wire fences, he'd be an old man, and she would likely be in her grave. When Seth entered that heavily guarded, dull and dreary fortress, he carried something with him the guards didn't notice. They didn't find it in their search. He passed through the gates and carried it with him everywhere he went. It was stowed away inside him. It was Rita's heart.

In the weeks following Seth's incarceration, Rita became severely depressed. She ate very little and drank far too much. After a month of denying herself proper nutrition, she found herself in the hospital.

Rita's youngest brother, Ellison Logan, was the only sibling with whom she stayed in contact. Once he found out his only sister was in the hospital, he dropped everything in his life and steadfastly stayed by her side. Both night and day, he faithfully remained for a week, doing his part to lift Rita's spirits and nurse her back to health. He'd stayed a while longer but a demanding job, a nagging wife, and two pre-school heathens beckoned him home to Colorado Springs.

Ellison didn't try merely coaxing Rita to come live with him and his family - he practically demanded it. Unemployed, depressed, and alone, she quickly gave in to the badgering. It was time to leave Virginia in search for a new and better life.

After two weeks in her brothers inadequately sized house, Rita knew she'd made a mistake. She had two choices - get out, or go insane. The sister-in-law was a thoroughbred drama queen with special and demanding needs. She constantly reminded Rita's brother that he didn't earn enough money. She wanted his undivided attention and when she didn't get her way, no one in the house was happy. If that wasn't enough, there were the two unruly children whom both parents felt compelled to obey. Compared to being in the house with her brother's dysfunctional family, living alone and being depressed seemed the logical choice.

By the end of week four in Colorado, she had gotten herself together and landed a job at a Junior College. She began teaching entry-level math and English 101. The pay was peanuts, compared to what she'd made working for the Commonwealth of Virginia as a psychologist. The job came with a cozy little apartment however. It was situated on the edge of the campus, convenient to both work and shopping.

She was eating right again, had put back on a few of the pounds she'd lost, and had stopped drinking the booze altogether. For the first time since before Seth went to prison, she noticed how pretty the sunset was.

Being a very attractive woman, she was approached often by men who wanted to get close to her. As often as not, the men were married. Her brother was also trying hard to get her fixed up with a co-worker. Rita wasn't interested in any of them. Perhaps if given enough time, the precious memories of Seth Boone would fade and a prince on a white horse would ride into her life. For now though, she was determined to live alone and date no one. Until all the phases of the grieving process had worked their course, trying to develop a relationship with a male would be a failure.

For the first month, the job went well. It was something new, a challenge. It wasn't anything she'd ever imagined doing for a living. The novelty soon wore off, however. Rita discovered that working with individuals, getting to know them, digging into their souls to help them resolve issues, was her cup of tea – not teaching.

Most of the students in her English classes weren't bad. The math classes that took up half her day were different though. They were filled with adolescent deadbeats who were only attending college classes because mommy and daddy were footing the bill. The parents had hopes that Sally or Junior would walk across the stage and be handed a diploma someday, miraculously having earned a college degree. The majority of those deadbeats were more interested in good weed than good grades.

Dissatisfied with her new job, Rita began sending out resumes. Colorado was fine, but she missed the lush green mountains of western Virginia. She couldn't go back there though. She had no idea what would happen next. She had no direction at all, but knew she must continue going forward. She only had two requirements in seeking a new job. Moving to a warmer climate and returning to the kind of work that suited her.

During the day, she was doing much better than before. By keeping busy for long periods, thoughts of Seth were pushed to the back of her mind. At night, when she was alone in her apartment though, it was different. She stayed up late many nights, hoping to quickly fall asleep when her head hit the pillow, but that didn't work. As soon as she laid down, Seth's memory would flood her mind. Her heart would ache to see him, and tears would begin to flow.

She was still holding on to a thread of hope that someday far in the future she'd get to see him again. Perhaps there would be an appeal and he'd somehow be exonerated by some newly discovered evidence, but that wasn't likely to happen. The chance of an appellate court considering Seth's case was about as likely as receiving a presidential pardon.

The single thread of hope Rita was clinging to come crashing down one morning. She felt like a wounded bird, falling hopelessly through the sky.

She began each day with a cup of coffee and a bagel, sitting in front of her computer as she read the national news. Half way down the front page of a Washington D.C. newspaper was a headline that read 'Murderer Attempts Escape – Dies in Inferno'. She was about to skip the article. Things like that never interested her, but then she saw the first line that read – 'Radford Virginia'.

When Rita saw the name Seth Boone, her heart all but stopped. Her blood pressure bottomed out and she felt light headed. Her respirations doubled as her eyes shifted back and forth across the screen, reading what had to be some sort of fabrication. The article described a prisoner at Radford serving two life sentences for killing his parents. He'd recently killed five inmates in a cold-blooded attack inside the prison library.

It described how Seth was being transferred to Leavenworth Supermax Prison in Kansas when he attempted an escape. Two corrections officers narrowly escaped death when the prisoner somehow managed to obtain one of their handguns and began firing wildly. The officers bailed out of the van through a blaze of gunfire. The vehicle ran off the highway and down a steep West Virginia mountainside. The van's gas tank was ruptured during the gunfight and no sooner had the vehicle left the highway, it burst into flames. Seth's body was burned beyond recognition.

When Rita awakened, she was on the floor. Her right forearm was stinging badly from hot coffee that had spilled over it. She got to her knees, but as soon as she tried to stand, the dizziness returned. The room was spinning and she felt like she was going to throw up. Managing to crawl across the room, she reached the patio door. She needed fresh air. The door wasn't locked. Using her fingernails, she was able to slide the door open far enough to crawl through the opening.

The fresh air felt good. Suddenly, Rita lost what breakfast she'd eaten and then things went black.

Rita's neighbor, Jane Lew, had worked at the college in the music department for four years. Although they'd never had a conversation, they waved at each other several times when passing. Jane happened to be on her own balcony that morning. She didn't have to be at work until ten, so she was sitting on the balcony drinking a cup of hot English tea and enjoying a novel started the night before. When she heard the sound of a patio door opening, she instinctively looked over toward Rita's balcony. She thought Rita was stepping outside and perhaps they could finally find a minute in their busy lives to be properly introduced.

Jane didn't see Rita at first. She was looking over the railing. Then she saw Rita crawling across the concrete pad, heaving her guts up. Jane stood from her chair, just as Rita's face fell to the concrete, her eyes closed and her movements ceased.

Ten minutes later, the landlord was rushing to open Rita's door with the master key. An ambulance with its siren wailing was approaching the complex. Jane and the landlord went inside. Rita had awakened by this time and had crawled back inside the apartment. She was sitting with her back propped up against the wall.

A short time later, Rita was signing a release form, after refusing to allow the ambulance crew to take her to a hospital for evaluation. She insisted that she was fine, and had only passed out. After everyone finally left and she was alone, Rita broke down. She spent several hours going back and forth from rereading news articles about Seth, to laying on the floor crying. It was the epitome of agony and grief.

Two days later, Rita got a call from a hospital in Longview, Texas. She had applied for a job in a Longview hospital as a Clinical Psychologist. Her resume had been reviewed and the selection committee was impressed. After an hour and fifteen minute phone interview, Rita was offered the job at a starting salary of $185,000 per year and a $12,000 moving allowance.

Rita had only been to Texas once in her life, switching planes in Houston. She had no idea about the culture, the layout of the land, or the climate, but she expected it to be much warmer than Colorado Springs. She had requested a day to give her decision but called back within the hour and accepted. Within a week, Rita Logan was sitting behind her new desk. Her brother said she was running from her past and should give the job at the college a bit more time. Rita knew he was partly right, but she needed to earn more money. Besides, at this new job she would be in her element, doing the kind of work she loved.

Rita made a few phone calls and using part of her relocation allowance, paid to have Seth's remains buried in a cemetery in the town where she grew up. She knew he wouldn't have wanted to be taken back to Abingdon.

There would be no memorial service and no funeral. All of Seth's family was dead and there were no friends to pay their last respects. Rita was the only person in the world who loved Seth Boone, there were no others. She wrestled with herself, trying to decide if she should make a trip back east and say goodbye.

In the end, she decided not to go. Instead, she visited a church and had her own private service for Seth. She placed his picture on the altar and read a tear soaked letter. The pastor stood in the shadows and fought back his own tears.

The love letter she'd written was nothing less than beautiful. He was puzzled though, hearing it was for a convicted felon, the soul of which he expected now lay in the abyss, awaiting judgment day.

42

Rita left her office in Longview, Texas at 4 p.m. She was out of the building and headed across the parking area, pressing the unlock button on her key fob as she walked. She noticed a man and a woman standing beside a motorcycle, a dozen spaces from her car. She felt they were watching her and it gave her an uneasy feeling. She purposely increased her speed. Just as she was about to reach down and open the car door, she looked up. The woman who had been standing at the motorcycle was coming toward her.

"Rita Logan," the woman said, now only a few paces away.

Rita hesitated, undecided if she should quickly get into her car, or reach for the container of pepper spray in her pocketbook. The reason for the hesitation was that the woman had called her by name.

Rita froze in place. The woman was only a step away now. She had long blonde hair, neatly pulled back and tied in a ponytail. She was wearing black leather boots, black chaps, and a black leather vest. Rita didn't think she looked like a rough hardcore biker babe though. Her arms weren't covered in tattoos, she was smiling, and she had nice teeth. What caused Rita to pull her head back and her eyes to widen was the woman's face. *Oh my Lord*, she thought. *Minus a few lines near the eyes and a slight change of the cheekbones, I could be looking in a mirror.*

The woman extended a black leather gloved hand holding a white envelope. Rita hesitantly accepted the envelope from the woman's hand. Without any explanation, the woman turned and walked back toward the man who was now sitting on the motorcycle. Rita quickly got into her car and locked the doors. She watched as the woman climbed on the back of the motorcycle and the two strangers roared away.

She tossed the envelope into the passenger seat, started her car, and pulled out of the parking lot. She drove straight home, continually looking in the mirrors, expecting to see the motorcycle following at a distance. As she approached the parking lot of her condo unit, she looked once more in her mirrors. She'd not spotted the motorcycle, nor anyone else who appeared to be following her.

As she was getting out of the car, Rita picked up the envelope and stuffed it into her purse. Five minutes later, with her doors locked, shoes kicked off, and a diet Dr. Pepper in her hand, she flopped down on the sofa with the envelope. She'd already been thinking about the contents, feeling certain someone was being sued and she'd just been served a subpoena to appear in court.

The two people on the motorcycle didn't look anything close to what she thought gang members should look like. They were likely a couple of undercover cops, taking a break from some sting operation to perform other assigned duties. Rita could still see that woman's face. The resemblance to her own appearance was unnerving.

The envelope didn't contain an official document. Instead, it was a handwritten letter. Rita unfolded the paper and began to read.

"Rita,

I purposely didn't speak to you when handing you this letter. Forgive me for being rude. It was for good cause. As far as I know, you aren't in any sort of danger, but you are being monitored. There's a good chance your car, house, even your clothing and shoes could contain some sort of listening devices."

"How stupid!" Rita said loudly. She thought this was some sort of sales gimmick to get her to purchase a new alarm system. This was a new approach and a new low for salesmanship. She was about to toss the letter into the trash can, but her curiosity got the better of her.

"We are here to let you know Seth Boone is alive. Yes, that's right. He's alive and well, living in Mississippi. He didn't die in a shootout with authorities, as you likely read in the newspapers."

Rita stopped reading and threw the letter down with disgust. She was trying to think of who the sick son-of-a-bitch was that would play such a cruel and sick joke. She was furious. She took the letter to the kitchen and laid it on the counter. She began digging in her purse for her cell phone. She was going to call the police and report this. "THIS IS OUTRAGEOUS!" She screamed loudly. She was out of control, way beyond mad and holding back tears.

She looked at the list of emergency numbers on the magnet stuck to the side of the refrigerator and began calling the Sheriff's Office. She stopped after punching a few numbers, unsure of what she would say. She put the phone down and tried to gather her senses. She picked the letter back up and continued reading where she left off.

"I can prove to you that Seth is alive. He told me while the two of you were spending time together in Damascus, he would often call you Rita Lovin, instead of Rita Logan."

Rita felt her blood drain to her feet. She felt light headed, and made her way back to the sofa. Seth had indeed called her that many times, but only when they were alone. "Oh my God," she said, as a thousand emotions swept through her mind.

She read on, now deeply engrossed in the contents of the letter.

"Seth thinks about you constantly. He loves you deeply and his greatest desire is to be with you. He can't contact you however. He's working undercover for a government agency, and they monitor his every move. He used an unregistered computer to find out where you lived. They found out about it, and that's when he knew you were being monitored as well. You can surely see the complications if a 'dead man' were to be in contact with someone from their past.

If you want to find out more, meet us tonight at 7:00 p.m. at The Steak Authority restaurant, on Stanley Street. We'll be sitting at the bar. We thought you would consider a crowded public place an okay place to meet. Wear old clothes, something you pulled out of storage. Examine your shoes for anything odd - listening devices are very small these days. Leave your phone in the car, wrap your keys in a sock and stuff them deep inside your pocket, they could have a listening device as well.

Give us a chance and we will prove to you beyond a shadow of a doubt that this is real – Seth is alive!

If you don't show up by 7:30, we'll leave, go back home, and I promise, you'll never hear from us again. If you decide to come, we will reveal who we are and how we are involved. You'll hear Seth's story.

If anyone finds out about this, it could endanger everyone, including you and Seth.

If you no longer love him, please, please, please, burn this letter and by all means, don't contact the police."

Rita read the letter a second time. Her head was spinning. She didn't know what to do. She thought, perhaps the man on the motorcycle could have been in prison with Seth. *Perhaps he was Seth's cellmate. Maybe Seth told him about calling me Rita Lovin. Maybe they're here to sucker me in so they can rob me, maybe even kill me! What if it's real? What if Seth really is alive? Could it be? Is that possible? Would the FBI or CIA have made up the story about Seth? I read about Seth's attempted escape in a dozen newspapers, and they all said pretty much the same thing? What if I'm being watched? What if my apartment really is bugged? Oh God, please help me? Please help me!"*

Rita's stomach was cramping. She rushed to the bathroom, barely making it before her bowels exploded. After she was past the nausea and diarrhea, she stripped off her clothes and stepped into the shower.

She put her head directly in the jets of the refreshing water coming from the showerhead. *This is a hoax. No, this is real. No one could ever guess that Seth called me Rita Lovin. Who were those two people on the motorcycle? I can't believe how much that woman looked like me. How weird is that? I don't know what to do!*

The shower felt great, but contrary to what she'd hoped for, it did little to clear her head. She was torn, not knowing what to do about the letter. She wanted to believe it was true, that Seth was alive. There was no way though. Whoever fabricated this pack of lies was out to hurt her, and thus far, they'd done a good job. She picked up the phone again to call the police then hesitated. Her brain was crying out for justice, wanting to summons the police and have the two criminals who approached her picked up for questioning. Her heart was working in the other direction, however. It wanted her to meet the couple on the motorcycle and find out more.

The thought of being kidnapped crossed Rita's mind, but if the couple had intended to kidnap her, they could have easily done so back at the hospital parking lot. *Oh God, what if Seth really is alive? I've got to find out!*

Living alone and keeping to herself, both at home and work, Rita hadn't attempted to make friends since moving to Longview. There was this one girl at work she'd spoken with a few times, Hanna Summers. She was a sweet, soft-spoken young woman who worked for Dr. Womack, across the hall from her own office. Rita remembered that when she'd first moved to Longview, before her office phone was set up, everyone called her on her personal phone. Hanna had been one on those callers, welcoming her to the building and inviting her to lunch, but she'd declined. Rita searched her phone and saw Hanna's number was still there. She had saved it for some reason, now she knew why.

Hanna answered on the second ring. After a minute of chitchat, Rita asked Hanna if she'd like to join her for dinner at The Steak Authority around seven.

"I've never been there," Hanna said with excitement in her voice. "I don't get out much. Wow, that doesn't leave me much time to get ready. Sure, I'd love to. See you there at seven."

Rita was happy she wouldn't be going to the restaurant alone, but hoping and praying she wasn't leading Hanna into something that could get them both hurt. She felt bad, knowing that was a possibility, but she had no one else to call. If they got to the restaurant and things turned ugly, she'd act as if the two of them weren't together, or she'd yell out to Hanna to run. She couldn't believe she was actually going through with this.

The entire thing with this man and woman on the motorcycle was just too weird. She wanted to just forget about it, watch some TV and go to bed, but couldn't. If she didn't find out what was going on, it would eat at her forever.

Before leaving her condo, Rita looked back at her bed. It was piled high with clothes. She'd ransacked her closets and pulled things out of every drawer, unable to make a decision on what to wear. Her mind was too occupied, she couldn't think. All she knew to do was look for some old clothes, something no one would have ever thought to bug. *This is the most ridiculous thing I've ever done in my entire life!* She brushed her hair back as she dug through yet another box of clothing from her closet.

Wearing a pair of knit slacks that shouted 1970, Rita strolled across the parking lot at The Steak Authority to greet Hanna. Her blouse was old, worn, and a gross mismatch to the slacks. The sandals on her feet looked like they'd been recently unearthed at a landfill. She was such a wreck she'd forgotten to comb her hair. It was a tangled mess.

Hanna had always seen the well-dressed Rita, always showing up for work dressed like a million bucks. Everything was always in place. Most days she looked like a model in a glamour magazine. Hanna was stunned, and at first wondered whether it was Rita walking toward her or someone else.

"Baby girl. I thought we were here to pick up a couple of men," Hanna said bluntly. "You got looks that can turn any man's heart to mush, but we gotta take you shoppin. You ain't never gonna get a date dressed like a hobo."

Rita smiled. "I just needed to get out tonight. I'm not interested in picking up a man."

The two women walked toward the entrance of the restaurant. Several more cars were pulling into the parking lot that was quickly becoming full. Rita felt a slight sense of relief. She expected at least a couple of dozen redneck oil and gas workers would be inside, any number of which wouldn't think twice about rescuing a damsel in distress.

She noted several motorcycles in the lot. She'd not paid a lot of attention to the color and type of motorcycle the strange man and woman had been riding. She hoped if the couple was there, that they weren't part of a larger group of gangsters. Thinking about such a thing made her nervous and her palms were wet with perspiration.

She was having second thoughts of going inside the restaurant, but was driven by the thought that Seth could still be alive. It was almost twenty minutes after seven. It was possible the couple's motorcycle wasn't even there. Perhaps they had never shown up, or had already left. Her head was spinning. She was a nervous wreck.

A large lump formed in Rita's throat as she and Hanna entered the noisy restaurant. She could feel the back of her blouse becoming moist from perspiration. Her heart was pumping fast. She was hoping the dim lights inside would camouflage her pale face. Hanna was cheerful, hungry, and glad Rita had called. Since Rita was most certainly dressed down, Hanna was hopeful some young cowboy with muscular arms and a handsome face would notice her instead.

425

Hagel and Renee had arrived at the restaurant early. They'd been sitting at the bar for well over an hour, talking about their trip and having met Rita. Renee had been as surprised as Rita when they met face to face. Tyler, rather Seth, had mentioned many times how closely she resembled Rita, and it turned out to be true.

Renee was anxious, and had her fingers crossed. *Was my letter convincing? Was it too much? Did Rita even read it? If she did read it, does she still love Tyler and if so, will she show up?*

Hagel was excited. This was like a dream come true. He was playing a role in a spy movie, where the stakes and danger were both sky high. When Renee had first mentioned going to find Rita, he'd balked at the idea. The more he thought about the adventure though, the more he liked it. It was dangerous, thrilling, and more exciting than anything he'd done in years.

Renee looked at her watch. It was 7:19. The hope that Rita would show up was quickly fading. She and Hagel were getting antsy, and didn't know if they could actually wait until 7:30, as promised in the letter. Hagel was expecting that any time now, two, three, or maybe even a dozen police officers would storm the restaurant. They'd lead Renee and him out in handcuffs. People would stop eating and watch, wondering what horrible crime they'd committed.

Hagel had gone many years without having a run-in with the law and was hoping to avoid one now. At his age, he didn't think he could survive being in jail. It had been hard when he was younger. Back then, prisoners would get into a fight, throw some punches, and it was over. Now, they killed each other over the smallest of quarrels. An old man in that environment wouldn't stand much of a chance. Even worse, he couldn't bear the thought of his precious Renee being incarcerated. She was a tough old gal, but she was no match for the gangs of women in prison who dreamed of fresh meat to abuse in every sordid way imaginable. For the first time, he was regretting they'd come.

The police were only a minor concern though, compared to the rogue secret government vigilante group to which Tyler had become connected. The longer he sat there, the more he realized how much this adventure hadn't been thought through properly. It was dangerous, extremely dangerous. They weren't playing with amateurs. He reached for his wallet, ready to throw cash down on the bar for their meal plus tip. It was time to go, get out of Dodge and ride back to the safety of their small, but comfortable, home in Mississippi.

Renee grabbed Hagel's arm, just as he was about to rise off the barstool.

"She's here!"

Hagel turned and looked toward the door. Rita was coming through, but she wasn't alone. Even worse, she had her cell phone in her hand. This was something they'd not anticipated, and it was definitely a problem.

"It's a set up," Hagel said sharply. "Let's go now - out the side exit over there."

"Wait," Renee said.

He held back, his feet ready to run, but willing to give Renee a few seconds more to convince him everything was going to be fine.

Renee had come too far not to play this high-stakes game to the end. She had been so excited about this trip. She wanted Tyler to be happy and that meant taking risks she wouldn't normally consider. If anyone could convince Tyler to run and hide from the devils who held him captive, Rita could, and Renee wanted that to happen. Rita could lead him away from the killing, and see that he never harmed anyone ever again.

Rita and the other woman were being seated only a few tables away from the barstools where Hagel and Renee were nervously watching. Rita glanced their way twice, producing something between a grin and a forced smile.

"Can I get you folks anything else?"

The voice was coming from behind Hagel. It was the bartender.

"Yeah, more coffee, for both of us," Hagel replied without taking his eyes off the table where Rita was sitting.

"What's she doing?" Renee said to Hagel, loud enough to overcome the multitude of voices, TV blaring over the bar, and a hundred or more forks and knives clattering against dinnerware.

"Since the police haven't stormed through the door yet, I guess she's just checking us out," Hagel replied. "Can you imagine how confused and scared she must be?"

"I'm not confused, but I'm scared out of my wits!" Renee replied.

Hagel and Renee tried not to stare, but found themselves glancing over at the table where Rita sat every few seconds. Rita was doing the same, quickly turning away when their eyes met.

As soon as the waiter had taken their drink order, Rita announced to Hanna she'd spotted an old friend at the bar. Hanna thought that was odd, knowing Rita had no old friends in Longview, but didn't say anything.

"Would you mind if I stepped over and spoke to her for a few minutes?

"No, no. Go right ahead," Hanna said, her face now buried in the menu.

Rita stood. "Whatever you are having, order the same for me."

"Here she comes," Renee said, squeezing Hagel's hand.

"She left her cell phone on the table, so that's a good sign," Hagel replied.

Rita walked toward the couple at the bar. The two people she'd seen in the parking lot were still decked out in leather, but looking at them more closely than before, they looked even less like hardened bikers. They looked to be every bit as nervous as she was.

The man was on the right and the woman was on the left. Rita was locked in on the empty barstool to the woman's left. She walked with her head high. She was determined to be brave. She approached the barstool, but didn't sit down. She stopped, put her hands on the seat, and looked directly at Renee, only inches away. The two women looked into each other's eyes, both thinking how unbelievable it was that they looked so much alike. Anyone sitting around them would surely think they were sisters.

"OK. I'll give you five minutes of my time," Rita said sternly, a tinge of harshness in her voice. "Convince me you're not a pair of reprobates playing some sick joke - or here to commit some hideous crime. Otherwise, my friend over there is prepared to scream bloody murder and have every able-bodied man in this joint pounce on the both of you."

Renee's adrenaline level had never been this high. Hagel had often joked that Renee could speak at twice the speed of sound when excited - but do it with clarity. He'd tried a few times to get her to apply for a job doing car commercials, knowing she could rattle off the fine lines and disclaimers at the end in a New York second.

In far less than the five-minute time Rita had allotted, Renee told the entire story that had taken Tyler over two hours to spit out. The story had only begun when Rita realized this wasn't a prank, a sick joke, or some form of a well-planned scam. She wrinkled her forehead as she listened close to the speed-speaker who touched on numerous things only Seth Boone would have known about her.

Rita was speechless. She slid over the barstool and sat down. She had a ghostly look on her face. The bartender noticed how she looked and asked if she was okay. She nodded yes then asked for a double gin and tonic.

No sooner had the bartender placed the drink on the bar, Rita leaned over, grabbed the glass and chugged down the contents. She wiped her lip with the back of her hand then sat up straight. Thirty seconds elapsed as Rita and Renee locked onto each other's eyes. Rita believed the story she'd just heard, but it was like some sort of dream. She was expecting to awaken at any moment, finding herself sitting up in bed, a cold sweat covering her body.

"I buried Seth Boone over a year ago," Rita said. "I've worked hard to erase his memory and was making a small amount of progress. Now, here I sit at a bar, staring at a stranger, who's telling me he's not dead. I'm overjoyed, but forgive me - I'm bewildered and confused in the most complicated fashion!"

Hanna was getting irritated. It was one thing to walk over and speak to someone you knew - but it was something else to totally neglect the person you'd invited to dinner. After another minute of waiting for her ill-mannered, so-called friend to return to the table, Hanna stood and stormed toward the bar. After making a loud, attention-getting statement that included, hands waving, head shaking, and in the end producing a bird only inches from Rita's nose, Hanna turned and quickly left the restaurant. There wasn't a soul at the bar or sitting at a table with any doubt about the way Hanna felt regarding being ignored.

Rita was embarrassed by Hanna's loud outburst of anger and the drama she'd displayed. Still, she felt horrible that she'd treated a new friend in such a manner. She wanted to run out the door after her, but she was too interested in the couple she was sitting with at the bar and the information they had just relayed to her. There would be time to apologize to Hanna later, and somehow try to make amends. For now however, she could focus on nothing more than the news she'd just been convinced was true – Seth Boone was still alive! She was euphoric!

Rita turned back to look at Renee, and took a deep breath. "I believe what you've just told me. You know too much for it to be some fabricated story. Still, I won't be fully convinced until I talk to Seth, or Tyler, as you say his name is now."

"We thought about that," Hagel said, speaking for the first time since Rita approached them.

Renee pulled a cell phone out of her purse and handed it to Rita.

"I just bought this today. It's a prepaid disposable phone with 500 minutes of talk time. Tyler doesn't have one yet, but he will as soon as we see him again."

"He doesn't know you are here, does he?" Rita asked.

"That's right," Hagel answered. "He would never have allowed it, knowing how risky this is. Renee and I have come to love that 'ole boy. He needs help – your help! I've heard so much about you, Rita, and now that we've met, I'm convinced that you're his only hope. I think we can all work together and figure out a way to get him free from these gangsters who have such a stronghold on him."

"This is so surreal," Rita said, her eyes glazed over and looking at the ceiling. "It's like something straight out of Hollywood."

"Hagel and I feel the same way," Renee said.

"So, those are your names, Hagel and Renee?"

"Yes," Renee answered.

Rita took another deep breath, took her eyes off the ceiling, and looked directly at Hagel and Renee. "I love him with all my heart."

"Take the phone and keep it out of sight," Renee instructed. "It might take a day, maybe a week, but as soon as Tyler has one like it, he'll send you a text. If you're at home or work, step outside. Buy some new clothes and shoes too. Put them on when you talk on the phone. I know that sounds crazy, but it's better to play this safe."

"Try to remember – these characters Tyler's tied up with are pretty nasty players. They play for keeps," Hagel stressed.

Rita was shaking from the nervousness that was taking her body over. She looked back to the table where she and Hanna had been sitting. Her cellphone was still sitting there. She wondered if someone listened to all her calls. *Is my condo bugged? What about my car? Is it possible to bug your clothing?* She knew technology had advanced to the point that almost anything was possible. Those thoughts gave her a sick and uneasy feeling. She felt violated.

"And, you don't think Seth is working for the FBI or CIA?" Rita asked.

"He says no," Hagel answered. "He said they don't have an official name. They're funded by crooked politicians and a bunch of rich tycoons."

Rita shook her head sideways. "What have I gotten myself into now?"

"I know it's hard not to worry, but try not to," Hagel said with as calm a voice as he could muster. "I don't think this outfit has too many agents. It's likely they monitor you electronically, not with troops on the ground here in Longview. Just try to act normal, but be careful what you say. If they think Tyler has contacted you, we could all end up in some deep shit."

"We've got to get back to Mississippi," Renee said. "As soon as we see Tyler, he'll be calling. Reply to his text, but don't call back immediately. Get to a safe place first, and be sure to wear old clothes, just as we told you," she warned.

"Anything you want us to tell Tyler?" Hagel asked dutifully.

"Yes. Tell him there's never been anyone else, he's always been the one, and he'll always be the only man in my life." She paused, wiped a tear then said, "Tell him he still holds my heart, and that I've never stopped loving him."

43

Arriving back at the airport in Jackson, Tyler grabbed his bag from the baggage carousel and headed for the parking garage. No sooner had he gotten into his Yukon, someone tapped on the passenger side window. It was Foreman. Tyler unlocked the door and Foreman climbed in.

"I thought you were in D.C.?"

"I was. Meetings with senators don't take a lot of time, especially on holiday weekends. So, how was south Florida?"

"Everything went as planned," Tyler answered. "I was surprised. At the time I pulled the trigger, it brought me pleasure. I loved seeing those animals breathe their last breath, but now...I just hate this killing for a living."

"That's a good thing. If you reach the point where killing someone doesn't bother you -" Foreman said, stopping in mid-sentence. "I wish it were different for you. This isn't how I wanted or expected things to turn out."

"I like you, Foreman. There's a bond between you and me. So, can I ask you something?"

"Sure, but I may not be able to give you an answer."

"Will you truly let me go when my debt is paid?"

"I thought we had this conversation before," Foreman said. "It's not entirely up to me, but I do have some influence. It's more up to you than anyone. You have to keep your head on straight."

"You were there, at Sarah's wake. I spotted you a few other times too, outside the fence at school or other places, always in the shadows. Why didn't you recruit me then? Why wait until I was in prison?"

"I never intended to recruit you at all. I did it to save your life. It was very difficult getting you out of prison."

Foreman had a far away look in his eyes. He became nervous and didn't seem to want to talk about this.

"I'm more confused now!" Tyler said, trying to read Foreman.

Foreman was looking out the windshield, unable or unwilling to make eye contact. A minute later, he regained his composure and was back to business.

"Go home and take it easy for a while," Foreman said. "There's something in the works, dealing with some suspected terrorists in Michigan that we'd like to see lying in a pine box. I may need your services if the green light is given. I don't think you'll have any issues taking out foreigners planning on killing innocent Americans?"

"No, I won't have any problem with that," Tyler stated. "So, you're fairly sure I won't be called for a few weeks?"

"At least one week. These things are sensitive and people higher up want to make sure they have their ducks in a row," Foreman said. "Don't get any bright ideas about time off though. Remember, Texas is off limits. Find yourself a hot babe and get laid, maybe that will help."

Foreman reached over and gave Tyler his usual tight squeeze. "Gotta go, big guy." He opened the door then stuck his head back in as always.

"Tell me the numbers, I want to hear them."

Tyler knew what he meant. They were the numbers secretly given him back at the ranch. He still didn't know what was so dang important about the set of numbers. He rolled his eyes and played the game. "11-19-30-50-40. My favorite game is 9 ball."

"Wonderful," Foreman said.

The door closed and Foreman performed his magical disappearance act.

Well, that was a memorable and exciting meeting. Why did Foreman come all the way here for a five-minute meeting? I'll never understand it all! I wonder what those numbers are. If Mississippi had a lottery, I'd buy a ticket and use them. I can only imagine what would happen when The Company looked at the newspaper and read about Tyler DuPont winning the jackpot.

Tyler put the Yukon in gear and drove home.

Monday was Memorial Day. Tyler slept in then went to the pool for a short time in the afternoon. Several people in the apartment complex were grilling out. The air was filled with the delightful aroma of hickory smoke and sizzling meats, making everyone hungry.

Between hunger pains and tiring of a hundred or more noisy children splashing about in the pool, Tyler decided to seek what he considered a quieter place to hang out. He changed clothes and headed to the pool hall where he was now recognized as a frequent customer. To his surprise, the place was nearly deserted. He ordered a beer and a club sandwich then shot a couple of relaxing games of billiards. It was just what he needed.

On Tuesday morning, after his normal routine of exercise, shower, and breakfast, Tyler drove down to Campbell Custom Cycles. The open sign was lit, so he opened the door and strolled inside. He was hoping to hear Hagel and Renee had gone out of town for a few days on a vacation instead of an emergency trip to see a seriously ill family member.

Hagel was rummaging through a pile of rusty rims in the storage area above the showroom. The room was large enough for a dance hall if empty. Instead, it was packed to the rafters with a lifetime collection of old motorcycle parts. The place was a motorcycle junk man's dream.

After handshakes and hugs, Tyler began a conversation.

"Where you catbirds been? I didn't know you guys were heading out of town."

"Let's go over to the house and I'll tell you."

Tyler followed Hagel down the stairs, out through the back of the building, and across the small yard to the house. Hagel was unusually quiet, which worried Tyler. He knew something terrible must have happened to Renee's sister.

"Is Renee's sister okay?"

"Yeah, she's fine as far as I know," Hagel replied as they entered the living room. "Sit down here on the couch now, I need to talk to you."

Tyler sat down cautiously. He feared something was seriously wrong, but didn't have a clue what it was.

Renee was in the bedroom. She hollered out when she heard Tyler's voice, and soon appeared, carrying a small shopping bag. She practically jumped into Tyler's lap, gave him a long kiss on his right cheek, and giggled like a little girl."

"You have no shame, do you Renee?" Hagel barked. "Why don't you go ahead and give him a lap dance while you're at it?"

She and Hagel both laughed as they watched Tyler blush.

Renee got out of Tyler's lap and joined Hagel on the loveseat.

"We've got news to tell you," she said, almost unable to contain herself.

Renee pulled a cell phone out of the bag and tossed it to Tyler.

"I programmed a number into the contact list," she said. "You need to send someone a text."

"Who?" Tyler asked, oblivious about what was happening.

"Rita!"

Renee began telling Tyler about their trip to Texas. Hagel held her shoulders, as if she were about to jettison off the couch at any moment. Watching the expressions change on Tyler's face, Hagel kept reminding her to slow down, as well as reminding her of a few details she'd skipped.

Tyler was stunned, speechless, overcome with emotion. They could have gotten themselves plus Rita killed, but they didn't. He quickly dismissed those thoughts, realizing their scheme had worked. They had accomplished what he thought was impossible. He now had a means to contact Rita!

Hagel and Renee watched Tyler's hands shake as he nervously fumbled with the phone. He soon enough hit the send button and his first text was on its way. The message contained his new phone number, and read, "I'm overjoyed. I want to hear your voice! I love you!!!"

"Get on out of here now," Hagel said. "I'm sure you want some privacy. She'll be calling you soon."

"Yeah. And, I don't suppose I need to remind you to be in a bug free environment," Renee added.

Tyler left in a rush, promising he'd let them know what happened. With the new phone in his pocket, he quickly drove over to the city park. He left the Yukon in a parking area and walked around the lake to a bench where there was no one around. The phone gave a distinct tone, indicating a text had been received. It read, "Twenty minutes!"

He stared at the display for a long time. He couldn't believe this was real. The text had come from Rita Logan, the woman he loved more than life itself. He stood up and paced back and forth, looking at his watch as the seconds slowly crept by. He rubbed his fingers over the screen of the phone, as if he were touching her. His heart felt as if it would burst out of his chest at any moment. Finally, the phone rang. Tyler jumped, as if he wasn't expecting it to ring. He answered with a simple yet excited. "Hello!"

"Seth. Is this Seth?"

Tyler felt his heart hit fifth gear. His mind was in a spin. His veins were filled with adrenaline. The voice he heard was a voice from his past, one forever etched in his mind. He heard the sweet voice of his beloved Rita.

Sitting at the base of a sycamore tree in the field behind her condo unit, Rita listened on her new phone. She was nervous, pale as a ghost, and her heart was beating as hard as she could ever remember. Her back was already covered in perspiration, soaking her blouse. This call would tell all. This call would prove if Seth Boone was alive or not. When the voice on the other end said "hello" she wasn't certain. It sounded deeper than the voice she remembered.

"It's me, baby," she heard the man say. "I can't believe it! I'm hearing your sweet wonderful voice!"

Rita let out a shrill sound that sounded like a wounded animal, which was actually a sound of uncontrollable joy. Had anyone been standing in the vicinity, it would have scared them, thinking perhaps she'd been snake bitten. The voice Rita heard was deeper, but there wasn't an ounce of doubt, it belonged to Seth Boone.

"I can't tell you how wonderful it is to hear your voice as well," Rita said as she struggled past her tears. "Oh God, Seth. I can't believe you're alive!"

The emotions were too much. Rita burst into tears. She could hear Seth sniffling in the phone. Hearing Rita's voice was such a rapturous feeling. Seth could barely hold back his own tears. It was several minutes before they could compose themselves to the point of speaking complete sentences.

Four hours later, with their tongues tired, and their bladders crying for a break, the two lovers reluctantly said goodbye. The time had been filled with an equal split of laughter and tears. They hung up their phones, temporarily pulling away, with promises of a call the following morning. Each would find a store to purchase more phone minutes to make sure they didn't run out.

After a bathroom break and a long shower, Tyler drove back to the Campbell's house. He hugged his friends tightly, and gave them the details about the most wonderful phone call he'd ever gotten. For supper that evening, Tyler treated Hagel and Renee at 'Jonah's Whale' in downtown Meridian, the best fresh seafood restaurant in central Mississippi.

The following morning, Tyler was back at the city park and Rita was sitting beneath the same sycamore tree where she'd spent yesterday afternoon. They had plenty of minutes in their phones and were ready for another heart-to-heart marathon. Rita wanted to hear more about what Seth had been through in prison, and the miraculous escape that had killed Seth Boone and breathed life into Tyler DuPont. She wanted to know about life on the ranch, and life in Meridian. Tyler held back in one area. Just as he had done with Hagel and Renee, he didn't disclose details about the killings he'd done as a puppet for The Company.

Listening to Seth's story, she was horrified, disgusted, and sickened. The man she loved had been abused by the prison system and was now being forced to play the role of a hit man, a cutthroat, a cold-blooded killer. She stopped short of thinking of Seth as a murderer, however. The word seemed too harsh, although she knew it was fitting. She loved Seth beyond measure. She couldn't change what had already happened, but she was willing to sacrifice everything to help him break away from the life he was living. She knew she must learn to live with what Seth had done - she just didn't know how.

She agreed with Seth's conclusion that The Company would never let him walk away once his dues were paid. Having Tyler DuPont terminated would be easy. They both realized that. No one would miss a man who was already dead.

When Rita mentioned to Seth about them running away together, it reminded him of a similar plan that had been laid out only a few years ago. He and Sarah would run away, then sneak back and secretly steal Julian away from the Boone house of horror. Seth was moved that Rita loved him enough to give up her job, her family, her life, all for him. She'd told him her love was unconditional, and he knew it was true. The only way either of them would ever be happy was if they were together, but getting it all worked out was going to be complicated.

Being on the run would require some grand strategic planning. He had no idea how many agents Foreman and The Company had at their disposal to hunt them down. He suspected The Company goons would never give up though. They'd search the world over until it was announced he and Rita had been found and were dead.

Living on the run as a fugitive would also take a boxcar of money. They'd have to move often and there was no way they could get jobs. The nest egg he'd been building wasn't small, considering the loot he'd taken from the Nashville job, but it wasn't enough to sustain two people living in seclusion for very long. He and Rita weren't interested in material things. A meager lower-class lifestyle would suit them fine. Still, considering they could be in hiding for fifty years or longer would take a substantial amount of cash.

It could take years to save enough, and they didn't have that kind of time. Tyler and Rita set a goal. In six months, they would take the plunge. No matter how much or how little they'd saved, it would have to suffice while they worked things out. They would meet and disappear together, somehow disguise their appearance, and if all went well, they'd never run into any of the discerning eyes of an employee from The Company. Neither were fans of cold weather, but they were considering a place in the backcountry of Alaska to begin their lives together.

They wanted to meet, but it wasn't possible for now. It was much too risky, not knowing with any certainty how each was being monitored. Until they could make their escape, they'd talk every day if possible. They would refine their plan and only hope their lustful desires to be together could be put at bay until it was time to vanish. They longed to look into each other's eyes, touch each other's skin, and hold each other tight.

44

On Sunday morning, Tyler was putting on his running shoes, ready for a quick 5K run. He was to call Rita at noon and wanted to complete his exercise routine before spending hours with her on the phone. The talks had been so wonderful. Each day it was a challenge to find the strength to hang up. Each night it was a struggle to wait patiently until the next day when they could talk again.

He tied his shoes and was ready to jump from his chair and head for the door when his cell phone rang. Tyler looked at the table where his phone sat vibrating toward the edge. He never received telemarketing calls on that phone, never received calls from anyone with a wrong number. The only time that phone rang was when he was about to be sent on a mission. Foreman had promised two weeks or more before being called on again, but it had only been seven days.

"Hello," he said indignantly.

"You got a text coming in about five minutes."

The phone went dead. It was a different voice than expected. It was the same person he'd heard on the phone that gave him the room number of Sarah's parents. He couldn't believe his bad luck. He wanted to think the text would give information about some future event, but knew better. The text would be a set of coordinates where he was supposed to be within the next four hours.

It was exactly five minutes later when the text came. As expected it was numbers, representing a set of state plane coordinates. He plugged the numbers into the app on his phone and within a few seconds, a map appeared.

Studying the map, he kept zooming in closer. This was certainly different then the past meeting places of Hattiesburg and Philadelphia. Switching from the map to satellite image, the meeting place appeared to be an old gas station on the outskirts of Biloxi, Mississippi. He wondered why they chose to meet in Biloxi. *Why Biloxi, a city that's 170 miles from Meridian? Why such a long drive?* He felt uneasy, something didn't seem right. *Foreman mentioned something big might be coming down. Could this be related? I wouldn't think so. The job Foreman mentioned was going to take place in Michigan.*

He laid the phone down on the table and untied his shoes. A beep came from the phone, indicating a new text had arrived. Tyler looked at the message. "Big pool party tonight - bring your own toys." Back at the ranch, he'd been taught to read between the lines. He was being told the job would be at night, had something to do with water, and he was to bring weapons.

After sending a long apologetic text to Rita, explaining why he couldn't talk that afternoon, and perhaps not for a few days, he packed and headed out the door. His two suitcases were filled with a pair of boots, black clothing suitable for nighttime operations, a pair of night-vision goggles, black makeup, a variety of disguises, and a host of rifles and handguns. He knew better than to speed and be pulled over by some suspicious traffic cop. If he were caught with the weapons in the back of his Yukon, he'd be as good as dead.

There was no way he could take the phone he used to call Rita. He couldn't afford to leave it at the apartment either. If someone from The Company searched his place while he was gone and found the phone, his and Rita's lives would be in peril. He drove to Hagel's, all the while thinking about the dangerous game he was being forced to play.

It was an absolutely, gorgeous Sunday morning. Hagel and Renee weren't home. They'd left early that morning for a long day of motorcycle riding on the Natchez Trace Parkway. Tyler had a key to the motorcycle shop. He left the phone beside the open cash register with a note about where he was heading.

When he got to the meeting place in Biloxi, he slowly drove past the old gas station, checking it out. It was most certainly abandoned. The awning out front had partly collapsed and the platforms where gas pumps once stood were nothing more now than islands of deteriorating concrete. Grass was growing through cracks in front of both garage bays, and sun faded sheets of plywood covered every window.

A quarter mile past the station, Tyler turned and headed back. As he was pulling off the road, the left garage bay door opened. An old man, who looked to be at least seventy, waved him inside. He hesitated at first, thinking the man by chance thought he was someone else. After another wave then putting his hands on his hips out of frustration, Tyler did as the man was suggesting and pulled into the empty bay. The other bay was occupied by a white television utility company van, with the front end pointing toward the door.

"Thought I was going to have to drag your ass in here," the old man said as Tyler was climbing out of the Yukon.

The old man's voice was deep and gruff sounding. It was the voice on the phone when it rang hours earlier. The old man extended a hand and greeted Tyler. "I'm The Mechanic," he said.

This was Tyler's first job without getting his instructions from Foreman. He wondered where Foreman was.

"Is that your name because you work on cars, or is it Mechanic like the slang term for a hit man," Tyler replied.

"We all have a past, DuPont," The Mechanic said smugly. "I don't know you, but I don't figure you're any different than I was. You didn't get involved with this outfit for stealing hubcaps."

The man most certainly had been an assassin at one time. That meant operatives for The Company did survive beyond their usefulness as killing machines. *Of course*, Tyler thought. *The Company needs people like this old man behind the scenes.* That was how his apartment was set up. That was how his Yukon was waiting at the airport when he arrived in Meridian. There had to be a group of workers for logistics.

For the first time, Tyler gave thought to remaining with The Company once his obligation was fulfilled. Perhaps they would need a runner of sorts, a setup man, someone working behind the scenes. Staying on with The Company would mean never ever being with Rita though, so he quickly dismissed the idea.

"I normally meet with Foreman," Tyler said. "Do you know him?"

"Know him well. So you're his protégé, huh? Well, he can't be your babysitter on every job you do."

Tyler had just met The Mechanic - but had already formed an opinion. He didn't like him.

"Open your hatch. Let's see what you brought along," The Mechanic said.

Tyler opened the hatch on the Yukon and dropped the tailgate. The old man went through Tyler's bags and pulled out the Sig Sauer pistol.

"Hold onto this, it might come in handy," the man said as he handed the pistol and three extra clips to Tyler. He then pulled out a small bag of C-4 explosive blocks Tyler had brought.

"What the hell you gonna do with this?" the old man barked.

"Hey," Tyler replied, becoming irritated. "I wasn't exactly given detailed instructions, so I brought most of everything I had."

"Well, you're going to blow something up tonight, but not with these firecrackers," the man said as he stuffed the C-4 back into the bag. "Alright. Get dressed in your black pajamas and bring along those night goggles."

"Where are we going?" Tyler asked, feeling his anger rise as he listened to the man who apparently was born without a personality.

"Throw your junk in the front of that van. Then meet me inside the office over there." The man was pointing to the door that had once led to the cashier and waiting area of the old gas station.

Tyler changed clothes in the garage and put the rest of the gear he was instructed to bring along in the passenger seat of the white van. He then went through the doorway where the old man was waiting. A dust-covered fluorescent light hovered over the ancient sales counter, where a map lay unfolded.

"Let me tell you about the job, then we'll look at the map," the man said. "Two days ago the Mexican government conducted a raid on what they believed to be the top cartel headquarters in all of Mexico. Someone tipped the cartel off though. When the Mexican police arrived, the compound was a ghost town. Not a single soul around, no people, no guns, no money, no drugs. The kingpins lit out, looking for a place to hide and regroup. Well guess what? They're only a few miles down the road. That's right. The four big cheeses of the cartel are camped out here in the US of A. Ironic, isn't it. Just south of Mobile, Alabama is a little place on the coast called Bayou la Batre. They're holed up there at a beach house. If you drove by the place on any given day, you'd never suspect it was a safe house for drug runners, but that's exactly what it is."

The Mechanic paused while he pulled a pack of Camels out of his pocket and lit up. He blew a smoke ring in the air then continued.

"We don't think they'll be there long, so we got to get you in there tonight and take them out."

"Why not send a SWAT team in and arrest them?" Tyler asked.

"Shit boy. Why spend millions of taxpayer dollars and years in court trying to put these vermin away? Somebody decided the best thing is to kill their dirty drug-selling asses and be done with it. Can't send anybody legit in there though. It has to look like another cartel did the hit or a gas leak took them out. By the way, the gas company has gotten three anonymous calls today from people smelling gas as they drove down Shell Belt Road. That's the road in front of this drug house. The gas company sent some folks out. They smelled methyl mercaptan, the compound used to give natural gas its odor, but they never detected any gas."

"I suppose you had nothing to do with that?" Tyler asked sarcastically.

The man smiled for the first time, revealing a gold tooth sitting between old yellow teeth that looked like the last brushing came sometime in the previous century.

"You'll find most of what you need in the back of that van in the garage. The rest you brought with you. You'll find something very special in a black bag. Handle it with care. It's four five-pound bricks of AMZ-412."

"Never heard of it," Tyler said

"Few have. It's highly classified. The bricks in that black bag left Redstone Arsenal last night in a special delivery truck. One of those five pounders has the explosive power of fifteen cases of TNT. I don't know a lot about it, only that it contains white phosphorus and some secret compound of aluminum shavings embedded with mercuric chloride. All I know is it's supposed to make one hell of an explosion and temporarily generate temperatures that approach that of the sun's surface."

"I'm not sure I want to touch the stuff," Tyler said, his eyebrows raised.

"Just be sure to get the hell as far away as you can once you set the trigger. The explosives are shaped in rectangular blocks, little bigger than an ordinary brick for house construction. There's a tube of resin glue in the bag, cover the bricks with the glue and stick one on the exterior wall of all four sides of the house. There's a gas meter on the west side of the house, make sure the brick you use on that side gets attached to the meter. From what I've been told, once this shit explodes, it doesn't leave any traces that it existed except for a few minute fragments of superheated aluminum. Nothing any fire marshal can identify as coming from a bomb."

"I gather nothing happens until after dark," Tyler remarked. "Any alarms or landmines for me to worry about? And, how many people are in the house?"

"Hold your damn horses, son. I'm going to cover everything for you. The house sits about a hundred feet off the highway in the front. Behind the house is a large sandy lot, then scrub pines all the way back to the railroad located five-hundred feet behind the house. They got three cameras in front, and three in the back, hidden in trees. Go down the railroad then hit the woods before reaching the property and enter from the side. You'll miss the cameras that way. This is a drug-runners house, not Fort Knox. The place is supposed to look inconspicuous, and it does."

"I don't know," Tyler said. "You make it sound like I can just walk in there, distribute the charges and walk away. It can't be that easy."

"Of course it ain't that easy. They don't have an elaborate alarm system, but something better - three badass dogs. Dobermans. They're fast and they're lethal, trained to go for the throat. If you don't take them down before they reach you, you'll die when they do."

"Oh great! How am I supposed to take out three vicious dogs and remain unnoticed?"

"There's a high-powered air operated tranquilizer gun in back of the van and ten darts. That's far more ammo than you'll need. I sighted the gun myself at a hundred yards. That's about the range of the gun. You might get off three, maybe four shots before those butt sniffers have you down on the ground. Take the dogs out first. I suggest you climb a tree. Use it as your platform until the dogs are out of the picture."

"I'm already getting pumped for this adventure," Tyler said with extreme sarcasm. "By the way, why bring my own guns and ammo if you have everything in the van already?"

"I didn't make that call. As far as I'm concerned, all you need is that 9mm for close action. I would have provided that as well but I'm sure that gun hidden beneath your jacket is used at least a couple of times a week on a firing range. If I gave you a new one, it might not fit your hand right or shoot straight. Always best to bring your own piece to a gun fight, Sonny."

"So how many people in the house?"

"We think the four cartel bosses, plus five or six bodyguards or other players. None of them will be there for long. I expect they've already made plans to get back to Mexico once the heat there dies down."

"So, besides the dogs, I also have bodyguards to worry about!"

"Yeah. I give you one chance in seven of making it out of there. One in five if that storm in the gulf moves inland and gives you a little more cover."

"Wow. That makes me feel great. And, thank you for such confidence in my abilities."

The Mechanic looked at Tyler indignantly.

"Suck it up, kid. You don't always get a cakewalk when the call comes through. Take the van, drive by the place and check it out. Keep your phone in your pocket and on vibrate only. Once it gets dark and I get confirmation the players are still at the house, move in. The bricks have a button on the end, covered with a piece of tape. Once you remove the tape, the trigger goes live. A fob, about the size of a matchbox, is in the black bag. It sets everything in motion. Hit the button on the fob three times and you have one minute before the world comes crashing down. Don't be anywhere near the house, unless you have a desire to look like a piece of burnt toast. If you make it out of there, come straight here, exchange vehicles and get on back to wherever it is they got you shacked up."

Tyler gave The Mechanic a look chocked full of malice. He wanted to punch the old man in the face, but resisted. This job gave him a hollow feeling inside. It was a mission impossible scenario. A thousand things could go wrong. He might never get his chance to see Rita again. *What a waste if it all ends now. The old man gives me cause to believe that's a good possibility.*

45

As Tyler drove past the house where the Mexican cartel members were allegedly holed up, the wind whipped against the van, nearly pushing it off the road. A major storm front that had been lingering over the Gulf of Mexico was quickly working its way inland. It was far from a hurricane or even a tropical storm, but nonetheless, the dark, approaching clouds and stiff wind had emptied all the beaches and most highways. The impending storm was about to bring darkness over the land an hour early that day.

There was an electrical grid sub-substation located just off Duckbill Road where the railroad crossed. Tyler parked the van there. It was less than a half-mile trek down the tracks before he reached the back of the beach house property. The rain and darkness that were only minutes away from pouncing down on him and everything between New Orleans and Orange Beach, Alabama didn't concern him. To the contrary, he welcomed it. If rain set in, it would provide cover, and keep the bodyguards at the beach house indoors instead of outside roaming about.

Total darkness had taken over before he left the van and headed down the railroad tracks. A black bag was slung over his shoulder, a Sig Sauer 9mm pistol holstered underneath his jacket, a pair of the latest night-vision goggles covered his eyes, and a tranquilizer gun he'd never shot was cradled in his arms. The first drops of what was about to become a torrential downpour hit Tyler's face as he trudged through the thick gravel alongside the railroad.

By the time he left the tracks and worked his way into the thicket of scrub pines behind the beach house, the rain was coming down in sheets. The rain wasn't cold, but it was miserable. At the edge of a cluster of scrawny pines, he looked past the half-sand, half-grass covered back lawn toward the house. The tree he was under didn't look sturdy enough to climb. It wasn't strong enough to support his weight. There weren't any other trees around that looked any sturdier. If the killer dogs came after him and he shot and missed, they'd eat him for their midnight snack.

The beach house stood at a full one hundred yards across the expanse of the lawn. Tyler knew a good run was better than a bad stand, but it would take his best effort and a head start to outrun the bloodthirsty canines if a chase began while at the house. He stood behind the tree and watched the house for a while, trying his best to endure the heavy rain being pushed by a stiff wind.

Lights were on inside the house, and he could see silhouettes of people through the shade covered windows. Apparently, the dogs were hunkered down inside the house, along with the bodyguards.

The only purpose of the dogs and the bodyguards, were to protect the ruthless drug lords. He was praying that he could take them all out without an incident occurring, but the odds of that happening were slim to none.

All he could do now was stand and wait until he got a phone call from the Mechanic. It seemed absurd, standing outside in a downpour with a thirty mile per hour wind whipping about. He had dressed for night operations, but hadn't given foul-weather gear a thought. The black cotton-polyester blend coveralls had sucked up at least two gallons of water and he was soaked to the core.

After twenty minutes of trying to focus on the windows of the house, Tyler began looking around for a better tree to hunker beneath, but there were none. The storm seemed to be centered directly over his head. Every few seconds he had to blow rainwater away from his mouth. The heavy rain, accompanied by the wind, reminded him of the torture he'd endured from a fire hose many times back at Radford Prison.

Thirty feet to his right, looking past the barely translucent sheets of rain, he saw some sort of low-lying manmade structure. Working past the thick growth of small trees and bushes, he saw that it was an old storm shelter. Only a few feet to the left, was a long row of old cinderblocks, nearly covered with weeds, tall grass, and pine needles. A house had stood on that site many years in the past.

The steps leading down into the storm shelter were surprisingly clear of debris. Standing in the downpour waiting for the phone call was irrational. He decided to check out the shelter.

The hinges on the metal door swung open easily and he stepped inside. Using a flashlight swinging on a cord attached to his belt, Tyler took a good look around. There were no snakes or rats, and surprisingly only a few spider webs. It was strange - the six by eight-foot shelter was half-filled with old cardboard boxes. 'Christmas Decorations' was written on each box in large bold letters.

The storm shelter was remarkably dry, a welcoming site from the storm raging outside. Tyler made up his mind to stay put there until the call came to move in. He was hoping the call would never come though. There was always the chance that the cartel bosses had bugged out. From the activity seen in the windows though, that wasn't likely the case. Soon enough, he'd be placing himself in danger of being shot by some cartel gunslinger with a sub-machine gun, or trying to fend off three ferocious dogs, hungry for the taste of human flesh.

Fifteen more minutes passed as he stood waiting for the call. Searching for something to pass the time, Tyler pulled out his knife and opened one of the cardboard boxes. It contained age-old tinsel, and a variety of antique glass bulbs used for Christmas tree decoration. Many of the bulbs were broken and mingled in the maze of tinsel, creating a hazard for anyone who dared stick their hand in to sort through the mess.

He set the box aside and out of curiosity began to open more boxes. One contained a few old decorations, a half-box of used Christmas Cards, and an assortment of broken toys that had been well used. He wondered about the family that had lived there and how their lives would have been so much different from those in the electronic world of today.

A much larger box sat in the corner. It was also new, unstained by time like the others. Setting other boxes aside, he reached the big box. Tyler slid his knife through the tape sealing the top of the box and pulled the flaps back. Inside was a large green duffle bag. He tugged at the bag, struggling to raise it out of the box. He estimated the bag weighed a hundred pounds, perhaps more.

After laying the bag on the floor, Tyler peered out the metal door. He halfway expected to see three growling dogs, their gums drawn high, revealing sets of razor-sharp teeth.

There were no dogs - just sheets of rain. The storm hadn't let up. If anything, the rain was coming down harder than before.

Turning back to the bag sitting on the concrete floor, Tyler held his flashlight with one hand and unzipped the bag with his other. Not really knowing what to expect, he took a step back when he saw the bag's contents. It was stuffed to the max with banded together stacks of twenty, fifty, and one-hundred-dollar bills.

"Hot damn!" he said loudly. "This is drug money."

The bag must have just been put here. I imagine the drug lords brought it with them and hid it here in case the house was raided. Or perhaps this is where they hide the money collected from meth and coke sales, waiting until an opportune time to smuggle it across the Mexican border where it can be laundered.

He counted the number of bills in one of the hundred-dollar stacks. There were a hundred, totaling ten-thousand dollars. Thumbing through the stacks of money, he estimated the bag contained somewhere in the neighborhood of two million dollars.

No way was he going to leave there without that bag. It was the key he and Rita needed to unlock the door to a new life. He had been told by Foreman he should collect any loot he found during assignments. This was the jackpot! He was elated. He wanted to jump up and down and shout for joy, but dared not. Thinking about what the money could do for Rita and him, he could hardly contain himself.

The excitement of finding the treasure chest, created an enormous amount of adrenaline. He needed to calm down and concentrate on where he was and what he was doing there, but his body refused to surrender. He wanted to leave now, hi-tail it out of there with the loot, but resisted. He had to play this the right way - sticking to his and Rita's plan. This grand find was certainly going to put their escape plan in motion much sooner than expected. He couldn't wait to talk to Rita.

Just then, the phone vibrated in his pocket. He nervously dug into his pocket and pulled the phone out. He hit the 'accept call' button and listened.

"You there?"

It was the Mechanic's voice.

"Yes, I'm in position," Tyler reported, feeling like an army commander in the field ready to send his troops into battle.

"It's a go. Good luck."

The phone went silent. Tyler stuffed the phone back in his pants pocket and zipped it closed. He looked back down at the duffle bag, split open like a giant green pea pod, filled with legal tender. He struggled against the fullness of the bag to get it zipped closed. He was hesitant to leave his treasure, as if it would grow legs and walk away. Knowing no one could get to the bag without going through him first, he opened the metal door and climbed the six steep steps leading to ground level.

The wind had died down for the moment, but the torrential rain was still coming out of the clouds as if the rain god was angry at earth. Working his way back to the tree where he stood and observed the house previously, he looked toward the dim lights of the beach house. The night goggles were working, but the heavy rain was creating distortion. It didn't matter, because without the goggles, he could see nothing at all.

Tyler saw the shadows near the house a few seconds before he spotted the dogs. There were two of them. They'd not smelled an intruder, but they'd either sensed or spotted something.

The rifle was lifted into position and the safety latch released just as one of the dogs focused on something at the edge of the woods. The dog's ears perked up and his chest rose slightly. The other dog thought he spotted something to the right, and was walking off in that direction. Firing at the dog honing in on Tyler's position, the dart fell four feet short, dragged down by the rain. The dog hesitated for a few seconds, unsure of the sound it had heard and what had landed and buried itself in the soggy ground a few feet away.

The hesitation was all the time Tyler needed to make an adjustment. The second dart hit the dog squarely in the chest. The dog might have growled, but Tyler was too far away and in a driving rainstorm, so he couldn't tell. The animal sprang forward, toward Tyler, making its charge.

Tyler's rain soaked hair stood out straight on the back of his neck. He thought he'd hit the dog, but apparently had not. Now it was charging, and even in the rain-soaked ground, the dog had amazing speed. It was gaining twenty feet or more with each gallop, and there was no time to reload.

Suddenly, the dog's legs went out from under it. The big animal flipped, landed on its back, and stopped moving. Tyler's heart was racing. He had hit the dog with the dart and it had fallen. Under the weather conditions and distance of the shot, it was a remarkable feat. He wanted to celebrate the victory, but there was no time.

The second dog had walked to its right and acted as if it were going to walk toward the front of the house. Then it had taken notice of the pinging report of the powerful air rifle and that the other dog had shot forth into the darkness, toward the back of the property. Without hesitation, it too turned and took off in that direction.

The Doberman stopped briefly to see what had happened to his friend, laying silently on the ground, perhaps dead, perhaps injured. Tyler had nervously reloaded. He steadied, pulled the trigger, and hit the second dog broadside, just above the belly. He heard a quick yelp, watched the dog jump forward, then fall over, only a few feet from where the first dog had tumbled to the ground for a four-hour nap.

It took a minute for Tyler to calm himself down. He let out a long sigh. It had been a close call with the first dog, and would have been with the second if not for getting an accurate shot at a closer range. There was more danger ahead, and this job had only begun.

Using the zoom on the night-vision glasses, Tyler studied the beach house and surroundings. The third dog, if indeed there was one, was nowhere in sight. More lights were on inside the house now, but none of the bodyguards had stepped outside. The noises made by the dogs and the air rifle had been muffled by the falling rain, alarming no one.

Moving forward, squishing noises came with each step, produced by the mud and sand mixture beneath his rain-soaked boots. It was miserable, but still, he was thankful for the rain and deep darkness it brought. It provided much needed cover for a lone assassin going against a dozen or more gunmen plus killer dogs. The loud thumping in Tyler's chest was a distraction, and if not for the rain, he felt certain it would have been heard by those inside the beach house.

The house happened to be one of the older ones along Shell Belt Road. It wasn't on stilts like most strung out along the highway. The foundation construction was cinderblocks, stacked four high. The exterior was dark cedar, horizontal planks. It looked more like a rustic cabin than a beach home.

Time was of the essence. The dart gun had been left behind, standing against the tree. If the third dog showed its face now, he was in serious trouble. Crawling beneath the back deck, Tyler dug into the black bag and pulled out one of the aluminum colored bricks. The tube of glue was found, and he removed the cap. Squeezing the tube, a stream of two liquids separated by a thin membrane began mixing to form a quick setting epoxy.

He squeezed out a couple of lines on the block then slapped it onto the side of the house. It stuck firmly. The small piece of tape from the end of the brick was pulled away, allowing the trigger mechanism inside to pop up and set the detonator in live mode. The brick was ready to explode once that trigger was activated. Crawling from beneath the deck, he moved to the east side of the house and put another brick in position.

Voices could be heard inside the house. Tyler, versed in Spanish, could make out a few of the muffled words. One man was complaining about the miserable weather, another was complaining about the cheap liquor, and yet another was saying something about a shipment of product being delayed.

The front of the house was wide open. There was no deck, only a stoop by the front door. There were plenty of windows for viewing the beach lying across the highway in front of the house. The light from those windows lit the front lawn, making Tyler's wish to remain unseen more difficult. The shadow of a man standing at the storm door was being projected onto the grass. Tyler waited impatiently until finally, the shadow disappeared.

As soon as the coast was clear, he moved like a cat, quickly slapping one of the five-pound aluminum bricks against the house only a few feet away from the front door. He got a quick look inside the door as he flashed by, and saw two Latino men sitting at a table in the living room playing cards. Further into the house was the kitchen. He could see the back half of a dog lying on the floor, likely sleeping, while its comrades did the same outside in a torrential downpour.

There was a large window on the west side of the house, directly above the gas meter, situated only a foot from the foundation wall. The window gave a perfect view of the kitchen, located in the west corner. Tyler got a full view of the dog, indeed fast asleep on the floor. Three rough looking men, two of which were carrying assault rifles, stood with their backsides pressed against the kitchen countertop, deep in conversation.

The rain was pushing in from the west, still coming down hard, driven by a wind that was beginning to pick up again. The glue wasn't working. Tyler couldn't get the last explosive brick to stick to the gas meter. He pulled the tape off, allowing the trigger to become alive, then shoved the brick back inside the black bag. Using the carrying straps of the bag, he wrapped the strap around the gas pipe and fastened it as tightly as possible.

Tyler stood to leave, but his foot was stuck in the mud. He grunted as he pulled himself free of the boot sucking mire. It was just enough of a sound to perk up the ears of the dog lying on the kitchen floor.

Wasting no time, Tyler took off in a dead run, splashing water with each step. The fob was in his right hand. Using his thumb, he pressed the button three times. In one minute, all hell was going to break loose. He was hoping to make it to the tree line and take cover. Along the way, he would grab the tranquilizer gun in case the dog somehow got out of the house.

The dog was fully aware now that an intruder was outside. It was growling and showing its razor-sharp teeth.

"Que' pasa?" (What's going on?) One of the men said to the dog.

"Que' esta pasando?" (What's happening?) Another guard said.

The dog headed to the back door and barked loudly. The door opened and the dog shot out, followed by the two gunmen. The dog looked past the heavy rain and saw Tyler, with a fifty-yard lead. Tyler heard the dog barking at the backdoor and the men shouting. Things were going to get ugly fast. No way could he make it to the tranquilizer gun in time. He pulled the Sig Sauer from the holster as he continued running. Releasing the safety, he turned and saw the dog coming at him in a full sprint. He had two, maybe three seconds before the swift animal took a giant leap and landed on his chest.

In a barrage of gunfire, Tyler continued pulling the trigger, firing the shell in the chamber and fourteen rounds stored in the clip. At least three slugs hit the dog, only a second away from reaching Tyler and sinking its teeth deep into his jugular. There was a sharp, loud yelp as the dog came crashing to the ground, less than five feet from where Tyler was standing.

The two gunmen were out on the covered deck. They saw the direction the dog had run in, but struggled to see past the rain and darkness. They'd questioned themselves earlier about where the other two animals were, but knew those two preferred being outside, even if there had been a hurricane pounding the coast. They were now wondering why the dogs hadn't sniffed out the intruder.

As soon as the gunmen heard the report of the gun and saw the muzzle flashes from Tyler's pistol, they knew something bad was happening. They instantly raised their assault rifles and readied to fire.

The first few bullets hit in front of Tyler, sending mud and sticks flying in his direction. He flung himself to the ground and began crawling feverishly to the side and toward the tree line some thirty feet away. Another quick burst of gunfire erupted, but the bullets were hitting past Tyler's position. The shooters, unable to find their target, were firing aimlessly at the area where they'd seen the muzzle flashes.

Tyler being on the ground is the only thing that saved him. His head was buried in a pile of mud, facing away from the blast. For a few seconds, it felt like he'd been thrown inside a blast furnace. The heatwave rolled past and dissipated as it spread further out. Even the tops of the rain-drenched trees were scorched. With his eyes closed, Tyler still witnessed a bright-white flash of light. He was certain that if he'd been looking at his arms or legs, it would have been like studying an x-ray film.

Seconds later, the sky was as full of falling debris, as it was raindrops. Rushing to his feet, Tyler stumbled along before reaching the storm shelter. Diving down the steps and bursting through the door, he was inside just as chunks of brick, mortar, wood, and human flesh, came raining down on every square foot of the surrounding land.

Grabbing the heavy green duffle bag, Tyler slung it over his shoulders, his knees bending slightly under the load. He quickly climbed back out of the shelter and began looking for the tranquilizer gun. It was lying on the ground, having been blown five feet from where it had been standing against the tree. The air was already filled with horrible odors, including the stench of death.

Looking back toward the house, there was nothing left. The air in that vicinity was full of smoke, mingling with the falling rain. Everything up to and including areas far past Tyler's location was littered with pieces of what had moments ago been a beach house with people inside. The blast broke out windows of other houses up to a quarter of a mile up and down the road.

Dropping the bag temporarily, Tyler ran to the two dogs he'd taken down with the tranquilizer gun. He found the darts, pulled them out, then ran to the dog he'd shot with his pistol. He hurriedly dragged the dog far into the pines - hoping investigators wouldn't find it. He dropped the dog behind a pile of brush. The darts were thrown onto the wet ground and stomped into the sandy soil. He took a deep breath, sighed, then ran back and collected the bag and the tranquilizer gun.

Moving as quickly as possible down the middle of the railroad tracks, Tyler struggled beneath the heavy bag on his shoulder. It took him twenty minutes to arrive back at the van, still sitting at the substation, somehow untouched by the debris that seemed to be everywhere. He threw the duffle bag and rifle into the back of the van and slammed the door shut. A minute later, he was heading west, away from the sirens and flashing lights coming toward him.

He was exhausted. His clothing clung to his skin. The black makeup he'd applied to his face and arms was streaked, giving him a creepy sinister look. His mind was already replaying the entire event, and he was hoping he'd done everything right. One thing was certain - anyone in or around the house, including the armed men who had been shooting at him were burnt to a crisp.

46

Back at the abandoned gas station, Tyler stripped down, washed his face, and changed his clothes. It felt good to be dry and he was beginning to get warm again. Mechanic was watching, saying few words, but amazed Tyler had pulled off the job and had made it back in one piece. Tyler was hoping to hear some sort of positive comment, at least a 'Hell of a good job, son,' but got nothing.

The only thing the old man seemed concerned about was the green duffle bag.

"I had to kill one of the dogs," Tyler replied. "I put it in this bag I found and plan on giving it a proper burial."

"Dead dog, my ass," the old man said.

As quickly as he could get his things transferred into the Yukon, Tyler was in the driver's seat and heading toward I-10. He made a mental note to ask Foreman about the old jerk who called himself, the Mechanic.

Arriving back at his apartment, Tyler looked at his watch. It was 2 a.m., and he was exhausted. Unwilling to leave his treasure at the peril of some thief, Tyler dragged the heavy duffle bag up the stairs to his apartment and laid it beside his bed. He took a long shower then collapsed on top of the covers. When he awakened, the steady rain that had followed him home was still coming down. It was noon before he could find enough energy to get out of bed. He wanted to go by Hagel's, collect his cell phone, and send Rita a text. He was hoping she could get off work early and spend some time chatting with him. He couldn't wait to tell her about the money he'd stumbled across. Their secretive plan of escape had just reached high gear.

Turning on the radio while driving, Tyler searched the stations, hoping to hear news about a gas explosion that had wiped out a beach house and everyone inside. He found nothing but sad country music, some oldies stations still making their money off AC/DC and the Eagles, and several stations blaring filthy rap, which he refused to call music.

Hagel wasn't in the shop. Tyler grabbed his cell phone, still sitting where he'd left it, and sent a long text message to Rita. He told her he was back, how he loved her more today than yesterday, and how much he missed hearing her voice. He wanted to send a message about the money he'd stumbled upon, but decided to wait and tell her that over the phone, instead of through a text. He spent several more minutes in the shop before heading over to the house to see if Hagel and Renee were there.

Renee was out grocery shopping but expected back at any time. The rain had finally stopped. Hagel and Tyler sat on the front porch drinking a cup of coffee and sharing small talk. When asked, Hagel said he had heard several news reports about a suspected gas leak blowing a house apart. He'd also seen a news crew on television. They were standing behind a line of wide red plastic ribbon the police had stretched across the highway near the blast area. Little was known about what happened at this point, but police felt certain people were inside the house when the blast occurred.

When Hagel finished telling all he knew, a light bulb turned on in his head. He looked at Tyler, grinned, and said, "You were there, weren't you?"

Tyler didn't answer, but the look on his face spoke volumes.

Realizing he wasn't going to obtain any of the details, Hagel changed the subject. Renee returned home, and was overjoyed to see Tyler. Business was slow at the shop, so Hagel sweet-talked Renee into watching it for a few hours while he and Tyler went for a motorcycle ride. Tyler got excited the moment Hagel mentioned the ride. The roads were nearly dry already. A relaxing ride on a motorcycle, with a cool sounding powerful engine beneath him and the wind in his face was just what he needed.

Tyler had just finished receiving a huge hug and a large kiss on the cheek from Renee. He was about to strap a helmet on when his day suddenly took a turn for the worse. His cell phone rang. He started not to answer, but was scared not to. He stomped out of the garage, allowing Hagel and Renee to see his frustration.

"Yeah!" Tyler answered.

Receiving a call so soon made him furious. He suspected it was Foreman, wanting to meet and chitchat about the events of last night.

"Drop whatever you're doing and meet me at the Meridian airport - pronto!"

It was Foreman's voice as suspected, but he sounded serious. Tyler began to protest but Foreman cut him off. "I need you to leave now!" Foreman demanded. "Hanger 4. The guard will let you in the gate."

The phone went dead.

"Well, crapola!" Tyler screamed out, the veins showing in his muscular arms as he waved them about in frustration. He looked back at Hagel and Renee, who were watching him from inside the garage.

"I have to go," Tyler said, storming back inside the garage.

He pulled out his other cell phone, typed in a quick text to Rita then extended the phone to Renee. "Will you hold onto this until I get back?"

"Sure, honeybuns," she said, reaching for the phone.

Tyler gave his dear friends a hug, then shot for the door, muttering something Hagel and Renee couldn't make out.

§

The private jet that had carried Tyler both to and from the ranch was sitting in front of hanger 4 with the engines running. A man, who didn't look as if he were airport security, opened the gate and waved Tyler through. He parked beside two other cars sitting by the hanger and got out. Foreman, as usual, appeared from nowhere.

"Let's go. I'll fill you in on the plane."

The two men ducked down as they entered the plane and the door immediately shut behind them. The wheels were rolling before they took their seats. Foreman looked like he hadn't slept since Tyler had last seen him. Having gotten several hours sleep, Tyler was feeling refreshed.

"Where are we going?" Tyler asked, as he was buckling his seat belt.

"You packing a weapon?" Foreman asked, not answering Tyler's question.

"No. I was out running around when you called. You said you wanted me here fast, so I didn't go back to the apartment."

"Good. I'm dropping you off at New Orleans International then I'm heading on to Corpus Christi."

"Again, what's going on?"

Foreman pulled a photo out of his pocket and showed it to Tyler. It was a picture of a hard looking Latino man.

"You're looking at Jose Antonio Torres. He's the kingpin of the cartel gang you took care of last night. He was supposed to have been at the beach house, but was across town at a titty bar when the fireworks went off. Word is he's heading back to Mexico as fast as he can get there. As we speak, he's in one of two places, either a drug safe house in central New Orleans or a safe house in Corpus Christi. We don't do Mexico, so we gotta take him down before he gets back across the border. You drew New Orleans, and I got Corpus Christi."

"I'm rested but still tired, Foreman. Not too many hours ago, I was only a few seconds away from death's door. I had killer animals and cartel gunman coming at me. Not to mention, I was nearly toasted when a small nuclear bomb went off. Don't you have a dozen other agents who can take care of this?"

"This was our assignment and our mess. We have to mop it up ourselves. Look, my neck gets put on the line too, it's not all about you."

"I don't even know how many points I scored last night," Tyler said, continuing his loud protest.

"Believe me. You did well - damn well, and I'm proud of you. I should be able to get you forty or fifty points shaved off your bill, but not unless we can finish this."

Fifteen minutes into the flight, tempers had cooled off and voices had returned to normal. Foreman handed Tyler a set of keys and informed him a car would be at the airport parking garage ready to go. Everything he needed would be inside the trunk. He was to drive to the location where Torres was thought to be, scope everything out then report back to Foreman as soon as possible.

If the target was found holed up in New Orleans, Tyler was expected to make a move in broad daylight in an attempt to take out the notorious drug lord. It would be made to look like any other drug deal gone bad. It was very risky, but necessary. Someone, likely a Washington politician, wasn't satisfied with Tyler having wiped out only three of the four key players the night before. He or she wouldn't rest until they'd killed the final and main player, Jose Antonio Torres.

§

Following Transportation Security Administration (TSA) regulations, Tyler was required to go inside the terminal for screening before being allowed to go on his way. He had forgotten about a folding six-inch knife in his pocket. It was confiscated by the not so happy agent who checked him over. Tyler's explanation about just getting off a private jet and not being there to board another flight seemed to ease the tension.

After that small delay, Tyler rushed down the concourse on his way to the main terminal then the parking garage. Thousands of people were in the airport that day, but as Tyler turned the corner into the main terminal, he spotted someone who caused him to do a double take. He stopped dead in his tracks. Moving along the walking sidewalk was a man with an unforgettable face. Tyler wasn't one-hundred percent certain, but felt compelled to take the time to investigate. He quickly stepped onto the moving conveyor and hurriedly walked forward, passing several people content to ride along standing still.

The man was accompanying a woman. Just past the end of the moving sidewalk, the man said something to the woman then disappeared into a restroom. When he'd turned to look at the woman, it gave Tyler a good look at the man's face. His heart began to pound and he could feel his blood starting to boil. He could hardly believe it. The odds of them being there at the same time were a zillion to one.

He was trailing a man who had made his life a living hell. It was a man who had tortured him, and ordered his death by lethal injection. He was trailing none other than the infamous Warden Pendleton. The despicable slimy rodent was apparently vacationing in The Big Easy.

Several men were standing at urinals, but Pendleton wasn't one of them. Only one stall door was closed. Tyler kicked the door open. In one giant move, he grabbed Pendleton by the throat, dragged him out of the stall and pressed him against the wall. The look on Pendleton's face gave Tyler the highest degree of satisfaction. It was a startled look of 'No – You're dead!' It was a stunned horrified look. It was the look of a man drowning, realizing he'd drawn his last breath.

Tyler had dreamed of a moment similar to this many times. In his last days at Radford, he had succumbed to accept being killed by the guards if it meant getting his hands around Pendleton's throat. The setting here was different, but the result would be the same. Tyler squeezed tighter and saw Pendleton's eyes begin to roll back in his head.

Easing the chokehold, Tyler allowed Pendleton to draw another breath. The man gasped, sucked in a huge lung full of air, and immediately began speaking. He pleaded with Tyler, promising him anything he owned if he would let him go. The only thing Tyler wanted was to see the vermin suffer. He wanted the man to suffer for what he'd done to Shanghai, suffer for the pain and agony he himself endured at the command of this heartless, cruel, sadistic man.

Pendleton had been a merciless man all his life. Tyler knew he and Shanghai weren't the only victims of this spiteful brutal animal, who wasn't capable of compassion or loving anyone other than himself.

Three businessmen in suits entered the restroom at the same time, cheerfully talking about the positive results from a board meeting they'd left earlier. They stopped dead in their tracks when they saw what was happening. All three ran out, shouting, hoping to draw the attention of authorities. The thought crossed Tyler's mind to let Pendleton go, hunt him down again later, with promises he'd be back to finish the job. It would cause the vile, detestable man to toss in his bed at night, incessantly worrying when and where the attack would come.

A commotion could be heard outside the restroom. Suddenly, Tyler realized it was now or never. In reality, he'd never get another chance to even the score, to rid the world of this scum. He'd deprive the despicable animal of his last years, where he'd only serve to harm others. Pendleton lost control of his bowels. The pungent stench of urine and feces filled the air.

The warden realized this was it. He had awakened that morning for the last time, seen his last sunset, drank his last beer. Pendleton's eyes were locked on Tyler's but his focus was elsewhere. His mind was playing a film, a movie of the evil he'd done in his life - it was a triple feature.

Tyler looked closely into Pendleton's pleading eyes as he tightened the grip. Pendleton had both his hands clenching Tyler's strong right arm, seeking desperately to break free - but it was proving to be futile. Pendleton's back was pressed hard against the wall and his feet were two inches off the floor. He kicked feebly about, his strength fading fast.

"This is for all the inmates at Radford, past and present," Tyler said sternly then spit in the warden's face. "Say hello to your daddy - the devil!"

Pendleton's face turned expressionless and his body went limp. Using both hands, Tyler snapped the man's neck. He let go and watched the warden's lifeless body as it slid slowly down the wall then fall across the tile floor.

A TSA agent entered the restroom as Tyler was turning to walk out. He ran toward Tyler, drawing his gun as he cautiously moved forward. Tyler had two choices, neither of them good. He could give up, be arrested and be killed by The Company before the day was over - or he could fight. Either choice likely would end with the same result - death. At least by fighting, he had a slight chance of escape.

In the split second the TSA agent took to look down and observe Pendleton's body lying lifeless on the floor, Tyler made his move. He leaped forward, planted his left leg, as his right leg shot upward. Tyler's foot landed squarely under the officer's chin. It was a precise and powerful blow. The gun discharged into the floor at the same time the officer went flying through the air.

Running out of the restroom, Tyler entered the busy spaces of the airport just as alarms and sirens began sounding everywhere. TSA officers were running frantically in every which direction, not yet knowing who or what they were looking for. In only a few short minutes, everything would be made known. Cameras at every corridor were already scanning the crowd, looking for anyone moving too fast, anyone who appeared to be on the run. A massive manhunt was about to get into full swing.

The doors were locked. Those inside the airport couldn't get out, and those outside rushing to catch their flights, couldn't get in. Panic set in, and several thousand people inside the airport were running about. It had taken less than a minute for total mayhem to take over. Tyler worked his way at a pace equal to the surrounding crowd. Spotting an emergency exit, he quickly shot out the door and closed it behind him. This action set off another alarm, but fortunately, its blaring sound wasn't loud enough to overcome the noise of the crowd.

Using the key fob Foreman had given him on the jet, Tyler pressed the unlock button over and over as he ran through the parking garage. The car was supposed to be on the second level, which it was, but located at the far end near the exit ramp. He sped forward, in a hurry to get away, but when reaching the car, took time to open the trunk and look inside. He found two Smith and Wesson .40 caliber pistols, loaded, and each had four extra clips. He grabbed the guns and clips and tossed them into the passenger-side seat.

The car was likely bugged with a GPS location device. He would have to ditch the car as soon as possible, and find some other mode of transportation. His cover had been compromised. He was now on the run. The escape from The Company was much sooner and far different from anything he had been dreamed about.

He needed time - time to think about what to do. He thought he could outrun and outmaneuver the police, but he didn't think he could hide from the agents of The Company. All four tires on the car squealed as Tyler sped down the circular ramp. Just before reaching the bottom, he flung The Company cell phone out the window. The only thing the phone was good for now was in aiding other assassins trying to track him down. With or without the phone though, he figured he was doomed.

He ditched the car in the Castle Hills area, near the mall. He set out on foot, hoping the TSA was still searching for him inside the airport, thinking they had their suspect cornered. If they didn't have it already, the local police would soon have a photo of the man who murdered a passenger at the airport and nearly killed a TSA agent. Tyler's head was spinning. One lone act of revenge was about to bring heaping piles of red-hot coals down on his head.

Walking down a back alley, Tyler checked his watch. It was 5 p.m. It had been one heck of a long day, and it was far from being over. He came across a group of black men and boys playing basketball on a homemade court. It was a rough looking crowd, and Tyler had invaded their turf. They sized Tyler up and decided it best to be cool and let this man walk on past.

Tyler didn't stroll on past however. Pulling out a twenty-dollar bill, he asked if anyone was willing to allow him a one-minute call on a cell phone. A tall scrawny man, who appeared to be the oldest of the group, left his friends shooting hoops and came over to negotiate. He wanted fifty dollars for the call, but Tyler stuck to his original offer.

A minute later, Tyler was on the man's phone calling Rita. She didn't answer. Of course, she wouldn't, not without a text coming first. He gave the man another twenty, got a giant smile in return, and began typing with his thumbs.

In a few short sentences, he let her know he'd been compromised and was in serious trouble. He told her if she truly loved him and was serious about living a life on the run, to be ready when he got there. He had no idea how that was going to happen, or how long it would take, but that was his plan. If he made it to Longview and Rita said no, it would break his heart, but he would understand. He'd rejected her once, and now it was her turn to decide if they should be together or say goodbye forever.

"Hey, you know anyone who might be willing to drive me to Texas," Tyler asked the man who had rented him the phone.

"TEXAS," The man said. "Damn, we be a long damn way from Texas. What part?"

"Longview."

"Don't know where that be."

"Not far from Shreveport."

"Damn man. That a long way. Where your car be?"

"It's a long story. Do you have a car?"

"Yeah man, I got a car - a 99 Charger," he said proudly.

"I've got almost a thousand dollars on me. I'll give it to you, plus this gun."

Tyler pulled one of the .40 calibers out from beneath his jacket and showed the man. The man whistled and dipped his shoulders back and forth.

"Damn nice piece! It hot?"

"No, it's not hot."

"You some kind of cop man?"

"No, but it's only fair to tell you, I'm running from them," Tyler said honestly.

"You make it two-grand, and I'll see that my boys over there make the Po Po think you never left town."

"I don't have two-grand. I got a thousand and that's it. Take the deal or leave it, either way I gotta move - and fast."

47

Just over an hour later, Tyler was going through Baton Rouge, riding shotgun in an old Dodge Charger in need of shocks and a new muffler. The driver was a talker, and kept Tyler's mind off the dangerous situation he had foolishly brought upon himself. His name was Montgomery Brooks, nicknamed Saxman.

"So, you play the saxophone?"

"No dude. This brother don't put his lips on no damn horn. I get that name cause I like sax man, get it?"

Saxman laughed for two minutes. Tyler failed to see the humor and wondered why the man's nickname wasn't Sexman. He thought it best to drop the subject, there were much greater things to worry about.

Saxman, was twenty-three years old. He'd dropped out of school the day he turned sixteen, and had been living off welfare and street crime ever since. He was a fugitive in his own right, wanted by a host of New Orleans drug pushers for selling fake molly on Bourbon Street during Mardi Gras and other events that drew in large crowds of tourists.

Using Saxman's phone, Tyler sent several more text messages to Rita, but got no answer. She was either refusing to respond to the messages coming from a number she didn't recognize, or had bailed on him, deciding life on the run wasn't the way she wanted to live after all.

After arriving in Longview, they stopped twice for directions to Pipestem Manor. Finally locating the complex, Saxman dropped Tyler off in the parking lot.

Having bought all the gas, plus snacks and a twelve-pack of beer to keep Saxman satisfied, Tyler paid the man eight-hundred and fifty dollars, which was all he had left. Saxman wasn't very pleased, but Tyler told him the Smith and Wesson handgun was worth that much and more. Seeing that was all he was going to get, Saxman gave Tyler a firm handshake, wished him luck, and left.

It was a nice neighborhood, quiet, clean, and no one was stirring about. Tyler found the 300 building and made his way to unit 336, Rita's condo. He was nervous, unsure if she were home, unsure if she still wanted to be with him under the circumstances, and unsure how he would react when he saw her beautiful face. It had been a long time since that day back in Spotsylvania County when they'd said their final goodbyes. With his fingers crossed, he trudged forward, hoping this day would end with her in his arms.

He looked around. Seeing no one, he knocked on Rita's door. He was nervous, scared, and a lump was moving into his throat. No answer, so he knocked again. Still, there was no answer. Rita had jokingly told him over the phone more than once that if he ever decided to swing by one evening a key would be waiting for him under the doormat. He stooped down, pulled the mat back, and there it was. Perhaps she was out with friends, or was working late. He'd just looked at his watch however and realized it was nearly midnight.

Sliding the key in, he turned the lock and opened the door. The hallway was dark, but there was a light in the room ahead to the right, which was likely the kitchen. He closed the door behind him but left it unlocked. With a squeaky voice, he said. "Rita, you home? It's me Seth!"

The place was quiet. He approached the room ahead and walked in. His heart nearly jumped out of his chest. It was indeed the kitchen. On the far side of a table sat Rita, the woman he loved. She was tied to a chair, and her mouth gagged. Even with a horrified look on her face, she was every bit as beautiful as he remembered.

"Damn if you didn't take your sweet 'ole time getting here," a voice said from behind.

Tyler froze in place. He recognized the voice. He didn't have to turn to see who had addressed him. He knew who it was. It was Trainer.

"Try one of your martial arts moves or go for that pistol under your jacket and this will end faster than you expected," Trainer said.

It was over and Tyler knew it. He was fast with his feet and a quick draw with his gun, but no more so than Trainer. The man had taught him many things back at the ranch, and both knew the other's abilities. After everything that had happened, here he was, back with the love of his life, but they both were about to die.

"We've got one hell of a mess to clean up back in New Orleans, thanks to you," Trainer said in the most condescending way. "You just couldn't let it go could you? The damn rookie runs into someone from his past and gets stupid. You're so predictable. The first thing you did was run here to your lover girl. I thought you were smart, but it appears you think more with your dick than your head. I was looking forward to a good long chase, but you even managed to screw that up!"

Tyler remained frozen. He wanted to make a move, wanted to fight, but this was Trainer. The slightest offensive motion on his part and Trainer would pull the trigger.

"You were Foreman's favorite," Trainer continued with his speech, as if he felt obligated to say a few words before he killed them both. "Foreman thought highly of you, fought hard with our superiors to get you out of prison. I thought it was a crazy idea, busting you out. The military is packed with grunts who could be recruited easily. Once we started training you though, I saw where Foreman was coming from. I was impressed. You never did get your head on straight though, so here we are today, in one hell of a jam. I wish I could let the girl live, she's a hot one. Damn it, DuPont, I hate what I have to do, but it's your own damned fault!"

Three rapid shots were fired. It was the distinct sound of a silencer connected to the barrel of a large caliber handgun. Tyler flinched then looked down at his torso, expecting to see his blood and guts oozing out. Instead, he felt and saw nothing, then Trainer fell against him and they both tumbled to the floor.

"Are you alright?" another familiar voice yelled out. It was Foreman. He was standing in the doorway holding a 9mm pistol. Smoke was still coming from the barrel.

Tyler rolled Trainer away and jumped to his feet, shocked by everything that was taking place. He wasted no time. He didn't know what was going on or what was about to happen next. All he could think of was untying Rita and setting her free.

485

Foreman looked at Trainer, shook his head, pulled out a chair from the table, and sat down. He lowered his head to the table, exhaled deeply and let out a long sigh of despair.

Tyler removed the duct tape from around Rita's body and removed the gag from her mouth. She said nothing. She was in shock.

"I knew this was bound to happen someday," Foreman said, slowly raising his head off the table. I knew you wouldn't last, you're strong and smart, but you're not cut out for this life. I knew there wasn't any other woman for you besides Rita, knew you'd never given her up."

"I don't know what to do or say," Tyler said, hardly able even to find those words.

"I've known Trainer for many years," Foreman said. "He was a good man, a friend."

Tyler was helping Rita to her feet. He heard what Foreman had just said, which made him even more confused.

"We don't have a lot of time," Foreman said, looking at Tyler. "There's a white Subaru Forester outside, the keys are in it. Take Rita and drive to Dallas/Fort Worth International. There's a variety of makeup, clothes and such in the trunk. Use what you can to disguise yourselves."

Foreman reached into his jacket pocket and pulled out a thick envelope.

"Like I said, I knew this would happen. There's a passport for both of you in the envelope, plus enough money to buy plane tickets and get you out of the country. Use the names on the passports, not your own. There's a letter inside the envelope with instructions on where you need to go and what you need to do. After you read it, tear the paper into shreds or better yet, burn it. My best guess is you have three hours, four tops, until everybody we've got comes looking for you."

"I still don't understand," Tyler said. "And what about you?"

"I'll stay here and do what I can to throw the gang off your trail. If I'm lucky, I'll catch up with you in a few days. If not – well, you'll never know for sure."

Tyler started to protest, but Foreman waved him off. "Go!"

Tyler was holding the love of his life. She was able to walk, but otherwise unresponsive. He led her out of the apartment to the Subaru sitting in the parking lot.

48

Rita's hair was tucked away beneath a head wrap. She had a ghostly look on her face and needed help getting aboard the plane. Everyone on the plane suspected the poor woman had just gotten out of the hospital after a long hard dose of chemotherapy. She was assisted by a hippie looking hunk who didn't seem her type. He sat beside her, dark glasses covering his eyes, wearing a Dallas Mavericks' cap.

Beneath Tyler's cap was a longhair wig, purposely tangled, and pulled into a ponytail behind his head. Their passports said they were Randall and Joy Thacker, a couple from Abilene, Texas, on their way to a much needed vacation in Costa Rica.

The envelope Foreman had handed Tyler contained the passports, plus four-thousand dollars cash. The note gave instructions to fly to Costa Rica, stay a day then fly out to Buenos Aires, Argentina. He was to get a hotel room at the Hilton and book it for one week. If Foreman didn't join them by then, the instructions were to drive south to Mar del Plata, go to the Carnerillo Bank, and ask for a man by the name of Leopoldo Flores. He was to present himself at the bank as Tyler DuPont.

Everything was a giant puzzle. He wondered how Foreman found the time to write such a letter and give him detailed instructions? *The letter must have been written on the jet, on his way from Corpus Christi to Longview. As far as my trouble in New Orleans, Foreman would have been notified immediately of that debacle, so that was explainable.*

Tyler scratched his chin several times thinking about the passports. *How on earth could Foreman have made up passports, not only for me, which would have been odd enough, but for Rita as well? Foreman said he knew this would happen someday, so at least part of the escape was planned in advance, but why, and how?*

Tyler wanted answers but knew they'd never come. It had been that way since he arrived at the ranch, which seemed like eons ago.

It was near the end of the day in San Jose, Costa Rica before Rita finally started coming around. She clung to Tyler as if he were her life support, which, in fact, he was. After hours of just holding each other and at times shedding tears, Rita finally managed to produce a smile.

The shock of being kidnapped, thinking she and Tyler both were about to be killed by a gunman, then seeing the intruder die before her very eyes, was an experience that would haunt her forever. That man, Foreman, the one Tyler liked oddly enough, arrived just in time and saved them both. It was so strange. Neither of them could figure out why Foreman would show up and kill an old friend, just to save Tyler and herself.

Life would never be the same, and it would take a very long time to adjust. She had Tyler back in her life, however. She felt that with Tyler, Seth, or whatever name he wished to call himself, she was safe. They were free at last, free to be together every minute of every day, to love and cherish each other, for as long as they both shall live.

Tyler was anxious, afraid, but at the same time filled with joy beyond imagination. He couldn't stop staring at Rita, and liked the fact that she wouldn't let go, even for a minute. It was what he had hoped for and wanted for so long. He had experienced many living nightmares in his young life, and a few good dreams. This was the pinnacle of good dreams, the sweetest dream possible. Nothing could ever surpass it.

He was perplexed at the way his life with The Company had ended. He failed to understand why Foreman would sacrifice everything for him. He liked Foreman a lot. More some days than others, but Foreman was a friend, someone he respected. He owed the man his life. After all, according to Trainer, Foreman had fought with The Company to break him out of prison, saving him from death by lethal injection.

Foreman had cast the final die now, and he failed to understand why. Why would Foreman kill his long-time friend to save an operative who had only been in the organization for a short time? Tyler had certainly created several headaches for the man, like when he tried to contact Rita using the computer. Perhaps Foreman had seen something that reminded him of a time when he too had hopes of breaking free from The Company's bonds. Who knew? It was all so strange.

The second night after arriving in Buenos Aires, Tyler and Rita made love for the first time ever. Tyler had long ago shut out the horrifying experiences he had went through with his stepmother and gotten past the mental anguish it had caused. It was nothing like the abusive sex he'd suffered not so many years ago. It was pure unwavering love making in its greatest form. The two lovers, who had waited so long, never thinking they'd ever be together as one, finally exhausted all their energy and fell asleep in each others arms.

The days rolled past, as Tyler and Rita spent hours walking on the seashore, running in and out of shops, and having long lunches in quaint little cafes. Seven days flew by, and Foreman was nowhere to be seen. Tyler expected the worst, fearing there was no way Foreman could cover up what he'd done to Trainer. Foreman was supposed to have been in Corpus Christi, looking for the fleeing cartel boss, just as he was supposed to have been doing in New Orleans.

There was no way Foreman could explain why he'd aborted his mission and somehow arrived in Longview just as Trainer was about to blow the heads off of Tyler DuPont and Rita Logan. Trainer was there because he'd been handed down the order. Foreman, however, would never be able to explain his presence.

Tyler wished he knew the mind of Foreman, a man born in Meridian, Mississippi as Samuel DuPont. He wondered how the man came to be brought into The Company. He thought the man's life would make a good book, but it would have to be Foreman doing the writing. No one else knew enough about him to complete even one chapter.

They were to leave the Hilton that day and drive along the coast to Mar del Plata, a city to the south. Tyler wondered why Foreman wanted him to use the name Tyler DuPont at the bank. He wondered why Foreman didn't want him to use the name Randall Thacker, the name on his new passport?

As Tyler and Rita were checking out, now known by the hotel staff as the honeymooners on the ninth floor, the clerk remembered that a letter had arrived for Mr. Thacker yesterday. He handed the letter over, along with an itemized bill showing the hotel charges over the last week.

On a sofa in the spacious lobby, Tyler and Rita looked at the envelope. There was no return address, but 'Foreman' was written on the upper left corner. The letter was postmarked June 8th, a week ago. It was the day after the nightmare, when Foreman had killed Trainer in Rita's condo. They had arrived safely in Costa Rica that same day, on their way to a better life, or so they hoped.

The letter was opened, and Tyler began to read.

Dear Tyler:

I have much to say, and find it hard as I search for the right words. I've revised this letter at least a hundred times over the years, most of the revisions coming in the last few months. What you are about to read will certainly be a shock, but I swear on my life it's the truth. It's the truth I wish you could have heard many years ago, but didn't.

I trust that you and Rita have arrived safely. I hope you will find Argentina and its people to be as wonderful as I found them to be. I've been there many times and selected it as the best place to hide if I chose to run.

I hope to see you again one day soon, but the odds are stacked against me now. I'm either, on the run myself trying to evade those wishing to kill me, or I'm already dead. Regardless, I need to make a confession, something I've held inside for far too long. Back in the courtroom in Virginia, you were shocked by the news you had been adopted. The adoption part was true, but the part of who your real parents were was a fabrication. That information was presented to the prosecutor, who was so eager to use it to promote his case that he never even verified the source.

The truth is - your mother did die giving birth. She was a wonderful woman, much like the one you have found and fallen in love with. You ask how I know these things – because I'm your real father. Take a moment to let that sink in before going on.

This is hard for me.

You were named Tyler for the baby brother I lost. You know that story already. When you were born, I was already working for the agency. Your mother and I were secretly married. If they had found out about her or about you, chances are neither of you would have lived. As wrong as all that was, that's the way things were. I couldn't get out, and there was no one to raise you. The Boones were looking for a child to adopt, and it all fell together.

I didn't know about the abuse you were suffering until you had already taken action yourself that night in Julian's room. If I had of known, I would most certainly have spared you from having to take things into your own hands.

At every opportunity, I secretly came to Abingdon, which wasn't often enough. The times I saw you, my heart ached to run, wrap you in my arms, and tell you how much I loved you. It was so hard not to, but I couldn't expose you. I had to keep you safe.

I watched you grow, and saw how you developed into such a strong young boy. You're built like me, but with your mother's brains, which is good.

It was never my intent to drag you into the agency. I had dreams of you growing up to be a doctor. I know that was your dream as well. When you were arrested, I tried to help. There were too many people involved and little I could do. I had to work behind the scenes alone, and my efforts went nowhere. The adoption thing was inevitably going to come up, so I helped throw it off course. If the truth had been found out, you wouldn't have made it through the end of the trial, and I would have been dead as well.

While you were in prison, I worked hard with the agency recruiters. A convict had never been brought into the agency before. Most agents come from the military, ex-Seals or Green Berets. I worked hard, and it took a lot of persuading. I convinced them you were strong, had the brawn plus the brains to go with it, which isn't a lie. After that night in the library, I thought it was over.

After pleading with my boss, he looked into what happened. He was impressed that you took on five assailants who wanted to kill you and walked away unharmed. I was given the green light, but had to plan and arrange the escape myself. If it had gone south, that too would have ended it for both of us.

I won't make this already long letter any longer. I've given you a lot of information and many things to think about. My only desire is that you not hate me for what I did. Please believe me when I say if I could have changed it all, I would have. I loved being with you back on the ranch and wish that could have gone on forever. All things change though, so goes life.

Go to the bank and do as I instructed you to do. The agency only has a few people to send out looking for you, and it's a big world. Don't get me wrong, they'll make a good attempt to find you. Being small in number though, it's hard to put together a sustained mission, so that's in your favor. They figure if you're gone - you aren't going to talk. In a few years, they'll give up the search, but you can't ever come back to the States, that would be suicidal.

You're free son, and you're with the love of your life. Get married, and live happily ever after. If you ever have a son of your own, I hope you will consider the name Samuel.

I love you with all my heart and soul.

Foreman

49

Rita drove the rental car to Mar del Plata. Tyler sat on the passenger side staring out the window. He was speechless, as stupefied as Rita had been when he'd put her on the plane back in Longview. There were so many things to think about, so many things to consider. He'd gotten some answers to questions, but it would take a long time to sort through it all. The letter sent by Foreman would be read many times, and be highly treasured - forever.

Rita and Tyler were both nervous as they walked into the Carnerillo Bank. Their request was made at a teller-window. The young girl behind the glass smiled, made a phone call, then ask them to have a seat in the lobby. A few minutes later, another woman came and led them through a door and down a hallway to an office.

They were greeted by a short, chubby, balding man with a thin black mustache. He spoke decent English, which pleased Rita, who spoke no Spanish, but knew she had to learn.

"I am Leopoldo Flores," the man said, as handshakes were exchanged. "So, what can I do for you, Mr. DuPont?"

"My father sent me here," Tyler responded, feeling awkward but proud.

"Your father?"

"Yes. His name is Samuel DuPont."

"Do either of you have an account in our bank?"

"I'm not sure," Tyler answered, his nervousness increasing. He wondered why Foreman would send him to this man if he'd never heard of Tyler or Samuel DuPont.

"Let me see," Leopoldo said.

He began typing on his keyboard as Tyler and Rita sat across from his desk watching.

"Aha. I know Samuel DuPont," he announced. "The name didn't ring a bell, but his picture does."

The monitor was turned for Tyler and Rita to see. Along with bank information, was a photo of Foreman. The man then turned the monitor back to face himself and typed more on the keyboard.

"Ah, yes. The account is in two names, Samuel and Tyler DuPont. Do you wish to make a deposit or withdrawal?"

"How much is in the account," Tyler asked.

"That is a fair question," the man said. "Before I can tell you more though, I will have to verify some things. Do you have any identification?"

Tyler handed him the Mississippi driver's license bearing Tyler's photo.

"Good," the man said. "Now, follow me."

They were led back to the lobby area and into a small room to the left of the teller desks.

"I'm sorry for this inconvenience," Leopoldo said. "Any accounts that come through Swiss banks require this verification procedure."

The nervousness had abated slightly when the driver's license was accepted. It had returned now. Tyler sensed something else was going to be required. He didn't have a passport with the name DuPont and the only other thing he had bearing that name was a VISA card, which he dared not use. The thought reminded him to destroy the card as soon as possible.

"Please place your right thumb on the pad in front of you," Leopoldo said.

Oh no, Tyler thought. *This won't work.* He hesitated, but then placed his thumb on a small device that looked like a hollowed out computer mouse. The computer monitor that Leopoldo had been typing commands into confirmed it was a match for Tyler DuPont.

Tyler had a surprised look on his face.

How the heck could that happen?" Tyler thought.

Rita was just as impressed. Foreman had somehow set this up. The man was a genius.

"Now, Mr. DuPont. If you will please - type in your passcode."

"What passcode?" Tyler said, once again alarmed.

"Your two digit, five number passcode, sir," Leopoldo said with a concerned look on his face.

Tyler's mind was racing a mile a minute.

"Son of a gun," he said aloud as the thought hit him.

Tyler walked up to the keypad and punched in the numbers 11-19-30-50-40. The computer beeped and indicated the numbers were correct. Tyler took a deep breath and looked over at Rita. He could see the perspiration on her forehead and the astonished look in her eyes. He smiled at her. Everything was going to be fine.

"Just one more thing and we are complete," Leopoldo said, ready to type on the keyboard.

"It's 9-ball," Tyler said.

Leopoldo typed in the answer as he nodded up and down. A beeping sound was made and a verification affirmation popped up on the screen. Leopoldo typed in a new command and the printer to his left came alive.

"These are your account figures," Leopoldo said, handing Tyler the paper. I'm assuming you would like to withdraw some money today?"

Rita stepped in close to look the paper over as well. Their eyes lit up at the same time.

The amount was thirteen million dollars.

50

Two years later

Tyler DuPont, the young man they'd welcomed into their home and learned to love was long gone. Hagel and Renee spoke of him often, during mealtimes especially. They missed their friend and hoped he was safe, wherever he was.

A month after Tyler's disappearance, the two of them took a motorcycle ride to Longview, Texas, and went to Rita's apartment. Rita no longer lived there. When they'd knocked, an elderly woman and two cats came to the door. They suspected Tyler had broken free from his imprisonment, picked up Rita, and sailed off into the sunset. They worried though that it may have turned out differently and both Rita and Tyler were dead, buried somewhere in the mountain of trash at the city dump.

Campbell Custom Cycles had fallen on hard times. Two franchised dealerships had opened in town and chipped away at Hagel's already shaky business. He was selling a used motorcycle here and there, a few parts, and a considerable number of new tires, but it wasn't enough to keep the business afloat.

Custom motorcycles were his specialty and anyone who had purchased one had nothing but good things to say about Hagel's work. The fact was though, the economy wasn't doing well, and custom-made motorcycles were expensive. Orders were few and far between.

Renee made a few dollars with her computer skills, but that too wasn't enough to pay off the ever-mounting debt and still put food on the table. They were both too young for social security and too old to look for another job.

After much debate, they decided they had no choice but to discount their inventory, sell off the goods, and close up shop. Hagel had made a trip over to the newly opened Harley Davidson Motorcycle store, spoken to the manager, and put in an application as a mechanic in their repair shop. They didn't have any openings at the time. He was told they'd keep him in mind in case someone quit.

Motorcycles were all Hagel knew or had ever done, and he'd always worked for himself. The thought of punching a time clock every day sickened him. The way things were going however, he may never have to worry about that. The mechanic crew at the Harley shop was young, and had been through special training. Unless the owners got desperate, Hagel would never get the call.

In the storage area above the showroom, Hagel and Renee began taking inventory of the junk collection and putting prices on each item. Some things would be sold downstairs. Others would be photographed and sold online. It was painstakingly hard for Hagel to let go of his lifetime collection of rusted metal and faded plastic, piled to the rafters in some areas.

After almost a week of hard work and long hours, they finally made their way to the front of the storage area, which faced the entrance of the showroom below. The dirty, dust covered windows provided little light, so Hagel installed two fluorescent lamps he'd robbed from the now empty show room.

In the right corner was an unorganized stack of various sized boxes, containing everything from old carburetors to rusty spoke rims. Renee stood by with camera, inventory list, and price tags as Hagel painstakingly went through each box, barking out names and numbers.

"Well, there's a box I don't recognize," Hagel said as he uncovered more of the heaping pile.

Renee laughed. "Hagel Campbell. You can't remember what you had for breakfast this morning, much less a pile of trash that's been sitting up here since you were wearing diapers."

"I remember marrying your pretty ass. I just can't remember why!"

Renee hit him hard over the head with her clipboard. They wrestled around on the dirty floor. Hagel was willing to allow her to win until she started playing dirty and tickled him. He ended the fun and demanded she get back to work.

Using a box knife, Hagel sliced through the tape on the big box. He folded a flap back and saw a letter sitting on top of some crumpled up newspapers. He picked up the letter and thinking it contained an old invoice slip, tossed it to Renee. She opened the envelope and pulled out a one-page letter. Hagel was turning back to dig into the box when Renee said.

"I don't believe this!"

"What is it?" Hagel asked, turning back to look at Renee.

"It's from Tyler."

"Tyler. Why would he have put a letter up here?"

"I don't know," Renee responded. "Hush for a minute and I'll read it."

"You have no idea how hard it is to love you," Hagel fired back.

My dearest friends:

If you have this letter, it means I'm gone and not coming back. If I never got a chance to tell you before I left, let me now say how much I appreciate all you did for me. You two wonderful people openly accepted someone who society had cast away and made him feel special and loved. I could never thank you enough for all you did, or tell you on paper how much you both mean to me.

I've left you a small token of my appreciation – enjoy.

I love you both forever.

Tyler.

Hagel turned and slid his knife down the corner of the box. He pulled the two sides apart, revealing money, jewels, some rare coins - and a bulky large green duffle bag.

THE END

Author's Note

This book is a work of fiction, dreamed up and wrote down over a period of months.

I've visited the towns of Abingdon and Radford, Virginia, many times. They're quaint southern towns filled with history, charm, and great people. As far as I could determine, Abingdon never catered to bootleggers during prohibition, and Radford doesn't have a prison.

Meridian, Mississippi is another wonderful southern community. If you ever visit there, be sure to drive up to the city park and take a stroll around the scenic lake.

Spending the first forty-six years of my life in Wild, Wonderful, West Virginia the state is near and dear to me. The surnames and given names of practically every character in this book are the names of communities, towns, cities, or counties, situated in the beautiful and bountiful Mountain State.

I hope you enjoyed the book and found it entertaining - that was my intent. I also hope you've enjoyed my other books, and if not, there's no time like the present!

I'll keep writing these wild tales for your pleasure. I've really nothing else to do, because I can't dance, and it's too wet to plow.

Enjoy the rest of your day.

Mingo Twain